PRAISE FOR

Janice Kay Johnson

"Ms. Johnson's rich-toned characters and solid
conflict make for very good reading."
—*Romantic Times BOOKclub* on *The Woman in Blue*

"Janice Kay Johnson's *The Baby and the Badge* works on
many levels comprised of mystery, emotional power
and strong female characters."
—*Romantic Times BOOKclub*

"Janice Kay Johnson writes a strong relationship drama...."
—Harriet Klausner on *With Child*

Dear Reader,

It's hard to believe that the Signature Select program is one year old—with seventy-two books already published by top Harlequin and Silhouette authors.

What an exciting and varied lineup we have in the year ahead! In the first quarter of the year, the Signature Spotlight program offers three very different reading experiences. Popular author Marie Ferrarella, well-known for her warm family-centered romances, has gone in quite a different direction to write a story that has been "haunting her" for years. Please check out *Sundays Are for Murder* in January. Hop aboard a Caribbean cruise with Joanne Rock in *The Pleasure Trip* in February, and don't miss a trademark romantic suspense from Debra Webb, *Vows of Silence*, in March.

Our collections in the first quarter of the year explore a variety of contemporary themes. Our Valentine's collection—*Write It Up!*—homes in on the trend of alternative dating in three stories by Elizabeth Bevarly, Tracy Kelleher and Mary Leo. February is awards season, and Barbara Bretton, Isabel Sharpe and Emilie Rose join the fun and glamour in *And the Envelope, Please....* And in March, Leslie Kelly, Heather MacAllister and Cindi Myers have penned novellas about women desperate enough to go to *Bootcamp* to learn how *not* to scare men away!

Three original sagas also come your way in the first quarter of this year. Silhouette author Gina Wilkins spins off her popular FAMILY FOUND miniseries in *Wealth Beyond Riches*. Janice Kay Johnson has written a powerful story of a tortured past in *Dead Wrong*, which is connected to her PATTON'S DAUGHTERS Superromance miniseries, and Kathleen O'Brien gives a haunting story of mysterious murder in *Quiet as the Grave*.

And don't forget there is original bonus material in every single Signature Select book to give you the inside scoop on the creative process of your favorite authors! We hope you enjoy all our new offerings!

Marsha Zinberg

Marsha Zinberg
Executive Editor
The Signature Select Program

MINISERIES

Janice Kay Johnson

Patton's Daughters

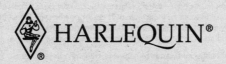

HARLEQUIN®

TORONTO • NEW YORK • LONDON
AMSTERDAM • PARIS • SYDNEY • HAMBURG
STOCKHOLM • ATHENS • TOKYO • MILAN • MADRID
PRAGUE • WARSAW • BUDAPEST • AUCKLAND

ISBN 0-373-83686-4

PATTON'S DAUGHTERS

Copyright © 2006 by Harlequin Books S.A.

The publisher acknowledges the copyright holder of the individual works as follows:

THE WOMAN IN BLUE
Copyright © 1999 by Janice Kay Johnson.

THE BABY AND THE BADGE
Copyright © 1999 by Janice Kay Johnson.

www.eHarlequin.com

Printed in U.S.A.

Janice Kay Johnson is the author of thirty-eight published or forthcoming books for children and adults. She is a former librarian who now lives north of Seattle, Washington, with her two teenaged daughters. When she's not chauffeuring her daughters to play rehearsals or piano lessons, Janice is writing, quilting, gardening and volunteering at a no-kill cat shelter. She also serves as doorkeeper and can opener for more cats and dogs than she cares to admit to sharing a home with.

CONTENTS

THE WOMAN IN BLUE

Since this book is about family, it seems
right to dedicate it to Karl. Whatever distance there may be
between us, you'll always be my beloved big brother.

CHAPTER ONE

HAVING YOUR DOG present you with a human skull was a hell of a way to start a day.

Daniel Barnard had thought it was going to be a good morning. He'd awakened with the rooster, whose crow rang just the right note as far as he was concerned. And the weather was perfect, he saw as soon as he stepped out onto the front porch with a steaming mug of coffee in one hand. He sat down, as he always did, on the rustic Adirondack chair that faced due east.

The back porch was for evenings, when the sun set like liquid gold over the Sisters, a trio of mountains as sharp and cantankerous as the elderly Robb sisters in town. But the front porch was for morning, when the sun poured glorious colors over Oregon's high desert country as if trying to make it the most beautiful place on God's earth. And maybe succeeding.

The coffee warmed him from inside until the sun's rays touched his face like a gentle hand. He set down the mug and thought about the morning's chores. These days, Daniel had enough help on the ranch. He no longer felt as if twelve hours weren't half long enough. He didn't shovel much you-know-what in the barn anymore; that was the job of hired hands. He concentrated on tenderly caring for the mamas waiting to foal and training the stock that had made the Triple B famous for world-class cutting horses. Back right after Granddad disappeared his father died, and times had been tougher. A hell of a lot tougher.

But no reason to remember that right now. The day was too full of promise for dark memories.

Daniel stood and saw Lotto trotting across the scrap of lawn he watered and mowed just to please his mother, who said a house wasn't a home without grass. The big yellow Lab had something in his mouth half the time; he liked tennis balls or branches so big he couldn't get through doorways. At the creek, he'd dip his head all the way under to pick up rocks that would probably wear his teeth down. Lately, he'd even taken to fetching home some weathered bones. A long-dead deer or elk, Daniel figured.

But today…what in tarnation did he have? If it was a rock, it was a damned big one. And grayish-brown, not red like the dirt around here. Something about the perfect curve of the top made Daniel uneasy.

He whistled. "Lotto, here, boy."

The dog came obligingly. He didn't mind showing off his treasure. Daniel's uneasiness grew as the Lab neared, that oval, dirty…something clutched awkwardly in his broad jaws.

By the time Lotto galumphed up the porch steps, Daniel knew. Even with soil clinging to it, he knew. He crouched and held out his hands.

"Let go, boy."

The dog whimpered, his brown eyes anxious, and held on tight.

"Lotto," Daniel said sharply.

The yellow Lab reluctantly released his prize, and

with a sigh sank onto his belly on the painted porch floor. Daniel was left with the skull in his hands.

He turned it to face him—truer words had never been spoken, he thought with sick humor. Empty eye sockets stared at him. The lower jaw was missing, but the upper teeth were pretty much intact, and when he tilted the skull he saw something that made his stomach turn. Metal in one of those teeth. This was no ancient Indian burial. And that hole in the top suggested things he didn't like to contemplate. Especially since he guessed he knew who this was.

"Granddad," he whispered. "It's you, isn't it?"

RENEE PATTON strolled into the office that still felt like her father's but now belonged to the acting police chief, Jack Murray. She'd known Jack most of her life, though he was two years older, her sister's contemporary rather than hers. He and Meg had been high school sweethearts, but he'd never come calling after Meg had run away from home. To this day, Renee had no idea whether Jack had known Meg was going, or whether they'd broken up before she'd left. He'd never mentioned Meg to Renee, never asked if she heard from her sister, and Renee sure as heck hadn't brought up Meg's name.

What she did know was that he'd also dated Abby, Renee's younger sister, a few times about a year ago. Apparently Jack had a thing for Patton women. Just not for Renee, the plain sister.

Oh, yeah. It stung.

He glanced up now, one dark brow lifted. "Catch the punks?"

She snorted. "You kidding? Long gone."

They got calls like this twice a week on average.

Vandalizing mailboxes was a favorite recreation for local teenagers. The county deputies faced the same thing. Not much could be done; even within the Elk Springs city limits, country roads abounded. Houses stood far apart, traffic was sparse. But lately one particular neighborhood had been victimized every few days. Some folks had given up and had canceled mail delivery. A few put out portable mailboxes and took them back in come late afternoon. Others had fortified theirs with concrete and metal pipes, which functioned as a red flag waving does for a bull. The vandals had done some creative work on those boxes. Post office security had asked for help, and she was darned if she was going to admit failure.

"I'm thinking about setting up a video camera," she said, perching on the edge of Jack's desk.

He grinned, softening a face rough-hewn enough to be called homely. Not that any woman in her right mind would think such a thing.

"Go for it," he said.

Her heart rate accelerated, but she ignored what had become an automatic response. Aside from the fact that Jack wasn't interested in her—never had been, never would be—he was too much like her father. He'd become more so since he'd moved into this office. She knew he was campaigning to keep it, which was fine with her. Becoming police chief was something of a dream of hers, but she wasn't ready yet. She knew the city council wasn't ready to hire a woman, either. But Jack would move on; he liked the power that went with the job, and soon he'd be chafing at the limitations of the Elk Springs Police Department compared to the bigger county sheriff's force that patrolled the area outside the various city limits. Heck, for all she knew, he lay awake nights lusting after an FBI badge.

Elk Springs was all she wanted. Maybe this town hadn't been good enough for Meg, but it was for Renee.

"Hey, Jack," called the dispatcher, whose desk sat just outside his office. "Here's a good one. Daniel Barnard says he has a human skull."

"The rancher?"

Renee swiveled to better hear the answer.

"Yup. Says his dog brought it home."

Jack grunted. "If it's human, it's bound to be from some old Indian burial. Still, somebody better go see." His gaze fell on Renee. "It's all yours."

She rose with alacrity. A human skull. Now, that sounded more interesting than a mailbox bashed in with a baseball bat. "Do I know Daniel Barnard?"

"His dad was Matthew Barnard. The Triple B?"

"Oh, yeah." She frowned. Seemed as if she remembered a Barnard boy about Meg's age, too, but she couldn't seem to picture him. "I can find the place. It's in the city limits?"

"Yeah, Matt kicked and screamed because when they redrew the line his taxes climbed, but the city wanted Butte Road because they were talking about taking cinders from that little lava cone past his place. Then they opened the quarry at Ponderosa Butte instead, but they couldn't be bothered to take back what they'd done, even for Matt."

Renee recalled hearing about that, too. "On my way," she said cheerfully, sauntering out the office door.

The whole city police department—all fifteen officers—drove Bronco 4x4s. Winters here in eastern Oregon were long and cold. Heavy snowfalls at this elevation only came two or three times a season, but the ice stayed.

Of course, that long cold winter was also bringing prosperity to Elk Springs, in the form of a new ski area on Juanita Butte. The influx of outsiders brought more crime, which made life interesting for a cop, but also changed the personality of a town where you used to be able to leave your doors unlocked. Renee curled her lip as she passed an espresso stand. Seemed as if one stood on every corner. A steaming cup of coffee wasn't good enough for folks anymore. At least, not the urbanites who came from Seattle and Portland to ski.

She was glad to leave the central district, cross the Deschutes River, low from summer and fall, and find herself almost immediately on ranch land. Except, even here big fancy houses were cropping up on every bare ridge. More than 5,000 square feet, some of them, and they were vacation places! Renee couldn't imagine that much space echoing around her. She liked to feel enclosed, snug. As it was, by herself in the house Daddy had left jointly to her and her younger sister, Abby, Renee was rattling around like a lone pea in a pod.

The Barnard spread was the last on Butte Road; if you went on past their gate, you'd come to the foot of the area's smallest cinder cone, red with scrubby ponderosa pine clinging here and there. Target shooters came out now and again, maybe a few teenagers who liked sliding around on the steep slope of loose cinders near the bottom, but otherwise the road was a dead end, in more ways than one.

At the turnoff, letters burned into a slab of wood supported by two peeled poles announced the Triple B Ranch. Renee didn't mind seeing that the road to the house was packed firm with red cinders. Yesterday's rain had left most unpaved roads shin-deep in rust-colored mud.

The ranch was picture-perfect: split-rail fences, gray-blue barns and an old ranch house nestled among the grove of cottonwood near the creek. A second house had been added some distance away, on a spine of ancient crumbling lava exposed to winds and driving snow. The small patch of green lawn in front was incongruous, sur-rounded as it was by the bare knuckles of lava and the gray-green sage. Beyond the barns, broad green pastures were the product of huge rolling irrigation sprinklers.

A shiny blue pickup sat outside the newer place; a modest sedan down by the old one. At the Y, Renee turned toward the modern house with its big porches and shingled, natural cedar siding. A yellow Lab raced alongside the Bronco, barking the whole while.

As she parked and turned off the engine, a sharp whistle silenced the dog, who reluctantly went to the man who came down the porch steps. Squirming, the Lab stayed behind his master.

Renee never liked being dwarfed by a man. No mystery why she felt that way, but insight didn't always help. She tended to be her stiffest when she came up against somebody like this rancher, a solid 6'4" if he was an inch. Big shoulders, big chest, lean hips, strong legs. Short dark hair. His face was saved from being uninter-esting by his eyes, an electric blue. It wasn't just the color, either; they were intelligent, perceptive, intense. She darn near squirmed just like the dog.

The man nodded. "Officer." His gaze touched on the name plate pinned to her chest. She'd never been so glad not to be buxom.

She didn't bother to introduce herself. "Daniel Barnard?"

"The same." His voice, slow and deep, went with his looks.

"I hear you found a skull."

He nodded toward the house. "Come on in."

She followed, appreciating the simplicity of the porch railing and the front door, topped by a window shaped like a fan. Inside, she knew right away no woman had had anything to do with the decorating. The entry was half mudroom; a rain slicker and a parka and an olive-green duster buried a coat tree, and several pairs of boots lined the wall. She caught a quick glimpse of the living room to the right. Wood floors, plain white walls and leather furniture weren't softened by pretty cushions or knickknacks. Big windows, wood-framed, let in floods of light that touched on the one spectacular painting above the couch and some smaller, quieter ones—pencil sketches, she thought.

But Daniel Barnard led her the other way, into a kitchen so neat she had to shake her head. Maybe there was a woman around, after all.

"Coffee?" he asked.

Attention riveted on the dirty, discolored skull that sat smack in the middle of the maple table, Renee shook her head.

"Your dog brought you this."

"Yup." He leaned against the island countertop and watched her. "Some other bones, too. I just didn't pay any attention to them. I rounded up what I could find. They're in that box there."

She glanced. One long heavy bone that might be a femur, which she seemed to remember was a good thing as it could be used to determine height and maybe gender. A cluster of others as dingy as the skull. A couple of ribs—she could see the arc.

Renee circled the table to see the gaping eye sockets. No lower jaw, which wasn't surprising if this skull had kicked around out there for Lord knew how many years. And definitely human, unless Sasquatch really existed.

"Any idea where the dog got these?"

He shook his head. "Not a clue. I'll try following him, if I can do it without him noticing."

"Chances are, it's an old Indian burial." Those cropped up from time to time, exciting everybody until the coroner took a look at the bones.

"Not unless this fellow's shaman moonlighted in dentistry," the rancher said.

She gave him a sharp look. For the first time she noticed how tense he was. Shook up. For all his casualness he was too still. The hand that gripped the edge of the tile counter showed white knuckles. A muscle danced in his jaw.

Interesting. And gratifying. She hadn't liked feeling as wriggly and timid and obedient as his dog.

Back to the skull. Renee guessed she ought to pick it up to see what he was talking about. Irked to discover she was capable of squeamishness over something so long dead, she lifted the damn thing. It was lighter than you'd think, dry and grainy.

And, yup, an upper molar had a filling, the kind most people ended up with.

"You're right," she agreed. "It looks modern to me." Gingerly, she turned the skull in her hands. A pale groove and several gouges made plain where the dog's teeth had gripped.

"About ten years ago, my grandfather disappeared." Daniel Barnard met her eyes when she looked up. His tight jaw betrayed emotions he'd otherwise clamped down. "Senile, but my mother wanted to keep him at home. He just wandered out one night, in December. We never found him."

Bet that had made for a jolly Christmas.

"I'm sorry," Renee said simply, and he inclined his head in silent acknowledgment. She tilted the skull back and studied those teeth again. "I doubt this is your grandfather's…uh, remains, though."

Without even looking, she felt him go on alert, like a Labrador retriever spotting a quail. "Why?" he asked.

"Come here." Renee held the skull higher, waiting until he covered the few steps to her side. "Except for those two fillings, these teeth aren't bad." A thought came to her. "He still had his own? Your grandpa?"

A frown drew Daniel Barnard's dark brows together. "Yeah," he said doubtfully. "I'll have to ask, but I don't think he wore dentures."

"Still, most old people I know have had lots more dental work than this. Bits have broken off, and they have bridges, caps…" Renee shrugged. "These are in better shape than my teeth."

"Or mine." He exhaled. "I should've seen that."

"It's natural, when you know a man disappeared on your place, to figure this is him. Question is—" she carefully set the skull back on the table "—who else has disappeared?"

A small silence followed as they both stared at the empty eye sockets and crumbling bone. After a moment she gave herself a shake. "Well. I'll just take these with me."

"You know anything about bones?"

"Not much," Renee admitted. "Some basics are covered at the police academy. I've done a little reading. The coroner is good, though. He can tell an amazing amount from a femur. I'm hoping that big one there is a human femur."

"Could be deer and cow bones mixed in. Lotto isn't very discriminating."

The dog had stayed on the porch. "But he's brought these home recently?"

"Yeah, I've noticed him carrying bones around just this last...oh, week, ten days. I just figured it was an antelope or cow." He grimaced. "Until this morning."

She nodded. "We'll have more questions, once we know something about this fellow."

The rancher's gaze followed hers. "Or gal."

Now there was a thought. The uncomfortable reminder of her own mortality shuddered right through her. Someday, that's all she'd be. Right then, she hoped as she'd never hoped before that her minister knew what he was talking about.

"Would you like a bag?" Daniel asked. "To put that in?"

She'd felt his eyes on her; he must have read her morbid thoughts. The offer showed some sensitivity. No reason the skull couldn't just sit on her front seat, but she didn't much like the idea of it looking at her, or gazing ahead as if hoping it could see out the windshield, and turning it to face the upholstery seemed sort of...cruel.

Another shudder touched her. "Thank you. I would."

He produced a brown paper grocery bag and even set the skull in it for her. She thanked him again and reached for it. His voice stopped her.

"You're Meg Patton's little sister, aren't you?"

Was she? She didn't even know if her older sister was alive.

"I'm the middle sister."

His eyes stayed trained on her face. "What ever happened to Meg?"

"I have no idea," Renee said shortly.

He apparently didn't notice she didn't want to chat about her family. He made a sound. "I can see a resemblance."

Distant, she guessed from his tone. Her throat closed, and she had to grit her teeth. Hurt, after all these years? she marveled. Or was what she felt grief?

"Meg was the pretty one," Renee said carelessly.

"Was she?"

Saints above, he actually sounded surprised! As if he had never noticed. Renee suppressed a snort. Maybe those vivid blue eyes didn't see as much as she'd thought.

"In a dress," he mused, "I think you'd be plenty pretty."

She was standing there surrounded by bits and pieces of a dead man, and Daniel Barnard was… Well, she wasn't sure what he was doing. Flirting with her? She had trouble believing that. Insulting her? Probably.

"You don't think women belong in a uniform?"

His eyes opened wide, ostensibly in surprise, although this time she sensed some pretense. "Did I say that? I just thought, in some floaty dress, or maybe one of those crinkly skirts…" He shrugged, nodding toward her dark navy uniform. "That outfit just looks too much like a man's."

Definitely insulting her.

"No, it looks like a police officer's," Renee said through her teeth. "Man *or* woman. Now, if you'll excuse me, I'll be on my way to the coroner."

A groove deepened in one lean cheek. "I didn't mean…"

"I'm sure you didn't." She set the bag with the skull atop the bones in the cardboard carton.

"I'll take it," he said, voice tight. Before she could argue, he hefted the box without a glance at its contents and strode toward the door. Not much she could do but trail him, like the little woman.

Everything deposited in the Bronco, she climbed in and slammed the door, rolling down her window just a bit.

He bent down. "You'll let me know?"

Renee eyed him narrowly. Was he really so naive? Hadn't it occurred to him yet that skeletons weren't strewn in everybody's backyards? Sure, a few people went missing for reasons that didn't involve a crime, like his grandpa. Most dead folks not tucked in a grave, however, were dumped somewhere because they'd been murdered. Which meant she'd have a few thousand questions to ask.

Assuming, she reminded herself, with an involuntary flicker of a glance toward the brown paper bag set atop the box on the passenger side of her front seat, assuming those bones told the coroner enough to give any grounds to ask those questions.

"We'll be in touch," she agreed, and drove away.

BOBBY SANCHEZ laid the bones out on a table, more or less in order. "Mostly less," he said with a chuckle. "Lot of gaps here."

As she watched, he discarded a number of bones. "Deer," he'd remark, tossing one aside, or, "Cow."

Balding and potbellied, the coroner had kept his position for the past ten years without much opposition when elections rolled around. Partly, that was because of police support. With training in forensic anthropology, he knew his stuff and was genuinely useful to police investigations. Today was a good example.

Renee waited, outwardly patient, while a half hour dragged into an hour, then more, as he examined the small collection, measuring the bones and turning them in his hands and humming to himself.

Inside, she was anything but. One thing bothered her most. Hadn't anybody missed whoever these remains belonged to?

She'd spent the past few hours shying away from that speculation. She of all people knew how easy it was, if someone walked out of your life, to assume that person had gone of her own volition. If someone you trusted told you she'd left because she didn't want to be bothered with three kids, you shrank inside. You didn't say, *Wait a minute! Mom wouldn't have gone this way, without even saying goodbye!*

Those were the kinds of thoughts Renee had had on her way back to town, with that box of bones on the seat beside her. She couldn't forget that those teeth looked as if they belonged to a fairly young man or woman. Renee had been just a little girl when her mother, Jolene, had deserted her family. And Jolene had been only thirty-three years old then. Renee had nothing but her dead father's word that her mother had chosen to leave.

The hamburger and fries she'd had for lunch weren't sitting too well by the time she passed under the Triple B arch and turned onto the highway. Renee swallowed the acid in her mouth and stole a glance at the rough knob where the femur would have connected to the pelvis. It was poking over the edge of the carton as if taunting her.

What if these bones turned out to be a woman's?

Her brooding was interrupted when the coroner spoke for the first time in more than a mutter to himself. "I'll fax you a report, but I can tell you the basics if you'd like."

"I'd like." Why else did he think she'd been sitting here on her hands for two hours?

He was succinct. Male, the coroner was certain.

"You're sure about that?" she asked, telling herself she'd known her mother wasn't dead. What she felt was curiosity, not relief.

"No question," Bobby Sanchez said. He continued. The victim had been 5'9" to 5'11" tall. Rangy, not real muscular. Teeth in good shape; he'd seen a dentist regularly—two small fillings meant the cavities had been caught early. Late teens to thirty years old, tops. Hard to tell how long he'd been dead; ten years at least, most likely not over twenty.

"And chances are he was murdered," Bobby Sanchez concluded. "See?" He showed her the vee-shaped cut in the rib.

"But animals must have been gnawing at all these," Renee protested. "What's different about this spot?"

"The teeth marks formed tiny U-shaped gouges," he informed her, making sure she saw the difference. "And by the time animals got to the bones, they would have crumbled, like this hole in the cranium. They wouldn't have had the elasticity to shave clean the way this did. Nope. Had to have happened right about the time of death. Or not long before, because there is no sign of regeneration."

Renee left in a hurry, hoping to catch Jack Murray before he went home for the day. She pulled into the parking lot behind the station just as he reached his car. When he saw her, he leaned against the fender and waited. She had to give him credit; he never looked impatient. He must really love his job.

Jack listened as she reported the coroner's conclusions.

"Bobby's sure?" he said at last.

"Sure as he can be. That's a quote. He'd like more bones."

"I'll bet he would," the acting police chief agreed dryly. "He's welcome to go hunting."

"Shouldn't we?" Renee tried not to sound too eager. The only murder cases she'd ever investigated were the garden variety kind: a shot fired during a bar brawl, a domestic dispute gone uglier than either husband or wife had intended, a cashier in an all-night gas station/grocery executed during a holdup. Not a lot of mystery, just lives lost or ruined because of hot tempers and panic. But this one, the victim dead ten years or more, identity unknown—this one made her want to find out who the bones had belonged to and why someone had killed him.

Jack frowned. "How long has this guy been dead?" he asked. "Bobby have any idea?"

"He thinks ten to fifteen years. Twenty years at most. Somebody has gotten away with it for a long time."

Jack grunted. "Have you checked to see who might have gone missing within that time frame?"

"I'll do that next. The only one I know of is Daniel Barnard's grandpa," Renee reminded him. "But the coroner says this victim is too young to be him. Not more than thirty years old, he thinks."

"I'd forgotten about that." Jack seemed not to be seeing her anymore. "I hadn't been back in Elk Springs long. Dan's mother called. Hysterical, of course. She'd turned her back for a minute, and the old man was gone. He was getting pretty confused, and some new medication was making him worse. It started snowing just about the time he slipped away. Covered any tracks and confused the dogs." He shook his head. "After the first hour or so, we knew in our hearts that we were looking for a body, not a lost old man. It was so damned cold, we had to give up, though we hated to with her carrying on the way she was, sure the whole thing was her fault. Nobody could convince her that turning on the news and watching for a few minutes wasn't a sin. We looked again the next day, and the day after, and then when the snow melted. Never found him."

Renee shivered. With October around the corner and dusk fast approaching, the air had a wintry bite to it for the first time. She pictured a dazed, elderly man, maybe in his shirtsleeves and slippers, just walking away from the lighted house, powdery flakes of snow clinging to his lashes and hair, clouding his vision. Where had he thought he was going? Had he seen someplace else, a mirage that lured him on and on?

She'd read about old people doing that. Nursing homes lost residents pretty regularly. You could understand that; who'd want to stay in one of those places, especially once you'd regressed far enough to forget that you hadn't wanted to be a burden to your children?

But to walk away from your own home, into a snowstorm… Maybe it was instinct, like an animal going off to die. But it was cruel, too, leaving the people who'd loved you to wonder and to imagine you slipping and staggering and finally going down.

Renee shivered again. Those bones were not his, she reminded herself. Any more than they were her mother's.

"Yeah, okay," Jack finally said, straightening and reaching for the car door handle. "Find out who went missing during those years, see if you can come up with any more bones without using much manpower. Ask at the Triple B. Maybe Daniel's mother remembers a ranch hand taking off one night and leaving his stuff behind. At the very least, I'd like to see us put a name to those bones."

"I'll do my best," Renee agreed.

Hurrying into the station, she started thinking about the questions she'd ask. Something told her Daniel Barnard wouldn't like them.

And he'd like even less that she was the one doing the asking.

CHAPTER TWO

DANIEL REINED THE MARE into a whirling pivot to the left, her hindquarters bunched and her front hooves flying as she propelled herself in a circle. Responding to a slight touch of the rein on her neck, the mare reversed direction, spinning to the right. Daniel sat loose in the saddle, feeling the power gathered beneath him, the sweet willingness to do as he asked.

When he let the rein go slack, she went still, waiting for the tightened legs that would send her surging ahead. This mare could stop on a dime. Better yet, she used her head. She could read a steer better than Daniel could. Not quite four years old, Marian B Good was going to be one of the best.

Daniel slapped her neck and murmured a few words. Her mobile ears swiveled to listen.

When he lifted his head, he realized he had an audience. The lady cop watched from the other side of the corral fence, her arms crossed on the top rail, one black-shod foot resting on the bottom rail.

Daniel wondered if he could scare her. Without pausing to examine the childish impulse, he urged his horse into a dead run, straight at Officer Renee Patton.

She never flinched, even when 1,500 pounds of horseflesh slid to a stop with whiskers tickling Renee's hand. All she did was nod, cool as the snow that stayed atop Juanita Butte year-round. "Mr. Barnard."

"Officer," he drawled, inclining his head.

"I promised to be in touch."

He'd expected a phone call. Those bones had been out there a long time. This wasn't like finding a body with blood still sticky. How interested were the police really going to be in a scattering of weathered bones?

Daniel had kind of hoped for a visit, though; Renee Patton interested him. He'd known enough about her old man that he hadn't been surprised when her sister had run away before graduating from high school.

Funny, though, that nobody except, presumably, her sisters had ever heard from Meg Patton again. After talking with Renee the other day, now he wondered. Runaways were a dime a dozen; when a rebellious teenager vanished, people just assumed she'd gone under her own steam. But he remembered the time Meg spent with her sisters, walking them to school, taking them out for ice cream, bringing them along to the swimming hole on the Deschutes. What would have made her go out the door and never come back, even to see them?

Renee stroked the mare's velvety muzzle, not seeming to mind the steamy breath Marian puffed out with a nicker. The lady cop was as pretty as he remembered, all delicate bones and eyes as big and greeny-gold as a cat's. Her pale blond hair was long, but pulled back so tightly it must hurt.

Her mouth thinned, as if she didn't like his scrutiny. "I need to ask you and your mother some questions."

She'd been wrong about the teeth, Daniel thought instantly, stomach clenching. Those bones had been Granddad's, after all.

"What did you find out?"

"The bones belonged to a young man, between five foot nine inches and five foot eleven. No weightlifter. Probably lean, the coroner thinks."

"Then…definitely not my grandfather," Daniel said slowly.

"Not your grandfather," she agreed.

His stomach should have unclenched, but it didn't. Meg was still on his mind—Daniel remembered her as being tall. "The coroner is sure the bones are a man's?"

Something flickered in Renee's eyes. "He's sure," she said shortly. Was she trying to squelch him, or her own uneasiness?

"I do have questions to ask," she repeated. "I'm told that your mother lives here on the ranch?"

"Over there." A frown coming on, he nodded toward the modest white house where he'd grown up. "My sister's here for a visit right now with her son, too."

"Oh? Well, she might remember something worthwhile. If you can make time for me later, I'll start with them."

Daniel shifted in the saddle, and Marian B Good quivered under him. "Remember what?" he demanded.

Her gaze didn't waver. "Those bones mean a young man died around here, maybe even on your place. Nobody but the killer ever knew what happened to him. It's like your grandfather. Somewhere there's family who's been wondering all these years. I want to know—"

Her words took a minute to sink in. When they did, he interrupted, "*Killer?* What makes you think something like that? The dead guy might've been some drunken drifter who fell asleep in a snowbank. Or a Vietnam vet living up in the foothills."

"He had a knife cut in one rib. Made around about the time of death, the coroner says."

Daniel swore under his breath. *Murder.* In his backyard.

The mare moved restlessly and he realized his legs had tightened. He soothed her with one hand while he said aloud, "It can't have happened here. Unless it was…jeez, thirty, forty years ago? I mean, I've been here most of my life. My parents have owned this spread since 1959. We'd have noticed if someone upped and disappeared."

"Ranch hands must come and go."

"Yeah, but…" He stopped. She was right. They did. Logical assumption: one of them had killed another after a Saturday night trip to town to hit the bars. Fight over a girl, maybe. "You never did say how long ago the…" He hesitated.

"Victim," Renee supplied.

"Yeah. The victim. You never said how long ago he died."

"Ten to twenty years is the coroner's best guess."

Daniel had recently turned thirty. This murder had happened so long ago, he'd been a kid.

He must have expressed his thought aloud, because the lady cop said crisply, "A twenty-year-old isn't a child."

Daniel grunted, not much liking the speculation in Renee Patton's eyes. What was she thinking? That at twenty he'd have been plenty old enough to commit murder? He went rigid in the saddle and the mare fidgeted under him, edging sideways, tossing her head. He hardly noticed.

God Almighty. The cops would be out here asking questions. People in town would soon be talking. Next time his mother went shopping, folks would hush up when she neared, but she wouldn't have to hear the whispers to know what was being said. Locals would be remembering her husband's sudden death, and the way she'd let her father-in-law just up and wander out into the cold night, never to be seen again. Now a body had been found out on the Triple B, but not Joshua Barnard's. A lot of dying out there, people would say; maybe those others weren't accidents after all.

"Your horse is getting antsy," Renee Patton said, stepping back from the corral fence. "I'll head on down to the house and talk to your mother."

His mother's twin losses, not that many years apart, had weakened her fiber. Maybe she never had been strong, although when he was a child she'd seemed that way. He knew she still cried sometimes, for no reason anyone else could see.

"You're not talking to her without me there," Daniel said flatly, urging Marian B Good toward the gate. As obliging as ever, the mare went through, then turned sideways without him asking so he could close it behind them. He swung off the horse's back and led her to the barn, the cop trailing him.

When he called, a young cowboy came out and took Marian's reins. "Walk her," Daniel said, and Warren nodded, looking curiously toward Renee. Daniel didn't explain her presence.

Renee fell into step with him as he strode between paddocks. "I wasn't planning to grill your mother," she said mildly.

He'd like to believe her.

Daniel said abruptly, "I never told her about the bones."

"Never told her...?" Renee lifted her eyebrows. "Why?"

"Until I was sure it wasn't Granddad…" He stopped. "I figured I would when we knew more."

"She's going to be sorry this isn't your grandfather."

"Sorry?" he began incredulously.

"Never finding a trace is worse than having some bones to lay to rest." Her tone was flat; her face averted now.

The sense of what she'd said penetrated, and Daniel hunched his shoulders. The uniform Renee Patton wore was mannish, but she had a woman's instincts and way of driving to the emotional heart of a matter. She was right—a real funeral would assuage his mother's grief, if not her terrible sense of guilt.

Down at the house, he knocked once, then opened the door. "Mom?" he called.

"Why, Daniel!" His mother appeared from the kitchen. The welcoming smile on her plain, gentle face wavered when she clapped eyes on the woman beside him, then settled into place again. "I'm sorry, Officer, I didn't realize…"

"No reason you should," the lady cop said. "I'm parked over by the barns."

"Is there trouble?" His mother's gaze turned anxiously to him.

Only old trouble that should have been buried ten, twenty years ago.

"No," he said. "Not exactly."

"I need to speak to you," Renee interjected. "If you have a few minutes to spare."

"Of course." His mother's ingrained courtesy kicked in. "Why don't you come into the living room. Can I get you coffee? Tea?"

"I'm fine."

His mother looked at him again; Daniel shook his head.

The front room was more like an old-fashioned parlor: rarely used, a formal configuration of wing chairs and high-backed sofa, dark wood end tables dotted with china figurines Daniel's father had bought for his wife. The only incongruous note was the bright painted wooden blocks scattered in front of the couch. As kids, he and his sister hadn't been allowed to play in here. His mother must be more permissive with her grandson.

Renee chose a chair; Daniel sat beside his mother on the sofa and took her hand. Fine and fragile, it trembled in his. He didn't give the cop a chance to break the news.

"Mom," he said gently, "lately Lotto has been bringing home bones. I, uh, I realized they were human and called the police. I didn't tell you because I wanted to know more first. Officer Patton brought me an update today, and it turns out this doesn't have anything to do with us. The bones are a young man's, and they've been out there a long time."

Somewhere in this speech, her pupils dilated until her eyes were huge and dark and unfamiliar. At the end, she sagged a little.

Her voice was faint with relief. "You mean, like an Indian burial? Or some settler?"

"No, Mrs. Barnard." Renee was watching his mother with an intensity that scared Daniel, but her voice was kind enough. "The coroner thinks this man was murdered. Knifed. Probably ten, fifteen, maybe as much as twenty years ago. His body might have been dumped here, but we can't rule out the possibility that he was one of your ranch hands, say. You must have had ones up and leave unexpectedly. Maybe even without taking their stuff."

A moan rose from his mother's throat. "Fifteen years ago?" she whispered.

Renee edged forward in her seat, her expression like Lotto's at the sight of tall grass shivering from the movement of some small creature. "What happened fifteen years ago?"

Mrs. Barnard stared blindly. Whatever she saw, it wasn't in this living room here and now. She kept making that sound, a soft keening that raised the hair on Daniel's arms.

"Mom!" he said sharply, his fingers biting into her hand. "What's wrong?"

She swung toward him, the keening becoming small gasps. "Wrong?" she echoed, as if not understanding the word.

"What is it?" His throat hurt. Dear God, did he *want* her to say, with a cop sitting here hanging on every word? A wild glance told him that Renee wasn't feeling compassion; she looked predatory. And it was his mother she was hunting.

Not that Daniel knew what he feared; his mother couldn't have hurt anybody, she even trapped spiders and buzzing flies and carried them out of the house to tenderly release them. But it sure as hell sounded as if Mom knew something. About his father?

She looked back at the cop, then him. A shudder worked its way up her thin frame, and she closed her eyes for a long moment. When she opened them again, the pupils were almost back to normal.

"I…" She wet her lips. "You're certain this man was young? He can't possibly have been my father-in-law?"

After an infinitesimal pause, Renee leaned back in her chair, apparently willing—for now—to accept that Mrs. Barnard's distress had been for her father-in-law. "The coroner is quite certain. From the bones he has to work with, he thinks the man might have been anywhere from teenage to thirty at the most. He says that he was under six feet tall, maybe as short as five nine. Probably wiry."

Mrs. Barnard didn't blink. "How can you possibly identify him from that vague a description?"

"Dental records will help."

He'd have sworn his mother's cheeks blanched. He also had the unpleasant feeling he wasn't the only one to notice.

"Mrs. Barnard, Mr. Barnard." Renee sat unmoving, her clear eyes missing nothing. "I'm going to need you to find your employment records from back then. We might be able to follow up, see if we can trace the men who worked here. Of course we'll be checking neighboring spreads, too. I don't know if your dog wanders that far…"

Daniel would have liked to lie. But the Rosler ranch, the nearest, was a mile and a half away. Lotto liked to keep Daniel in sight. He was never gone long enough to have left Barnard land. Reluctantly, Daniel shook his head.

"Mrs. Barnard, do you remember anything at all that might shed some light on this crime? Any talk, back then, about someone disappearing, or a fight, or ugly feelings? Did your husband complain about a hand who didn't show up to work one morning? You must have a pretty good idea what goes on around here."

Body rigid, his mother said expressionlessly, "Ms… excuse me, *Officer* Patton, hands come and go and my husband was always complaining. After fifteen years, no one story sticks in my mind. We've had as many as half a dozen men working for us at any one time. Sometimes, after a Saturday night in town, one of them will have a black eye or be walking real careful. But, to be truthful, I can hardly even remember names and

faces from that long ago. Maybe—" she rose to her feet
"—once I find the records they'll nudge my memory.
But I can't promise."

It didn't take much perception to realize that Officer
Patton was being gently dismissed. Whether she'd have
gone if she hadn't been ready to leave anyway was
another question. As it was, she, too, rose to her feet.

"Thank you, Mrs. Barnard. I'll be stopping by again.
Perhaps I can speak to your daughter then, too."

The air seemed to quiver, and his mother stiffened.
"My daughter?"

"She'd have been a child, but children hear things."

Mrs. Barnard's mouth pinched, but she gave a single
formal nod. "Yes. Very well. If you'll call ahead, I'll ask
her to be here."

Daniel walked Renee to the door. "I assume you
remember the way," he said.

Her eyes met his; plainly, she knew why he didn't
want to accompany her back. "Of course," she agreed.
"I'm sorry that I upset your mother."

"Murder isn't a pleasant subject."

She didn't look away. "No. It isn't. Is it?"

"For God's sake…" he growled.

"Good day, Mr. Barnard." She went down the stairs
and walked away without a glance back.

He disliked her a great deal just then, but he also
watched her go longer than he should have, because of the
way her hips swayed inside uniform trousers that fit her
rump snugly. They'd probably been designed for a man.

Daniel swore under his breath. So the lady cop was
pretty. She also had a gaze that measured guilt and sized
it for prison bars. She didn't give a damn what she did
to his mother's fragile sense of peace.

When he went back in, he closed the front door and, for a moment, stood just inside, listening. Had his mother gone back to the kitchen?

But when he went to the archway and looked into the living room, he saw that she'd sunk back onto the couch and sat, spine ruler straight, staring ahead with wide unblinking eyes. Fear laid cold fingers on his nape.

"Mom?"

Her head slowly turned toward him; more sluggishly yet, her eyes focused. "Daniel?"

She sounded as if she couldn't remember why he was here. The fear walked a few icy steps down his neck.

He went into the living room and sat next to her again, taking her hand. It was as cold as he felt inside.

"Mom." He waited until her head swung toward him, until her wide distressed gaze acknowledged his existence. "What happened here fifteen years ago?"

RENEE FOUND, as she'd expected, that it was tedious work following up on the dozens of missing person cases that fell within the ten year span that Bobby Sanchez had suggested.

Some could be eliminated because of gender or age, among them Daniel Barnard's grandfather. She took a few minutes to read the stark police report on the night Joshua Barnard had disappeared into a snowstorm. It added nothing to Jack Murray's recollection. Searchers had indeed combed the ranch land for days; not even a footprint was found. Where had the old man gone? Why?

Just thinking about it gave her the willies. Sure, he'd been senile. But still, he'd chosen to go out that door, walking away from what he knew toward something imagined or real that seemed better. Not so different than what Renee's mother had done. What her sister had done.

Why did anybody shed a life as if it were old skin, unneeded and uninteresting? How could you just let it fall to the ground? Kick it aside as if it were nothing, as if the scars on the discarded skin didn't represent pain, the birthmarks your heritage? As if you hadn't touched other people in that old life?

From long habit Renee was able to wall that familiar emptiness and hurt behind everyday busyness. She searched records, made phone calls, eliminated as possibilities another fourteen men who somebody had thought was missing, back all those years ago. Two had died; one had been discovered dead behind the wheel of his car, which had gone off an icy, little-used road into a canyon. One case resulted from a misunderstanding; the guy had never really been missing. Most had come home again.

One of those, interestingly, was the son of the rancher whose spread bordered the Barnard's. He'd had a police record. Petty stuff, but Gabe Rosler sounded as if he'd been a troubled teenager and young man. When he dropped from sight thirteen years ago, the family panicked, but only a few weeks later he surfaced in San Francisco. Too bad. He'd have been a likely prospect.

But just as interesting was one of Gabe Rosler's buddies who'd vanished about the same time. In fact, people had assumed they'd gone together, only Gabe showed up again, and Les Greene didn't. Greene was into drugs, although he liked hallucinogens, not today's more popular crack. According to his description, he was a little on the tall side—six foot, according to his mother and the high school, where he'd played football before he got tossed from the team for drinking. On the other hand, in Renee's experience, males tended to exaggerate height as much as women tended, when asked, to admit to substantially fewer pounds than they really weighed. Mothers were given to exaggerating, too, as were high school athletic departments.

Besides, given how few bones the coroner had to work with, couldn't he be wrong an inch or two one way or the other?

Greene's mother, she discovered, had died two years ago. Cirrhosis of the liver. Her son had come by his vices naturally, it appeared.

Renee put Les Greene's file on her stack of possibles, then called it a day.

Home was her father's house—she still thought of it that way—within spitting distance of the Deschutes River. The view from the back stoop, Renee told herself, was why she was still in the house despite too many empty rooms and the unsettling sight of her father's recliner sometimes giving an agitated rock on its own.

Chief Patton had kept the place in pristine condition. He painted the house every two years, power-washed the roof every fall, mowed the lawn twice a week. So far, she'd done the same. How could she not, with him looking over her shoulder? His ghost would never let her sleep nights if the windows were smudged or the grass untrimmed along the fence.

Tonight the darn place felt even lonelier than usual. She almost wished she'd hear a clank of handcuffs as her father's ghost strode down the hall.

She stood in the living room—with the same furniture that had been there all her life—and said aloud, "I should sell the house."

Of course she should. She didn't even know why she hadn't. Her younger sister Abby wanted her to. Dad had been dead…six months. Not long, for the loss of a dearly beloved parent. But Renee hadn't loved him.

She didn't stop in the living room tonight, any more than she ever did. She hadn't sat in there in six months. How could she curl up in the armchair and read, when she could *feel* him in that damned recliner, rustling his newspaper, making edgy comments, working up a head of steam about something.

Even the brief image of him was enough to prickle the tiny hairs on her arms. Renee shivered and hurried into the kitchen, which had always been the domain of the girls. Nowadays, she practically lived in here. She'd even moved the TV to the dining room table.

She stuck a frozen, prepared dinner into the microwave and set the timer, then leaned against the counter waiting. She hadn't cooked dinner in six months, either. Not a real, oven kind of meal. Microwave was good enough for her. Some nights she brought home Chinese takeout or a pizza or even just a burger and fries. Not nutritious, but she'd become sick of cooking. And the only recipes she knew were those her father had liked. Meat loaf. A few casseroles. She could mash potatoes, grill a steak. Her beef stews were probably very good; Dad had always grunted when he dug in, which she'd taken for approval.

What fond memories he'd left her, Renee thought bitterly. He hadn't given hugs or quiet words of praise. No, her best memories were of silence or a grunt.

She reached for the telephone without thought, dialing a number she knew by heart. Her younger sister answered on the first ring.

"I was just thinking about you," Abby said. "What's up?"

"What were you thinking?" Renee countered.

"Just that I haven't seen you in two weeks. Shall we have dinner one of these nights? Tomorrow? No, shoot, I can't do that. How about Thursday?"

Renee consulted her mental calendar. "Sounds good."

They discussed where, made plans to meet. Then Abby asked, "How are you?"

The microwave beeped. Phone held between her ear and her shoulder, Renee took the dinner out, peeled off the plastic top and dumped it onto a plate. She felt like being civilized tonight.

"Oh, I'm okay."

Her sister waited.

"I've just had a weird couple of days. It's this case. Do you know the Barnards? I think Daniel was Meg's age."

They rarely talked about their sister. Abby said only, "No, that doesn't sound familiar. But I don't remember very many of her friends. Don't forget, I was only eleven when she left."

And had seemed younger. In one of those quick flashes, Renee saw Abby curled in a small ball in bed, face wet with tears. Feeling terribly young herself, Renee had still known that, at fourteen, she was now the mother. She'd slipped under the covers and held her little sister, spending the night in that narrow twin bed. Perhaps she'd needed the comfort as much as Abby had.

"Well, Daniel Barnard is a rancher. Quarter horses. The place is called the Triple B." She told Abby about the dog bringing home the skull, and about Joshua Barnard going out into the snowstorm one night and not coming back, and how interesting Shirley Barnard's reaction to the news of the murder had been. Finally she told her sister about the sheaf of missing persons reports she'd been reading.

"It's all made you think about Mom," Abby diagnosed.

"And Meg." Still leaning against the counter, Renee looked down without interest at the cooling lasagna. "Both of them, just disappearing like that… Don't you ever wonder?"

Abby was quiet for a moment. "Whether they're alive?"

"Yeah."

"Of course I wonder!" Unexpectedly, Abby sounded mad. "When I was little, I convinced myself that Mom was dead, so I could believe she'd really loved us! Because if she's *not* dead…"

"It means she didn't care very much about us."

"Which is probably the truth."

"But we know Meg loved us."

"Oh, sure," her sister said, the anger gone but her voice wry. "I remember the stuff she did with us, and the way she used to shield us from Dad. But, you know, when she left she was only sixteen. Even if she did love us, she was probably still glad to be gone. Away from him. And you were a pain about then, always talking back and making Dad mad, and then you'd yell at her when she tried to head you off."

"Blame *me*, why don't you?" Renee said hotly. As if she hadn't blamed herself often enough.

"I'm not!" Abby denied. "I'm just saying, Meg wasn't an adult like Mom. She hadn't *chosen* to have three kids, then leave them. I mean, how can we blame her?"

Easily, Renee thought. *You weren't the one who had to take her place because she couldn't be bothered with it anymore. You weren't the one who had to become an instant grown-up. Have dinner on the table when Dad walked in the door at 5:45 every day. Take the brunt of his anger.*

But all Renee said was, "She could have written us. Or called."

Again, her sister was silent, speaking at last in a small voice. "Yeah. She could have."

Renee sighed. "I didn't mean to get you down, too. I just…when I saw that skull, I thought it might be Mom. Or Meg, I guess, except at least I saw Meg packing. Mom was just…gone."

"Maybe someone else should handle this case. If it bothers you so much."

"No," Renee said swiftly, surprised at her instant resistance. "No, I want to see it through. If I can't accomplish anything else, I'm determined to give this guy his name back."

"In case…" Abby stopped.

She didn't have to finish. They both knew what she'd been going to say. *In case Mom had been buried somewhere in an anonymous grave. In case they'd never heard from her because she'd died and no one had known who she was, so they couldn't notify the family.*

"Anyway, it's my job," Renee said more pragmatically.

She hung up a moment later, thinking fate had sent her out to the Triple B. No one else in the department would care anywhere near as fiercely as she did.

Acknowledging, even to herself, how strongly she felt, how much she cared about having a name to put on a gravestone, embarrassed her.

It was probably just her mood, she decided. Tomorrow the whole thing would become a puzzle she had to put together. No more.

"Hey," she said aloud to the silent kitchen. "Investigating a murder beats staking out a mailbox."

She only wished Daniel Barnard wasn't involved. The way he charged her on his horse today had been a challenge, whether he knew it or not. When she didn't flinch, his eyes had held respect. That had meant more to her than she wanted to admit.

But the respect had been gone later. While she questioned his mother, he'd looked at her as if she were some kind of monster. He wasn't going to be any help on this. In fact, he'd be fighting her all the way.

Oh, well, she told herself. It wasn't as if he'd noticed her as a woman. Men didn't. Not the way they noticed Abby. Which was okay by her.

That's how she wanted it.

Renee dumped the now cold lasagna in the garbage, rinsed off the plate and turned on the television.

LISTENING TO THE SOUNDS of her son's departure, Shirley Barnard glanced down at the dish towel in her hands. She had picked it up only to look busy, as if she were herself again, ready to bustle around the kitchen. When the front door closed behind him, she let the towel drop as if it were a piece of trash and went to the round oak table in front of the bay window, where she sank into one of the chairs. The fraying cane seat gave comfortably, shaping to fit her. As it should. Why, she'd sat in this very same seat, three meals a day, for thirty years now! She didn't even have to count back; she'd been pregnant with Daniel when Matt had his grandmother's oak chairs freshly caned for his wife of two years.

In her memory it was only yesterday. She looked at the empty chairs, seeing in her mind's eye countless dinners, Daniel and Mary in high chairs, then as chattering school-age children, and finally teenagers. Joshua, after his wife had died and he'd moved in with Matt and Shirley. And Matthew, always Matthew, presiding over the table, his enormous shoulders filling the worn denim shirts he favored, his blue eyes sparkling with humor and that hint of something private she had to call lust, always just for her. She'd never been afraid of him straying, not Matthew. He'd sworn to love her for keeps, and he had. Even during that awful year when she hadn't wanted him on top of her, when the very idea made her stomach heave, still he had loved her and looked at her with desire and affection along with sorrow.

Shirley had never ever been glad Matt had died. How could she? she thought, shocked even though right this minute she *was* glad. She had loved him with all her being. When Daniel came to the house to tell her Matt had gone over a horse's neck—Matthew! Of all people!—straight into the wall of the arena and was unconscious, she'd rushed out without a coat even though it was winter and ridden in the ambulance with him to the hospital, holding his hand the entire way, terrified by his white still face. He'd stayed unconscious for two days, then died without ever waking up. He was brain dead, they'd tried to tell her, but she hadn't believed them. She'd talked to him, and squeezed his hand, and waited for his eyes to open and that slow sweet smile to curve his mouth when he saw her. His heart was beating—wasn't it—and he was breathing. So how could he be dead, the way the doctors said? It was like the night when Joshua wandered out, leaving the front door open and snow blowing into the front hall. They wanted to give up, and she wouldn't let them. How far could he have gone? He had to still be alive, just cold and lonely and confused. To this day she thought of him that way, huddled out there somewhere.

Daniel had tried to gently pull her away from her husband's side at the hospital. She had screamed at him to let her alone. Oh, how she'd loved that man! How could he die so stupidly, doing something he was so good at?

But now she had to be glad, because it would be worse, so much worse, if he'd been arrested and dragged off to prison. And it would have been her fault, because if it hadn't been for her he wouldn't have had to do what he'd done. Matthew had been a gentle man, not given to violence. Stern sometimes, and not wishy-washy in his beliefs, but his quick temper cooled just as fast.

But that night… Oh, that night…

Shirley stared dully into space. She'd buried all this fear and guilt ten feet under, where it belonged, never thinking to meet it again. Matt and she had agreed that putting it out of their minds was the best thing they could do. What good would talking about it do? If they pretended none of it had happened, pretty soon it would be as if it hadn't.

The bad thing about their not having talked was that she only knew part of the story. Her part. She hadn't wanted to know any more, not then. What you don't know can't hurt you, the scared child inside her had whispered. Don't ask.

But if she knew what had really happened that night after Matt stormed out, before he came back splattered with blood, she would be able to handle this. The finding of the bones. That police officer, here asking questions.

What you didn't know could hurt you, she realized, and the child didn't try to argue. That part of her was gone. Dead. No, not dead, just all grown up. Mourning her husband, but glad he wasn't here to speak out. For above everything else, he'd been honest. He wouldn't let blame go where it didn't belong.

If she had asked, he would have told her.

Tears were running down her cheeks, blurring her vision, so the past was all she *could* see.

"Oh, Matt," she whispered. "What did you do?"

CHAPTER THREE

"WHAT HAPPENED fifteen years ago?" Shirley Barnard echoed Renee's question without so much as raising her eyebrows. Looking unnaturally calm, she sat primly on her living room sofa, her hair softly curled, her face made up, no trace of yesterday's distress to be seen. She'd made an effort today, replacing the everyday housedress with a going-to-town one. "As I said," she continued, "nothing in particular happened fifteen years ago that I can recall. Why, have you pinpointed the…death to that year?"

Renee wondered if she was imagining the tension that had crept into the older woman's voice with her last question.

"No." Renee glanced down at her notebook, where she'd written precisely nothing. She looked back up, expression suitably bland. "You were the one to mention that date. And you did seem quite agitated."

"Are you certain you wouldn't like a cup of coffee?" When Renee declined, Mrs. Barnard said with that same false calm, "I'm afraid I upset my son, too. Having bones found here, on our place—" She broke off. "It just brought it all back. I felt—I still feel responsible for my father-in-law's death."

"I understand, Mrs. Barnard." Although she didn't,

Renee reflected, understand why a subject that had shattered Daniel's mother only yesterday could today be discussed as if it were less important than the weather. "But from what I read, it really wasn't your fault. You couldn't be expected…"

Mrs. Barnard lifted a hand. "Please, Officer Patton. You can't say anything that hasn't been said a thousand times before. My conscience doesn't believe any of it. I was alone with him. I let myself be distracted. He might have been gone as much as forty-five minutes before I noticed. If only I'd been able to call the police sooner…" She took a breath. "But that has nothing to do with your business here."

"Your father-in-law didn't disappear fifteen years ago."

"That's true." She went still. "I don't know what you're driving at."

Renee said conversationally, "I'm merely curious about why, when you became so upset, you specifically said 'fifteen years ago.' Not ten years ago, when your father-in-law died. Fifteen."

Now Mrs. Barnard did raise her eyebrows. "Wasn't it you who said fifteen years ago?"

"I gave a range. Ten to twenty."

"I'm certain you mentioned fifteen. I could only have been repeating the last thing you said."

Renee couldn't shake her. She also didn't believe her. Mrs. Barnard knew or suspected something that she had no intention of telling. At least, not telling Renee. Her son, however, might be another story.

She had already met and interviewed his sister, a slender dark-haired woman who had left the house immediately thereafter with her toddler, destination undisclosed.

Mary Stevens—her married name—had been wearing no makeup, and dark circles under her eyes suggested she wasn't sleeping well.

She didn't offer apologies or explanations, merely answered Renee's questions succinctly. Ten years ago she'd been seventeen. Yes, she thought she would have noticed if any ranch hands had vanished unexpectedly.

A shadow of a smile touched Mary's pale lips. "I was at an age when I was all too aware of any young man in denim and cowboy boots."

"What about when you were twelve?"

She made a horrible face. "I was slow maturing. *Really* slow. At twelve, I was still hoping I wouldn't have to bother with breasts." Mary glanced ruefully down at her chest. If her bra wasn't a C cup, Renee missed her guess. "So the answer is no. I had no interest whatsoever in the help, with a few exceptions."

"Exceptions?"

"Oh…" She shrugged. "I barrel raced. Dreamed of doing the rodeo circuit, much to my parents' dismay. One guy who worked here had been a bronc rider. I don't remember his name, but there was something a little dangerous about him. Now, if I'd been sixteen, I'd have probably been in love. Instead, I pumped him for details about rodeo life."

"Any others?"

"There were a few who were willing to indulge me. I'd follow them around." Her blue eyes were as clear and penetrating as her brother's. "But I don't see how this helps you."

"I don't suppose it does," Renee admitted. "But I want to know the name of the man who died out there, apparently never missed by anybody. He might have been a drifter, but chances are he worked around here."

"Most likely at the Triple B," Mary said slowly. "That's what you mean, isn't it?"

"Or at a neighboring ranch. Or he might have been someone who came out here to drink with one of your hands."

"In which case, someone who worked here was a murderer."

"That's a possibility," Renee said evenly. "Anybody occur to you?"

Unlike her mother, Mary looked as if she was giving it some serious thought. But she ended up shaking her head. "I'm sorry. The idea of a murderer... The guys I remember... I just can't see any of them bashing a man's head in, or shooting him, or... How did it happen?"

"A knife, we think." Interesting that neither her mother nor brother had told her. Renee sidestepped to an earlier thought. "You said there was something 'dangerous' about the one fellow. What did you mean?"

Daniel's sister actually laughed at that point. "I suspect what my twelve-year-old self was trying to put into words is that he was sexy. You know, one of those guys who would raise a mother's warning flags. I know mine didn't like me spending time with him. Not that he'd have looked twice at me, even if I had been interested. At that age, I could have stood in for a fence rail."

"Me, too." Renee was momentarily surprised that the admission had slipped out. She rarely got personal with interview subjects. "Well," she said briskly, "I guess that's it. If you think of anything..."

"Of course." Mary stood, then hesitated. "You know, this is upsetting my mother dreadfully. Is it really necessary for you to talk to her again?"

So Daniel wasn't alone in feeling protective toward his mother.

"I'm afraid so," Renee said. "She's the only one still here who was an adult when the crime was committed. She would have seen things differently than you or your brother did."

Mary accepted the answer, although she looked troubled when she left the living room. Yet she bundled up her boy and departed rather than staying to offer moral support to her mother.

Not that Mrs. Barnard appeared to need it. Today her facade never cracked. Renee wondered if she was as fragile as her children seemed to think.

Daniel was expecting her up at his house, Mrs. Barnard informed her at the end of the interview.

"His office is there. He has the boxes of old personnel records I'd stored in the attic."

"Fine. Thank you. I'm sorry to have had to bother you again."

Mrs. Barnard's dark eyes, so unlike her son's and daughter's, met Renee's with a kind of pleading. "This may have nothing to do with us."

"That's true," Renee agreed, moved to both compassion and curiosity by the other woman's veiled desperation. "But I have to start somewhere. You understand."

"They—" she swallowed "—the bones...*he* was found here. On Barnard land. Of course, I understand."

Renee didn't tell her that she would undoubtedly be back. Nothing would convince her Shirley Barnard's terrified, grieving response to the news that a murder had been committed here on the Triple B fifteen years ago had a thing to do with the old man who had chosen to die out in the wilderness rather than in a recliner in front of the TV.

When she rang Daniel's doorbell, she had to wait for several minutes before he opened the door.

"Sorry," he said curtly. "I was on the phone."

With his mother? Renee wondered.

His flannel shirt was unbuttoned over a faded blue T-shirt. As she followed him, this time through the living room, she saw that his dark hair was damp and his jeans clean. Her uniform shoes clicked on the wood floor; he padded silently in stocking feet. Again his very presence, his height and sheer bulk, moved her to uneasiness edged with something she'd rather not identify.

Large and uncluttered, his office had the same feel as the living room. Renee took in the gleaming birch floors, ceiling-high bookcases, oak filing cabinets, desk and computer, the screen glowing blue-white. A dhurrie rug in rust and sage and desert sand added just enough color. On the far side of the room, a big leather chair faced the picture windows.

Once in the office, he stood to one side. Aware of him behind her, she crossed the room and looked out. The expansive view explained why he'd built his house on the ridge. To the south, she could just see Rusty Butte, a small red cinder cone. Directly west were the barns and pastures laid out like a child's model. Beyond them was the dry gray-green high desert country, not beautiful like the mountains to the west, but compelling.

She made a sound and turned. "Wish we had a view like that from the station."

He didn't comment, only jerked his head toward the desk. "The files you asked for are right here."

"Thank you." Renee hesitated. "Will you be around if I have questions?"

He grunted. "I'm not going anywhere."

Oh, good. She could spend the whole afternoon with her nerves prickling from that uncomfortable awareness. Dismay drove her to say casually, "In that case, why don't I take these out to your kitchen table? So you can keep working."

"I'll bring a card table in here." He disappeared immediately, eager either to accommodate her or to keep his eye on her. She suspected the latter, considering the chill she'd felt from him today.

He set up the card table, pulled a straight-backed chair over from in front of his desk, and dragged the boxes to the table.

"Thank you," she said again.

Daniel nodded in acknowledgment, then bent to peel the tape from the flaps on one of the cartons. "These are payroll records. The other box has personnel files." Seeing her expression, he said, "Don't get excited. Basically, all we keep are the original applications, maybe a letter of recommendation, a few notes. We don't do written evaluations like a big company."

To be thorough, she started back twenty years ago, taking notes when she came to anyone who fell in the right age range. No comments had been written when an employee left, although she discovered that sometimes a new hire started immediately, and sometimes several weeks passed before a new name and social security number appeared. From that, she could deduce when notice had been given and when someone had most likely quit unexpectedly. Or just flat out disappeared.

At first the records were all handwritten. The paper

had yellowed and the ink faded. After scanning a couple years' worth, Renee took a break from the payroll ledgers and opened the box that held personnel files.

She had deliberately sat with her back to Daniel, at his desk. The intermittent clack of computer keys was sandwiched between long periods of silence.

When she stretched, he said immediately, "Would you like a cup of coffee?"

"Do you have something cold?" Renee asked without turning. "Pop?"

He made a noncommittal sound and went away, coming back after a few minutes with a glass of ice and a can of cola. "This okay?"

"Wonderful." She smiled at him.

He didn't smile back. She was still in the doghouse. He also didn't return to his desk, however.

Renee asked idly, "Is your sister here for a visit?"

"No." For a moment it appeared he would say no more. At last, looking reluctant, he continued, "She's having problems with her husband. They needed to cool off."

"I'm sorry. She seems very nice."

The groove in one cheek deepened. "Yeah. She is."

Still he stood there, towering over her. She wondered if he was making her feel small on purpose. Reminding her that he didn't think a woman should be a cop.

"Well," she said. "Back to work."

He took the hint and retreated, although she wasn't sure how far. He moved so quietly. And she was damned if she was going to turn to look. What if he were watching her? She wouldn't let him see that he made her self-conscious.

Damn it, she didn't know why he did.

The personnel files were marginally more interest-

ing than the financial ledgers had been, although Daniel
was right: they weren't a treasure trove of information.
No photographs, just a bare application asking for a
minimum of background data—previous jobs, education, two names for references. Age was asked, although
a few had left the space blank. On the back of most, the
date of employment and termination had been written.

"They don't stay long, do they?" Renee murmured.

Behind her, Daniel said, "Low pay, hard work."

She turned in her chair. He was leaning back in his,
long legs stretched out, stocking feet on the desk. Hands
clasped behind his head, he contemplated her. Had he
been staring at her for the past hour?

"Is there any way of telling the ones who actually
said goodbye from the ones who just upped and left?"

"Probably not." He didn't move. "I remember
some of them."

"Your sister mentioned a cowboy she thought was
'dangerous.' Her word, not mine. She said your mother
didn't like her talking to him."

He frowned and put his feet back on the floor. "Did
she say how old she was?"

"Um…twelve, I think."

"Ah." His mouth tilted into a faint, crooked smile.
"Yeah, I remember him. Let me think." He rubbed his
jaw. "Seems like he went by initials. Uh, L.J., P.J.—no,
T.J. Yeah, that was it. T. J. Baxter, though I might have
the last name wrong."

Renee flipped back through the files. Baxter. There
it was. She'd already glanced through it; T. J. Baxter was
one of those who'd left abruptly, or so it appeared.

"Why didn't your mother like him?"

"He flirted with anything in skirts. Even Mom.

Baxter liked Mary, though I never saw anything wrong in it. He was patient, indulgent...you know, as if she were a kid sister. But he made Mom nervous."

Renee could see why. Young Mary Barnard hadn't been far from physically developing. If T. J. Baxter, with his glamorous past as a rodeo bronc rider, had still been around when Mary did develop an interest in young cowboys in tight jeans, Baxter would have been a real danger.

"So, did he get fired?"

"Yeah, Dad lost patience. Baxter was good with horses but lazy. You couldn't trust him to keep working when no one was watching. Dad told him to clear out."

"You heard? Saw him packing?"

Daniel frowned. "No, his bunk was empty one morning, and Dad said he'd told him to go. You saying my father lied?"

Lying went hand-in-glove with murder. But Renee didn't remind him of that fact, since she had no reason at all to suspect the late Matthew Barnard of either offense.

"Just hoping to eliminate him as a possibility," she said neutrally.

He didn't comment, but the creases between his dark brows didn't smooth out.

"Thanks for the info," Renee said pointedly, opening the next file.

He gave only a brusque nod before picking up a pen and returning to work. Or to staring at her. She didn't know, since she didn't look over her shoulder to check.

She worked steadily from then on, her pile of notes growing. Given the social security numbers, she ought to be able to find out which of these men had started another job elsewhere after leaving the Triple B. And which one hadn't, because he'd never left Barnard land.

When Renee flipped the ledger closed, she glanced at her watch. Six o'clock. The shadows were dropping low in the sky. In another hour, the picture windows would frame a glorious spectacle.

She rotated her head, working some kinks out of her neck, then stole a surreptitious glance over her shoulder. She was alone in the office.

Returning everything to the boxes, she closed the tops and restuck the tape as best she could. Then she took her notes and made her way back through the quiet house. Had its owner left her alone altogether? At the front door, she called, "Mr. Barnard?"

He appeared from the direction of the kitchen before she could feel silly, shouting in an empty house.

"All done?" he asked.

"I think so. I appreciate your cooperation." She sounded wooden, worlds from how she felt. His magnetic blue eyes made her want to hang her head like a shy adolescent.

"I was about to put dinner on the table." He nodded back toward the kitchen.

Renee became consciously aware of the delicious aroma that had probably hurried her through those last files. Pot roast, she guessed. And biscuits? Was he expecting someone? Hinting that he'd be glad to see her backside?

Daniel rocked onto his heels and shoved his hands into the pockets of his jeans. "Can I talk you into staying? I get tired of eating by myself."

He wanted *her* to stay to dinner? Astonishment made her blurt, "Your mother would probably appreciate your company." Wasn't that graceless, even for her? she marveled.

One dark eyebrow rose, making her feel even more gauche. Smoothly, Daniel said, "I'm sure she's sitting down to her own meal by now. We keep early hours."

"Oh. Um, I had plans for dinner." What lonely company pride could be.

His expression closed, becoming remote. "Ah. Well, enjoy yourself."

Exasperated, her stomach growled. Whatever he was making for dinner *did* smell awfully good. And he *had* asked her, which was something men rarely did. He undoubtedly wanted to know more about her investigation, or else he was just being polite, but it didn't hurt to be sociable, did it? He wasn't a suspect, for Pete's sake.

Impulsively, Renee admitted, "My plans were for a microwave dinner. Lasagna, I think. That's the best."

Daniel's mouth twitched. "Undoubtedly," he agreed.

"Your dinner smells better."

"Pot roast."

"I thought so." She took a deep breath. "If you really mean it…"

"I don't say things I don't mean."

Her father hadn't, either. Which was why he'd never given compliments. If Daniel Barnard hadn't said she was pretty, even implied she was as pretty as her sister Meg, Renee would have figured he was grudging with them, too. He didn't seem the slick kind to use flattery to disarm an opponent. But she had heard him say it, a mistruth so blatant that now she was suspicious. *You're not so bad-looking,* Renee might have bought. As pretty as Meg—never.

Except…there might be a man somewhere who

'hought she was. Men and women both had incompre-
hensible tastes sometimes, she'd seen that for herself.
Fortunately, nature had the common sense to shield
people's vision with blinders.

More likely Daniel Barnard had forgotten what Meg
looked like, and the compliment had been an idle
remark, the kind of thing people say without meaning
much. Not a lie exactly, but not words to hold close to
your heart, either.

Still, it wouldn't hurt to stay to dinner to see, would it?

"Well, then, thank you," Renee said. "A man who can
really cook is a wonder I've got to behold."

A slow smile warmed his face, making her see it in
a different light. That first time, she'd thought him plain
except for those extraordinary eyes. But now, with a
smile dipping the crease in his cheek deeper, creating
tiny crinkles beside his blue, blue eyes, giving a sexy
twist to his mouth, she knew she'd been wrong.

Or else nature was in the process of manufacturing
a pair of blinders for her, custom fit.

Scary thought.

She followed him back to the kitchen, where her
offer to help was refused. He poured her some wine and
insisted she sit back and admire.

"Besides," he confessed, "it's ready. Not much else
to do. Unless you want a salad?"

"Not if there are vegetables in with that meat. And
potatoes. I never have potatoes anymore, except
French fries."

Using quilted oven mitts, which were kind of cute on
a man, Daniel carried the cast-iron pot to the table where
he set it on a trivet. In the very spot the skull had sat,
come to think of it. But she wouldn't let that bother her.

She blinked and realized he'd said something. "What?"

"I asked why you never have potatoes anymore."

"Because I'd have to cook 'em. I quit cooking after my father died."

Now, why had she told him that? He'd want to know how she'd felt about her father and what his death had meant to her. And she didn't know. Wouldn't want to say if she did know.

But Daniel surprised her. "Were they his favorite food?"

Renee blinked. "I guess so. Well, meat and potatoes."

"A man after my own heart."

Oh, she surely did hope not.

A basket of hot biscuits joined the main course on the table. Margarine in the wrapper—how typical of a man not to gussy it up. Then he joined her.

After the first bite, Renee gave an ecstatic sigh. "You can cook."

"Did you doubt me?"

His tone was serious enough to make her wonder if he was really talking about his ability in the kitchen. She looked up to find him regarding her with an expression just as grave.

"I have no reason to doubt you," she said after a moment, carefully.

Their eyes held. At last he nodded, as though satisfied, then picked up his fork. "Good."

She buttered her biscuit and discovered that it was melt-in-your-mouth perfection. Why wasn't a man who could cook like this married?

She didn't quite dare ask that.

"I hear your horses have quite a reputation," she said instead, almost at random. "Jack Murray says they've won national championships."

"That's the goal, if you really want to breed or train horses." Daniel savored a bite, then continued, "I rarely show them myself beyond the regional level. That's not what I want to do. I get them to a certain point, then sell 'em. The new owners make my reputation."

She tilted her head to one side. "Which means, I suppose, that you have to pick the new owners carefully."

"Right." He flashed a grin that almost stopped her heart. Definitely not plain. "I would, anyway, because I don't want to hear that one of my animals has been mistreated. But when I have a good horse, I'll only sell it to someone who has the ability to make it a champion. If Triple B horses aren't popping up in the top ten regularly, my asking prices would have to drop."

"Your father trained horses, too?"

"Yes, but on a smaller scale. He never made much money. I figured the business should be more than subsistence. Besides—" another quick smile "—when I do something, I want to be the best."

She contemplated what that said about him. "And your quarter horses are."

"I got lucky, to start with." He leaned his elbows comfortably on the table. "A colt my father almost sold turned out to be the smartest horse I've ever known. He went all the way, the one time I've competed at a national show. He's still standing stud here, along with one of his sons. That mare I was riding yesterday is a granddaughter. She's going to be the best."

"You love what you do," Renee said, amazed.

"Why else would I do it?" he said simply.

The answer came without thought. "Because you inherited this place. Because your father did it."

"Is that why you're a cop?" His eyes told her he'd see through any lie. "Because your father was?"

Renee looked down at her nearly empty plate. "Partly," she admitted. "It's…what I grew up with. Becoming a cop felt natural."

Instead of pursuing it, for which she was grateful, Daniel said mildly, "I suppose it's the same for me. I was put on a horse before I could walk. But that's not all of it. The same was true for my sister, but she's a nurse. Says she can't imagine spending her life on fun and games."

Amused at the outrage he couldn't hide, Renee smiled. "She has a point. Cutting horses aren't used much anymore on cattle ranches, I hear."

"The day an all-terrain vehicle can outthink Marian B Good is the day I hang it up."

"Marian be good," Renee mused. "Did you name her?"

Daniel sat back in his chair looking wary. "Yeah."

"Was it wishful thinking? Like, you could substitute any woman's name? Susan be good? Jennifer be good?" *Renee be good?* she couldn't help adding to herself.

"Her mom was Good Golly. Her grandma was Marian B."

"Oh, I see." Renee gazed innocently at him. "Strictly a family thing."

"Damn it," he growled, but with amusement narrowing his eyes "I'm as good in the kitchen as any woman. So don't accuse me of being a sexist pig."

She raised her eyebrows. "I seem to recall something about how a police uniform wasn't made to fit a woman. Care to comment?"

"It's ugly," he said bluntly. "It's not that I think a woman belongs in an apron. Or satin and lace. You, for example. I think you'd look fine in tight jeans. Or a doctor's coat. Don't read into my words what isn't there."

Not totally reassured, she asked, "Does Jack Murray look bad in this uniform?"

"I've never given a thought to how Jack looks. Now, you…" For the first time, he let his eyes blatantly caress her.

No man had ever hungered for her. She couldn't believe this one was. Stiffly, she said, "Well, give it a thought now."

"You're a tough nut to crack, aren't you?"

A tough nut. That was her. God forbid she be a desirable woman.

"That's right," she drawled. "So, what do you think? This—" she thumbed her lapel "—look okay on Jack?"

Now annoyance flickered in Daniel Barnard's eyes. "Yeah. The fabric is heavy, sturdy, utilitarian. Masculine."

It stung. She couldn't lie to herself. But she didn't have to let him know how much. "So," she said insolently, "the truth comes out."

A muscle in his jaw jerked. "The uniform is masculine. The job isn't necessarily."

She didn't back down. "The uniform's a symbol. Like the badge. It's all a package deal."

"Maybe so." He turned his wineglass without picking it up. "I like what's inside the package better than I do the wrapping paper."

She opened her mouth and closed it.

A smile appeared in his eyes. "Deflated all that righteous anger, didn't I?"

Renee struggled with the unpalatable fact that he was right. Oh, she did hate to admit that. "Yeah," she grumbled. "You took the fun out of my evening."

His gaze didn't leave her even as he sipped wine. "Now, why were you so all-fired sure I was a jerk? Didn't Meg like me?"

"Actually, she had a crush on you for a while. Before she and Jack started going out."

She'd expected him to look gratified. He only arched a brow. "Okay, then. Why the preconception?"

There had been no preconception. She'd taken his words wrong because she wanted to. Because disliking him was easier than wanting him.

"I guess I've just gotten prickly," Renee said. "I meet plenty of jerks who really think I have no business wearing a badge or a gun. The way you put it about the uniform…" She shrugged. "Like I said, I guess I'm too sensitive."

Somehow she'd convinced him. He grimaced, nodded. "I can see how that would happen. Okay. Can we start from square one?"

"You mean, I can't finish my dinner?"

His slow warm smile was just for her. "We just jumped forward to square three real quick."

"Square three being a display of hospitality."

"No." Raw intent darkened his eyes. "It's a woman and a man breaking bread together."

Her heart felt as if it might bounce right out of her chest. She tried to sound insouciant, but her voice squeaked. "I hate to think what square four is."

"Well…" Daniel's gaze touched her mouth. "We might get there yet tonight, who knows?"

Lord Almighty, she thought. Was he talking about kissing? Did he *want* to kiss her?

CHAPTER FOUR

WELL, HE HADN'T GOTTEN so far as kissing her, but Daniel was otherwise satisfied with the evening. In that drab uniform, Renee Patton was like some neglected, winter-pastured horse, brought in with hip bones showing and coat dull. Given a month or two and the right care, that mare would become round and shiny and fit, an eyeful of magnificent horseflesh. Renee's spring hadn't come yet, he sensed; her father was dead, but she hadn't yet blossomed away from his harshness.

Or maybe, Daniel told himself, he was reading more into her few remarks about Patton than they deserved. For all he knew, she was mending from a heart broken by another man. But somehow he didn't think so. He remembered as a kid going to the movie *Cinderella*. He had never seen such innocence until he met Renee.

Sexual and romantic innocence, that is. Where her job was concerned, she was all too knowing. Young as she was, she already had cynicism in her eyes, an expectation that people would lie to her.

That his mother would lie.

God help them all, she was right. His mother was lying, although he thought it wasn't easy for her. But if she was concealing something that had happened fifteen years ago, she must have told plenty of lies in those years. Even to him.

Mary had tried to talk to their mother, too, with no more success.

"Maybe it is just thinking about Granddad that has her upset," his sister had said without much conviction. Her two-year-old son toddled toward Daniel's kitchen. Mary rose from the couch, corralled the boy and continued above his howls, "You know Mom. She wouldn't have…well, had anything to do with that dead body."

She couldn't say it either—Mom wouldn't have had anything to do with *murder.* Impossible. But then, why was she lying?

"Maybe not," he said. "But you know how much she loved Dad. And he had a temper."

Short-lived and never resulting in more than roars of displeasure, but if someone had hurt one of the horses or threatened his beloved family, he might have lashed out.

It was the knife part that had Daniel's imagination balking. Stabbing someone had to be planned. Feeling the blade bite flesh, sink in, scrape bone… Continuing to thrust every sickening inch. Hate, not temper, would lead you to do that. Or else no conscience at all.

"Not Dad," his sister said, as if she'd followed his thoughts as clearly as a trail through the high desert scrub.

"No," Daniel agreed, but he could see in her eyes that, same as him, she was thinking, *Then why is Mom lying?* Partly to distract her, he asked, "You been talking to Kurt?"

Tension quivered through his sister's fine-boned frame. "Yes. He says he misses me."

Not, he misses me, but he *says* he misses me.

She changed the subject immediately, so Daniel let

it go. A few minutes later Mary hoisted her son onto her hip and left, looking pleased when he invited their mother and her and her son, Devon, to dinner that night. Renee's sharp little comment had reminded him he hadn't done so yet, and Mary had been home going on two weeks now, with no sign that she was thinking of returning to her husband.

Daniel had never liked Kurt Stevens, though for his sister's sake he'd hidden his feelings. Mary's husband was one of those men who seemed stuck knee-deep in adolescence. Daniel had been in the car with him once when he decided another driver had cut him off. Instead of shrugging and accepting that some folks had bad manners, Kurt had chased the other driver down, gotten out of his own car, stalked forward and slammed a booted foot into the door of a shiny red Subaru with a ski rack on top. Scared the hell out of someone. Kurt was lucky, Daniel thought, that the "someone" hadn't had a loaded gun under the front seat.

Daniel wasn't sure what had gone wrong with his sister's marriage. He'd been trying to find out, but she wasn't talking. It would be their business, he figured, unless his suspicions were right and the bastard had taken some of that rage out on his wife or son. Then it would become Daniel's concern. A sister had a right to her brother's protection.

As did a mother to her son's. There couldn't be any doubt, next time Renee Patton came calling, of whose side he was on. He might want her with surprising fierceness, but his family still had to come first.

He could only hope Renee didn't put him in the position of having to choose. Wouldn't you think she'd give up soon? The murder was an old one. The present day had enough bloodshed and burglary and car wrecks to occupy the small police force, surely.

When his mother didn't call in a tizzy the next day to let him know the policewoman had been back, Daniel began to relax. Renee would follow up on all those names she'd collected and get nowhere. Find out that every one of the ranch hands had moved on to work elsewhere or died natural if early deaths like his father. With the social security numbers, it should be easy, shouldn't it?

Yet another morning came with no police car turning in through the ranch gates. He figured curiosity was a good enough excuse to call her by that afternoon. When she came on the line promptly, Daniel identified himself and asked if she was having any luck.

"Not as much as you'd think," Renee grumbled. "The computers were down all morning, and I do have other cases."

Good, Daniel thought. Maybe she'd let this one go. Without answers, he might always wonder, but sometimes that was better.

"Any chance you could have dinner with me tonight?" he asked. "I'll take you out for potatoes."

"You mean, you don't already have something good cooking?"

"Day's been too busy."

"Mine, too." Weariness sounded in her voice. "Do I need to get dressed up?"

Itching to see her in a swirly skirt, Daniel was still gentleman enough to say, "Nah. We'll save fancy for some other night. How about Mario's?"

"Do they have potato pizza?" she teased. "You did promise me…"

He liked the picture he had of her rocking back in her chair, smiling.

Doing the same, he said, "We can always go to the Black Angus."

"No, pizza sounds good. Might as well eat there as often as we can before ski season opens."

Which was only two months away, he reflected; by Thanksgiving weekend, the population of Elk Springs would have doubled, and the wait for a table at the best restaurants would stretch to forty-five minutes or more. Locals tended to stay home during the winter.

To his disappointment, Renee suggested they meet there. "I don't know if I'll have time to go home first," was her excuse, although her tone was evasive. Well, he couldn't blame her if she was cautious on first dates— or even second ones, if you counted dinner the other night. Although he wasn't exactly a stranger; she'd said herself that her own sister had had a crush on him in high school. He remembered Meg Patton's little sisters often trailing behind her, skinny and blond, the both of them. Still, he shouldn't take it as a mortal insult that Renee didn't want him to know where she lived.

They agreed on a time. He settled all four legs of the chair back on the floor, put down the cordless and reached for his phone book, flipping it open to the middle.

Patton. His finger moved down the listings. Two Pattons. One was nobody he knew; the other was Renee's father, whose name would disappear from the next directory, assuming someone let the phone company know about his death—2568 River Drive.

Had the house been sold? Renee might have a cozy condo somewhere. Maybe she and the younger sister lived together. But the way Renee had talked, it sounded as if she'd cooked for her father up to the end. So she might still be there.

Feeling low, he nonetheless chose a circuitous route to Mario's, one that happened to take him down River Drive. Idle curiosity, he justified his nosiness, as he glanced at house numbers. 2556. 2562. There it was ahead, a big white Colonial-style house, police car in the driveway. He put his foot down harder on the gas, even as he craned his neck to take in the mature shade trees, leaves golden and orange, the long sweep of grass, smooth as a putting green, the white picket fence, repainted in the recent past. She must hire someone to keep the place up, Daniel decided. She couldn't do all that raking and mowing and painting herself. Even so, it wasn't the house for a single woman. Kids should spill out of it. Or it could be a bed-and-breakfast.

Why wasn't a For Sale sign at the head of the driveway?

Hell, maybe she loved her home, Daniel thought, irritated at himself. Maybe her younger sister *was* married and had a brood, and they all lived in Daddy's house. And maybe it was none of his damn business.

No surprise that Renee was five minutes behind him in arriving at Mario's, or that she had been home to change clothes. Not into a skirt, he was disappointed to see as she paused in the doorway, scanning the dimly lit room while shrugging off her coat. But black corduroy jeans fit as snugly as his hands itched to, and her juniper-green turtleneck sweater clung almost as closely, ending with a ribbed hem at her slender waist. She wore earrings tonight, too, he saw as she turned her head and silver shimmered. Hair still up, but maybe a little looser, a little more feminine. She'd made some effort for him, he thought, pleased.

He lifted a hand and she spotted him then, coming right over. When Daniel started to stand, she waved him back.

"Have you ordered?"

"Just the beer. Didn't know how you like your pizza."

She settled herself on the bench across from him and propped her elbows on the table. "Oh, I like anything. Well, almost."

They negotiated about the pizza and he went up to the counter to order. When he turned around, he saw that Renee had swiveled in her seat and was watching him. Though he wouldn't have sworn to a blush in this lighting, she swung back around mighty quick, embarrassed—he'd have been willing to bet—by being caught staring.

Daniel just hoped she liked what she saw.

She'd poured herself a glass of beer, but barely touched it. Instead, with her fingertip she traced pictures in the condensation on the glass, not looking up until he'd sat down. Definitely a blush, he decided, contemplating her pretty face.

"I don't remember your little sister's name," he said, choosing an easy wedge to loosen any resistance she had to talking about her life.

"Abby."

"That's right." He sipped his beer. "She was—what?—a couple years younger than you? What's she doing these days?"

"Three years younger. And, believe it or not, she's a firefighter." His face must have showed his incredulity, because Renee continued in a defensive tone, "Abby's taller than I am, and more athletic. She passed all the tests with flying colors. Don't tell me you think a woman shouldn't be a firefighter, or we'll quit getting along."

Heaven forbid. He chose his words carefully. "Is she

really strong enough to carry a two-hundred-pound man out of danger?"

Her eyes narrowed a flicker. "She wouldn't be doing the job if she couldn't."

Daniel raised one hand. "Whoa. Don't get testy on me. I was just asking."

"Why do men all assume…"

"Maybe because I can't picture you being able to sling me over *your* back," he said mildly.

Her gaze measured his shoulders, shifted to her own slender frame. She looked back at him, her nose scrunched. "Why do you always have to take the wind out of my sails?"

"Because I'm such a reasonable guy, I don't deserve all that anger a bunch of jerks have stirred up in you. That's why."

"Oh, all right." She pretended to grumble, then gave him a sunny smile that snatched his breath right out of his lungs. "Did your mom sit you in a corner every time you told your sister she couldn't do something as well as you did?"

Suppressing his gut-level reaction to her, Daniel thought back. "Mom didn't have to. Even though Mary's younger than I am, she was always better at school, which shut me up. She's a gifted horsewoman, too. I never did understand how she could reject the ranch as a way of life."

Renee didn't say anything immediately, and he wasn't sure she was really seeing him for a second there. Then she gave her head a small shake. "Funny, isn't it," she said, tone faraway, "how you can grow up with sisters and never really know them?"

He reached out and gripped her hand. "You're thinking about Meg, aren't you?"

She looked at where their hands met and color blossomed in her cheeks again, a blush of wild rose. But she didn't try to pull free. "Sometimes I go weeks or months on end without thinking about her, and then for a stretch I can't get her out of my head. I guess this is one of those stretches."

"Do you know why she left?"

A tiny breath puffed out and her eyes became unseeing again as she gazed into the past. "Oh, sure. She and Dad fought all the time. Over boys or makeup or how clean the house was, or if dinner was a few minutes late… Over us, too—Abby and me. She'd defend us, you see.

"All I know is they had a really awful fight, the worst ever. The school called because she'd slipped away at lunchtime—it was a closed campus in those days—and somebody saw her. I think she had a friend over to the house, maybe a boy. I don't know. I just know that I got home from school and she was packing. Dad had—" Renee caught herself. "Well, her face was bruised and puffy from crying, and she had the most terrible look in her eyes. I've never forgotten." After a silent moment she shivered. "She kissed me goodbye, and hugged me so hard it hurt, and promised to call or write."

"Did she?" he asked quietly.

"No." For an instant Renee could have been a little girl, eyes pleading with him for an answer that he didn't have. *Why?* she asked silently. "Not once. She just…went."

He rubbed his thumb over the back of her hand. "You've never looked for her?"

"No." She averted her gaze. "I figure she needed to make a clean break. Meg was too young to have as much responsibility as Dad dumped on her. Maybe she got so she hated us, too."

What a son of a bitch Ed Patton had been. Daniel had guessed at some of it, but this story still came as a shock.

Grittily, he said, "And then he dumped it on you."

"Yes. But that's not Meg's fault."

"She was old enough to know that's what would happen."

"She was sixteen. That's all. Was she supposed to sacrifice herself for her little sisters?"

He heard too much passion in Renee's voice. She'd had this argument before. With herself?

"Maybe. Weren't you angry?"

Her eyes flashed. "Yes. Yes, I was angry! But I was a kid, too, then. Now I understand why she had to do what she did!"

"Do you." He didn't make it a question; the unintended curl of his lip said what he thought.

Renee wrenched her hand free from his. "What do you want me to say?" she demanded. "Yes, I'm still mad as all get-out? I'd spit in her face if she walked in this door? Fine. Consider it said. Yes, sometimes I hate her for leaving me the way she did. But that doesn't mean I can't understand."

"No." Daniel gave a crooked smile that held anything but amusement. "You're right. I just wanted to hear you admit how you really feel. I figured we might as well have honesty from the start."

She stiffened. "The start of what?"

"Who knows?" Daniel made his tone easy, as if he were soothing a spooked horse. "Whatever we make of it."

"There is no 'it.'"

"We're having dinner together," he said. "For the second time."

She gazed at him with her brow crinkled and what

seemed like genuine perplexity in her eyes. "Why are we?"

He set down his beer glass. "What the hell does that mean? Are you asking why I *wanted* to have dinner with you?"

She took to tracing patterns on her glass again, attention on the swirly lines and not him. "I guess I am. I just thought we should get it straight from the first. Are you wanting to keep up on the investigation? I don't mind, but you don't have to buy me dinner to get a report."

His jaw almost dropped. Yeah, okay, he'd used a question about her progress as an excuse, but what woman couldn't tell when a man was in hot pursuit of her?

This one, apparently, and he knew who to blame. Too bad the bastard was in the grave and beyond Daniel's reach.

"I called for a report," he said evenly. "I asked you to dinner in hopes I'd get to know you and the evening might even end with a kiss. There. I'm laying my cards on the table."

Her eyes were huge and dark. "I'm a cop."

"Yeah. And a woman. Or so's my impression."

"And not all that pretty."

"I could argue with that. I will, at the right time and place." He let her absorb that. "I'm not much to look at myself."

"I didn't think so, either, until—" She stopped so fast, she should have had air bags. The rose in her cheeks deepened to scarlet.

Until. He savored the suggestion that she'd changed her mind.

"Until when?" Daniel prodded, his male ego, if not yet his heart, on the line.

She seemed unable to look away from him. "Until you smiled."

Maybe he'd been wrong about his heart. It damn near stopped, the result of one too many electrical jolts.

Renee's expression changed to pretend or real affront. "You're doing it now."

"Doing it?"

"Smiling."

She was right. He was grinning like a kid who just knew what he'd find under the tree on Christmas morning. A kiss. *That's all I want, Santa,* he thought, even as he knew better. Christmas was a while away yet; by then he hoped her sweet kisses would have him putting a much bigger present on his list.

"You know," she said, "I think that must be our number they're calling. Over and over again."

"What?" He jerked back from dreams of sugarplums and a naked woman sprawled on his bed. Swearing under his breath, he slid off the bench. "It's probably cold."

Renee gave a saucy smile of her own. "Fortunately for you, I like cold pizza."

Not pretty. How could she think that for a second? Didn't the woman ever look in a mirror? Maybe the pain when she yanked her hair back so tight distorted what she saw.

Not pretty. He was still marveling when he brought the pizza back.

"Ouch," she said, reaching for a piece. "It's not stone-cold yet."

"Nope," he conceded, dishing up his own. "Would you like a soda instead of that beer?" He nodded toward her glass.

"No." Renee took a deep swallow, as if to show him.

"I was just a little nervous. I didn't want to…well, let my tongue get too loose. Now I guess I've said so much, why worry?"

"I like honesty," Daniel reminded her.

"Well, good." She sniffed the pizza appreciatively. "Because I'm lousy at hiding what I think."

"I didn't get that impression when you were talking to my mother."

Her eyes met his, wary again. "It's my job. I'm a cop."

"So you said."

"You don't seem to want to believe it."

If he were to be honest, the way he claimed to want, now was the moment to admit he wished she were anything but. Because, if she kept doing her job out on the Triple B, she'd soon discover that he'd chosen sides, and it wasn't hers. Coming from her background, would she understand? Didn't seem like either of her parents or even her big sister had put family first. How could Renee have learned that's how it ought to be?

So he lied—no, prevaricated. "I'm just trying to reconcile the cop with the woman sitting here eating pizza. Which one is the closest to who you are inside?"

Her laugh was a little uneasy. "Well, that's a deep question. Even if I knew the answer, I'm not sure I'd want to tell you."

"I'll find out on my own."

"You do that," she suggested without any sign of discomposure, then bit into her pizza with apparent relish.

He'd deserved that. A second date, and he was trying to figure her out the way he did a new horse. A little more subtlety was called for with a woman, he guessed.

They chatted after that, like two people getting to know each other ought to. About the changes coming to Elk Springs with the new ski area, about why they'd stayed when most of their high school classmates had long since shaken the gritty soil of eastern Oregon from their heels. About movies and books and cats. Not about family, or jobs, or weathered bones. But Renee laughed a few times, and smiled often. Daniel began wishing even harder that he'd picked her up at her house. How was he going to kiss her good night out on the sidewalk?

The weather hadn't cooperated, either, he discovered as they stepped out of the restaurant. The night was dark and cold, with the smell of rain in the air. She wouldn't want to linger.

Renee shivered right away. "I'm already looking forward to spring."

"I thought you said you were a skier."

"A fair-weather skier." She struggled with the zipper on her coat. "I hate being cold or wet."

"Where's your car?"

"Around the side." Renee nodded toward the narrow parking lot tucked between Mario's and the two-story brick building next door. "What about you?"

"I'm the other way, but I'll walk you to your car."

"You don't need…"

As if a firm hand on the small of her back wasn't enough to silence her, he said mildly, "I want to."

She walked fast. Daniel had to stretch his legs to keep up. Renee stopped at the bumper of a red 4x4 not so different from what she drove on the job. A man's vehicle, he would have said, which was sexist as hell of him and better left unspoken. The truth was, it was practical transportation for a woman who didn't intend to stay in front of her fire knitting when bad weather hit. His mother had always had a man to depend on, first her husband and then her son. Renee was on her own now, and he guessed she always had been in most ways that count.

"Thank you for dinner," she said almost as quickly as she'd walked. "I enjoyed myself. I'll call you as soon as I know anything about the investigation…"

He withdrew his free hand from his pocket and wrapped it around her nape, tangling his fingers in her hair. "I enjoyed dinner, too," he said huskily. "I'm hoping you won't mind if I kiss you."

His heart sank when she stayed still and silent for a long moment. Maybe he shouldn't have asked; maybe he should have kissed first and let her protest after. But that wasn't the way he did things.

"I guess I don't mind," she conceded, voice low and grudging, just when he was about to release her.

"Well, there's a welcome a man could warm his hands over," Daniel murmured, though he hadn't taken offense—he knew shyness when he heard it.

He moved closer, liking the way she lifted her face, the back of her head nesting in his cupped hand. A car passed on the street, its headlights momentarily illuminating her, eyes closed, lashes fanned on her cheeks, her warm breath puffing a small cloud in the chilly night air. He made a sound and bent his head, his mouth finding hers.

Her cold lips warmed under the pressure of his. They softened when he nibbled. She didn't so much kiss him back as…accept. But his other hand had found her throat and felt the leap of her pulse, and he heard the vibration of a whimper when he lifted his head. She was as innocent as he'd imagined, as uncertain how to respond, but, oh, she wanted to. He felt it.

"I'll call you tomorrow," Daniel said. "Do you have your keys?"

"Keys?" Her immobility lasted long enough for awareness to return. "Oh. Of course I do. Right here in my pocket." She groped for them, dangled them under his nose. "There. I can make it home. Good night, Daniel."

"Good night," he said, amused and satisfied. Her snippiness, he figured, was in direct proportion to how swept away she'd been.

She unlocked the door and hopped in to start the engine.

Daniel stepped out of the way and watched as she backed out, lifted a hand and drove away.

Next time he'd definitely pick her up at her house.

DANIEL'S GENERAL STATE of smugness lasted for exactly twelve hours. Long enough to lie in bed having some nice fantasies that drifted into better dreams. Long enough to awaken with a glow of anticipation as he wondered whether he ought to call first thing or wait until lunchtime. Even long enough so that he could convincingly reassure his mother when she stopped by the barn midmorning, new lines beside her mouth and a tremble to her hands.

Hell, he wasn't even bothered by the mixed snow and rain falling. Well, this was October 2, a little early, but with El Niño and La Niña and all their cousins, you didn't know what to expect these days.

He'd worn a rain slicker to the barn, then hung it over a stall door. A heavy sweater and fingerless wool gloves were enough to keep him comfortable as long as he worked the horses in the smaller indoor arena.

At eleven o'clock on the nose—he knew, because he looked at his watch—one of the hands leaned against the gate and announced, "Hey, boss. That cop's here again. She's heading for your mom's house."

CHAPTER FIVE

SHIRLEY BARNARD came to the door herself, wrapped in an apron. Flour coated her hands as if she were breading them to go in the oven. Alarm sparked in her eyes when she saw who the caller was, but the next second her expression held only polite inquiry. "Yes?"

"Mrs. Barnard? I wonder if I might come in." Renee always liked to phrase it as a question, although it wasn't really. Most law-abiding citizens wouldn't dream of refusing admittance to a police officer.

"Why, yes, of course." For a moment the other woman didn't move, which was undoubtedly a more accurate reflection of how she felt than her conventional response. She did finally, grudgingly, inch back.

Renee stepped inside. With a nod at Shirley's white hands, Renee asked, "You're baking?"

Dumbly, Daniel's mother followed her gaze, as though her own hands were unfamiliar to her. "Oh. Yes! Yes, I'm kneading bread." Her mouth pinched. "I suppose you'll have to come back to the kitchen."

"I don't mind," Renee said mildly, although she could tell that Shirley did. The front parlor was probably for outsiders, for the enemy; only friends and family would normally be welcome in the kitchen. It seemed that Shirley was between a rock and a hard place. Let the partially kneaded bread go to waste, or sully the warm heart of the house with that irritating police officer's presence?

The bread won.

"I'd like to get my dough to rising, so if we can talk while I'm working, I'd be grateful," she said stiffly.

"Of course," Renee agreed.

The kitchen was big and old-fashioned. A chrome-trimmed wood cooking stove for winter heat shared space with a modern gas range. A long oak table filled the tiled expanse. A timer ticked beside the pale lump of dough resting on a flour-dusted breadboard.

"Tea or coffee?" Shirley Barnard asked with automatic courtesy.

"I'd love some tea." Renee waved her away from the stove. "Just tell me where everything is. You don't want the dough to decide not to rise."

Her hostess settled her hands as gently and firmly around that dough as if it were a baby. "Mugs in the cupboard to the right of the sink, tea bags in that copper canister. Water in the kettle was boiling just a minute ago."

Renee poured herself a cup of tea, found the sugar and added a spoonful, then took it around to the table. "You don't like the bread machine?" she asked, nodding toward the appliance sitting on the counter.

Shirley leaned on the dough, flattening it, then with practiced hands pulled it toward her. The rhythm seemed to loosen her up, and her talk flowed as though they were friends, not adversaries.

"Oh, I use it once in a while, but the bread just isn't as good, though you can argue with me if you want. Daniel does. He says I'm wearing myself out for no reason, just sheer stubbornness. But I like my own home-baked bread, and with my daughter and grandson staying here, we're going through plenty."

"Kneading makes for strong hands." Renee smiled. "Besides, it's relaxing. I always find it frees my thoughts."

A hitch in the even motion—shove, ball the dough in her hands, pull it back, start over—showed Shirley's surprise. "You make your own?"

"When I have time. My father liked it."

He'd grunted with approval when fresh hot bread appeared on the table. Renee hadn't baked bread since he died, but she didn't say that.

"Daniel doesn't understand. This is time to myself," Shirley said. The timer went off, but she ignored it, having lost several minutes to let Renee in. "I can daydream without feeling guilty."

"Sometimes I wonder if men do," Renee said on impulse. "Daydream, I mean. They always seem to be thinking about something practical."

Shirley looked startled, then thoughtful. "Matt—my husband—never did. You know that song? The one that says you can't have a dream come true if you don't have a dream in the first place? He used to laugh and say if you waste too much time dreaming, you never get anything done and not a single one would come true. He wanted simple things, and usually got them. I thought it was just him, but maybe all men are like that."

Renee opened her mouth to respond, although what could she say? She didn't want to use the same yardstick to measure her father and Matthew Barnard, who by all accounts had been a decent man. And she didn't know any other men all that well.

She didn't get a chance to say a word, anyway, because the sound of the front door opening and slamming was followed by heavy footsteps. Daniel burst into the kitchen. His wet hair clung to his head and he shook water and melting snowflakes from his wool sweater as if he were a dog giving up on a swim.

Frowning thunderously, he demanded, "What's going on here?"

His mother kept kneading. "You usually knock."

"Someone told me he'd seen a police car."

His narrowed gaze rested on Renee, who returned it as expressionlessly as she could, considering how her heart was pounding. She should have called him, but she'd feared he might think she was making an excuse to talk to him, or even angling for another invitation. And, how she wanted one, even after seeing him wet and angry, his presence filling the big kitchen.

Shirley glanced at the clock and stopped kneading. "Pour yourself a cup of coffee," she suggested. "You know where the towels are if you want to dry off." After draping a cloth over the dough, she went to the sink to wash her hands.

Daniel swung on his heel to face Renee. "What do you want?" he asked bluntly.

"Help from your mother."

"She's told you everything she knows."

Renee seriously doubted that, but she wasn't here to cross-examine his mother today, anyway. "I've run across some problems with your personnel records. A couple social security numbers were fakes, or the names the men gave were. I'm just following up. That's all."

His mother gave him a look that said, *See?* "Who?" she asked with apparent willingness, pulling up a chair at the table. "Daniel, don't tower over me that way. If you're going to stay, sit down."

Still glowering, he tugged off fingerless wool gloves and tossed them down, then went to the stove. Focusing on his mother, Renee tried not to be so damned conscious of his every move.

After a glance at her notes, she said, "Bill Hodgkins was one. He worked here from May 1978 to July '80. Longer than some. But the social security number I got from the files belongs to a ninety-year-old woman named Pearl Bishop who lives in Atlanta, Georgia."

"Well, now." Shirley gazed reflectively into space, seemingly unaware when her son thumped a mug of coffee onto the table, yanked a chair back and sat, his dark stare still pinning Renee. "Bill. I remember him because he was black." Her tone became apologetic. "I don't mean that in a bad way. It's just that we don't see many. The boys who come out here looking for work are usually white. He had a Southern accent, too. Not strong. Texan, maybe. He did know horses. But he was trouble. He'd steal money from the other hands. That kind of thing. Petty, but it made for bad feelings. Matt finally let him go, even though he could ride like no one since, my husband thought."

Renee concentrated on her notebook. She jotted down "black" with a question mark. Could the coroner tell race from those few bones? Had he said in his report?

"You never heard about him afterward?"

Shirley's eyes widened. "Why, I do seem to remember Matt saying something. Bill was riding in a cutting competition somewhere. Let me think." Her brow crinkled. "For someone we know. Up near Pendleton is where Matt saw him, seems to me." Her face cleared. "John Randall. That's who. He had a spread up that way. I don't think Matt said anything to him about Bill. He always hoped for the best, you see. He thought maybe Bill would have turned over a new leaf after losing this job. But I'm sure that was it." She gave a nod. "John Randall." She turned to her son. "Has John retired?"

"His daughter mostly trains their horses now, but he hasn't let up on the reins completely." His mouth closed tight; he'd answered his mother, but he wouldn't willingly go any further.

Although she would have liked to ignore him, irritation and the knowledge of how much time he could save her made Renee ask, "Would you happen to have his phone number?"

"I might."

"I'd appreciate it if you could find it." Only an idiot wouldn't hear sarcasm in her syrupy tones.

Daniel wasn't an idiot. His hand tightened on his mug as if he wished it was her neck.

Shirley's amusement let Renee see that she might be just a flat-out *nice* woman when she wasn't scared.

"You said a couple numbers were wrong?"

Renee didn't have to glance back at her notes on the ranch hand whose employment at the Triple B had ended, one way or another, exactly fifteen years ago. She looked Shirley right in the eye and said, "Yes. T. J. Baxter."

Daniel's mother shot up from her seat. "I think I'll get myself some tea. Do you need a freshener, Officer?"

Renee found herself looking at Shirley's back as the older woman reached into a cupboard. Coincidence she'd chosen that precise moment to fuss in the kitchen? Frowning, Renee said, "Thank you. No."

"Now, what was that name?" Shirley asked as vaguely as if she really hadn't heard Renee in the first place.

Renee repeated the name.

"Now that one…" Shirley stopped as if thinking, the teakettle poised above her cup. "How long did he work here? I don't know that I recall him."

"Sure you do, Mom." Daniel intervened unexpectedly. "He was that bronc rider Mary worshiped when she was, oh, twelve or thirteen. Handsome devil."

"Oh, yes," Shirley came back from the stove, mug in hand. "I was glad Mary was young for her age. T.J.? Is that what his name was? I don't recall why he left."

Renee didn't buy it. Daniel and Mary had both remembered this one particular ranch hand instantly. He'd made an impression. He'd have made just as much of one on Shirley, the mother of a pretty twelve-year-old girl. And hadn't Daniel even remarked that T. J. Baxter flirted with all women, including his mother? Surely that would have startled the wife of T. J. Baxter's employer. Especially since Shirley would have been in her late thirties. Men couldn't have been flirting with her every day.

But Shirley was gazing at her now with an air of pleasant inquiry. "And his social security number wasn't right?"

"Apparently not. You have no idea where he went when he left here?"

"No, I don't." The tone of finality was unmistakable. "Was there anyone else?"

"No, just those two." Renee had already heard Daniel's remembrance of why Baxter had left, but she turned to him, anyway. "If somebody had called or written for a reference, would your father have made a note?"

Daniel shook his head. "Not if it was a call. But I'm sure Dad fired him. This'd be the last place Baxter would give for a reference."

Unfortunately, that was probably true.

"He didn't have a nickname? Something that might have suggested another name?"

Daniel frowned. "Far as I know, T.J. was what he went by. I never even knew what it stood for. Mom?"

The pleasant, vague expression on her face didn't change one iota. "I didn't even remember him. How would I know if he had a nickname?"

Keeping a surreptitious eye on Shirley, Renee closed her notebook. "Well, it sounds like a dead end where T. J. Baxter is concerned."

Some emotion welled in Shirley so high she blinked several times, quick and hard. Relief?

"Unless he left any possessions behind?" Renee ventured.

Shirley bowed her head.

"If he had, we wouldn't have kept them long." Daniel shrugged. "After a few months, Dad would have taken anything to the Salvation Army."

"Well, then—" Renee pushed back her chair and rose to her feet "—if you can find that phone number for me, I'd appreciate it. Thank you both for your help."

"I didn't mind a bit." All smiles—damn it, *nice* again, relaxed—Shirley started to stand.

"*I'll* walk her out," her son said in a voice that had his mother's mouth opening in an O of surprise even as she sank docilely back into her seat.

Renee didn't think she cared for that voice. But it lacked the plain meanness her father would have imbued it with, so she didn't say a word as she preceded Daniel to the front door and out onto the porch, where Lotto waited with tail thumping. There she stopped dead. Hail pelted the ground and drummed off the top of her 4x4. She'd have to make a run for it.

But first… Renee shivered and reluctantly turned to face Daniel.

His expression was harder than a basalt outcropping. "You said you'd keep me updated. Why didn't you call me?"

"I didn't see any reason to bother you." How weak that sounded!

A muscle worked in his jaw. "I thought I made it pretty clear last night that you aren't a bother to me."

He meant the kiss, she knew he did. She hadn't been able to think of much else since. The way his big hand had lifted her jaw, the tenderness of his mouth on hers, her own befuddlement… But it scared her, too, knowing she would have done anything he asked right then.

And how did she know he wasn't angry today because he'd figured he'd solved any problem she posed? Hey, the cop was a woman. Wine her, dine her and kiss her, was probably his strategy. He'd said himself she was a tough nut to crack. That wasn't what you thought about a woman you wanted.

Temper and deep-rooted insecurity flared. "Not a bother? What you mean is, you romanced me in the hopes it'd keep me away from your mother."

He took a step closer, crowding her. "Damn it, you know that isn't what I meant!"

"Do I?" Renee held her chin high.

He swore under his breath, making his yellow Lab whimper. "You think I'm that calculating?"

"I didn't," she said coolly. "But after the way you came roaring in here today just because I had the gall to knock on your mother's door, I have to wonder."

His eyes glittered. "Just like I have to wonder if you

didn't call ahead because you hoped you could sneak by and corner my mother alone."

Renee opened her mouth to snap back, but guilt stopped the words. She *should* have phoned him. He was the one who'd found the bones in the first place. He'd been decent about this, even though it was upsetting his mother and Renee hadn't hidden the fact that she thought Shirley was lying about what she knew. Just last night at dinner she'd agreed to report to him when she knew anything. And then today…

Oh, Lord. How could she admit she'd felt *shy?*

"No." She fixed her gaze on the collar of his sweater. "Really. I wasn't sneaking. I just wanted some information. I wasn't trying to put her on the spot."

"Then why *didn't* you call first?"

Renee didn't know whether his expression had softened. She'd lifted her gaze only as far as his throat, strong and tanned. If he ever kissed her again, she'd put her hand there, feel the pulse beating, the smooth skin on his neck and the rough up above where he shaved.

"I…" She licked her lips. "Well, I thought your mother could answer my questions as well as you could. And I don't want to keep pulling you away from work for every little thing."

"A murder isn't 'every little thing.'"

"An investigation can take a long time. You don't want me calling constantly."

His voice had an odd intonation. "You sure about that?"

Oh, she was sure enough. Though she remembered that kiss again and trembled a little inside.

With incredulity, she heard herself declaring, "Maybe it's a mistake to have any kind of personal relationship until this investigation is brought to a close."

Quicker than a blink, Daniel closed the small distance left between them. Lifting her chin, just as she'd remembered—though his fingers hadn't been so cold last night—he asked, "Do you think I murdered whoever the hell this guy was?"

"I… No," Renee faltered.

His head bent; his mouth hovered just above hers. "Are you attracted to me?"

She tried frantically to think of an out. "This isn't the time or place…"

"Okay, how about dinner tonight?"

Her mind was fogging just like the windshield had on her way out here. "I can't let you influence how I conduct an investigation…"

She thought he swore before he kissed her, but it didn't really register. She was too busy flinching from the icy touch of his lips, then reveling in the way they warmed, and at last in the heat her whole being tried to soak up. This kiss was simply erotic: he nibbled and suckled on her lower lip, stroked her tongue with his, pressed her hips up against him, making it impossible for her to pretend unawareness of the hard ridge under the fly of his jeans.

By the time Daniel lifted his head, she was shaking and weak-kneed. And angry, once understanding flooded her.

"You're doing it again!" she snapped in a voice too tremulous for a cop's. "Using—" her hand waved, encompassing them "—*this* to influence me!"

"This?" His brows drew together. "You mean sex?"

"We haven't *had* sex!"

"But we're working our way toward it, aren't we?"

They were?

But even to herself she couldn't pretend ignorance that complete. Wasn't sex exactly what she'd been thinking about all the way home last night? What had kept her awake, made her too shy to phone him in a business-like manner this morning?

"Just tell me," she pleaded, "why you're doing this. Even if you get me in bed, it won't make me softer toward your mother…"

He backed well away from her, his hands balled into fists. "Is it just me, or do you distrust all men?"

All men. The answer came, swift and shocking. Oh, she'd known distantly that she was looking for her father in the men she dealt with, and not in a nostalgic way. But this…this instant certainty that Daniel Barnard couldn't be treating her nicely because he liked her… If nothing else, it made her understand why she was alone when the friends her age from high school were wives and mothers, or at least girlfriends. She wasn't beautiful, she knew that, but she wasn't ugly, either. She could have had a man if she'd wanted one.

But it appeared that she'd been so certain they were all like her father, she hadn't let them get to first base.

Until this week.

Question was, why now? Why this man?

"Say something."

She realized abruptly that Daniel had stepped forward again and was gripping her upper arms, giving her a little shake. She must have been staring at him like an idiot.

"All men," she said.

"What?" Now he stared.

"I guess maybe I'm not inclined to trust men."

He had her in his arms in a heartbeat, just cuddled close as though she needed shelter. His voice held a growl of rage that vibrated deep through his chest. "That bastard," he said clearly.

Renee soaked up the bliss, his warmth and strength and anger, the fact that he still *wanted* to hold her. But finally she tugged herself free.

"Yes, he was," she said straight out. "Assuming you meant my father."

Daniel's mouth was tight; his hands automatically gripped her upper arms again, as though he were unwilling to let her go far. "Did he hit you?"

"Sometimes," she admitted, the first time she'd ever let herself say that to anyone but her sisters. "But mostly not. He just…froze me with his disapproval. Nothing was ever right. I couldn't come home and tell him about an unfair grade or a friend who'd snubbed me. He'd be mad, I'd screwed up again. If I got an A or won the science fair, he'd grunt. And I learned early on that if I told him anything, he'd use it against me. Or against Meg or Abby, if I'd been stupid enough to admit something about one of them."

She'd always thought it a cliché when someone wanted to drown in a pair of eyes. But right this minute Daniel's were like that, so blue she couldn't look away. Blue should be a cold color, bringing to mind one of the high mountain lakes nestled up in the bosom of the Sisters, but his eyes were more like the lick of blue in a fire: warmer than the hot springs or the glowing coals in a stove.

"Your mother?" he asked, voice low and rough.

Renee gave a small helpless shrug. "She was scared of him, too. I don't blame her for leaving him. If that's what she did." Another shock; she'd expressed a secret fear that she had only just told Abby.

"You think she might be dead?" He processed that, took the next logical step with startling speed. "Those bones…"

"I wondered for a minute," Renee admitted.

"Do you have any reason to think she's dead?"

"No. Just that she's gone so completely. She and Meg both. I've never heard another word from either of them. Of course, my father would have destroyed any letters. He had the mail delivered to the post office, not the house, so it would have been easy. Maybe that's why he did it."

"The SOB must have realized what it would mean to a kid to get a letter from her mother—" Daniel broke off. "We're standing here freezing our butts off. Let's go to my place."

She was shivering and hadn't even noticed. But panic set in. She'd said too much, too fast. They hadn't settled anything; he was a good listener, but that didn't mean he hadn't been using her attraction to him to manipulate her. She was cold, but the heater in her Bronco would unthaw her hands and feet.

"No," she said quickly. "No, I've got to get back. This isn't my only case."

"Then what about dinner?"

She owed him that, didn't she? After not calling this morning, and accusing him of…well, of kissing her in cold blood, which he might still have done, but then what if he hadn't? What if he really did want her?

That thought warmed her belly, if not her numb hands. Dinner wouldn't hurt. She'd find out sooner or later what his motive was. Once he noticed that his kisses didn't result in the investigation being shelved, well, then she'd know, wouldn't she?

"Dinner," she agreed.

His kiss was brief and cold, but it still affected her. Enough so that she had a revelation when she walked into the station twenty minutes later to find Jack Murray in her office stripping off a wet button-down shirt and yanking on a dry sweatshirt, giving her a front-seat view of well-developed muscles and soft, dark chest hair that trailed on down his belly to the belt of his pants. In other words, to a sight that would have induced some wild if hopeless fantasies not so long ago. In fact, just a few days ago. Before Daniel Barnard.

Only, now it was After. A.D.B., she told herself frivolously. And now her admiration of Jack's fine physique was purely aesthetic. Her heart didn't flutter, her blood pressure didn't shoot dangerously high, and no desire curled in her stomach.

In fact, Renee thought, she was cured.

Too bad the cure was only a symptom of a new disease.

While Jack's head was buried in the sweatshirt, she strolled in and perched on the edge of her desk. "You going to change your pants, too?"

His head emerged. "In your dreams."

Just a few days ago, that would have hurt. She could only be grateful that he had no idea she ever *had* dreamed about him. Or curdled inside every time she thought about him wanting both her sisters but never her.

"Oh, yeah, that one keeps me awake," she mocked.

He grinned, then let it go. "You were out at the Triple B?"

"Yup," she agreed. She gave him an update. "Daniel promised to call me with a phone number so I can follow up on Bill Hodgkins. This Baxter…well, I'm at a dead end right now. I'm going to keep putting pressure on Shirley Barnard. Baxter's the one who makes her nervous."

Jack ran his fingers through wet, dark hair. "Damn it, Renee, you might be making a mountain out of a molehill. Maybe she had an affair with him!"

"You don't get hysterical remembering an ancient affair," she retorted. "She could have even privately admitted it to me. Her husband's dead; I wouldn't have told her son or daughter. No, it's more than that. Murder's good at causing hysteria."

"That's an easy answer." Jack frowned at her for a long abstracted moment. "You don't really think that nice lady stuck a knife in somebody."

"Nice ladies do sometimes."

His mouth tilted in acknowledgment. "Usually their husbands. Not some drifter or ranch hand."

"Anyway," she said, "I don't think Shirley stabbed anyone. I just think she knows who did."

"You're guessing her husband."

She looked coolly back at him. "I'll wait till she tells me."

Jack ruminated, frowning the whole while. "Okay," he finally agreed. "You stick with it for a little longer. But I do mean 'a little.' These bones are old news. We can't waste too many man-hours on something as cold as this trail."

Her stomach churned, as if he were on the edge of firing her. This mattered that much. "In other words, make progress or forget it."

Jack lifted an eyebrow. "Ten more mailboxes were bashed in last night. People are getting mad."

"Let the post office handle it themselves," Renee snapped. "Or tell people to pick up their mail in town!"

"Oh, that'll be a popular proposition in the dead of winter." Jack grabbed his wet shirt from the back of her chair. In the doorway of her office, he glanced back. "Keep me current."

"Oh, sure."

Once alone, she sank into her chair and put her feet on the desk.

How much time was a little? One day? Two? A week, if she was lucky?

How, in one week or less, was she going to find out who the handsome, ex-rodeo bronc rider had been? The one who flirted with every woman and lied about his social security number? T. J. Baxter, whose very name scared a nice woman like Shirley Barnard?

T. J. Baxter, who had left no clues behind to his existence.

Aloud, softly, she put into words her suspicion. "Except maybe his bones."

CHAPTER SIX

RENEE HADN'T LIED to Daniel; she did have other cases. In fact, she'd intended to spend the afternoon visiting pawnshops in hopes of tracking down several items stolen from a house in the Heights. A phone message had been left on her desk this morning, reminding her that the homeowner was waiting to hear from her.

But she didn't have a deadline on that one. And she suddenly, passionately, didn't care who'd broken the window and stolen jewelry and antique clocks as well as the ever popular electronic equipment. It'd turn out to be the usual—teens out for a thrill and the bucks to let them indulge in some high-risk activity. Maybe drugs. Maybe just snowboarding, if they came from the wrong side of the river and Mom and Dad couldn't afford the lift tickets.

Renee would get them. For the Elk Springs P.D., the clearance rate on crimes like this was eighty percent or better. This side of Portland, there just weren't that many places to fence stolen property. Teenagers in particular would be unwilling to sit on the stuff for a while, which would have been safer. Instead, they'd choose some seedy pawnshop, take a fraction of what the VCR or diamond ring was worth, and never guess that the pawnshop owner would willingly ID them.

Tomorrow would do just as well, she decided, putting her feet back on the floor. Today, she'd return to the R & R, the cattle ranch bordering the Triple B. She wanted to ask Marjorie Rosler about her son's friend, the one who'd dropped out of sight only a couple years after T. J. Baxter vanished from the Triple B.

In comparison to the Barnard ranch, the R & R looked run-down. Fence posts needed replacing, barbed wire was rusting, and the siding on the barns was weathered instead of freshly painted. On the other hand, running cattle wasn't the same kind of operation as raising world-class quarter horses. Dick Rosler culled his herd and shipped the cattle to market; buyers didn't come to him. And who knew? Maybe he'd lost heart when his son opted for a life that didn't include ranching with his father. The other day, Renee had asked about the ranch name.

"I'm former military," Dick Rosler said. "It was a joke."

But his wife had bowed her head, and Renee guessed the R & R had been intended to stand for father and son.

Mounting the front porch steps of the white farmhouse, Renee wondered about the son who'd disappeared so abruptly only to surface in San Francisco. Talk about culture shock. Why San Francisco? Did he have a buddy there? Say, Les Greene? And what had precipitated his flight?

It wasn't Gabe Rosler she was interested in, but Renee couldn't get him out of her mind. Unlike her mother and sister, Gabe did write to his parents. But he'd never come home, either.

Would his mother tell Renee why he'd gone if she asked? Of course, it wasn't any of her business, Renee admitted, so long as the Roslers weren't lying about those letters.

Drying her hands on a dish towel, Marjorie came to the door alone to answer the bell. She didn't open the screen. Her face was a blur through it. "Officer Patton! Are you looking for Dick?"

"No, I just had some questions about a boy your son would have gone to school with. I figured you'd know the answers better than your husband would, unless Gabe was given to talking to him."

Her laugh had a bitter ring. "No, they never did get along. You know how it is sometimes, with a father and son. Sure, you come on in." She pushed open the screen and stepped back.

This front room looked lived in, unlike the Barnard's, yet oddly sterile. His and hers recliners, showing their age, were planted in front of a TV. Renee would have been willing to bet nobody ever sat on the couch. The oil paintings and knickknacks somehow weren't personal; it was as if someone had filled the empty space twenty years ago and had never really thought about what was there since, except to dust. Only the framed photos on the fireplace mantel gave any real clues to this family.

Renee crossed the room to look at them more carefully than she had the last time she was here.

"Your son looks like you," she observed.

Marjorie Rosler stayed beside her recliner. "Yes, he does," she agreed, sadness and warmth both in her voice. "He especially looks like my father did as a boy."

Gabe was blond and blue-eyed like his mother. Fine-boned, like her. Almost pretty, when he was about twelve. How he must have hated that!

"Do you hear from him often?" she asked casually.

Marjorie was wringing her hands. "No. Only about

once a year. At Christmas time he always writes. Just to let us know how he's doing. He's an E.M.T.," she said, pride warring with her grief. "You know, an emergency medical technician? He always did love to watch an ambulance go by."

"Yeah, I'm pretty fond of those guys," Renee said with a smile. "I don't know where we'd be without 'em. Some of them are real heroes."

"Well." Still an attractive woman despite the grief worn like makeup she never washed off, Marjorie said, "Why don't you have a seat?"

Renee chose the couch. The recliners didn't seem to welcome anyone but their owners. Marjorie perched uncomfortably at the other end.

"Who was it you wanted to know about?" she asked.

"Your son had a friend named Les Greene." Renee knew because the two had been arrested together as teenagers and neither had ever acted to have their criminal records sealed. "I understand he disappeared about the same time your son moved to San Francisco."

"That poor boy." She sighed. "I never did like him. That sounds awful to admit, doesn't it? I know it wasn't his fault, the way he was. He didn't have a father, and his mother was a drunk. He had a couple of cigarette burns on his back. I saw them once. I mean, they were scars by then, but I could tell what they were. He made some excuse, but it just gave me the willies. You know? Sometimes his mother had some man living there."

"Were the boys friends for a long time?"

"Oh, I think maybe it was sixth or seventh grade when they got to be friends." She frowned, thinking back. "I don't know how they hooked up. Having such different backgrounds, I mean. Les wasn't a very good influence on Gabe. At first I thought maybe it would work the other way around, but it didn't. Gabe was going through a difficult stage right then—mostly just adolescence, but he and his father fought a lot, too. Sometimes I'd swear he would go out of his way to provoke Dick." She shook her head. "Then I'd see Les, standing there in the background smirking. I swear, I could almost hate him."

Because she couldn't afford to let herself hate the man who was helping make all their lives a misery?

Renee had no trouble disliking Dick Rosler, though she hardly knew him. It was no stretch to see her father in him.

As a teenager, she'd been the one to go out of the way to push her father's buttons. Some of it was just blind anger. She hated him, and she wanted to yell and scream and maybe even nurse a bruised cheek, because then she could hate him even more. But now she thought that wasn't all there was to it. Stupid as it sounded, every time she picked a fight she hoped for a grain of understanding or patience or affection. She had to test him, over and over.

Her guess was, Gabe Rosler had been testing his dad, too. And maybe getting madder and madder. More and more hurt. Until one day he finally saw there was no point in wasting hope, because his father wasn't going to change.

The difference was, Gabe Rosler had had one parent who did love him, unless Renee missed her guess. And that was a big difference. However angry at his father, how could he never come home again to see his mother?

Well, that wasn't her business, Renee reminded herself. Les Greene was.

"Do you remember whether Les went away before or after your son left home?" she asked.

"Later, because when Gabe disappeared I went to see Les, to find out if he knew anything. I thought he might have gone, too, but he was home. He was working on his car, I remember. You know, feet sticking out from under it, but when I said, 'Les, is that you?' he wheeled out on one of those little trolleys. He had grease on his face and his hands. He looked surprised when I asked if he knew where Gabe was. He claimed he hadn't known my son had run away. It was strange." She fell silent.

"Did you ever see him again?"

"What?" Seemingly lost in the past, Marjorie looked blankly at Renee, who repeated her question.

Marjorie shook her head. "After Gabe called—and then I got a letter from him—I went to tell Les, in case he was worried. His mother was the only one there. She'd been drinking, and she just shrugged and said he was gone for good and she didn't know where he was. Didn't care, either." She paused, amazed by the very notion. "Can you imagine?"

"There are a lot of parents out there like that," Renee said gently. "Gabe was lucky to have you."

She looked away. "Well, I guess he doesn't think so. Though he does write."

"You're the one who reported Les missing to the police."

"Yes." She stared down at her hands, folded so tightly in her lap they must hurt. "I knew his mother wouldn't. If his car had been gone, I wouldn't have, but I couldn't believe he'd left that Chevy. He loved it so. I think it was the only thing he did love."

Renee made a note. She'd known boys like Les Greene. Ones who spent half their lives under the hoods of their cars. Like Marjorie Rosler, Renee couldn't imagine a boy like Les leaving his behind to rust in his mother's driveway, or for her to sell to buy jugs of wine. Even if something unexpected or traumatic happened, why would he have taken a bus or hitchhiked when he could have driven?

The investigation had been cursory, as far as she could tell from the notes. Les had been seventeen. The officer didn't find it surprising that a poor student hadn't hung around to graduate. Les hadn't bought a Greyhound bus ticket, at least that anybody recalled, but a wild kid like him was more likely to have hitchhiked, anyway. His mother had no idea whether he'd taken some clothes or not. In the end, the officer concluded that he'd packed a duffel bag and gone out to the highway to stick out his thumb. There was no reason to suspect foul play, nor any reason to track him down, given his age. The file was closed.

"One last question," Renee said thoughtfully. "Do you happen to know what dentist his mother took him to?"

"His mother?" Marjorie snorted. "You mean, the social workers. I don't know, but they must keep records, don't they?"

Yes, they did, Renee discovered shortly thereafter. Within an hour a young woman returned her call with the name of the dentist Les Greene had seen several times. The man had retired, but Dr. Clifford, who'd bought the practice, still had records of former patients. Renee took over photographs and X rays of the skull's upper teeth, and within another hour had her answer.

"Nope," said Dr. Clifford, shaking his shaggy hair regretfully. "Whoever you've got there, it isn't Les Greene."

Peering at the X rays, hung side by side in one of those light boxes, Renee had no trouble concurring. "I don't suppose you can tell me anything more from these. Age, say."

He frowned and leaned closer. "With the weathering that's taken place—and of course I'm used to judging a mouth by the health of the gums, too... No. I'm afraid not. I'd agree that this was a young man. Could have been as young as Les Greene when he disappeared. Could be a man ten years older, too." He switched off the light and unclipped the X ray, handing it to her. "Sorry."

"Don't be. I appreciate your time."

Okay, forget Les Greene. Although she surely would love to know where he'd disappeared to. It occurred to her, as she drove, to wonder if he'd held any summer jobs as a teenager. Maybe she could get his social security number, run a check on him.

Quietly, she cautioned herself. If he caught wind, Jack would tell her to drop it. Bad enough she was wasting time on a case that had no fresher clues than a long-scattered skeleton. Never mind an ancient missing persons report unconnected even to that case.

And he had a point. For Pete's sake, Les Greene would be—she had to think—twenty-nine years old now, a year older than she was. That required a mental adjustment on her part. She'd been thinking of both Les and Gabe Rosler as teenagers still, looking about like they had in that mug shot taken fourteen years ago.

She did stop at two pawnshops on her way back to the station, and hit a row of little red cherries at the second one. Shown photographs of the antique clocks, the owner slapped his hand down hard on the countertop. "God damn it. I bought the story hook, line and sinker."

"What story?" Renee asked, leaning against the glass-topped counter.

"Inherited them from his mom." He made a sound of disgust. "Didn't know what they were worth. Said all he knew was the damn things used to tick, tick, tick all over the house. Drove him crazy. Then come midnight, every damn night, it was New Year's Eve in Times Square all over again. I've never had anyone admit they hated something they were pawning. Usually they want to claim how valuable the stuff is."

Now, that was interesting. The name on the pawn ticket he produced didn't ring any bells, but who gave a real name anyway?

"What'd the guy look like?" Renee asked.

The answer was exactly what she'd expected to hear. Half an hour later, she handed the homeowner a box containing most of his missing possessions. Along with it, she broke the news that his nineteen-year-old son had faked the burglary and pawned Daddy's precious clocks along with Mommy's beloved diamond jewelry.

Daddy went through the usual stages of disbelief, shock, rage, and finally hurt. He declined to press charges, not at all to her surprise, thanked her profusely and hurried her out the door.

The crime had turned out to be a little more interesting than usual. You had to wonder why a kid from a family this wealthy had felt he needed the money. Or maybe money never had been the point. Maybe hurting his parents had been the kid's sole motivation.

She'd agreed to have dinner again with Daniel, so she went straight home to change clothes. He'd pressed until she also agreed to let him pick her up here.

Renee didn't even totally understand why she'd been reluctant, or why she hustled out the moment he rang the bell, making him back up quick to allow her room to lock the door. She just knew she didn't want him inside. Didn't want him to see that living room and realize it was some kind of morbid museum, untouched except for cleaning since the day her father had died.

Daniel quirked an eyebrow. "Uh…hello. I'm glad you're eager."

"The phone was ringing," she lied. "I didn't want to answer it."

"Don't you have a machine?"

"Yes, but I feel guilty and can't ignore a voice. If we leave, I won't feel obligated."

"Ah." He seemed satisfied with her explanation. Escorting her to his truck and holding open the door, he added, "Pretty big place to live in all by yourself."

"Too big," she agreed, scrambling in. "I inhabit a few corners and ignore the rest."

He went around to the driver's side and slid in behind the wheel, starting the engine. "Are you thinking about selling?"

"Yes." How bald the one little word sounded, not suggesting in any way how conflicted she felt over the whole thing.

Sell. Walk away, common sense insisted. But another part of her felt obligated to keep the home fires burning, or something equally ridiculous. As if Meg and her mother wouldn't be able to find her if strangers occupied the house. As if the only hope of them ever coming home was for her to keep the house intact, untouched. A museum.

"You lived there your whole life?"

She'd almost forgotten Daniel's presence. Renee blinked and pulled herself together.

"Mmm-hmm. I guess that's why I've put it off. Abby

keeps urging me, but…oh, it's only been six months. I just didn't want to jump. You know?"

He gave her a peculiar look, but said agreeably, "Sure. Makes sense."

Renee was grateful when he didn't pursue it. Probably he hadn't because it *did* make sense not to make any hasty decisions after a loved one had died. Which meant that she was only being sensible. Taking into account, of course, the one hundred percent wrong assumption that she'd loved her father.

Over dinner—tonight at a Chinese restaurant—she and Daniel tacitly agreed to stay away from the subject of his mother and the investigation of the bones his dog had brought home.

Instead she told him—without naming names, of course—about the rich kid who'd ripped off his parents' valued possessions.

"What I can't figure out," she said, "is whether we'll see the kid again. I mean, will he start breaking and entering as a regular habit? Maybe move on over to his parents' friends' houses? Or will the fact that he got caught so easily this time scare him?"

"Scare him?" Daniel popped a bite of spring roll in his mouth. "Depends on how his parents handle this. If they don't do anything more than have a little talk with him, scared is the last thing he's going to be."

"Um." She frowned, imagining herself in that father's shoes. "Hard to know what they should do. Prosecuting your own son—that'd be hard. But grounding him doesn't somehow quite cover it."

"Reform school hits the right note." Daniel didn't sound sympathetic. "But, yeah, you're right. I wouldn't want to be in that spot. Family should take care of family. Question is, why does the kid hate his parents so much?"

Renee sighed. "I thought I'd call children's services tomorrow. See if they've been involved before."

He stirred a sugar into his tea. "Otherwise?"

"What can I do?" She spread her hands.

Daniel grunted. "You must face this a lot."

"Not being able to fix a problem? Yeah. If we had time, and better ties to social services, we could do more. We try."

"Here." He handed her the bowl of sweet-and-sour prawns. "Have you had any of these?"

She had, but she took a couple more anyway. "How was *your* day?"

Lousy, it turned out. He'd gone into the barn that afternoon to find a colt down in his stall, hind leg shattered.

"It happens." His jaw set. "It's just one of those freak things. Somehow he got tangled up, or kicked the wall wrong. It was a messy break. We had to put him down."

"I'm sorry," Renee said softly. "Was he…was he a favorite of yours?"

"He had promise." Daniel didn't sound expansive. A typical male, not wanting to admit to emotion?

"Are you trying to tell me you don't get attached to your horses?"

"It's a business," he said stolidly. "I sell horses. I'd be a fool to make 'em all pets. That doesn't mean it doesn't hurt when they suffer or die."

"Of course you're right." She made a face. "I have a feeling I wouldn't be very good at shutting myself off that way."

"Are you sure?" His eyes, unnervingly perceptive, zeroed in on her face. "You're philosophical about the people you wish you could help but can't. Isn't that the same thing? You know what you can let yourself care about and what you can't." He shrugged. "It's reality."

Renee held up both hands in defeat. "Okay! You're right again. Darn it, are you ever *wrong?*"

"Hell, yes."

"Yeah? When was the last time you were wrong?" she challenged.

His expression became shuttered. "When I figured you'd give up on the case once you realized how long those bones had been out there."

Their pact had ended. A little tartly, she said, "Are you sure you've admitted to being wrong? You're not still hoping I'll hang it up?"

He met her stare straight-on. "What I'm hoping now is that you find out this guy had nothing to do with the Triple B."

"You must have known Gabe Rosler," Renee said on impulse. Funny, until this moment it hadn't occurred to her that the neighboring rancher's son was near to Daniel's age, too.

"Yeah, sure." Daniel frowned. "He was a year or two behind me in school. What's this got to do with anything?"

She wrinkled her nose. "As it turns out, nothing. Gabe had a friend named Les Greene…"

"I remember him. Tough kid."

"Well, around the time Gabe took off, so did Les Greene. Only he left behind his car which according to Mrs. Rosler, was the only thing in the world he loved. She filed a missing person's report. The kid's mother apparently didn't care enough to bother. Anyway, because of his age, the investigating officer took a cursory look around, couldn't find any trace of him, but also no evidence of foul play, and closed the file. I tracked down his dental records."

She had his attention now. Without moving a muscle, he still crackled with sudden tension. "And?"

"Your skeleton isn't Les Greene. So much for that brainstorm."

Daniel's shoulders relaxed. "Maybe he found out the damn car needed a new engine that he couldn't afford. Maybe he sold the car's guts for parts and used the money to start over."

It wasn't a bad explanation. Marjorie Rosler's whole case had rested on Les Greene's abandonment of the beloved car. Heck, it probably *had* been a heap of junk he kept going by sheer willpower. Maybe the thing had died the same day he had a final, ugly fight with his mother. Why not hit the road?

"I didn't think of that," she admitted. "It makes sense."

Daniel pushed away his plate and poured himself another cup of the fragrant, pale amber tea without which a meal couldn't be eaten at any bona fide Chinese restaurant. "Did his mother tell you why Gabe ran away?"

"She hinted at trouble with his father. That's the closest she got to an explanation. Do you know?"

"No, but I have my suspicions."

When he didn't go on, Renee leveled a look at him. "You're planning to leave it at that?"

He raised an eyebrow in what appeared to be genuine bewilderment. "Why would you care about Gabe's troubles?"

"Because I'm nosy!" she said in exasperation. "I like to hear every detail connected to a case. You never know what little tangent will turn out to be important."

Daniel grinned, the slow sweet smile that set her heart to thumping once it got over a missed beat or two.

"Okay, okay." Amusement still played in his eyes, although he tried to look grave. "Heaven forbid I frustrate you."

"Did I say you would?" Why did she suddenly have a feeling they weren't talking about Gabe Rosler anymore?

His gaze swept over her, slow and sensuous. "I'll do my best to be sure I don't."

Renee felt her cheeks warm. "You're flirting with me."

"Yup."

"I wish you wouldn't."

She'd wiped that *knowing* smile from his face. "Why? Damn it, I thought we were getting along well."

"We are. I just…" She looked down. "I don't know how to flirt back. You embarrass me."

He reached across the table and gripped her hand, his thumb circling on her palm. "The way you blush gets to me a lot faster than a little flirting would. I…like knowing you haven't had too much practice at this."

Her head shot up. "Why?"

"Why what?"

"Why are women supposed to want an experienced man, but men think a woman should be a…" The word stuck in her throat.

"Sweet innocent?"

"Yeah. Why?"

Brows drawing together, he said, "I don't know what men *should* want. I don't even know what my ideal is. All I do know is that I'd rather not think of you in bed with another man. If you haven't had a lot of practice at batting your eyes, I have to figure you haven't had much practice at bedding men, either."

Well! Renee felt as if she ought to be outraged. Wasn't it the same old stereotype? A woman should "save" herself for one man, while he could do anything he damn well pleased?

On the other hand, she *had* saved herself. Shouldn't she be glad Daniel wasn't hoping for an experienced bed partner?

Feeling the blush rise again at the idea, Renee hastily amended her thought. She should be glad, *assuming* she and Daniel ended up going to bed together. Assuming he really wanted to, and that she worked up her nerve.

"I'd give more than a penny to know what you're thinking about right now," he said softly, eyes narrowed.

Her cheeks must be flame-red. "What if I told you I was wandering down memory lane?"

"I'd say you were lying."

How she would have liked to argue! Considering, however, that he was right, dignity seemed to call for retreat without admission either way.

"Why don't you just tell me," she suggested, "why Gabe Rosler had to run away from home before he graduated from high school?"

"Chicken," Daniel murmured.

"I refuse to discuss my sexual experience on a second date."

"Third."

"What?" she asked, startled.

"Third date. You had dinner at my house."

"I thought we were 'breaking bread' together. Quote unquote. You didn't describe it as a date."

"You don't really think I work that hard on dinner for myself, do you?"

Ridiculous to feel so flattered. But she couldn't help it.

He'd gone to all that work without even knowing whether she'd stay? And then he'd schemed to persuade her?

"Really?" she asked shyly.

"The first time I saw you, I knew I'd ask you out." He searched her face. "That so hard to believe?"

Yes. Yes, it was. But she'd already admitted more of her insecurities to him than she should have. So she raised her eyebrows, trying to suggest a hint of disbelief, and said, "The day I came out to the ranch to look through your records, you didn't act as if you liked me very much. In fact, I thought you were mad as all get-out."

His expression changed, a subtle shift, but she felt as though he'd just closed a door in her face. "My mother had just called, upset. She's had a tough enough time without all this happening."

Yes, but why was this so upsetting to her? Renee wanted to ask. Discretion won.

"You've managed to evade my question again."

"Question?" Daniel's eyebrows rose before understanding resettled the lines of his face. "Gabe Rosler. Yeah, okay. This is just between you, me and the fence post, though."

"Understood."

"I think he was gay. Papa Rosler would not have been sympathetic."

She almost shuddered, picturing Dick Rosler, square-jawed westerner whose wife quivered into silence at a look from him. If his son, his only child, had come to him and admitted to being homosexual... No, the kid was better off taking a long hike and not coming back.

As if he'd followed her thoughts, Daniel added, "And remember, this was some years ago. No ski area here, no espresso stands, no yuppies telecommuting from Elk

Springs. I mean, Dick wouldn't have been alone. Not many folks hereabouts would have accepted Gabe."

"Did he *tell* you…?"

Daniel shook his head decisively. "There was just something about him. And something about his friendship with that Greene kid."

"You mean, you think…" Why so amazed? she asked herself. It was logical. Gabe's father found out. Maybe the boy went to tell Les and couldn't find him, so he split on his own. When Les found out Gabe had gone, he packed up and left town, too. Maybe they'd even arranged to meet, if their secret ever came out. Renee pursed her lips. "I wonder if Marjorie Rosler knows?"

"I have no idea," Daniel said flatly. "Now, how about if we forget Gabe and talk about something more relevant. Like whether you're going to let me beyond your doorstep tonight."

Oh, God. Did he mean for a cup of coffee, or to join her in bed?

She took a deep breath. He'd asked for honesty, hadn't he?

"No," she said. "I'm not. This is only the second—okay, the third—date. I have to work tomorrow, so I don't want to have a cup of coffee or a glass of wine. And…I don't know about anything else."

"Fair enough." He lifted her hand and kissed it, just a brush of his lips, but enough to send shock waves up her arm. "But it's damned cold out there tonight. We're going to freeze on that porch while I kiss you."

She batted her lashes—hey, maybe she could do this after all!—and murmured sweetly, "We could skip the kiss."

"Hell, no."

"Well, okay," she conceded. "One step inside, just to stay thawed. I'll give you two minutes."

That warm smile made her feel as limp as if she'd just crawled from a hot spring. "And I'll raise you to three."

Something told her he was right. Again. But she wouldn't admit it. She'd win tonight's contest if he didn't get beyond the front hall. If he didn't discover how bleak and empty her father's house was inside.

The thought came insidiously: if, by extension, Daniel didn't also discover the places *she* had inside that were just as bleak, just as lonely.

Or did he already suspect they were there?

CHAPTER SEVEN

"SO," HER SISTER SAID, turning casually away to pull aside the lace curtain and peer out the kitchen window, "why *do* you care what happened to Les Greene?"

"It's my job…" Renee began.

"Oh, come on." Abby swung back impatiently, letting the curtain drop. "It's not like you can save him now! I mean, he either made a new life for himself, or he didn't. Whichever, no one cares anymore but you. Well—" she made a face "—I suppose Les Greene does, if he's alive."

From her comfortable seat at the table, Renee watched her sister's restless prowling. Maturity and a job that required peak physical condition kept Abby looking like some kind of Norse goddess: tall, sleek, blond and blue-eyed. Maybe, if Meg were here now, she'd find she had lost her position as the prettiest Patton sister.

In answer to the question, Renee said honestly, "I don't know. I have to keep reminding myself he's not a seventeen-year-old kid anymore. Did I tell you what Daniel thinks?"

"'Daniel' now, eh?" Her sister threw a quick grin over her shoulder before she opened the freezer compartment and inspected its contents. "Jeez. You've won the title as Ms. Frozen Food Queen." She closed the freezer. "And, yes, you told me. Sure, it's sad the kid's own mother couldn't be bothered to file a missing persons report. And, wow, it would have been hard to be gay in good old Elk Springs back in those days—truthfully, it's probably still hard if you're in high school. That jock attitude prevails. Still, the bones aren't his. Good idea. Didn't pan out. You should move on. If you don't, Jack's going to think of something more useful for you to be doing."

Renee groaned and let her head fall back. "Such as picking up some twelve-year-old who's shoplifted a candy bar at the 7-Eleven."

"A hardened criminal in the making," her sister said with mock reproof. "It's important to intervene early."

"Yeah. Right." Renee grimaced. "Let me tell you about today's big excitement. We got this hysterical phone call. A teenage girl was home alone. Someone was trying to break in. I'm the closest, so I go over there, gun drawn, heart pounding, but whoever it was is gone. We call her parents home from work, everyone is all worked up over it, and I pin her down on what she actually heard."

Abby boosted herself onto the kitchen counter, eyes bright. "Yeah? What'd she hear?"

"The screen door on the enclosed back porch. It creaks and slams. Footsteps. Loud. Not somebody sneaking."

"*I'd* be scared."

"So I interview neighbors. A woman three doors down says gosh, no, the only person she's seen all day is the meter reader. Was just there, maybe half an hour ago."

Her sister had begun to laugh.

"Back to the house. Gee whiz, the meter *is* on the back porch. I check with the utility. Yeah, he had just been there. The parents look at the girl, she bursts into tears. Mystery solved."

When Abby quit laughing, she said, "I still don't blame her."

"No. I guess I don't, either."

A small silence fell. Abby tapped her fingers on the countertop, the nervous gesture reminding Renee of how energetic her little sister had always been. She'd never napped the way other toddlers did. Once she reached school age, she would burst in the door at the end of the day as fresh and ready to go as she had when she woke up in the morning. Meg used to groan and say, "Why didn't God share some of that get-up-and-go between the three of us? Why did *she* get all of it?"

"Hey," Abby said suddenly. "The snow's really coming down out there, you know."

Renee knew. Given that Halloween hadn't even arrived yet, how could she be oblivious to snow falling outside? Maybe that's why it felt so cozy in here.

"Let's go out and make a snowman."

"What?"

"Come on." Abby jumped down from the countertop. "Don't be a party pooper."

"But there isn't enough snow!" Renee protested, even as she knew she'd lose this argument.

"We can *try.*"

Renee rolled her eyes, but got to her feet. "Do we have to?" she mumbled, but obediently hunted for her gloves and hat and took her parka from the closet. Abby, of course, was ready and impatiently waiting for her.

On the porch, Renee surveyed the front yard. More snow had fallen than she'd realized; perhaps two inches of white blanketed the smooth sweep of lawn. Fat wet flakes floated down from a pale sky that would deepen toward dusk in another half hour.

Abby bounced down the steps and threw herself onto the ground, flapping her arms and legs to make a snow angel. She opened her mouth to catch some flakes, an expression of childish abandon on her face. "Come on. You do it, too."

"Maybe we should go down to the park," Renee suggested. "Like we used to."

Her sister sat up and stared at her. "Ding, ding. Dad isn't here anymore."

"I know, but…" His ghost was. How did she say that?

Their father had never let them play in the yard. When Abby was pitcher for the softball team, she couldn't practice at home; she might wear down the grass. Pets weren't allowed; they might poop in Dad's flowerbeds. He once trapped a neighbor's cat because it dared to use the soil on his side of the fence. The neighbor, thank God, retrieved her big orange tabby from the pound before it was euthanized, but she refused to speak to Renee's father ever again. Who could blame her?

And the girls had never been allowed to have snowball fights or build forts or snowmen in their own yard. The snow, just like the grass, must be pristine. "You tromp all over it," he'd growl, "it'll look like hell."

Still she hovered on the porch steps. "I know he's gone. This just seems…disrespectful."

Her sister hooted. "Excuse me? Who was the disrespectful one around here? What's gotten into you? You suddenly give a care what he thinks?"

"I always did." There it was: truth she'd always sidled away from. Not profound; kids had a way of wanting love and approval even from parents they thought they hated.

But not her, Renee had always told herself. How could you hate someone as passionately as she hated her father, and still want him to love you? It didn't make any sense.

It still didn't make any sense. It just was. She'd spent a lifetime fighting her father, all the while desperately needing his love and approval.

And she was still trying to get it.

"Well, here's a tip," Abby said without a hint of sympathy. "Quit. He's dead. If he were alive, you'd be the first one to tramp all over his snowy lawn, and to hell with him."

"*You're* a fine one to give advice," Renee said bitterly. "Daddy's little girl, always sucking up."

"You mean, *I* figured out how to get along with him." Abby picked herself up, only to bend over and pack a snowball in her gloved hands. "*I* didn't always talk back. *I* knew how to make him approve of me. You're just jealous."

Horribly. Renee ducked the snowball when Abby let it fly. Within seconds, she was down on the lawn, packing some snow into a firm ball. Abby ran, but the snowball smacked her right at her nape and slid down inside her jacket.

Shrieking, she made another and threw with that pitcher's arm. It splattered on Renee's chest, icy shards hitting her chin and bare neck.

The war was on.

By the time they collapsed, giggling, the snowy expanse looked as if a Cub Scout troop had held a rally on it, one interrupted by a bomb threat that had sent little boys scattering in panic.

"Too bad Dad already had a heart attack," Renee muttered. "Just think, we could have given him one."

"You really did hate him, didn't you?" Abby rose to her knees. "Come on. Let's make that snowman."

"Okay." Renee made a snowball, then gently set it down to roll. "Yeah. I hated him. Didn't you?"

"Nope." Abby had begun her own part of the snowman's fat body. "But I didn't especially love him, either. Not the way you did."

Renee digested that. She could see it now, so why hadn't she realized before that her little sister, the one Dad had indulged, didn't care about what she'd won so easily? Maybe that was natural; maybe you wanted most desperately that which you *didn't* have. Maybe anything achieved easily was to be despised.

"You're right. I'm jealous," she said, but Abby didn't hear her. She was rolling her ball in the other direction, leaving a grassy trail in her wake. If Renee didn't hurry, Abby's snowball would be the biggest, and therefore the base. Renee had been scrunched in the middle for too many years. The symbolism seemed suddenly important. *Hers* would be the biggest, the foundation.

Well, really the snowman's hips, but she wasn't about to let her little sister beat her.

Renee bent over and gave her ball of snow a shove to start it moving.

"SO BILL HODGKINS definitely did work for you after he left the Triple B." Phone wedged between ear and shoulder, Renee doodled on her pad of paper as the old man rambled on, repeating what he'd already told her. "For ten years?" she echoed politely. "And he has a ranch of his own down in Oklahoma now. Yes, I'm glad to hear he's done so well. I'll surely watch for his name in cutting competitions."

Renee glanced up to see Jack lounging in her office

doorway. She rolled her eyes and tried again to end the conversation. "Thank you, Mr. Randall. You've been a big help. His phone number? Oh, I don't think I need it… Well, sure." She wrote it down. "Again, thanks. I'll certainly call if I need more information." He was still talking when she firmly set down the receiver.

Jack grinned. "Chatty?"

"Reminds me of Abby when she was about four. She'd never shut up."

"Learn anything?" he asked.

She tensed inwardly. "Just eliminated another possibility."

"Sounds like you've eliminated all of them."

"You know these things are slow."

"It's looking like an early ski season." For the Elk Springs P.D., having the ski lifts start running was like opening day of the hunting season was for wildlife agents.

"This snow won't stay on the ground."

"Not in town. It may on the slopes."

They were starting to sound like two competing weather forecasters, Renee thought ruefully. Channels four and seven.

"Jack," she said, "it's October. We have a month to go, minimum, before ski season. You know that. I'm here when you need me. We don't exactly have a crime wave going on at the moment. This matters to me."

A frown gathered between his dark brows. "Law enforcement isn't supposed to be personal."

Uh-oh. She had to open her big mouth. "It's not that I have any stake in one person being guilty or innocent. I didn't know any of these people! I just don't want to let this one go. The more I dig, the more I'm convinced this wasn't just a drifter."

He still frowned, his dark eyes searching her face.

"Come on, Jack. What's so important I should be doing instead?"

"The gym wall at the high school got spray painted with obscenities last night."

She didn't have to say anything.

His grin flashed again. "Okay, our community won't crumble at the foundations if we don't catch the punks."

"Before we know it," Renee said, "they'll graduate— or not—from high school and be off to the big city."

"And another generation of punks will take their place. Yeah. I know."

"I'll tell you what, though," she said. "I'll go up to the high school today. Nose around a little. Heck, maybe I can scare 'em, if nothing else."

He nodded. "Go for it. As far as the other… Fine. Just don't step on too many toes. I've already heard from Dick Rosler. He didn't like having you up there."

That one came from left field. "Why?" she asked blankly.

"Didn't like you upsetting his wife."

Renee rocked back in her chair. "Funny," she said thoughtfully, "how this seems to be upsetting several people. You wouldn't expect that, considering what old news it is."

"Don't put words in my mouth." But his tone was mild. "And, yeah, I thought it was interesting, too. It's one reason I'm not ordering you to drop the investigation."

"Okay," Renee said. "I'm heading out to talk to Shirley Barnard again. I should warn you, Daniel won't like it."

"I hear you've had dinner a couple times."

Irritation brought her out of her chair. "Informers everywhere?"

"You know what this town's like."

"Well, if you're worried he's succeeded in bribing me, you can forget it. My price is higher than dinner."

"I wasn't worried—"

She cut him off. "Once I press his mother a little, I can kiss the dinners goodbye, anyway." She shrugged as if it didn't matter, even as she cursed herself for choosing the word "kiss." No more kisses, sweet, erotic, mind-drugging. No next step. No chance to find out what it would feel like to have Daniel's weight on hers, his hands on places no hands had ever touched, his... Never mind, she told herself hastily, about the time she noticed Jack's intrigued contemplation.

"Busybodies," she muttered.

"Yup." He tried to hide his amusement. "We're usually grateful for those same folks who notice everything."

"Well, I didn't commit a crime."

"Romance is just as interesting."

She mumbled an unprintable comment. He just laughed and disappeared from her doorway.

Renee dropped back in her squeaky office chair and stared at the telephone on her desk. Call Daniel and tell him she was coming back out to question his mother again? Or blindside Shirley Barnard, knowing full well how angry Daniel would be?

She closed her eyes, panic and depression weighting her chest in equal measure. She didn't need Daniel's smiles or kisses. Truth be known, they scared her some. It might be better this way.

So why, she asked herself as she quietly closed her office door behind her on the way out, did she feel like she had when her father's coffin had been lowered into the ground?

PROPELLED BY A SLAP on her rump, a cow burst through the gate, head swinging as she searched for a herd or escape back the way she'd come. The colt Daniel rode quivered at the sight of her, his skin rippling in fright or excitement. His ears swiveled like small radar antennae as he waited for a signal telling him what to do about this strange creature that now trotted toward them, following the fence in the round pen.

Daniel waited until the cow came abreast, then neck-reined the three-year-old in place just off the bony left flank of the cow. When the colt wanted to speed up, he eased back on the reins; when he lagged, Daniel tightened his legs.

The cow wheeled suddenly and took a few running steps in the other direction, still following the fence. With Daniel's guidance, the colt mirrored her movements. With no corner for the cow to hole up in, the round pen was best for an inexperienced horse.

Starting a colt like this wasn't demanding work, and someone else could have done it. But Daniel enjoyed this part, and he found he could make decent predictions about how far a young horse would go by observing these initial reactions to cattle.

This colt was pleasantly surprising him. Sometimes lazy, he was responding today to the tiniest shift of weight or touch of the rein. The cow fascinated him; his ears were pricked, his attention exactly where it should be. Within minutes he seemed to understand what was wanted of him. That's what Daniel hoped to see. A good cutting horse had to rely on his own instincts, not just on commands from his rider.

When the cow, frustrated, came to a stop, Daniel

gently backed the colt a step, then tipped the horse's nose toward the cow's hip. A couple of feet forward, and the cow became uneasy enough to resume her trot. Daniel could feel the horse's surprise and delight. He'd just discovered a new toy, and he was having fun.

Daniel didn't wait until the colt's interest diminished, ending the session even though he could feel reluctance in the powerful muscles beneath him. He'd bring in another young horse and start with a fresh cow; a bored one was tougher to work and less likely to pique the horse's curiosity.

He was just dismounting and handing the reins to Stan, one of the ranch hands, when Lee called from the barn, "Hey, Barnard! Your mom called. She wants you to come by."

She didn't often interrupt in the middle of the day. His dad had hated keeping a horse standing around, and she took for granted that Daniel felt the same. Something must be wrong.

"Cool him," Daniel ordered. When he passed Lee, leading out the three-year-old filly he'd been planning to ride next, Daniel said, "You start her. Let me know how she does."

Lee flashed a grin. "You betcha."

With ground-eating strides Daniel covered the quarter mile to the homestead. No police car out front. He hadn't any trouble interpreting the depth of his relief. Choices that had looked simple early on weren't so simple anymore. Now that he was beginning to understand the deep-rooted fears that made Renee prickly, he was more drawn to her than ever.

Drawn to her, hell! He wanted her like he'd never wanted a woman. The worst part was, he was dreaming about things that had nothing to do with his hunger to have her under him, her bare legs wrapped around his waist. No, he'd find himself imagining what she'd be like in five years, ten years, once he'd convinced her to trust him. How it would feel to know he'd healed her. He'd see her smile when she first opened her eyes in the morning. She'd laugh often, once she didn't have to guard herself from the world.

Except the one time he'd almost gotten married, Daniel had never thought more than a few weeks down the line where a woman was concerned. And that time— well, it was partly the fact he *couldn't* see ahead that had given him cold feet. By then, he'd been dating Carol Lynn for two years, sleeping with her for one. He hadn't so much asked her to marry him as they'd fallen into assuming they would get married.

Two *years.* He hadn't known Renee for two weeks and he was seeing her pregnant with his baby. He still didn't understand how he could be imagining a future with a woman he hardly knew.

But he couldn't deny that he was.

One of these days he'd have to tell his mother that he'd picked out a bride. Freely admitting to cowardice, he wasn't in any hurry to do it.

At her place, he knocked on the door. He waited, but heard no footsteps, no voice inviting him in. Mary wasn't here, either, he remembered, frowning. Taking her boy, she'd left this morning to go back over the mountains to Beaverton for either a reconciliation with Kurt or to collect more clothes—whichever seemed like a better idea at the time, she'd told Daniel wryly.

Starting to feel some disquiet, he hammered again on the door. His mother wouldn't have waited for him if she was ill, would she? Like if she were having chest pains? Surely she had the sense to call an ambulance, or at least tell Lee what was wrong.

The door wasn't locked. He thrust it open and went in, calling, "Mom? You here?"

The parlor was empty. So was the kitchen. She wouldn't have asked him to come over, then driven off to town, would she? Urgency had him taking the stairs two at a time.

Her bedroom door stood ajar. His breath whooshed out of him when he saw her sitting on the edge of the bed, her jewelry box open beside her. Her head was bent over something she held.

"Mom?"

All in one motion, she looked up and shoved whatever she held back in the polished mahogany box, snapping it shut. She jumped to her feet and set the jewelry box back onto her dresser as he came the rest of the way into her room.

"Daniel," she said breathlessly. "I'm sorry. I didn't hear you."

The way she looked scared him. It was as if she'd suddenly aged ten years. She seemed stooped, frail, her skin crepey and blanched. What in hell had happened? he wondered.

"What were you looking at?" he asked, curious.

"Oh, nothing. I…" She tried to smile. "I was just thinking about your father."

"I'm sorry." He tried to take her hand, but she backed away.

"What did you want?" she asked.

Now he was really scared. "You told Lee you wanted to see me."

She stared at him for a heart-stopping moment, during which thoughts of Alzheimer's and senile dementia crossed his mind with lightning speed.

She blinked. "Oh. I…I did leave a message, didn't I?"

"Was it important?" he asked, even as he debated whether he should call an ambulance. Or put her in the car and take her straight to her doctor's office.

She took a shaky step backward and sank onto the edge of the bed. "No, I… It was that policewoman. But I shouldn't have interrupted you, should I? It could have waited."

His gut tightened. "Policewoman?"

"She was here again." His mother knotted her fingers together, and tension made her voice tremulous. "She kept asking the same questions. About…about that rodeo rider. And what happened fifteen years ago. She doesn't believe me. I can tell she doesn't."

Feeling sick, he said grimly, "Apparently not. You didn't know she was coming?"

"She seemed so nice the last time she was here." His mother pinched together trembling lips. "I feel like… like some kind of criminal!"

"I'll talk to her." He sounded far away to his own ears, as if someone else was talking in that stony voice. "We'll get a lawyer if we have to. She doesn't have any right to harass you like this."

Hope filled his mother's eyes and stilled her writhing fingers. "You can stop her? I don't have to keep answering her questions?"

"We might have to get a lawyer, but I think you've cooperated more than enough. So long as you've told her everything you know." He didn't phrase it as a question, but it hung there as if he had. Daniel didn't know what he wanted—that she'd tell him whatever it was she was keeping secret, or that she'd convince him he'd been imagining things.

Either way, she bent her head to avoid his eyes and nodded. "You've always been a good son, Daniel. Taking over when your father died, the way you did… He'd be proud of you. He always was."

His father would have expected him to protect his mother, no matter what. Daniel knew that. He'd lied to himself earlier; he wasn't wavering on where his loyalties lay. He might be falling in love with Renee, though right this minute his former certainty about that *was* tottering. Sneaking out here to upset his mother like this, without calling him first… That was low. It made him question whether he was seeing in her what he wanted to see, not what was really there.

The last time they'd gone through this, he'd convinced himself she'd just felt shy after their date the night before. And she had genuinely seemed to be seeking information his mother hadn't minded providing. But this time, there was no misinterpreting why Renee hadn't phoned ahead.

Well, never again. He'd talk to her boss. He'd hire the best attorney in Oregon. Whatever it took.

But first he'd give himself the satisfaction of telling her what he thought of her behavior.

Now, when he took his mother's hand, she squeezed back. "Mom," he said, "will you call on over to the barn? Tell Lee I've had to go to town. I ought to be back in an hour or two."

Every word seemed to strengthen her, returning color to her cheeks. She nodded. "I'll phone right away."

"You'll be all right?" Daniel asked.

"Yes." She sounded more like herself. "Of course I will. I shouldn't have let myself get so upset."

Unless, he thought, *you really are hiding something. Unless you're afraid.* But immediately he felt like a traitor.

All her agitation meant was that his mother was blowing something way out of proportion. Hell, Dad could get pretty steamed when he thought someone had been careless in a way that might have led to one of the horses being injured. Mom was remembering some incident where Dad had ranted and raved and shaken his fists, maybe claimed he was going to string up that so-and-so, and now Mom was thinking maybe he'd been serious and gone and done it.

Didn't she know Dad better than that? Matthew Barnard was an honest, upstanding man. If he'd killed a man in a fight, it would have been an accident and he would have gone straight to the telephone to call the police. But to sink a knife into a man's chest, then dump the body… Daniel shook his head in instinctive denial.

He'd admired his father more than anyone on earth. Daniel knew damn well he wouldn't be the man he was if his father hadn't been there as an example. There was no way on God's green earth that Matthew Barnard had died with murder on his conscience. Daniel would stake everything he had and was on his bone-deep belief in his father's integrity.

Now, if Renee had been on her way to trusting Daniel the way he'd have liked, his word for it would have been good enough for her. As it was, he was going to have to march into her office breathing fire to stop her from tormenting his mother.

He didn't kid himself that Renee would see it his way, or forgive him anytime soon. Maybe she wasn't the woman he'd thought she was. Somehow that didn't seem like a great comfort right now.

It was going to be even less comfort when he got in his big empty bed tonight—the one he'd dreamed of sharing—and thought about her kisses and her innocence and her shaky steps toward faith in him.

Would she understand why he couldn't let her hurt his mother? Or would she believe he was just one more man who didn't hesitate to hurt *her*?

CHAPTER EIGHT

THE ELK SPRINGS Police Department was housed in a bland modern edifice that would have been interchangeable with the elementary school built the same year if it weren't for the jail. The new public safety building was part of a complex that included city offices, the library and a fire station. It was a big improvement over the old building, built in the twenties to intimidate the average citizen. Gray granite blocks, imposing stairs, wire-caged windows and the obligatory lions guarding heavy double oak doors had been right out of a Gothic novel. That old police station, two blocks away, was now an antique mall. This summer, Daniel had noticed the flower wreaths the lions sported around their necks.

Today he parked his pickup in a slot marked for visitors in front of the low building, then strode in, rage still simmering.

Just inside, a kid who looked about ten but was probably thirteen or fourteen slumped sullenly on one of a row of padded chairs, his expression imitating those on the faces that sneered from the Wanted posters hung above his head. A few feet away, a woman who was most likely the kid's mother stood talking to a uniformed officer behind a long counter. Her voice was rising, and although the boy was pretending indifference, his knuckles showed white where he gripped the arms of the chair.

Another uniformed officer approached him. "May I help you?"

"I'm here to see Renee Patton," Daniel said.

"I'll check on whether Lieutenant Patton is in." The policeman disappeared down the hall that led to rows of individual offices, a change from the old squad room where each desk had been separated by no more than a wastebasket and a chair to seat suspects.

Daniel knew. At fifteen, he'd been with a friend who shoplifted a pack of cigarettes. Both boys had been hauled down to the station. Daniel's genuine shock at his buddy's dishonesty must have showed, because his innocence was accepted and he walked out with his parents. His friend had stayed behind, his dad looking about like the kid's mother did today. As Daniel waited, he could hear her behind him.

"You stole a car? What were you thinking of?" The kid mumbled a brief reply Daniel couldn't make out. "Oh, God," his mother cried, "what did I do wrong?"

Daniel had been lucky. His parents had believed him. Of course, he hadn't had the cigarettes in his pocket. Or been sitting behind the wheel of a hot-wired car.

"Daniel!"

He quit eavesdropping in a hurry when Renee hurried toward him.

"What's up?" An open, inquiring expression didn't quite disguise her wariness.

"I want to talk to you."

"Well…I was about to go to lunch. Join me?"

"Fine," he said tersely.

Damn it, why had he agreed to make their talk social?

he asked himself, irritated, as he waited while Renee let somebody know she was leaving. What he'd wanted to do was flatten his hands on her desk, bend menacingly forward and say, "Get a warrant if you plan to come out to the Triple B again. Otherwise, you're not welcome." After which he'd stalk out.

Instead he found himself walking beside her and amicably debating where they'd eat—they agreed on the deli down the block. On the way, he kept sneaking sidelong glances, bothered afresh by her uniform and the holstered gun bumping on her hip. He had trouble seeing in her the woman he'd kissed. Yet he couldn't help noticing the delicate line of her cheek, the way her uniform shirt was rounded out, never mind the awkward fit of that holster because of the curves beneath. Even like this, she was pretty. Sexy. Daniel resented the fact that his anger didn't turn off his reaction to her.

The deli was a nice little place: antique tables and chairs, wallpaper with voluptuous roses and pink bows, an oak-and-iron coatrack in the entry and an old oak-and-glass case where pies were displayed and orders taken. The big disadvantage, he saw immediately, was that the tables were placed close enough together to eliminate any possibility of a completely private conversation.

Renee went for the special—minestrone soup with fresh-baked bread and a plate of fruit. Not hungry, Daniel ordered a sandwich and coffee.

She led him to a corner table, where between lacy curtains they could see down the riverfront park. They sat with their backs to the other diners.

The waitress brought his coffee and Renee's lemonade. Renee thanked her, then seemed to take a deep breath. Her eyes met his candidly. "I suppose this is about my having gone to see your mother this morning."

Jaws tight, he said, "I thought we'd come to an understanding."

Her eyes narrowed. "Really. And just what was that?"

"That you'd call me if you were coming out. Give me a chance to be there."

"And deflect my questions?"

He fought to keep his voice down. "Hear what the hell you're up to."

"And *I* thought I'd made it clear that our personal relationship wouldn't influence how I do my job."

"All I asked for was common courtesy," he growled.

"No," she said passionately, "you're asking me to dump this one in the unsolved files, because you don't want your mother bothered. Think about it for a minute. Every citizen in this country has the duty to cooperate…"

"You're accusing her of something without any evidence at all!"

He felt the stir as other diners turned. Well, let them listen.

"I haven't accused your mother of anything, and I don't expect I will. But you know as well as I do that she's hiding something. I want to know what it is."

"Thinking about the past upsets her. That doesn't mean she's lying."

"Don't kid yourself." Her voice was scathing. "You can't possibly believe she'd forgotten who T. J. Baxter was."

No, he didn't believe that. But his mother's conveniently poor memory didn't necessarily have anything to do with murder. His mother, a killer? His father? Never!

He opened his mouth to say something he probably

would have regretted, but was prevented by the arrival of the waitress with their food.

After depositing their lunches in front of them, she caroled, "Enjoy!" and trotted away.

Renee ignored her steaming bowl of soup. "Can you?" she repeated.

"Why the hell does this matter so much?" he heard himself asking. "Is it your first murder case? Are you afraid if you don't solve it, it'll show as a failure in your file?"

Her face was unreadable, her voice steady. "Maybe it matters to me because nobody else seems to care. Even you, and those bones came from *your* land. I want to know who he was more than I want to find out who killed him. I want a name on his gravestone."

"And you think my mother can put it there."

"That's right." Her gaze dared him to be honest. "And you think she can, too. You're just afraid to find out what she's hiding."

She'd nicked a vein with her accusation. It felt like rusty barbed wire biting deep.

"Maybe you're talking about yourself," he said, acid in his mouth. "Your father hid a hell of a lot, and you've spent a lifetime being afraid to find out what it was."

He was sorry the minute the words were out; fear and hurt pride were no excuse for striking where she was most vulnerable.

Her face paled.

He swore. "I shouldn't have said that…"

Color rose in her cheeks, vivid spots against the white. "No, you shouldn't have. But then, I guess you're willing to use any weapon to stop me, aren't you? Sweet words and kisses didn't work, so you're moving right along. Well, save it," she said bitterly. "Maybe you'd better go the legal route. Get your mom an attorney, why don't you? Admit she might need a defense."

She was in the act of rising to her feet, but he beat her to it. "Maybe I will," he snapped, "since you're obviously on a witch-hunt!" He yanked his wallet from his back pocket and tossed some bills on the table. "Enjoy your lunch." He walked out without looking back.

HUNCHED IN MISERY, Renee sat in her easy chair in the kitchen, knees drawn up and arms hugging herself.

Stupid, she thought. *Stupid, stupid, stupid.* She'd known all along why Daniel was interested in her. Of course he hadn't fallen madly in love with her at first sight! All she had to do was look in a mirror, especially when she was wearing her uniform. Helen of Troy, she was not. Heck, she probably had more in common with one of those Greek warriors. Achilles, maybe. Lord knew she'd discovered she possessed an unexpected weakness.

Not Daniel, she told herself. Vanity. All these years, she'd been the tough one. Abby charmed Daddy, and Renee refused even to try. Instead she tried to prove she could do everything as well as he did. Better. She wasn't soft; she didn't need or want anything that a woman had to coax from a man.

So, here she was, twenty-eight years old, and she was just discovering she'd lied to herself. *She* wanted tender words and flowers and passion, just like every other woman. She could become weak in the knees, too. No, weak in the head, Renee told herself in disgust. How could she have let herself crave approval from some man, to the point where she was tempted to surrender her convictions to get it?

"Which just goes to show," she muttered, "why I can't."

Because Daniel was right about that part, anyway; she *had* spent a lifetime being afraid. Not afraid of her father, exactly; rather, of who he was. Of what he might have done. Of finding out that her mother and sister hadn't just gone away.

What a mealymouth! She couldn't even put it into words. She was afraid of finding out that…

"He killed them." Throat thick, she felt the words lingering, as if they'd taken on bodily form.

What if she'd spent years desperately seeking approval from the man who had murdered her mother?

Renee shuddered and burrowed deeper in her own embrace. A grown woman trying with all her might to return to the womb. *Pathetic.*

Some sound made her lift her head. Was it…? Yes. The doorbell was ringing.

A kid trying to sell Girl Scout cookies. No. That was spring, wasn't it? Abby? But she had a key.

Whoever was there had abandoned the doorbell and was knocking now. She'd ignore it. Her. *Him.* Because she knew who it had to be.

He felt guilty. Or else he figured he could still string her along. Either way, she didn't want to hear it.

But he kept hammering, and after a while she heard his muffled voice, "Renee! I know you're home. Answer the door!"

Her father would have had a fit. She could just hear him bellowing, "God damn it, Renee, answer the door!"

"All right!" In her bare feet, she hurried to the front hall and flung the door open. "What do you want?"

"To talk to you." He glowered at her, dark brows drawn together. "I was getting worried."

To protect herself—ah, pride!—she tried for flippant. "What, you thought I committed suicide because you're mad at me? Well, sorry. I just wasn't in the mood for company. Especially yours."

In bulky parka and boots, Daniel looked even bigger than usual. Solid and sexy and scary, because he knew her too well. He could hurt her easily now, just as he had earlier.

"You're making it hard for me to apologize," he growled.

Renee crossed her arms. "Which part are you apologizing for?"

"That dig…"

"Fine. Consider your apology accepted."

His hand shot out, preventing her from closing the door.

"I want to talk to you."

"Come to my office tomorrow." Renee shoved at the door, gaining a few inches until he pushed back and regained every one of them plus more.

"Now," he said implacably.

A minor spurt of humor came to her rescue. To anyone else, they'd look as childish as she and Abby had the day before, each rolling bigger and bigger balls of snow until they couldn't make a snowman because both were too heavy to be lifted atop the other.

"All right." She let go of the door and stepped aside so suddenly he staggered and almost went down, a sight as gratifying in her current mood as she'd hoped. "Come in."

Daniel muttered something under his breath that she was just as glad she couldn't make out, then stalked ahead of her into the living room.

"Not here," she said hurriedly when he made a beeline for her father's recliner. *Not there.* She fancied it gave a small irritated rock. "Let's go into the kitchen."

Daniel stopped, but stood looking around. "You don't use this room, do you?"

"No. I told you the house was too big." *And this is his room.* She closed her eyes, for a moment fearing that she'd spoken aloud.

"It doesn't fit you."

Daniel had gone over to the bookcase, where he perused the titles, all true crime. Dad had loved that stuff, the gorier and sicker the better. He'd been known to muse aloud that it was too bad Elk Springs didn't have a *real* case like these.

Maybe he'd committed his own. The thought came unbidden, more readily than it once would have. It was getting easier to think of her father as the monster he'd been, whether he had also been a murderer or not.

"No," Renee said levelly. "This house doesn't fit me. But it's mine until I work up the energy to clean it out and sell it. So, can we go to the kitchen?"

"Cheery reading." Daniel shook his head. "Yeah, okay."

The minute he walked into the kitchen behind her, it came to her that she'd rather not have had him here, either. She felt like Shirley must have at the police intrusion. She'd gotten it wrong that day. It wasn't the presence of the enemy that made her uncomfortable, but rather the knowledge that this room revealed more about her than she wanted him to know.

His gaze went immediately to the dining nook, where the meager reality of her life was on display. There was the well-worn easy chair, the TV, the remains of her microwave dinner, the single piece of mail that had arrived today: a bill. Through his eyes, she saw it all and cringed. The lonely cell of a spinster.

"Were you watching something?" In his gentler voice, she heard pity.

"No." She'd forgotten the TV was even on; sunk in unhappiness as she'd been, she had no idea even what show it was tuned to. She stabbed the power button, bringing instant silence to the kitchen.

"All right." She didn't care if she sounded rude. "What did you want to say?"

He faced her, and she was confounded. The emotions in his electric-blue eyes were too complex to be labeled "pity." "I shouldn't have said what I did about your father. It had nothing to do with anything. I was angry. Trying to hurt you."

"I was getting personal, too," Renee felt compelled to admit. "Accusing you of being afraid to find out what your mother knows."

He swallowed hard. "But you were right."

She lifted her gaze to his. In a voice just above a whisper, she said, "You were, too."

"We all want to believe the best of our parents."

"I've never been able to do that."

"But you've tried."

"Yes." She gave a sharp, humorless laugh. "I've tried. Do you know, after that first day I never once asked Dad where my mother was? I still don't know whether I was scared of him, afraid of what he'd tell me, or trying to please him by implying that I didn't need her, that he was enough."

"And you're ashamed of yourself now." Somehow he'd moved. His hands clasped her upper arms, squeezing gently, massaging, comforting.

"Sure I am." Truer words had never been spoken. Her chest felt as if it might split open with the pain. "All these years I've hated my mother for deserting us, but I deserted her, too."

He swore and gave her a small shake. "You were a child!"

"Still, I could have hung on to her memory a little harder. Not gone along with pretending that she never existed, because that's what *he* wanted."

"Why not? He was here. She wasn't."

Irrational anger exploded. "And you think that was her fault? Did you ever meet him? He was…he was…" Oh, God. She pressed hands to her cheeks, finding them wet with tears.

Daniel pulled her into his arms. She went passively. Against her hair, he said roughly, "A son of a bitch. Yeah. I know. He was still your dad."

Anger and turmoil played tug-of-war in her chest, spilling those hated tears down her cheeks. She tried to wrench free. "Damn it! Why are you always so under-standing?"

He wouldn't let her go, though his grip never hurt her. "Because I know you well enough to despise the bastard."

She let out a choked sound. "Am I that messed up?"

"No. God." He closed his eyes briefly. "No. I just don't like to think about what you had to deal with. It's a miracle you came through whole."

"Whole?" Now, that *was* funny.

He scowled, not liking her laughter. "You did. You are."

Her bitter humor died. "You call this 'whole'?" Renee swept an arm in a gesture encompassing the kitchen, the living room behind them, the nook, her cocoon from the world. "It's weird. Why am I here? Why don't I have a nice condo like my sister does?"

Tone reasonable, he said, "Plenty of people live at home until they're twenty-eight. It's free."

"Oh, no." Her stomach clenched. "Not free. Believe me, nothing from my father was ever free. He extracted his price."

"He's dead. Gone." The compassion in his voice soothed, made promises. *Trust me,* he seemed to be saying.

Renee let herself believe, just for this minute. Still, she backed away from Daniel until she came up against the kitchen counter, needing the support, the distance. "Do you know—" the words just came, though she tried to say them lightly "—I'm not so sure he is."

He stared at her in open shock. "You're serious."

"Do you believe in ghosts?"

"No." His mouth closed tight.

"Well, I don't, either. I never did. But this house has just…soaked him up. Except out here. He only came in the kitchen to grab something from the refrigerator."

"So you hide here."

Her mouth twisted. "Something like that."

Pure rage flared in Daniel's eyes. "All right. Where is he?"

"Where…?" She gaped.

"Right now. Where is the bastard?"

"Do you plan to exorcise him?" Renee asked sarcastically. *If only it were possible.*

He stalked toward her. "Where is he?"

She threw up her hands. "It's my imagination! You know it is. He can't be here."

Daniel didn't hesitate. "But you feel him."

"I…yes."

"Where?"

Was he going to punch a ghost? she wondered wildly. What if she said, *Everywhere?* Would he burn the house down? She wouldn't mind; she'd been tempted herself. If she'd thought she could get away with it, walk away with the insurance money…

Her damned mouth opened itself. "Did you see the recliner rock when you went toward it?"

Daniel spun on one heel and went through the swinging door into the living room. Renee hurried after him. "What are you…"

Without a word, he grabbed the recliner and headed for the front door.

Sickening fear washed up in her throat. "Daniel! Where are you going with that? What are you *doing?*"

Her father… Oh, God, what would he say? The time she'd rearranged the living room and moved his chair ten feet to accommodate a pretty little antique chest she'd spotted in a store downtown, he had gone out to the garage, come back with an ax and chopped the chest into firewood. Then he'd looked at her and said coldly, "Clean this up and put the furniture where it's supposed to be."

That was when any illusion this was her home, too, had died stillborn.

"I'm throwing the damn chair out." Daniel set it down long enough to open the front door. He stopped its violent rocking by snatching it back up and wrestling it through the doorway. The muscles in his arms and shoulders bunched as he lifted the recliner and flung it off the porch. Renee heard a crunch.

Daniel turned to face her. His expression changed. "For God's sake, Renee! It's not some kind of altar." He stopped. "Or is it?"

Brushing past him, she clutched the porch railing and stared down at the chair, lying on its side on the wet lawn so that the mechanism beneath showed. A long wicked branch of the climbing rose had entangled it on the way down. Stuffing popped through one of the new tears. The branch was broken, its celery green heart showing. She would have to prune it at the base.

"No," she said slowly. "Not an altar. It was just…his."

"I'll load it in my truck when I go. Take it to the solid waste station."

She'd actually considered burning down the house, but it had never occurred to her to get rid of the chair. Giddily she thought, *I could strip the whole living room. Buy new carpet—something* he *would have hated. Teal. Periwinkle. Flowery, overstuffed sofa and chairs. Paint the heavy dark mantel white or cream. Have a dainty coffee table, instead of that ponderous mission oak he'd loved. Burn those horrible books. Fill the shelves with romances, fantasy, humor.*

Make this *her* room.

Do it now, an inner voice said. *Now, before you chicken out. Start thinking it's sacrilege.*

Feeling weirdly numb, Renee went back into the living room and scooped up an armful of her father's favorite reading. "Take these, too," she said, rushing out to throw them from the porch, watch them tumble and flutter to the soggy grass. She went back for more. "And these."

Without a word, Daniel helped her. When the bookcase was empty, she looked around. "And this. I hate it." The gun cabinet was too heavy for her. Daniel broke the glass and she dropped the row of rifles uncaringly on the brown carpet. She watched the cabinet crunch and splinter when Daniel flung it after the recliner. She remembered her pretty antique chest and thought, *What goes around comes around.*

The destruction was unexpectedly exhilarating, which worried her. Did she have a criminal bent? But, no—all she was doing was taking possession of what was hers. Dispossessing her father.

She and Daniel emptied the living room, moving a few pieces of furniture into the dining room or front hall, throwing out the rest. When Renee dropped to her knees and began wrenching up the carpet, Daniel went out to his pickup and came back with a hammer and screwdrivers.

"Get some big scissors," he said.

The stuff rolled up, revealing thin padding that she tore into shreds and heaped in a pile. Daniel pried up the carpet tacks and the staples that had held the padding. Renee cut up the carpet into manageable strips. They loaded what they could into plastic garbage sacks, carrying the rest out and shoving it into the back of his pickup. He obviously wouldn't be able to get all the furniture tonight, but she was glad when he loaded the recliner.

"Have you had dinner?" Renee asked recklessly. "I could make something."

"Actually, I have." Daniel sounded apologetic. "How about you?"

She remembered that microwave dinner and felt deflated. She'd wanted to cook something her father would have hated. Use the wok that had sat untouched in a lower cabinet since she'd bought it in a brave moment that didn't last long enough. Eat the dinner at the mahogany dining room table, where she hadn't sat since he died.

Not that she would have had the right ingredients.

When was the last time she'd bought staples, the stuff you needed when you really cooked? She knew, of course—six months ago.

"I've eaten, too," she admitted. "Daniel…"

He forestalled her gratitude. Taking her arm, he said, "Let's go see what we've wrought."

Furniture and carpet gone, the living room was an alien landscape. *He* wasn't gone altogether, but his presence was fainter, and she knew suddenly that it would be gone completely when she painted the mantel and bookcases on each side of the fireplace, tore down the heavy drapes, let in sunshine and light and color.

"Too bad Abby wasn't here," she said.

"She would have enjoyed it, too, huh?"

"She'd have loved throwing out his things," Renee said fiercely. "She can help me with his bedroom. Or maybe I should do it right now."

She'd taken no more than a step toward the staircase when Daniel's hand stopped her. "Tomorrow. You've done enough for one day."

He was right, she thought reluctantly, feeling the ache in her shoulders and back. The exhilaration was fading, leaving her drained. Not having second thoughts—oh, no, still glorying in the echoing emptiness that could be a beautiful room, a *new* room, but definitely weary.

"Yes. Okay." She turned to face him, wondering with sudden apprehension whether now he did think she was crazy.

He was watching her, worry in his eyes. Worry and tenderness and patience.

It was the patience that got to her. They were adults; why wait? She was in just the mood to do something *really* reckless.

She ought to go slowly, seduce him, let him think it was his idea. But tonight, she was taking charge of her own destiny.

Before she even opened her mouth, his expression changed. His eyes narrowed, the air became charged, as if he were so sensitive to her moods, he'd felt her decision before she could speak it aloud.

"Will you stay tonight?" She'd wanted to sound provocative, bold, but her voice squeaked. "I want you to make love to me."

Her fantasy man would have come to her in two long strides, kissed her passionately, then lifted her into his arms and carried her up the stairs to her bedroom.

The real man stayed stolidly put. A muscle jerked in his cheek, and he made a rough sound that might have been a groan. But his tone was controlled, even cool.

"That depends on whether you want me just because it would tick your father off royally."

Her minuscule store of confidence in her sexual appeal rushed out, as if someone had pulled the plug on it.

"Never mind." She shrugged as if his answer didn't matter, as if her impulsive invitation had been as trivial as a suggested lunch date. "We're both tired."

"Not that tired." Now he did take those two steps, and his big hand lifted her chin. "You know damn well I want you, Renee. I'm probably an idiot not to take what you're offering, no questions asked. Trouble is, I'd like sex between us to be about us. Not a dead man."

"I…" She stared up at Daniel, seeing the banked desire, the desperate honesty.

Was it about her father? He'd sneered at her every small effort to make herself look pretty. "Why would you put that crap on?" he'd asked when she tried mascara and blush. "A little paint doesn't turn a plow horse into a high-stepper." Oh, how he would tumble in his grave at the knowledge that a handsome man wanted her, that she was making love upstairs in this very house!

Suddenly shaky, weak-kneed, she had to lift her hands to Daniel's chest to brace herself. The answer came to her, searing, unexpected.

"No," she whispered. "No, it's not about my father. I was just using my anger to…to bolster my courage."

His big hands framed her face, and she felt the faintest trembling in them. His voice was gruff. "You're afraid of me?"

"No." Renee couldn't look above his throat. "Not you. I'm afraid of *this*. You see, I…" She had to stop, take a deep breath, finish in a rush. "Well, I've never done it."

CHAPTER NINE

STUNNED, Daniel froze. Dear God, she was a virgin. Twenty-eight years old, and she'd never had sex. Never, he had to guess, trusted any man or boy enough to let herself be that vulnerable. Or maybe, never believed anyone would want her.

This time the surge of rage was violent. So easygoing he'd never totally understood even his father's quick but short-lived temper, Daniel had never before wanted to hurt anyone. Not so seriously that he might have shoved a fist down her bastard of a father's throat if he could.

Now he knew what it felt like.

But she was still waiting.

"You're a virgin," he said aloud. *Brilliant.*

She flushed deep pink. "That sounds so…so medieval. I just thought you should know that I'm not very experienced. I mean, I'll probably disappoint you…"

His fingers bit into her arms and that edge of violence honed his voice. "Disappoint me? Don't you know what a gift you're offering?"

Renee stiffened under his hands. Tone combative, she asked, "Why a gift? Don't tell me you think it's okay for guys to play around, but girls should save themselves for their 'true love.' That's *worse* than medieval! It's…"

Daniel kissed her into silence. Drugged by her

softness, the tremor of her lips, the hitch in her breath, it was all he could do to raise his head.

"You always want to misunderstand me, don't you?"

Eyes wide and shimmery golden-green, Renee stared up at him.

"And I think we had this discussion before. No, I don't believe a woman should 'save herself.' But when she does give herself for the first time, the man she chooses ought to feel honored." He cupped her face, his thumbs moving in slow circles, teasing the corners of her mouth. "As I do."

"Oh," she whispered.

He kissed her again, lingering, nibbling gently, sucking on her bottom lip. "Is it okay," he murmured against her mouth, "if I delude myself that you must feel something special for me?"

"I…" Her head fell back against the support of his hand; her lashes swept down as she lifted her face to his. "I suppose," she said on a release of breath.

She loved him. She couldn't say the words, but she did. She must. The knowledge roared through him like an earthquake that could ripple tons of earth as if it were a sheet of cloth.

He groaned and took her mouth again, this time with savage need. That innocence… He had felt it, and now understood it. Even—though he would never admit to emotion so primitive—gloried in it. He was first. She was his.

Daniel bent, wrapped an arm under her thighs and lifted her up.

Renee gasped and clutched at his shoulders as though afraid to trust that he wouldn't drop her. Stiffening, she cried, "Daniel!"

"Indulge me," he said roughly. She might think she was tough, but she was a featherweight, all legs and fine bones and big eyes like a newborn colt. Despite her slenderness, however, she had plenty of curves, including a nicely rounded bottom nestled against him right where it tormented him the most.

Two or three stairs up, she relaxed and kissed his neck, a tiny shy peck that wrung a groan from him. Despite her inexperience, she apparently recognized pleasure when she heard it, because her mouth touched his throat again, more lingeringly this time. She trailed tiny kisses down to the hollow at the base. When her tongue flicked his skin, a warm damp taste, it was all he could do not to strip her right there, on the landing, and take her on the floor, to hell with gentle, patient foreplay.

Daniel reined himself in with a painful effort. *She's not ready,* he told himself grimly. *She can't be.* This was her first time, and he had to be sure it was good. He'd scare the hell out of her if she had any idea how close he was to breaking.

"Which is your bedroom?" he asked hoarsely.

"I…" She lifted her head and looked around, dazed, as if she had no idea where they were. "Oh. It's… Mine's the one on the right."

The white-painted, paneled door stood open. With an elbow he nudged the light switch. Inside was about what he'd expected, and feared: a room as innocent as she was. Walls a pale aqua, woodwork white, pastel rag rugs on the gleaming hardwood floor. White dresser, beveled mirror above. Stuffed animals lined up atop a tall bookcase, also white. Lacy curtains. Silver-framed photos on the bedside stand.

And a twin bed, covered with a pink and blue-green

quilt that looked old, in a good way: gently faded, frayed, but all the prettier for that.

He bit back a word that didn't belong in this room. Any more than hot sex did.

She began to stiffen again. "Is something wrong?"

"No. Nothing." He *had* to make love to her here, on her bed. If she knew that *he* was suddenly scared, she'd chicken out. Decide she was what was wrong.

And what was bothering him, anyway? She was an innocent; he knew that, he'd known it all along. This wouldn't be hot sex—it would be lovemaking.

And, God help him, he loved the girl who'd made this room and the woman who still felt at home here.

So what if his feet dangled off the foot of the bed?

"It's too short, isn't it?" As he let her slide to her feet, Renee looked at the bed. "And…and too narrow."

Husky amusement in his voice, Daniel said, "Definitely not too narrow. The short part doesn't matter. If, um, a man and a woman can have great sex in the front seat of a car, you don't need to worry about your bed being too small."

"Not very long ago, when I was out on patrol, I interrupted a couple of teenagers." She was blushing fiercely. "I shone the flashlight right in and…"

"And?" He quirked an eyebrow.

"The boy was on his knees and…" Her courage ran out.

"That works," Daniel said.

Shoot. He was getting randier by the minute. He wanted to try that with her. Her skirt—the one he had yet to see her wearing—up around her waist. Bare silky thighs, breasts pale in the moonlight, his pickup truck groaning as they rocked it…

"I went to a drive-in with a boy once." Musing aloud,

she didn't seem to have a clue what she was doing to him. "But we didn't…you know."

Daniel couldn't stand it another minute. He peeled off her sweatshirt and tossed it aside. The static he'd created fluffed tiny hairs around her face. And her bra… God help him, it was as pretty and sweet as her bedroom. Dainty, with scalloped edges and the hooks in back. His breath rasped out.

The pink on her cheeks crept down her neck. "I'm not very big…"

"You're perfect." He didn't sound like himself. His hands shook as he reached out and cupped her breasts, gently squeezed, ran his thumbs over the hardening nubs still hidden from his hungry gaze.

"Oh-hh," she sighed.

He turned her around and with hands that still trembled unhooked her bra. He slipped the straps from her shoulders, feeling the satiny skin, the fragility of her collarbone, the quick shaky breath she drew. And then he turned her back to face him.

She tried to cover her breasts with her hands; he pried them away. She was so pretty, with the snow-white skin that went with her pale gold hair. Pink nipples as petite as he'd imagined. He swallowed, touched her breasts. Her head bent as she watched, took in the contrast of his big, dark hands against her tender skin.

She swayed, then reached out and grabbed his shirt in two fists. "I don't think my legs want to hold me up," she whispered.

"Good," he said hoarsely. He lifted her and laid her on the bed. The sight of her sprawled there, half naked, was better than any fantasy he'd ever dreamed up.

He put one knee between her thighs.

"No fair," she murmured. "Your shirt has to go, too."

He fumbled with the damn buttons, popping one off before the shirt joined hers on the floor. He kicked off his boots, too, and peeled off the heavy socks he wore underneath. She'd already dropped her Swedish clogs on the floor, but he took care of her socks. Her feet were narrow with a high arch, and her toes curled in shyness.

He was smiling when he kneeled atop Renee. "You have sexy feet."

"They're…they're skinny!" she protested.

"At least you don't have hairs on your toes, like I do."

She giggled, then sighed when he nuzzled her breast. By the time he drew it into his mouth, she was arching up and whimpering. She didn't even seem to notice when he unsnapped the waistband of her jeans and eased down the zipper.

Her stomach quivered as his hand slipped inside her cotton panties, and her legs tried to tighten once she realized what he was up to, but then she had to cry out when he cupped her and rubbed gently.

He didn't dare take off his own jeans; he'd have been on her like a stallion on a mare in heat. The tight denim curbed him, kept him sane. Let him caress her and tell her how gorgeous she was and taste her breasts and kiss her smooth flat belly, and finally pull down her jeans and panties to reveal narrow hips and a silky vee of golden hair. She tried to cover herself there, too, but he only set her hand on his chest and stroked her thighs and tried not to picture himself between them.

She either didn't have the nerve to touch him, or didn't know he might like it, for which he was thankful. If she'd run her fingers down the painful bulge in the front of his jeans, he'd have reacted like a sixteen-year-old during his first sexual experience. And, damn, he wanted to be inside her before he lost it.

He teased and played and rubbed until her thighs parted and her hips rose and fell and she made urgent sounds that included his name.

"Daniel. Oh, Daniel! Oh, please." Her voice rose in what seemed a bewildered question. "Daniel?"

He pulled away from her just long enough to unbutton his jeans and rip them off. Renee came back to herself, rolling her eyes like a spooked horse, and he had to grit his teeth and hold on a little longer as he soothed her back to mindless wanting.

The next time she arched upward, he pushed inside her. Slowly, a fraction of an inch at a time, easing back, then forward. Nothing in his life had ever felt as good as this did, or as exquisitely frustrating. Damn near every muscle in his body locked with the effort not to thrust hard and fast, as deep as her lost memories.

Don't scare her. Don't hurt her.

He pulled back, waited until her hands clutched at him and she pushed upward herself.

She trusted him. He could endure anything.

"That's it, love," he whispered. "That's it. Just like that."

Her glazed eyes held his. "Daniel."

"You feel so good."

"Please."

He thrust. Felt the resistance, heard the rattle of her breath. But at last, at last, he was buried completely, part of her.

"I'm sorry, I'm sorry, I'm sorry," he groaned, even as he couldn't stop moving, had to retreat, push back, do it all over again.

She gave a hiccuping sigh, then, incredibly, smiled. "Don't be. Oh, Daniel."

She was there, moving with him, whimpering again, saying his name as if he could give her the world.

Slowly. Wait.

Her voice became puzzled, then frantic, as the need built and built and she didn't know what to do with it. But he did, moving as deliberately as he could make himself, holding back, waiting. Until her body squeezed around him and she cried his name one more time with all the wonder and joy a man in love needed. And then he convulsed inside her, pleasure blinding him and deafening him. It was like dying and being reborn.

Not sex. Love.

RENEE LAY CUDDLED against Daniel, her head on his shoulder, his arm wrapped snugly around her. His heartbeat drummed, slow and heavy, beneath her ear. One of her legs tangled wantonly with his, which felt coarse with hair. She'd dreamed of this, without knowing what it would really be like. It was…so *physical,* so sensual, so sweaty. And, oh, so glorious.

But scary, too. She didn't know him that well. And yet she'd let him see parts of her she'd never even taken a good look at herself. He'd touched her in shocking ways.

What was worse, she'd been noisy, she knew she had. The embarrassing knowledge prickled on her nerve endings.

Panic edged its way into her consciousness. Oh, Lord, what had she done? What must he think of her now? She'd practically thrown herself at him.

Had he really wanted her, or had it all been a big act to keep her away from the Triple B? Her humiliation reached a peak when she thought about how she'd put him on the spot. *Make love to me,* she'd said. *Will you stay tonight?* What could he do?

Her cheeks felt so hot, it was a wonder she wasn't burning him. Sizzling those tiny chest hairs that tickled at her nose. She prayed he couldn't see her face.

Before, she'd always been secure in her dignity. Now she felt stupidly vulnerable, stripped bare in more than one way. She hated knowing she'd made a fool of herself. Begging him to stay. Screeching like…like some cat in heat, just because what he was doing felt good.

He probably hadn't even enjoyed himself.

An image flickered into her mind, and she backed off. Well, she guessed he had enjoyed himself, sort of; she knew at least that he'd…*satisfied himself.*

Mealymouth, Renee thought scornfully, not for the first time. Some tough cop she was. She couldn't even use the words so common every thirteen-year-old used them without a second thought!

Daniel's hand moved, sliding up her back in a long, slow caress. Renee stiffened.

"Hey," he said softly. "I thought you were asleep."

Good excuse. "Mmm," she murmured. Could she turn away from him as if it were a natural shift, something a sleeping person did unconsciously? He wouldn't feel as if he could leave as long as she was hanging on him like a leech.

Renee lay still, breathing slow and deep, until she felt his muscles go lax again. He must have lifted his head from the pillow to look at her, and now he was lying back again. She gave it a minute or two, then sighed and burrowed her head as if seeking a more comfortable position. Finally, she just rolled away, hoping he would release her.

Smooth move, except she rolled herself right off the bed. Renee hit the floor with a bump and a shriek.

Daniel jackknifed up. "Are you all right?"

Renee stared up at him, horribly aware of how ridiculous she looked sitting naked on the floor. "I'm not hurt, if that's what you mean!" she snapped.

His face worked. Had she offended him? Then, indignant, she realized he was trying hard not to laugh. "I guess—" his voice was muffled with the effort "—I was wrong. Your bed is too narrow."

He looked good, lying there on his side, dark hair ruffled, blue eyes bright with laughter, a grin warming a face that was often too impassive. His shoulders were sleek, smooth skin over muscles that rippled as he laughed. Hips narrow, belly flat, thighs powerful. And what lay in between… Renee gulped. She hadn't really looked earlier. In fact, she'd squeezed her eyes shut tight so that she wouldn't!

It wasn't as if she didn't know what a man had between his legs. She and Abby had even gone to a porno movie once, feeling embarrassed but daring. It had been kind of disgusting, but…interesting.

Something up on the movie screen was one thing, though, and in real life another. It suddenly struck her: there was a naked man in her bedroom. In her *bed*. Right before having wild sex with him, she'd gutted the living room. Flung her father's books out in the slushy snow. Splintered his gun cabinet. If she went downstairs right this minute, she'd be walking on plywood.

Had she gone completely nuts?

"Learned anything?" Daniel asked.

She came to. "What?"

Humor and something more sensual roughened his voice. "You've been studying me real hard."

Studying? Oh, God. She'd been staring this whole time right at him. At his...

She swallowed. His penis wasn't limp anymore. Before her very eyes, it was changing. Thickening, lengthening.

"I..." Her throat clogged. "You're..."

He glanced down. "Yes. I am."

"Why?"

"I like you looking at me," he said simply.

"Oh." Now she felt even more foolish. "But we just..."

"Yeah. We did."

Was he laughing at her? she wondered suspiciously.

But his voice stayed grave. "We could again. If you'd like."

Warmth blossomed in her belly even as her mouth went dry. The first time, she hadn't been thinking. She'd been swept along by her sense of triumph, of freedom, of empowerment. But now...well, it was like waking up with a hangover. Totally stone-cold sober. Afterward, she'd have no excuse for her behavior.

"You can't stay the night," she blurted. "There's not enough room for both of us in my bed."

His mouth quirked. "No kidding."

She remembered that she was still sitting on the floor. But standing in front of him would be even more embarrassing.

"I'm not sure..."

His smile vanished. "That you want me here?"

"No! I didn't mean that!" Yes, she did, but at the same time, she didn't. A normally resolute person, she'd never been so rattled in her life.

"No?" The grooves in his cheeks deepened. "Then why don't you come back up here?"

"I…" She stared at his outstretched hand, frozen in indecision.

Into her mind flashed, *Oh, why not?* At least this time *he* was the one doing the asking. And, heck, if this turned out to be her only fling, she might as well make it a good one.

Eyes locked with his, she rose slowly to her feet. His gaze lowered, traveled slowly over her body, and her skin shivered at the passage as if the touch was physical.

"You're beautiful," he said hoarsely. "Wondering what you looked like without clothes has been driving me crazy."

She wanted to believe him wholeheartedly. His eyes said she could, but he was basically a kind man, one who'd lie under these circumstances. She'd never driven any man crazy before. Why would her effect on him be any different?

But tonight, just tonight, she would pretend. She would stretch, and revel in the hot awareness in his eyes. She would smile—yes, just like that—and sit next to him on the bed and wriggle her hips a little and pretend she didn't know she was pressing against him *there.* And maybe, oh, maybe, she would even wrap her hand around him, see if the skin felt as satiny as it looked, feel him quiver, those thick blood veins pulse.

"You don't look so bad yourself," she said throatily, like Rita Hayworth in an old movie, and curled one foot under herself as she sat on the bed. She stroked his chest, just for starters, and felt the groan rising from deep inside him. Hey, she wasn't doing half-bad.

Even if it was just pretend.

ABBY STOOD in the middle of the living room and stared, rotating slowly as if to take in the magnitude of what she was seeing. Finally she shook her head. "When did you do this?"

"Last night."

Seeing it through her sister's eyes, Renee was shocked afresh at what she'd done. She had lived in this house all her life, and the basic decor had never changed. Now she felt as if she'd wandered into a house under construction: raw, unfamiliar, uninhabited.

"Why?" her sister asked in genuine puzzlement.

It was fun was one possible explanation. *I was exorcising Dad's ghost* was another.

Renee took a breath. "I'm going to remodel. Paint all the woodwork white. Buy a new couch. New carpet." She gestured. "Teal, I think. Wouldn't that be pretty?"

Now Abby swung to face her. "But…are you planning to stay in the house?"

She had every right to want her share of the money from the sale of the house. To her credit, she'd been patient with Renee, and now she sounded disturbed, not angry.

"No-o," Renee said slowly. "I thought…well, that this would make it sell faster. And maybe make it easier for me to leave. It won't be *home* the same way. Does that make sense?"

"No." Abby's voice was flat. "Nothing you've done lately has made sense. You hated Dad—so why didn't you move out years ago? You hate the house, and we should have sold it this summer while the market was decent. It's not vacation house material, so it won't appeal to the skiers. Now we might as well not bother to put it on the market until May! You're irritating your boss because you can't get a few dirty old bones off your mind. You don't date, you don't have friends…" Abby gave her a look. "And it's not hard to see why. I mean, jeez, Renee, move on."

A sickening sense of betrayal hit Renee in the stomach, a fist of disbelief. "You don't like me very well, do you?"

Abby gave a careless shrug. "Don't be ridiculous. I'm your sister. Can't I tell you what I really think?"

Struggling to keep her voice even, Renee said, "Obviously, you can. You just did."

Abby cocked her head to one side. "You're mad, aren't you?"

"No." Hurt, not mad. Stunned. And chilled by her sister's emotionless expression. Either Abby didn't realize how much she'd revealed, or she didn't care.

"Good." Abby turned away to survey the bare room again. "Do you want company when you go shopping for carpet and furniture?"

"I suppose. I don't know. Maybe Saturday."

"Well…call me. Okay?"

Renee didn't say anything. Abby took one last look around, shook her head, rolled her eyes, and left. Renee fled into the kitchen to curl up in her easy chair in the dining nook. Her refuge.

Her sense of triumph was flattened. She'd wanted Abby to laugh and rejoice in what she'd done. She'd wanted to tell her sister about last night, about Daniel and the way he'd made her feel. About her cowardice afterward, when she'd pretended to be asleep when he got dressed and departed, about ignoring his phone messages today, about letting the phone ring only half an hour ago, though she knew it must be him.

But now she knew that her sister—her only remaining family—wouldn't have sympathized, wouldn't have understood. Inside, she would have scorned. She would have believed there was something wrong with Renee, who had never been able to deal with either their father or boys with Abby's insouciance.

Renee squeezed her eyes shut and hugged her knees. Was she so terribly neurotic?

She'd been doing fine until recently. Until Lotto brought home those bones, and they came to symbolize all the losses, all the mysteries, in her life. So many emotions had surfaced since then: grief and anger most of all.

She'd never let herself feel them before. Not until now, when it was safe. When she wouldn't be punished with her father's heavy hand or by being shut out emotionally.

Maybe she *needed* to feel all these extremes, everything she'd shut down all these years. Maybe the fact that she was letting herself meant that she was healing.

Maybe Abby didn't understand because she had grieved. After all, she'd been much younger when their mother left.

Or maybe, Renee thought with a twinge of unease, Abby, who didn't seem to let herself feel much of anything, was the one who needed help.

The phone shrilled again. Renee's head jerked up. As the ring stabbed at her, over and over again, she stared at the wall-hung telephone, fighting the urge to pick up the receiver, wanting to and afraid to at the same time.

Tomorrow, she promised herself. She'd talk to him then. When she decided what tack to take. How to be casual, friendly, flirtatious. How to hide what she really felt.

Because she'd discovered that among her tumult of emotions was love. She wasn't a casual person. She'd never made love with a man before because she'd never felt what she did now. And she had no idea how Daniel felt about *her*.

And she had no idea what would happen when he discovered that she wouldn't give up, that she had to find out who those bones had belonged to. As confused as she was, she understood this much: her quest was part of putting herself back together. She couldn't "move on," as her sister had so disdainfully put it, until she'd accomplished this one thing.

The one Daniel had begged her to let go.

The answering machine picked up at last. The caller didn't leave a message. Dry-eyed, Renee bowed her head against her knees.

It wasn't fair. How could he ask this of her? Why couldn't she have fallen in love with some other man? Why did it all have to happen now, before she was ready?

CHAPTER TEN

AFTER SENDING DANIEL on his way, Shirley started in on the dirty dishes. It had been nice having Mary and Devon here, she reflected, but it was good to have the house to herself again. Daniel and she, they hadn't used that many dishes. Think of the pile if there'd been two more at the table tonight!

She paused, hands in hot soapy dishwater, and looked at her reflection through the steam fogging the window above the sink.

She almost wished she hadn't suggested Daniel come for dinner tonight. First he'd said he had other plans, then tersely declared that he didn't after all.

Shirley could see her son's unhappiness and even knew some of the cause. Thanks to those bones, his faith in his father's worth was crumbling. *Like hers,* she'd been about to think, but that wasn't true. She knew why Matt had committed murder, if he had.

Oh, if only there was some way to find out for sure, without betraying him! But as far as she could see, there wasn't, so no point in thinking about it.

Daniel had more on his mind than just his father, though. Shirley could tell. It was that lady police officer. He'd fallen for her, and hard. Once upon a time he'd have told his own mother, but circumstances being what they were, he was keeping his mouth shut. But she knew. For one thing, Mary had mentioned that he was taking the policewoman to dinner.

Over the kitchen table this evening they'd talked about Lieutenant Renee Patton and her investigation. His voice caressed her name, but unhappiness showed bleakly in his eyes at the same time.

Last night Shirley hadn't been able to sleep, which was why she'd been up to see the headlights of his truck so late. Must've been two, three in the morning. She hadn't looked at the clock. Her Daniel never stayed out drinking to all hours, and he hadn't had a girlfriend in a while. He'd stomped out so darn mad yesterday, Shirley had known who he was after.

At the time she'd been hopeful he would talk Renee Patton into looking somewhere else for the killer. But at dinner Daniel hadn't sounded as if that was so. He'd suggested Shirley not talk to the police again without him there.

"And maybe an attorney," he'd suggested.

"An attorney?" Shirley repeated, not sure whether to be outraged or comforted by the idea. "They don't think *I* had anything to do with that man dying?"

"They think you know who did," he said bluntly, and she'd felt him waiting.

She *wanted* to tell him what had happened, but silence was a hard road to quit. And she still felt such shame and horror. Every time the memory of what had happened tried to slither up from the depth of her consciousness, her mind battled it back down, out of sight. She couldn't even bear to face the memory herself! How could she put it all into words?

But she hated to see Daniel so unhappy. What she

didn't know was whether she'd make anything better by telling. She wanted to do what was right for her son, and for Matthew. She didn't care so much about herself; she'd face anything if she had to—and if it was the right thing to do. But what was right? she worried.

What would Matthew want her to do?

Tonight she'd pretended that she hadn't noticed her son was waiting for an answer. She chattered about some other thing and ignored the searching look he gave her and the small frown between his dark brows. He was near the spitting image of his father! Sometimes that resemblance gave her a turn, letting her think for just a moment...

But of course Matthew wasn't back, wouldn't ever come back. She was on her own now, so far as this kind of decision went. Shirley almost wished she was crazy enough to believe that Matthew could answer her questions.

Tonight, looking at her misty reflection in the kitchen window, she felt a stir of painful humor. Heck, maybe she could *make* herself that crazy! Maybe Matt's voice would come to her, if she begged him loud and long enough.

She shut her eyes, so as not to see her own face looking back at her.

Voice as insubstantial as the steam rising from the hot dishwater, Shirley murmured, "Oh, Matthew, tell me how to do what's right for Daniel."

WEARING ONLY JEANS, Daniel toweled his hair dry as he walked barefoot down the hall to the kitchen. More crappy weather. He'd been working horses for a couple hours before his foul mood and numb fingers sent him back up to the house. Ten minutes under the hot spray in the shower had brought painful feeling back to his fingers without doing a thing for his mood.

Why the hell wouldn't Renee return his phone calls? Had she hankered to experiment sexually, and now that she'd gotten what she wanted, she didn't know how to tell him *adios?*

But he just couldn't believe that. She was shy; that had to be it. He latched onto this explanation, though he wouldn't be able to hold on to it long. These past two days, his mind wouldn't stop worrying the problem of what had gone wrong, like a dog nipping at a horse's heels. Every time he satisfied himself that he understood her, his certainty would bounce loose, as if that horse had kicked him good and hard.

Coffee bubbled gently in the pot. Daniel tossed the towel over the back of a chair and grabbed a mug from the cupboard. He was taking the first sip when his gaze encountered the answering machine. The red light blinked once, hesitated, blinked again, and his heart went still.

Daniel swore aloud. She'd called while he was in the shower. Didn't it figure? Why hadn't he taken the cordless phone into the bathroom where he could hear it?

Almost reluctantly, he pressed the play button. Probably wasn't her at all, he told himself without believing it for a second.

"Daniel, this is Renee." She sounded as if she were right there in the kitchen. He even heard the breath she took next. "I'm sorry I haven't called. Things at work…" She trailed off, as though even she realized how weak an explanation she was concocting. Then her voice strengthened, became formal. "I'm planning to come out and talk to your mother this morning. About eleven o'clock, in case you want to be there. Or you want an attorney representing her." Another pause, before she said in a rush, "This is something I have to do," and hung up.

Rage whistled through him like an icy north wind, and he wheeled to look at the clock. Ten-fifteen. If her call had come when he first got in the shower, she'd given exactly one hour's notice.

No wonder she hadn't called before! She'd been avoiding him because she wanted to spring another little surprise. She'd known damn well he would ask what her intentions were, and she hadn't wanted to lie. She'd probably hoped he wouldn't get this message until she'd been and gone, his mother in handcuffs if Renee had her way, he thought viciously.

Well, she'd made a big mistake, Daniel vowed. He wasn't letting her near his mother.

Coffee forgotten, he stalked back down the hall. In his bedroom he yanked on thick socks and boots, buttoned up a flannel shirt and grabbed a wool fisherman's sweater. He knew damn well she wouldn't take his call if he phoned, and he didn't dare set out to town to intercept her, in case she was early and took a different route than he guessed at.

He turned the heater in his pickup on full blast, and roared down the curving driveway from his place to meet the main ranch road. No sign of a police car yet in front of his mother's; Renee hadn't jumped the gun that much. Without stopping he turned right and sped the half mile to the Triple B gates, where he abruptly swerved and slammed on the brakes. The pickup bucked and slithered on the cinders, but came to a stop sideways. Blocking the way onto his property.

She'd better have a warrant if she thought she was going to get by him.

He waited, leaving the engine running for the heat and regretting the mug of coffee left sitting on the kitchen counter. 10:30 came and went. 10:40. He turned on the radio and George Strait's twangy voice came on, singing about love and loss and memories. With a muttered curse Daniel punched the button and cut George off mid-word.

10:55. What if she didn't come? He'd feel like a fool sitting here in the middle of his driveway. He hadn't called his mother and hadn't checked to see if her car was here. She wouldn't have gone to town to meet Renee without telling him, would she?

11:02. Daniel drummed his fingers on the steering wheel. Simmering anger was all that held boredom at bay. Anger, and the memories of her that kept playing in his mind: the long milk-pale line of her body as she arched her back in pleasure; the soft round weight of her breasts; her throaty cries; her hesitant kisses; the desperate need to tear out and throw away every physical manifestation of her father.

His fingers wrapped around the steering wheel so tightly his knuckles showed white. Nothing he knew or remembered about her, no touches, no doe-eyed looks, would weaken him today. By God, he *wanted* her to show up so he could tell her what he thought.

11:05. He lifted his head, and there was the 4x4 just turning into the Triple B, braking a nose away from his pickup.

He turned off the engine and shoved open his door. Jumping down, Daniel circled the bed of his pickup, strode to within a few feet of her door and waited, arms crossed.

Fiddling with something in there, she took her time before she climbed out to face him. Hell, for all he cared she'd called for backup. Uniformed, controlled, she said coolly, "What's the meaning of this?"

"You have a warrant?" he challenged.

"Your mother is not a suspect. She's helping me with my inquiries."

"She's done helping."

"She sent you out here?"

The way she looked at him with her gaze steady, not a flicker of remembrance or guilt or regret in her eyes, ate away at him. He didn't mean a damned thing to her. She was a cop, first and foremost; he'd apparently been a little fling, a boy-toy.

The answering ice in his voice was less slick; he wasn't as good at this. His voice could have scraped bare skin raw.

"This is my spread. I decide who's welcome."

Her eyes narrowed. "You've decided not to cooperate in a murder investigation. Is that what you're telling me?"

He widened his stance, not looking away. "We've co-operated. My mother has told you everything she knows. You can't figure out who that poor bastard was, so you're harassing her. I can't let you do that."

Her nose was turning pink from the cold and she stamped her feet to keep the blood circulating. "She's my best source…"

"She's told you everything she knows," he said inflexibly.

He'd gotten to her. The icy veneer of a law enforcement officer cracked. Temper spotted her cheeks with red. "Come on! You don't believe that any more than I do! Your mother is lying through her teeth. She has been from day one!"

A scene flickered before his eyes: his mother keening in despair or grief, all because unidentified bones had been found on their land. Then her denial that they meant anything to her, that anything special had happened fifteen years before.

With a shake of his head, he shut down the projector. He had to believe his mother, protect her. She'd have told him the truth if she knew anything.

The doubt he couldn't quite suppress lent whip to his voice. "You *want* to think she's lying to excuse your incompetence!"

Renee thrust out her chin, hurt buried quickly beneath fury. "Maybe you're lying, too. Is that it? So tell me. Why'd you call us in the first place if you're hiding something?"

"Because I didn't know my local police department conducted witch hunts!" he snapped.

"Oh, that's the oldest excuse in the book!" she scoffed. "How can you live with yourself, shielding a murderer?"

Like George Strait's song, her words cut too close to the bone. The pressure in his chest became unbearable, and Daniel shouted, "My father's dead and buried! Why the hell are you so determined to brand him a murderer?"

The shock in her eyes could have been a reflection of his own. What had he just done? Maybe she never had suspected his father. If not, he'd opened a new door for her.

Sick with turmoil, he braced himself as she stared at him.

When Renee finally spoke, it was more quietly. Her tone held an odd note. Compassion?

"Do you really believe your father killed someone?"

Daniel kept his mouth clamped shut. Couldn't do anything else. Nothing in his life had ever seemed to matter as much as her question. And he was such a god-damned coward, he wouldn't answer it, even to himself.

He was afraid to.

Now the compassion, or maybe pity, was open on her face. She even reached out to him. "Wouldn't you really rather know?" she asked softly.

He closed his eyes to shut her out. "Why?" he asked gruffly. "Why can't you let it go?"

After the briefest of pauses, she said in a curiously flat voice, "I'm atoning for my sins."

He understood and despaired, because his most gut-wrenching fear had met head-on her most desperate need. Attraction, sex, friendship—God help him, *love*—had no place here.

Into the darkness came her voice. "You think about it." The touch on his cheek had no more substance than a snowflake, but was a hell of a lot warmer. "Call me," she said, and he heard her swallow. "This time, I'll pick up the phone."

Still he said nothing. After a moment he heard the crunch of her footsteps on the red cinders, the slam of the car door, the roar of the Bronco's engine. He opened his eyes at last, now that she was blurred by the windshield, and watched her back out.

He could not sacrifice his father's honor or his mother's peace of mind to further Renee's quest. What if Matthew Barnard was branded a murderer? He knew how his mother felt about his father—her love and pride and constant, silent grief. What if everyone else condemned the man she'd spent her life loving?

Daniel let out a long ragged breath. Forget his mother. *He*'d spent his own life trying to live up to the man his father had been. If that had been a lie, it would be as if he'd spent years following the lines on a map, only to discover it was a fake, meant to deceive him; that all those years had been wasted.

He scrubbed his hands over his face. It felt…stiff. He didn't know how to move those muscles. How to smile or sneer. He was cold, down to his bones.

A groan rattled in his throat. He'd thought he could live with uncertainty, with the small quakes beneath the ground, so long as it didn't split open.

But now? Now, he wasn't so sure. Thanks to Renee Patton, he had a sickening feeling that he did need to know. One way or the other.

Whatever the cost.

RENEE MADE IT to the outskirts of town before a sob tore through her. Tears came in a hot, ugly cascade. She managed to pull over to the curb and yank on the emergency brake before she broke down completely.

She hadn't cried, not like this, in more years than she could remember. She didn't know how. The sobs just came, shaking her body, making it hard to breathe. Renee crossed her arms on the steering wheel, laid her forehead against them, and gave in to a force bigger than her.

New anguish and old piled atop each other. Looking in Daniel's eyes had been like seeing death. An end she'd brought on herself but would take back if she could. Why hadn't she known how much she loved him before it was too late?

Daniel! she cried. And then, *Meg, where are you? Why did you go?* And, *Mama, please stay!*

In as close to a fetal position as she could get, she cried for the emptiness in her life, for the people who'd left, and most of all for the man she'd driven away by her obsession with the past.

I love you. Come back! she begged, knowing she wouldn't get an answer, never had gotten one. Could she bear the loneliness?

With time the agony subsided, dulled, and the tears dried. Renee was left limp, face swollen, head aching, in emotional limbo. If she didn't open her eyes, she could imagine that she was floating in dark water. Utterly relaxed, almost peaceful, knowing only that she didn't want to be found.

But peace never lasted any more than tears did. A knock on the window jolted her back to life.

Renee lifted her head. Through puffy eyes she saw the fogged-up window and through it a face. A man with a red muffler wrapped around his neck was bent over peering in at her.

"Are you all right?" he called.

She stared stupidly. *Was* she all right? She thought that one over. Not really, she finally concluded. But, in a curious way, she was better than she'd been before the tears. All these years, she'd known a tight feeling in her chest, like a watch wound so much it quit working, the tension more than it—more than *she*—could bear.

The tightness was gone now. Instead, her chest hurt. But she also felt relaxed.

So… She rolled down her window a few inches. "Yeah. I'm okay. Thanks for asking."

The stranger's worried frown didn't go away. Her face must look like a drunkard's after a bar brawl.

"It was personal news," she explained reluctantly. "It just hit me. Nothing to do with the job. I hope you won't tell anyone that cops cry."

His frown eased; he almost smiled. "It'll be our secret. As long as you don't tell anyone that ambulance chasers do, too."

She watched him walk away, a tall man in a beautifully cut dark suit, the red muffler an incongruously human note. She imagined a wife winding it lovingly around his neck. Or maybe a daughter had knit it for him. She wondered what kind of law he practiced. If they met in court, she suspected he'd do no more than give her a small, acknowledging nod. *You're human. I'm human.*

The brief contact, the knowledge people did care, gave her the courage to look in the rearview mirror.

"Aagh!"

She had to go home before she went back to the station. A sink full of cold water, maybe a few ice cubes thrown in, might reduce the puffiness. A little makeup wouldn't hurt.

She turned up the defroster, released the emergency brake and checked for oncoming traffic. As she drove, the ache whispered at her—*Oh, Daniel!*—but she thought she could live with it, at least long enough to decide what was most important: settling with her past or working toward a future.

BACK AT THE STATION she found chaos. Members of the S.W.A.T. team had suited up in their dark uniforms and bulletproof vests and were running for their cars. The moment she stepped in the back door, she heard Jack bellowing down the hall.

"Goddamn it, you can't hesitate! What'd they teach you at the academy? To *negotiate?*" He spit out the last word as if it were loathsome.

Renee stopped in the door of his office, taking in the

sight of Jack Murray, hands flat on his desk as he leaned menacingly forward. The young patrolman stood with his shoulders square, but a frightened tic played piano up and down his jaw. Though she could see only his back, Renee knew the guy: twenty-two years old, smart, shy and determined to be a good cop. What had he done that was so terrible?

"What's happening?" she asked.

Jack turned his glower onto her. "Where the hell have *you* been?"

"Triple B."

He swore. "You're still wasting time on that?"

He'd known perfectly well she was, but under the circumstances she forgave him the irritation.

"What happened?" she repeated.

"Domestic disturbance that's turned into a hostage situation." He cast a look of dislike at the patrolman. "Thanks to Keller here."

"Sir, I felt…"

"I don't give a damn what you felt. What you should have *done* was slapped the bastard in handcuffs."

Patrolman Keller tried again. "I thought I could calm him. Defuse his anger."

Jack smacked his desk. Renee winced along with Keller.

"Defuse, hell!" Jack snapped. "That's a woman's tactic. Patton here might have to try that if she was too outsized. But you…you're a man, remember?"

Keller opened his mouth, thought better of it, and said only, "Yes, sir."

"Ah, jeez." Jack gestured disgustedly. "Go on. Out of here."

Renee waited until the door shut behind the patrolman. "You were a little hard on him," she said mildly. "And what's this 'be a man' crap?"

He went still. "Who says it's crap?"

She leaned back against the door frame. "I do."

Jack's eyebrows shot up. He wasn't used to her challenging him. She'd been inhibited by the crush she'd had on him. By the fact that he held her father's job.

To her surprise, he thought about getting angry but chose not to. "You know I respect your police work," he said gruffly. "I'm just trying to build some spine in this kid. Situation's ugly from the get-go. The husband's throwing furniture, tells Keller to butt out, backhands the wife when she grabs his arm. So Keller decides to take up counseling." Jack shook his head. "Instead of the bastard being behind bars where he ought to be, he's got a gun to his wife's head and he's threatening to kill their baby, too."

Renee digested the story. Bulling in and making the arrest sounded easier, she knew from experience, than it would have been in practice. Usually talking helped. Killed time, until the anger cooled, the booze wore off. Maybe until the wife grabbed the baby and slipped out. But that was her style. Jack's was to bounce the husband around a little, smack him against the wall and cuff him. He didn't cross the line to brutality, but he believed in coming down hard on criminals.

This time… Well, she just didn't know.

"Did you call in a negotiator?" she asked.

He was shrugging into his own bulletproof vest. "Cunningham," he said with a grimace. "He ought to be able to distract the guy while we go in the back."

"He's had good training." Renee kept her tone non-judgmental, even amiable. "Give him a chance to work."

"If I see a chance to do *my* job, I'm going to take it," Jack said curtly. "You're in charge here." He brushed past her and was gone.

Renee stayed where she was, in the silence of his office, musing on the oddities of life. Man's man that he was, Jack and the drunken husband were flip sides of a coin. Both thought a man should act, be physical; that talk was a waste of time. Difference was, Jack acted in defense of the vulnerable instead of abusing them.

You could have said the same about her father. Except that at home, he *had* abused his wife and daughters. He'd only hidden his ugly side with the collusion of Renee and her sisters, who dreamed up excuses for every bruise and even a few broken bones. Too bad *they* hadn't had the guts to act. Maybe then Jack Murray wouldn't have spent his career trying to win Chief Patton's approval. Maybe then he'd give the hostage negotiator a chance today, instead of emulating how his predecessor would have handled the same situation.

Would she and her sisters have been believed? she wondered.

She left Jack's office and went down the hall to her own. Heck, she thought with a new feeling of liberation, maybe she should find out. Once Jack was back from proving how a "man" did his job, she just might tell him everything Meg apparently hadn't mentioned about her father all those years back, when she and Jack had been high school sweethearts. He might be real interested to know why Meg had left town and never come back.

Renee sank down in her chair and swiveled it so that she could stare moodily out the small window across ten feet of space to the brick building next door.

You never know, she thought. Jack might turn out to be man enough to rethink his life.

Question was, could she do the same for her own?

CHAPTER ELEVEN

DANIEL URGED his gelding into an easy lope. Lotto had disappeared ahead, although every now and again Daniel heard a deep woof or caught a glimpse of a yellow tail wagging furiously behind a rock. He'd trailered Keegan, a fiery bay, up to Blue Lake, nestled at the feet of the Sisters. The trail, which circled the crystal clear mountain lake, was a favorite of his, a good place to think.

At this time of year the small parking lot at the trail-head was deserted except for his rig. Patches of snow replaced wildflowers in the open meadows, but the pungent scent of the pines was the same, and under a cold blue sky the lake water was as startling an azure as always and as clear. Fish darted, shadows among the rocks he could see several feet down. Above the meadow of thin grass reared a talus, boulders strewn like a kid's blocks after little sister had destroyed his tower.

The gelding moved at an easy jog and obliged with a lope whenever the trail was clear of snow and Daniel squeezed his legs. This beat endlessly circling an arena any day.

His thoughts here were more direct, less repetitive. In the arena, his mind tended to circle the same way, over and over a problem until he was dizzy and no further ahead than he'd been to start with.

Could he face knowing the truth? Did he want to find out for sure that his father had killed someone? Daniel asked himself. He shook his head in disbelief. Thinking about the man his dad had been, Daniel couldn't see it any more than he'd been able to a week ago. Damn it, Matt Barnard had been a good man!

Maybe he'd killed because he had to. It could be that, if he'd done the unthinkable, it was for a reason Daniel could understand. Daniel's mother had continued to respect and love her husband despite fearing— or *knowing*—what he'd done.

The time Daniel was unjustly blamed for starting a fight at school, his dad had listened carefully to him before he came to any conclusions. He hadn't jumped based on someone else's word or his own anger or fears. He'd given his son the benefit of the doubt.

Put it that way, and Daniel figured he owed his father the same.

He wasn't even sure why he'd been running scared. Smugness, maybe; he didn't want to believe his family was less than perfect. The Barnards had a solid reputation. They were old-timers in this community, respected. He admitted to himself that he even irrationally resented his grandfather vanishing the way he had, because afterward there had been whispers mixed with the pity and compassion. He liked having people look up to him. Was that such a sin?

The real question was, would he somehow be less of a man if it turned out his father had committed a terrible crime? Were the values Matt Barnard had taught his son any less worth living for, because the man who'd taught them had once violated his own beliefs?

Look at Renee, Daniel told himself. Her mother had

deserted her kids, her father had been an animal. Renee wasn't like either of her parents.

The saddle leather creaked as Keegan gathered his haunches and scrambled up a rocky incline made slick by snow. Automatically Daniel shifted his weight to help the horse.

He felt stupid, having the most basic of self-knowledge seem like a revelation straight from heaven.

Because he'd finally figured out that he didn't have to be who his father was. He'd rather remember him with respect and admiration, but if it turned out he couldn't, that didn't have to diminish his own self-worth.

What he didn't know was whether his mother felt so tied to her husband that she wouldn't agree. Or had she only been trying to protect Daniel and Mary from having to know their father had done something awful?

He guessed there was only one way to find out.

She didn't look real happy to see him when he went by after unloading the gelding and rubbing him down. Daniel had knocked and gone right on in.

The vacuum cleaner was running, but his mother turned it off when she saw him. "Daniel! What are you doing here in the middle of the afternoon?"

She didn't sound annoyed or even scared. *Wary* was closer to the mark.

"I wanted to talk to you," he said. "Can we sit down?"

"Well…" She drew out the word, every inch grudging. "I suppose so." His mother straightened some books in the case, then bent to unplug the vacuum cleaner and slowly rewound the cord. "Is something wrong?"

"I don't know." Daniel made himself sit, though he itched to pace. "I want you to tell me."

She perched on a chair as if ready to spring up at any

second. Her gaze met his with obvious reluctance. "What on earth are you talking about?" she asked, but without any real indignation or surprise.

"Mom…" He half rose, made himself settle back down. "What happened fifteen years ago? Did it have anything to do with Dad?"

He'd have sworn her cheeks blanched; he knew she swallowed.

But she marshaled herself enough to protest, "Are you going to start harping on this like that police officer, just because I was a fool and got upset at the idea of those bones out there? I thought you believed me."

"I *wanted* to believe you," he corrected her. "Probably for the same reasons you don't want to admit anything happened. But something did. I'm convinced of that. And I've decided I'd rather know what it was than spend the rest of my life wondering."

"Wondering," his mother said slowly, pure pain in her eyes, "is something you can put out of your head. Knowing…" Her mouth twisted. "Well, I'm not so sure once you *know* that you can ever forget. Maybe we're better off the way we are."

Not letting himself heed the lure she had thrown out, he leaned forward, seizing instead on the hope. "So you don't know for sure that Dad did anything."

The breath she released seemed to rack her body like a shudder contained for too long. "Daniel." With words and eyes both, she pleaded with him. "Are you sure you want to do this? Your father was a fine man. Can't we just leave it at that?"

"You're right. He was. And I have a hard time believing he would have done anything I couldn't understand or forgive him for."

"He was so angry…" Shivering again, she looked right through Daniel, seeing another man, another time.

Daniel moved swiftly, squatting in front of her and taking her hands. "Angry about what?"

"I…" She came back from the past and focused on him, though not without a struggle that squeezed his heart. "Are you going to tell that policewoman?"

"I think we should," he said carefully. "She's not going to let up until we do. She came again this morning. I headed her off, but I can't forever."

His mother's eyes searched his. "You like her, don't you?"

"Yes, but that's not why…" He stopped, wanting to be honest. A brief self-examination allowed him to continue more strongly. "Mom, you and I both know Dad would have been the first to cooperate with the police investigating a crime. How would he have felt about our covering up something that might be important? Anyway, who are we protecting? Dad's dead. Mostly Renee wants to know the name of the man who died. If we can help her find out, we should."

He was ashamed that it had taken him this long to come to the ethical conclusion. Whether Renee and he had any future, he didn't know. But he should have been helping out, not setting up roadblocks.

His mother bowed her head. She'd be fifty-four next month, but right now she could have been ten years older. Her hair had been turning silver fast lately, either because it was time or because she'd quit doing something to it, he wasn't sure. Worry had leached the pink from her skin; sleeplessness had left crepey bags under her eyes and a tremor to her hands.

Daniel felt a quiver of fear. What was all this doing

to her? Would it get better or worse once the whole story came out?

Ruefully he said, "That was easy for me to decide, wasn't it? I'm sorry, Mom."

She lifted her head, squared her shoulders and countered with surprising resolution, "No, you were right. Even back then, I *was* the one who didn't want anybody to know. I wouldn't even talk about it with your father. He wanted to go to the police."

That clutch of fear gripped harder and Daniel's voice became gritty. "Mom… What didn't you want anybody to know? *What happened?*"

"If you don't mind," she said with dignity, gently pulling her hands free from his, "I'd rather tell the story only once. Why don't you call your Officer Patton and see when she can come out here. Don't make her feel as though she has to rush." She rose to her feet. "It's not as if I'm going anywhere."

He stood, too. "Are you all right?"

"Why wouldn't I be?" She held herself straight, but resignation tugged at the lines of her face. She looked vaguely around. "Now, I really should finish the vacuuming. Especially with company coming."

"Yeah, okay." Daniel hesitated. "Mom, you could tell it all to me and I could pass the story on to Renee. That wouldn't be as hard on you."

"You know she wouldn't be satisfied with that. And—" her composure cracked "—I really don't think I can bear to do this more than once. Please." She turned blindly away. "Let me get back to…to…"

He touched her arm, but she shrank away, shutting him out. Her own son.

Daniel's fingers curled into a fist and he let his hand

drop to his side. He stood there for a moment, feeling helpless, and then turned and abruptly left. She wanted to be alone. He had to respect that.

Striding along the ranch road toward the barn—no, he'd go home to make this call—Daniel hoped like hell Renee was free to come right out. He felt sick with the need to know what terrible thing his father had done and his mother had kept secret for half her son's lifetime.

And now that he'd done this, forced his mother to admit to something she hadn't been sure she could bear to bring to the light of day, he wanted it over with.

What scared the hell out of him was wondering whether they'd ever be able to go back to the way they'd been.

"I HOPE YOU DIDN'T MISS dinner," Shirley fussed. "I told Daniel there wasn't any hurry. And I suppose he insisted you turn on your siren and rush right out here, didn't he? I could throw together some soup or sandwiches…"

"Thank you, Mrs. Barnard," the young policewoman said. "But I'm not hungry yet. I had a late lunch."

She was pretty, this woman Daniel looked at with such hunger and pain. Thin and strong, but also fragile. But not like china that shattered if you even knocked it against a crystal glass. More like those racehorses capable of such thundering speed and power, but with long skinny legs so vulnerable to snapping under the force of their own momentum.

Of course, pretty was only what made a man look in the first place. To break his heart, a woman needed to have more.

Well, it worked the other way around, too. Matt's broad shoulders and blue eyes had caught Shirley's fancy right away, the first time he came into the library where she worked. And then his smile, and the way he frowned, intent but also puzzled, over the books. And the way his big hands seemed clumsy turning the pages, but were so precise and strong and sure when he handled a horse. Or when he touched her, once she was ready. What got to her was his kindness and his laughter and his gentleness.

She was never quite sure why he'd fallen in love with her, or loved her so single-mindedly all those years. Some men had a wandering eye when their wives were pregnant, but not her Matt. Oh, no! He never saw any woman but her once they met, not even when… Though she knew she had to think about it, that the time had come, she shied away from the memory.

Maybe, she told herself hurriedly, it was knowing she loved him so completely, no part of her held in reserve, that Matt couldn't resist. How often did a person have a chance to be loved like that? Some people never did, she guessed.

"Mom." Daniel sat on the arm of the couch, beside her, his hand resting on her shoulder. "I think Renee is ready."

"Coffee," Shirley suggested, starting to rise. "I could at least get you a cup of coffee. It would only take a minute."

Daniel frowned at her and said sternly, "Mom."

But Renee Patton smiled as if she understood. "That sounds good. Can I help?"

"No, no. You just sit here and chat to Daniel." Shirley ignored his hand, which fell away from her once she stood, although she could tell he wanted to push her back down and make her talk as if she were a child wanting to slip away from explaining why she'd lied to her parents about something or other.

From the kitchen she heard their voices, her son's

sharp and aggressive, the woman's a hushed murmur. The softness of Renee Patton's answers comforted Shirley, helping her feel she was doing the right thing by telling what happened. Matt would agree, she believed; Daniel had talked most about the morality of it, but if her telling cleared the way for him to win the woman he loved, that was what Shirley cared about.

Maybe that was a flaw in her, putting her family first, above any kind of noble truth, but it was a woman's flaw, she thought, and maybe not such a bad thing, because a mother had to want to protect her children no matter what, didn't she?

"Matt," she whispered, "you do understand, don't you?"

No ghostly hand patted her shoulder, no lips brushed her cheek, but she felt no sense of protest, either. If Matt was there, watching over her, he was leaving this one to her.

Shirley carried the tray of coffee cups along with the sugar and creamer back to the living room. Daniel ignored it, but Renee smiled her thanks and stirred a dash of cream and half a teaspoon of sugar into her cup. Shirley did the same to hers, although she had no real interest in drinking the stuff right now; a cup of warm milk might have suited her more under the circumstances!

The policewoman sipped the coffee, set it down on the coaster and placed her notebook on her knee. With a pen poised above it, she said, "Whenever you're ready, Mrs. Barnard."

"Shirley."

"Shirley," she repeated, smiling again, as friendly as can be and with no sign that she was insincere.

"Well." Hand trembling, Shirley set down her cup

before the hot liquid spilled over her legs. "I think it's possible that T. J. Baxter is the one who died here." She hated even saying his name!

Something flickered in Renee Patton's eyes. "And why do you believe that?" she asked.

How hard it was to say! Shirley looked away from them both, the worry on her son's face, the keen interest and compassion on the policewoman's. She took a deep breath and said baldly, "You see, he raped me."

Daniel swore and came to his feet; Renee motioned him to sit down again.

"So it wasn't Mary he was interested in."

Goose bumps rose on Shirley's arms at the very thought. "Afterward, that was the one thing that really scared me," she confessed, "but when I talked to her I could tell nothing had happened. She was only twelve, you know, and really still a little girl. She couldn't have hidden such a thing. Oh, if he'd done that…!" Why, she would have killed him herself, and suffered no guilt at all! she thought fiercely.

"I remember the way he looked at you and smiled," Daniel said suddenly, his voice raw. "I didn't like it."

"He was always polite and proper when Matt was around," Shirley said. "If Matt had seen him smiling and…well, he would have fired him just like that! But I thought it was just Mr. Baxter's way with all women. You know? There's a kind of man who doesn't know how to talk to a woman without flirting. He…he made me uncomfortable, but didn't scare me. I never dreamed…" She shuddered to a stop.

Daniel briefly squeezed her hand. "How could you?"

"You never told your husband?" Renee Patton asked. With her eyes, Shirley begged for understanding from the other woman. "Matt couldn't believe that I hadn't complained about the flirting. But I knew my husband would fire him, and I thought he was harmless. He was good with horses, Matt kept saying he was one of the best, and I didn't like being responsible..." She tried again. "It didn't seem as though he should lose his job because he smiled a certain way at the boss's wife, or brushed against her." She felt Daniel stir restlessly and couldn't bring herself to look at him. "Afterward I knew I should have told, but..." Her fingernails bit painfully into her palms. "Oh, this is horrible to have to admit..."

"You were flattered." Renee spoke in a quiet voice that said she did understand. "Why is it horrible? He was a handsome man, you were in your thirties with teenage children. A woman likes to know she's attractive."

Shirley swallowed convulsively. Tears trickled down her cheeks. "It wasn't that he appealed to me. I never wanted any man but my Matthew. But it was nice to think I might still be pretty. Not that I encouraged him! I never did that!" She looked wildly from one to the other. They had to believe her; that was more important than anything!

"Of course you didn't, Mom." Daniel gripped her hand again, prying her fingernails away from her palm. "I know how you felt about Dad."

"Did Mr. Baxter ever make any advances?" Renee asked, tone gentle but clinical. "Did you ever have to say no?"

"He never...not once..." It was coming back to her now, the horror. She shut her eyes. "Not until that day."

"Will you tell us about it?"

She sighed. "Matt was away, trailering some horses he'd sold over to Springfield. I guess Mary and Daniel were at school. *He* came to the door. I opened it, never thinking a thing. He shoved the door open and just came in."

Shirley saw it, plain as day, her standing there with the door open a polite twelve inches, him putting a hand against it and pushing hard so she stumbled back. Once in, he shut the door behind him and locked it. At the solid *thunk* the dead bolt made, her blood had chilled.

"He said I was beautiful and he could tell my husband didn't appreciate me. He smiled and swaggered toward me—I'd backed up against the wall—and claimed I'd been smiling at him, too. He said, 'Today there's no jealous husband around.'" Terrified despite herself by something that was over and done with fifteen years ago, Shirley stared straight ahead and scarcely breathed.

She didn't see the policewoman move, but suddenly she was beside Shirley on the couch, holding her hand. "Would you like some water to drink?"

"No! No." Shirley squeezed Renee's hand. Her son's comfort she couldn't accept right now, but another woman—well, that was different, although she didn't know why. She couldn't even look at Daniel. "I'd rather finish."

"Okay." Renee's smile was infinitely gentle. "Did you tell him to leave?"

"Over and over. He kept saying he knew I didn't mean it. He…he grabbed me and kissed me." She was shaking all over now, just remembering. "Not like Matt kissed me. Nothing like that. He hurt me. I could taste blood and…and whiskey, I think. He wasn't staggering drunk, but he'd been drinking, though it was the middle of the day."

"Alcohol may have given him courage to do something he'd only thought about until then," Renee suggested.

Her head had hurt, grinding against the wall; he'd mashed her lips with his and bitten them and thrust his tongue in… "And then he ripped my blouse off, just tore all the buttons, and my bra. I fought, but he hit me." Reliving the shock and pain, Shirley fell silent for a moment. "I couldn't even scream, he didn't let me. He just…threw me onto the floor and came down on top of me and…" Hot tears scalded her cheeks. She could not, would not, describe the terrible things that happened then. "Afterward," she said starkly, "he stood above me, buttoning his jeans, and said, 'That was good, baby,' and then he left."

Daniel made a convulsive movement beside her, but she still couldn't face him. A son shouldn't have to hear this kind of thing about his mother!

"What did you do?" Renee asked. "Did you call anyone?"

Shirley shook her head. "I just lay there for…I don't know, hours, I think. I was so cold, and I hurt so much, and I was so ashamed."

Renee's eyes held hers. "You were in shock. And all rape victims feel the shame, even though what happened isn't their fault."

"But I should have made it plainer I didn't like him looking at me the way he did." The tears were weaker now. "Or told Matt. If only I'd told my husband…" She clasped a hand across her mouth to hold in a sob.

Renee touched her cheek. "You know none of that's true, don't you?"

"Yes," Shirley whispered. "It was *him*. But still, I can't help thinking…"

"If I give you the address and phone number, will you go to a rape counselor? Let her talk to you about these feelings?"

"Her? It would be a woman?"

"Yes. Anne McWhirter. She's a friend of mine, though closer to your age. She was raped herself, as a teenager. Will you talk to her?"

Shirley nodded numbly.

"Good. Now, do you feel up to telling us the rest? What happened when your husband found out?"

"Yes." She felt drained, and almost peaceful. The worst was over. Though the blood on Matt had frightened her, part of her had hoped Mr. Baxter was dead. It was what had happened right out there in the front hall that she had been determined to forget.

A box of tissues appeared in front of her, held by a man's hand. Daniel's. She took one and blew her nose. "Thank you."

He kissed the top of her head but said nothing, for which she was grateful.

She took a deep breath and continued. "It got dark and I crawled upstairs. I ran a bath and sat in it for a long time, until I was cold again. So I let the water out and ran more hot. I shampooed my hair and washed myself. I kept forgetting whether I already had and would do it again. The next day, I saw that I'd used half the bottle of shampoo. And my hair wasn't even dirty. But I *felt* dirty."

"Of course you did," Renee murmured.

"At last, because I was so cold, I put on long underwear beneath my nightgown and I got into bed. That's where Matt found me."

The front door had slammed and she'd started in

terror. Where could she hide? He'd find her in the closet, under the bed…

And then she'd heard her husband's roar of anguish and fear. "Shirley!"

"My clothes were still strewn around, you see. And there was blood. Just smears, but he was scared."

"Of course he was." She had such a soft voice, this woman Daniel loved.

"He…he made sure I was all right, and we talked about calling the police, but I just couldn't! To tell strange men, and know they'd think I'd brought it on, and then I wouldn't even have been able to go to the grocery store without people staring because they *knew.*" Still the idea was repugnant, although not so awful as it had seemed then. She took another tissue and mopped her eyes. "This won't be in the newspaper, will it?" she asked.

"No. I promise, this won't become public knowledge."

She nodded acknowledgment. "Matt left me then, and I knew where he was going. He didn't come back for a long time, it must have been an hour at least, and he had blood all over him. His hands and his shirt-front…" She swallowed convulsively. "It seemed like gallons of blood. And Matt said, 'He won't bother you ever again.' Just like that. Never another word." She lifted eyes freshly drenched with tears to Renee's. "I never asked what happened. I didn't want to know. I hated what I'd made Matt do. A peaceful man… He wanted me to talk about the rape, but I wouldn't. I said let's just forget it, and we tried. It was hard for both of us, hard on our marriage, because for a long time I didn't want—" She remembered her son's presence and stopped. "But Matt never said an angry word to me, never got impatient. And then one day we were laughing, and I felt different, and..." Through the tears she was blushing. "Well, time heals most anything. Sometimes I had nightmares, but mostly I did put it all out of my mind."

"Until you found out the bones of a murdered man had been discovered on your own land."

"And I thought it must be *him*."

"Was your husband given to using a knife? Did you find one missing from the kitchen later?"

"No." That part puzzled Shirley. "No, none of mine were missing, but there might have been a knife out in the barn. Matt did have a gun, for coyotes and such, though he didn't like using it. I suppose, if they were fighting, he might have snatched up a knife. Though you wouldn't think one would be lying around. A hoof pick, maybe, but not a knife."

"Daniel?" The policewoman looked past Shirley.

He sounded hoarse. "Dad carried a Swiss army knife. I, um, I use it now myself. But the blade wouldn't have been long enough. Otherwise, we have a machete out in the barn—we hack open bales of hay with it—and scissors and pliers and a leather awl, but a butcher knife..." Out of the corner of her eye, Shirley was aware of him shaking his head.

Renee's sigh was almost inaudible. "Well, our biggest trouble still is going to be identifying the bones. Without T. J. Baxter's real name or some fingerprints, I don't know how to locate dental records. Unless—" her voice altered "—you know of him going to a dentist while he was here?"

Shirley shook her head hopelessly.

"We don't provide dental insurance," Daniel said.

"If something of his was left around… Something he used…" She stopped, able to tell the anwer from their faces. "But you've already told me you wouldn't have kept it."

"So this didn't really help," Shirley said slowly.

"Of course it did! It gives me somewhere to focus. I'll have local dentists check records from back then, see if he did go to one of them. And if you think of anything…"

Shirley nodded dutifully.

Renee took her hand again. "Mrs. Barnard, I'm grateful you were able to do what you did today. I know this wasn't easy. I hope you'll end up being glad you told someone. If it turns out your husband did kill T. J. Baxter, most likely we'll just close the file. With everyone concerned dead except for you, there won't be an arrest or trial and I see no reason to go public at all. So I don't want you worrying about that."

Shirley nodded again.

"I have one of Anne McWhirter's cards in my glove compartment. I'll go get one right now. Will you call her, make an appointment?"

Shirley agreed that she would.

Daniel walked Renee out. Shirley wished he wouldn't come back in, not right now. Maybe tomorrow she'd be ready to talk to him, but now she wanted to be alone. She couldn't tell him that, though; he would be hurt. A good man like his father, Daniel would like to think he was needed.

Shirley sat where she was even when the living room was empty. She felt so tired, she could have gone straight to bed. Those tears had worn her out! But her exhaustion was the good kind, as if she'd worked hard all day and felt satisfied. She felt calmer than she had in weeks, more at peace. She had thought telling about such awful things would make them fresh again, tear open a wound healed but for an ache. But instead the telling had lessened the shame that had festered. She would call that counselor, Shirley decided. Talking about it all again wouldn't be so bad. Why, she might feel better each time!

Funny, she could think about T. J. Baxter now, as she hadn't been able to ever. She tested herself by seeing it all again. Opening the door, stumbling back as he advanced. That smile... Had she ever thought him handsome?

With pride, Shirley remembered how hard she had fought. She'd raked her fingers at his face, aiming for his eyes, like she'd read you should do. That's when he'd grabbed her around the neck...

No-o, that wasn't quite right, she thought, frowning. It had hurt—oh, it had hurt!—but not his hands... She sat up straighter. A necklace, that was it! She used to wear that locket Matt had given her on a silver chain around her neck. She never took it off, until that day. In a fury, T. J. Baxter had grabbed the locket itself and yanked it sideways until the chain cut into her flesh and made her violently gag. He might have strangled her, but the thin chain broke and he flung the locket aside.

She'd found it weeks later, Shirley remembered suddenly. She was moving the couch to vacuum when she saw it, lying there like a poisonous snake ready to strike. She'd almost called to Matt, but she didn't want to bring it all up again. She didn't want to see the wrenching pity on his face. So she took a tissue and picked it up and...

Shirley gave a gasp. She hadn't thrown it away! She'd stood there with it in her hand, and thought about how it held a picture of her and one of Matt, and how her husband had given it to her with love. But she couldn't bear to see it or think about it, not then, so she'd shoved locket and chain in a box she kept in her closet that held silly things like a history award she'd won in high school and a poem written to her by her first crush, an eighth grader who'd actually noticed her, only a seventh grader! And there that locket had lain, all these years, never touched.

Why, could that mean… Even before she thought it out, Shirley hurried out to the porch. The police car was just backing up.

"Daniel!" she called. "Stop her. I just thought of something."

He didn't question her, only stepped forward to put a hand on the hood of the Bronco. The policewoman rolled down her window, they exchanged a few words, and she turned the engine right off and got out.

They came toward Shirley together.

"I do have one thing he touched," she said in a rush. "If fingerprints last fifteen years, his should still be there."

CHAPTER TWELVE

RENEE DROVE BACK to town on autopilot, completely unaware of the passing scenery or any other cars on the road.

So now she knew, she thought, frowning straight ahead. Or did she?

Matthew Barnard had certainly had a motive for killing T. J. Baxter, no one would argue with that. If he'd been brought before a court at the time, any judge and jury would have been sympathetic to his reason for driving a knife into a man's chest, if not the cold-bloodedness of the act.

Gallons of blood, Shirley said. The heart could pump out a lot of blood. But so could the nose, if Matthew had punched the man who raped his wife before throwing him off the place. Her hysteria that night might well have exaggerated the quantity from a stained shirtfront to one soaked with a man's lifeblood.

Troubled, Renee asked herself whether she was making excuses. Did she not *want* Matthew Barnard to have killed anyone? Maybe because of Shirley? Daniel? Or maybe because the man himself sounded decent, a loving husband, a good father, a fine employer?

Well, no matter what, there wouldn't be a trial, she reminded herself. All she wanted was to *know,* once and for all. Part of her wished she could just accept Shirley's story and figure that now she did.

But she was bothered by a few things. A blade that nicked bone would have to be long, sharp and strong. Nothing dull would have made that perfect vee; not a hoof pick or leather-working awl, and not that small Swiss army knife Daniel had showed her. Was Matthew the kind of man who could have stabbed a man with one of his wife's kitchen knives, then washed it and put it back in the drawer to be used to carve the roast the next night? Renee couldn't see him that way.

Every single person she'd talked to described him as a real straight arrow, a good friend, a man with unshakable integrity.

Yes, but he'd tried, she remembered; according to Shirley, he'd wanted to call the police. His wife refused; was already hurt, terrified, wanting to pretend nothing had happened. So, did he let the man who'd raped his wife walk away? Or did he kill, though it went against his deepest beliefs, because his wife had begged for silence in which to heal?

Renee sighed heavily. She wondered what Daniel now thought, having heard his mother's story. Daniel wasn't his father, but he was a man with the same principles. What would he have done in the same spot? Could he have ruthlessly killed so that the woman he loved could retreat into pretense?

The woman he loved. The pain lancing her chest was sharp and breathtaking. Could she have been that woman? If she hadn't clung to some foolish, symbolic quest with no regard for who she hurt in her hunger to solve a mystery involving some long-dead stranger?

What was more important? she asked herself silently,

and knew the answer, couldn't believe she'd ever hesi-tated. But she also doubted Daniel Barnard had ever loved her. Wanted her, maybe; even pursued her, sure. But the kind of love Shirley described having with her husband? The kind with mutual trust, liking and hunger that could be satisfied by no one else… The kind that meant a man wouldn't look elsewhere, even when his wife was afraid of his sexual needs, that meant angry words were quickly forgotten, laughter and joy shared…

Renee wanted that. Oh, she wanted it fiercely! But there was nothing special about her, nothing that would make a man single her out, join into an undying bond with her. She could have felt like that about Daniel, she knew she could—maybe she already did—but she could also understand why he didn't reciprocate. Maybe his pursuit hadn't been totally aimed at deflecting her from his mother, but deep down inside that's surely what he was trying to do. And then maybe getting more involved than he'd intended, maybe sympathizing with her, wanting her sexually, even feeling hurt when she chose her duty—her quest—above him. But eternal love? She never had been any good at deceiving herself.

Today she didn't cry. She felt a great echoing emp-tiness inside, a desert where emotion shriveled up and died like a fresh green shoot denied water. Most of her life she'd known she had that arid space inside her, and thanked God for it. Otherwise, how could she ever have quit crying? Especially once Meg left, too?

It was dangerous, not letting any emotion swell to full growth or bloom, but she'd figured she was safe. With one sister left, she knew how to love, though she wasn't sure she ever wanted to let herself again.

Now it turned out Abby had secretly despised her

all this time, because she had refused to play games to get what she wanted from their father; because she had been clinging to her fears and regrets about him for so long. Abby understood, Renee had always believed, only now she knew Abby didn't, never had. Didn't feel the same way she did about the father who'd abused them.

But Daniel did understand. She didn't know how that could be, but despite everything that had happened since, she still believed he had. He'd understood even more than she had that her father's *things* had power over her.

Without his chair there to taunt her, she'd moved the television back into the living room last night. It sat on a kitchen chair, the lone piece of furniture in the room, but she had plopped down on the plywood floor with her back against the wall and watched one of her favorite programs. The best part was that she hadn't had any sense of defying him; he was just *gone*.

Now depression swamped her like sudden tiredness. Her father was gone, and she didn't care anymore. The hole wasn't one she could joyously fill. She wanted Daniel and Daniel alone to fill that lonely place in her life and her heart. She wanted to sell the damn house, to hell with her long-lost mother and sister. She loved Daniel's house, with the warm woods and the big kitchen and the windows looking out on forever. As Daniel's wife, she'd have a mother again, and Renee had a feeling Shirley would be wise, strong and loving in a way her own mother never had been.

Best of all would be waking up to Daniel in the morning, rubbing his sore muscles when he ached, being held when she hurt, talking about everything and nothing, having the right to kiss him whenever she felt like it.

She would have given anything to be the woman he would have and hold for the rest of his life.

But she guessed maybe it was time to do the best she could with her life. She would sell the house; it was time—past time. Make some new friends, find things she enjoyed doing. Follow Abby's example and live outside their father's shadow. Maybe, eventually, she would know herself to be stronger. She might even believe she *was* a woman a man might love the way Matt Barnard had loved his wife.

Voices had been crackling on her police radio, but the calls were all routine dispatches to fender benders, shoplifting, one household break-in. Now some officers were talking about the hostage situation.

Renee picked up her hand unit and called in. When Daniel had phoned earlier asking her to come out and talk to his mother, she'd left Lieutenant Pratt in charge in her stead. She wasn't needed right now, so she decided to stop by and check out the excitement.

The block of small shabby houses was cordoned off, but a patrolman moved one of the barricades to let her past. Squad cars were parked in a semicircle in front of a white house, the best-kept on the street. The lawn had been mowed late enough in the year to look decent over the winter, and browning foliage in window boxes suggested flowers had brightened the facade. Renee parked well back and approached the knot of officers huddled behind a dark-painted van belonging to the county S.W.A.T. team.

Jack saw her coming and jerked his head indicating she ought to hurry. Her heart sped up some and she ducked behind the van.

"Is he taking potshots at you?" she asked.

"Not yet, but you never know." Jack scowled. "What are you doing here?"

"Just curious."

Inside the van, she saw Lieutenant Cunningham, the county sheriff's department's balding middle-aged negotiator, wearing headphones and making notes on a pad in front of him. He was talking, and she saw by his expression of deep concern that he'd connected with the wife-abuser inside the small frame house.

When she peeked around the van, she saw sharpshooters positioned on rooftops and armed officers in place behind the squad cars. To all appearances, a terrorist was holed up in there.

"Any progress?" she asked.

"He's run out of beer."

"Maybe you should send him more. Let him drink until he passes out."

Jack gave her a look of dislike. "You sound like Cunningham."

Renee shrugged. "Seems pragmatic to me."

His voice hardened. "I tried to call you. They told me you'd gone back out to the Triple B. Damn it, Patton, I left you in charge and you're off chasing some kind of will-o'-the-wisp!"

She cocked a brow. "Why, Jack, how poetic."

He growled an obscenity.

"Pratt can hold down the fort as well as I can. Daniel Barnard called," Renee explained. "His mother was ready to talk."

His gaze sharpened. "And?"

"Fifteen years ago, a ranch hand raped her. She wouldn't let her husband call the police. All she knows is, Matthew went out for an hour or so and came back with blood on his shirt, saying she didn't have to worry about the man again."

"Matthew Barnard?" Jack sounded incredulous. "He's the last man I'd pick as a killer, even under those circumstances."

Renee spread her hands. "That seems to be the consensus. By the way, I promised his wife we'd keep this under our hats. She doesn't want everyone knowing what happened to her. I talked her into seeing a counselor."

Jack grunted. "After all these years? What's the point?"

"She's never dealt with it. This secret has been eating away at her all this time. She agreed."

Jack opened his mouth to say something, but was called away for a quick consultation that reminded her of a football huddle: men in a tight circle, heads together and backs out, voices barking. After a minute it broke up and he came back.

"So, are you satisfied?"

No. Her dissatisfaction was instant and emphatic. But she simply said, "We've gotten lucky. I hope. This T. J. Baxter who raped Shirley apparently grabbed a locket from around her neck. The chain broke, he tossed it away, and she found it under the couch a couple of weeks later. She didn't touch it, just wrapped it in a tissue and hid it in a shoebox in her closet. If we can lift a fingerprint…"

"You can find out who he really was."

"And whether he's still alive."

Jack's dark eyes narrowed. "You want him to be alive, don't you?"

Annoyed at herself—was she so transparent everyone could see right through her?—Renee said, "I want to know what happened. One way or the other."

"Boss!" someone called.

He turned away for another conclave, this time including Cunningham, who'd left his headphones on the table in the van. The excited buzz of voices made her guess something had happened. The negotiator and Jack were obviously arguing, although Renee couldn't hear what they were saying. Curious, she waited on the outskirts. Just as well she wasn't involved in the decision, because she knew darn well she'd be on Frank Cunningham's side. And she had a suspicion she and Jack were going to clash often enough now that she seemed to have become immune to his looks and to the knowledge that he usually made the same choices Chief Patton would have. Arguing with Jack had felt like disputing what was right and wrong with her father's ghost. She hadn't been able to question her father when he was alive, and until recently—until Daniel came into her life—she'd been just as afraid of her father dead.

Finally Jack barked some orders and the men broke off purposefully. The negotiator went back into the van and Jack came over to Renee.

"You're in luck. You may get to see the resolution." He didn't sound happy. From his gaze, pinned broodingly on the house across the street, she guessed it wasn't her presence that was bothering him.

"He's agreed to let his wife and child go?"

"He's coming out."

The policemen crouched behind the squad cars were holstering their guns and climbing into the cars, moving them farther down the street. Only the sharpshooters on the rooftops stayed put. Maybe the husband didn't know they were there. Watching the activity, Renee said, "You don't believe he means it?"

"He walks out now, the judge'll give him a slap on the wrist and suggest counseling," Jack said with disgust. "Scum like that, who'd hold a gun to his wife's head! And sure as shooting she'll welcome him back with open arms as soon as he's paroled. Hell, she'll probably bail him out!"

She shared some of his frustration, but not his obvious desire to storm the house, shoot the husband and heroically rescue woman and child. Ironic, when she thought about it, considering she'd been, in some sense, that child.

Words came out, words she'd never thought of saying to him.

"My father hit my mother. And Meg." She swallowed. "And me."

"What?" Jack swung toward her so violently, she flinched.

"You heard me." She held her chin high, jerked her head toward the scene across the street. "Your idol was as bad as that guy in there."

"I don't believe you." But he did, his eyes gave him away.

"Why do you think Meg ran away?"

"I know why—" He stopped so suddenly his teeth snapped together. After a rigid moment, Jack wiped a hand across his face and swore. "Why didn't she say anything? Goddamn it, why didn't *you?*"

"We were afraid of him," Renee said simply.

"Why didn't she tell me?" he said again, but not as if he were really asking Renee. Then he focused on her again, eyes and voice razor-sharp. "Did he hurt her? Really hurt her?"

"He didn't torture us or hold guns to our heads.

Just…lashed out when he was angry. He broke Meg's jaw once. Do you remember that? She told everyone she'd fallen down the stairs." Renee gave a brief, humorless laugh. "That's the oldest one in the book, isn't it? And you know, his hitting us wasn't the worst part. If sometimes he'd been happy with us… Proud of us… But he never was. None of us could ever measure up. You came closer than we did, maybe because you're a man. I don't think he liked women very much."

Jack groaned. "Why the hell are you telling me this right now?"

"Because of him." Like everyone else, she was riveted to the sight of the front door opening. "I'm sorry. This isn't a good time."

Jack swore again, but now he was focused on the man emerging onto the tiny porch. He bent over and set down a handgun, then straightened, arms above his head. Slowly, he started down the path. Except for him, nobody moved for what seemed the longest time. Maybe they were all paralyzed by his ordinariness; the monster was them. He was young, sandy-haired, weedy, freckled. Nice, Renee would have guessed, if she'd met him casually. Only, he stumbled, paused, swayed, and she remembered that he was drunk.

Cops closed in then, tackling him. He fell heavily and his face scraped the concrete of the narrow walk. He was yelling and cursing as the half dozen police officers cuffed him and hauled him back to his feet. Cheek and jaw raw and bloody now, he kept trying to turn back to the house.

"Lisa!" he bellowed, and his wife appeared in the doorway. God help them all, she was pregnant again, pregnant and holding a child who couldn't be over a year old. She was sobbing and the baby was screaming.

"I'm sorry!" he yelled. "I'm sorry. I wouldn't have hurt you. Lisa. I'm sorry." He was shoved into a police car, the door slammed, shutting him off.

Renee felt sick. "Have fun," she said tersely, and walked away.

BACK AT THE STATION, Renee left the locket, still wrapped in the tissue and enclosed in an evidence bag, with a fingerprint tech. Then she called Anne McWhirter.

The older woman had been a school counselor back when Renee's mother had walked out on her family. She'd helped all three Patton girls get through some tough weeks, and she'd continued checking on Renee every now and again since.

"Said goodbye to your father yet?" were the first words out of her mouth once Renee had identified herself.

Renee made a face. "Do you know, I think I have. Was I that obvious?"

"I worry about you," Anne said. "All of you."

"I've worked through some things lately." She took a breath. "I'm redecorating the house, and as soon as I've done the basics I'm putting it up for sale."

"Good for you," her friend said warmly. "Tell me what you're doing."

They chatted about carpet and stripping versus painting woodwork and where to buy furniture, finally agreeing that Anne would join Renee and Abby on Saturday to shop. Then Renee told her why she'd called.

"Will you let me know if Shirley Barnard *doesn't* make an appointment?" she asked. "I'd really like her to see you."

"You know I have to keep anything she says confidential."

Renee assured her she wasn't interested in what Shirley told the counselor. "But I really think she needs to see someone. I'm going to bug her until she does."

"Drumming up business for me?"

Renee smiled. "You bet. Heck, I'm trying to make up for never having stretched out on your couch myself."

"I don't do couches." Anne sounded amused. "Too Freudian for me. Besides, the last thing a rape victim or abused woman needs is to take a submissive posture or talk to some silent authority figure lurking off to the side."

"Anne…I've never thanked you."

"Don't thank me," she said crisply. "I knew your mother, you know. We were in the Garden Club together." She fell silent for a moment. "I wondered about your mother. She had bruises. I wish I'd done something. Offered to listen, if nothing else. She claimed she had such fragile skin, anything made her bruise, and I bought it, just like everyone else."

"She wouldn't have told you."

"Probably not. But her leaving the way she did, not even having the strength to take her own daughters with her… She's one of the reasons I went back to school for my master's degree and got into this kind of counseling. I thought you might like to know that."

Blinking back a sting of tears, Renee said, "It does make it seem…less pointless."

"Well." Anne's voice became brisker again. "I'll see you Saturday. Ten o'clock. Why don't we meet at McGillity's for coffee and a scone before we start?"

Renee spent the next hour catching up on paperwork. Police reports were boring to write and probably more boring to read, but a record was necessary for the long haul, and even the short. Details left an arresting officer's mind too quickly. One D.U.I. stop blended into another mighty easily, and it helped to go over notes and the official report before appearing in court. A glance at her calendar reminded her she had a court session herself tomorrow.

She heard the commotion in the hall when the troops arrived back from the day's excitement, but her office door stayed closed until Jack rapped and stuck his head in without waiting for her response.

"The wife swears she won't bail him out. Says 'sorry' isn't good enough. Do you believe that?"

"Nope."

"Me neither." He came the rest of the way in, but stayed beside the door, looking awkward. "Would you have dinner with me tonight?"

The emptiness she'd felt this morning washed over her again. "Jack, it doesn't matter. Maybe I shouldn't have told you. I don't know. But I thought maybe you should hear the truth. Anyway, there's nothing more to say."

"But I just can't believe..." He stopped, breathing raggedly. "I don't doubt you, Renee, I didn't mean that. But this is a big readjustment for me. I guess I'd like to know more. If you can bring yourself to tell me."

Who was he mourning? she wondered. His lost teenage love, or the father figure who had led him into police work?

Could she stand to cap off the day by talking about her father? Well, why not? Otherwise she'd just go home to that big lonesome house, eat a microwave dinner and watch TV. Here a man who used to make her heart beat faster was asking her out, and she was thinking of saying no?

"Fine," she said. "I can't tell you what Meg thought or felt when she left—we didn't have a chance to talk—but I can tell you anything else you want to know."

"Deal," he said. "By the way, Davies tells me he was able to lift a fingerprint from that locket. Now we just have to wait for it to be run through A.F.I.S."

Her moment of intense satisfaction was supplanted by wry awareness of that "we." *She'd* been chasing a will-o'-the-wisp, just wasting valuable man-hours. Now *we* were getting somewhere.

But she didn't care enough about who got credit for what to brood about it. Instead, once Jack was gone, closing the door behind him, Renee thought, *T. J. Baxter, now I'm going to find out who you really were.*

Or maybe not past tense. Maybe she'd find out who he now *was,* assuming those bones packaged up back in the evidence room didn't belong to him.

Knowing the FBI's backlog meant that the fingerprint ID wouldn't come back for weeks if not months had never been more frustrating.

THE PATTON HOUSE sat dark, the driveway empty.

Feeling like a damned fool, Daniel circled the block and came back to Renee's house, parking at the curb several doors down. He'd just wait for her, he figured. Maybe she was having dinner with her sister, or a friend. If it was a man…well, she wouldn't be looking for his pickup. With luck, she wouldn't spot him. He'd go home and cry into his beer.

A half hour passed. This felt all too familiar, except this time he wasn't gunning for a confrontation. He was… well, he didn't quite know what he was going to say, he knew only that he wanted to see her. Kiss her, if she'd let him. Explain his fears, and hope she understood.

He had a pretty good idea he was here with his mother's blessing, assuming he'd needed it. She'd as good as admitted that she'd told her story because she could tell her silence was getting in the way of his romance.

"It doesn't bother you that I'm seeing her?" he'd asked incredulously. "Don't you resent the way she's been riding you?"

His mother blinked in surprise. "Why would I resent her? She's just doing her job. She seems like a nice young woman. And so brave! I admire a woman who can take on a career that used to be for men only. In my day, we wouldn't have dared. Why, I just assumed I'd quit work altogether when I married your father. *He* was my work. But sometimes I'm sorry I didn't continue part-time. I enjoyed working at the library, you know."

"It's not too late," Daniel had pointed out.

"Don't be silly!" she declared, but her eyes had a thoughtful gleam.

He felt selfish not to have guessed she might be bored, having nothing to do these days but keep up a house for herself. Oh, she had friends and volunteer activities—years ago, she'd been on the library board of trustees, but they needed new blood, to use her words, and now all she did was help at the annual book sale.

Daniel glanced at his dashboard clock. 8:15. In his rearview mirror he saw approaching headlights. Two cars were coming. He saw the roof lights and E.S.P.D. emblazoned on the door as she passed and pulled into her driveway. Another police Bronco was right behind her. It slowed, she waved, and then it sped up, red taillights blinking at the stop sign down the block. Daniel watched her get out, check that the car door was locked, and let herself into the house. The porch light came on, then one in the living room.

Frowning, Daniel didn't move for a minute. He'd caught barely a glimpse under the streetlight, but he thought that had been Jack Murray following Renee home. Had they dined together? Was she turning her sights elsewhere? Or had something happened at work that had shaken her up, so Murray wanted to make sure she got home safe?

It was the last thought that decided Daniel. He started his pickup, drove the half a block and parked in Renee's driveway, right behind her 4x4.

The snow from a few days ago had melted, but the barometer was dropping again. It was damned cold. If snow fell tonight, the flakes would be tiny and dry, the powder that made skiing here in eastern Oregon world renowned.

He rang the doorbell, hearing the deep bong echoing far inside the house. Footsteps approached, hollow sounding now that there was no carpet to muffle noise. Daniel waited while she peered through the vee of glass high on the door, then unlocked.

"Daniel." Still in uniform, she looked tired and less than thrilled. "What are you doing here?"

He shifted uncomfortably. "Are you okay?"

"Oh, yeah. I'm just peachy." She didn't open the door any wider. "How about your mother? I called, but she didn't answer."

"Some friends were going to Portland and offered her a ride. She's going to stay with Mary. Mom wants to tell her what she told us."

"Good for her." Renee's expression warmed a fraction. "I imagine it'll get easier every time."

"Yeah." His breath puffed out in an icy cloud. "Uh, I was hoping we could talk."

"Talk," she echoed, as if perplexed by the idea.

"Renee, please. Can I come in? It's cold out here."

Still she hesitated discernibly, then at last, with every sign of reluctance, stepped back. He crossed the threshold and watched as she locked the door. Now that he was in, he heard tinny voices from the television.

"Did I interrupt a show?"

She shrugged and went ahead of him into the still-bare living room, where the television sat in lone splendor on a wood kitchen chair. Renee switched it off. "That's okay. It wasn't anything I cared about."

He turned his head. "You were sitting on the floor?"

"I'm shopping for furniture Saturday. New carpet is being laid Friday."

"What color?" Like he gave a damn.

"Blue. I'm doing the room in blue and white with some dashes of yellow or maybe rose, I haven't decided."

Sell the house, he thought. *Move in with me.*

They stood there, both stiff, uneasy. God, he wanted to kiss her, peel that damned uniform off, loosen her silky pale hair, find the woman beneath the cop.

He didn't dare touch her.

"I should have helped you," he said. "I shouldn't have tried to stop you."

Her eyes seemed to darken. "And I should have let it go, like you asked."

A groan tore his throat. "I've missed you."

"I've missed you, too."

They both took a step forward, meeting in the middle of that bare living room. Renee said something else, but softly, and through the roaring in his ears he couldn't hear it, but he wanted to imagine that it was, "I love you."

And then he was kissing her, and her arms were around his neck, and she was kissing him back.

CHAPTER THIRTEEN

MAKING LOVE was the easy part.

The fact that their hands were shaking didn't slow them from getting rid of clothes: a shirt draped over the banister, a bra tangled among the shoes kicked off down the hall, her gun and holster tossed on the bureau and his jeans on her bedroom floor.

The kisses, the sighs, the touches… His weight on her and her legs parting for him… The entry, long and deep and slow… Oh, that was easy. Natural and inevitable, like the sun rising in the morning or winter relinquishing its grip when bulbs burst through the soil come spring.

Afterward was the hard part.

Renee lay with her head on Daniel's shoulder and felt his chest rise and fall, the heat of his skin beneath her splayed hand, heard the heavy slow beat of his heart. He wasn't asleep, any more than she was. He just had no more idea what to say than she did, Renee guessed.

What a fool she'd been to admit she loved him! She was so afraid her impulsive words were what was stifling conversation now. She wasn't about to repeat them unless he reciprocated, and since he most likely didn't feel the same, he must be in a quandary about what to say.

What could he say? *I like you, and that was great sex,*

but I'm not sure about love. Maybe someday... They'd both know that was a lie. Or, worse yet, *Sure, I love you, too,* in a false hearty tone.

"I don't know what I was afraid of," he said abruptly, his mouth against her hair.

She went completely still. Even her heart seemed to stop beating. When he didn't continue on his own, she closed her eyes. "What do you mean?"

"You made me see how much I identified with my father. Too much, apparently." Daniel fell silent again, but only for a minute. Voice strained, he went on. "It was as if...oh, hell, as if *I* was morally responsible for anything he'd done. No. Worse than that. As if I was a continuation of him. If he'd done it, I'd done it. I didn't want to believe I could commit murder, for any reason." He shifted. "Does that make sense? Am I crazy?"

Was *he* crazy? A giggle hiccuped from her. No! She had to take him seriously! Reassure him, not laugh! But she couldn't help it. Another giggle tripped over the first, and then another.

He jackknifed to a sitting position, rolling her onto her back. "What the hell?"

"Are...*you*...crazy?" Renee managed to squeak out between side-splitting laughter. "Just...go down...and look...at my living room!"

He glowered at her for another moment. Finally a crease dented one cheek and his mouth compressed. "You've got a point," he conceded, a grin growing.

"Maybe...we're both..."

Suddenly he was laughing as hard as she was. When she didn't finish her sentence, he did. "Loco!"

"Nutty as fruitcakes." She wiped away tears and kept laughing, though her stomach muscles hurt.

"Ready for the loony bin." He swore. "I've got to pee."

"Race ya." Renee gave him a push and leaped from the bed, reaching the bathroom first.

She'd barely locked the door when Daniel whacked it with his hands.

"There's another one down the hall," she called.

"Now you tell me." She heard him retreat.

A moment later she flushed the toilet and stood in front of the mirror. Oh, Lord! Her hair was a tangled mess, her face so pale it was pasty. Maybe she should start wearing makeup to work. Just because a woman was a cop didn't mean she had to try to look like a man.

No wonder Jack Murray had never been interested! Experimentally, Renee yanked her hair back to mimic her daytime appearance. She made a horrible face at herself in the mirror. Had she been trying hard to make sure no man *ever* looked twice? Why the heck had Daniel?

An insidious voice whispered, *You know the answer. Because he was trying to influence you.*

Yes, but if that was true, why had he come tonight? *To justify his behavior? To have some good sex?*

Renee had sense enough to know she was listening to fears planted by her father. No, Daniel probably didn't love her, but he might like her. Maybe something *would* come of it. She could be optimistic, couldn't she?

She ran a brush through her hair and splashed cold water on her face, toweling it dry until her cheeks glowed pink. Then she opened the bathroom door.

Darn his hide, Daniel was already sprawled on the bed again, unashamedly naked, hands clasped behind his head. The moment she appeared, he let his gaze rove over her with purely masculine appreciation. Blushing fiercely, she dashed for the bed.

"Hey, slow down!" He rolled toward her nonetheless. "I was enjoying the overall effect. You could go back and do it again."

"Not on your life." She wriggled closer. "This is only the second time I've taken off my clothes for a man, and I'm not quite ready to parade around, posing."

"Next time." His hand roved from her waist to her hip. "This is good, too."

"Mmm-hmm." She kissed the hollow at the base of his throat. She still felt terribly self-conscious, lying here buck naked in front of a man, but it was fun, too. Exhilarating. A little shyly, she asked, "Are you still upset by the idea that your dad might have killed Baxter?"

Daniel's hand stilled. "I'm not excited about it, but... Hell, I can understand why he might have. Maybe I shouldn't be saying this to a cop, but as far as I'm concerned, Baxter deserved to die. That son of a—" He stopped, his voice a deep growl of rage. "If someone raped you..."

Her thrill of pleasure took Renee aback. She was a law enforcement officer, and she still had some kind of primitive reaction to the idea that a man would be willing to kill to protect her?

But she couldn't deny it. She *wanted* Daniel to feel that way about her.

Although there was no way on earth she could tell him that.

"I'm flattered," she said lightly. "I guess."

His throat worked. "You think I'm kidding?"

Their eyes met. "No," she whispered. "I think, just like your father, you would find it unacceptable for any woman to be treated like that. Especially one you...care about."

"Ah. So my father was just being a gentleman."

"I didn't say that."

Daniel studied her for a long time. Creases deepened between his brows. "My father would have gone to the police if the woman who'd been raped had been anyone but my mother. No matter how desperately the woman begged him to stay quiet. But Mom… He couldn't stand to see her hurt. He'd have given her anything…. His soul." He made a sound. "If he deliberately stabbed a man to death, that's exactly what he did give her."

"Now you sound as though you…oh, blame your mother. Or…or think the decision he made was terribly wrong."

Still his eyes searched her face with odd intensity. "I'd never have blamed my mother. A few weeks ago, I would have thought he should have stood by his principles and called the police no matter what. Now…" His mouth twisted. "Now I understand."

That same, atavistic thrill shot through her. Could he possibly mean what he seemed to be implying? Or was he just flattering her?

Or, she thought ruefully, was he not talking about her at all? Maybe he'd just meant that in these weeks he'd come to understand Shirley and Matt Barnard better as people rather than as parents. Learned to see them as a man and a woman who loved each other, who were basically good folks but who still weren't perfect.

"Your father might not have done this."

"Only it all fits."

"Except for the knife," she reminded him. "And for the fact that I'm still having trouble picturing your father driving a blade into a man's chest so hard it sliced bone. It's a crime of anger, but also one a man would need to steel himself to do. Would he have taken a knife to find Baxter? Why not a gun if he were going to bring a weapon? It would be a heck of a lot easier, physically and emotionally, to kill someone by pulling a trigger. Somehow I see your father storming straight out of the house to find Baxter, not thinking about what he'd do once he found him. Do you know what I mean?"

Daniel grunted. "Yeah, and I agree. Except he might have had murder on his mind."

"And so he detoured to the kitchen and took your mother's knife?" Renee said skeptically.

Daniel lay back and stared at the ceiling. "He might have had a bowie knife. It was a long time ago. Just because I don't remember him owning something like that doesn't mean he didn't."

"That's true." She hesitated. "Well, it looks like we'll be able to find out whether T. J. Baxter died on your place. I didn't get a chance to tell you, but we were successful in lifting a couple of clear fingerprints from your mother's locket. Now we're running them. The bad news is, it can take anywhere from a week, given a miracle, to three months to get the ID back. We've got a long wait ahead of us."

Daniel was silent for a moment. "Well," he said at last, "you were right. I'd rather know either way. I think Mom feels the same, now that it's come down to it."

"Has she called the counselor?"

"She said she did. She hoped I didn't mind, but she thought maybe she needed to talk about what happened some more. Why the hell would I mind?" He sounded genuinely baffled.

"She's been a wife and a mother a long time." Renee tried to be tactful. "I get the feeling she's used to deferring to first your dad and now you. Maybe not on little things, but on the big ones."

Shock showed on Daniel's face when he rolled his head to look at her again. "Defer? Maybe to Dad, but me? On the business side, sure, but…"

"What other side is there?" she asked softly. "The dinner menu? You don't even eat with her most of the time."

His brows shot together again, though he didn't sound angry. More…perturbed. "You think I neglect her?"

"No, I think she needs to get out more than she does. It doesn't sound as if horses are her thing. What is?"

She could see him groping for an answer and being bothered because he didn't have one. "It was always her family. The house." His shoulders moved, apologetically. "She gardens some. And reads. I guess books are something she loves. I know she worked in the library back before she was married. She's still active in the Friends."

"Well, what she does with her life isn't your choice, anyway. It's hers. I'm just guessing that, in her eyes, you've taken over your dad's role as authority figure. Unless she has her own income…"

She hadn't settled his perturbation any. "From the ranch," he admitted. "She owns half of it."

"So you write her a check."

"I deposit money every month in the same account she shared with Dad."

"Which might make her feel she has to clear her spending with you."

He swore.

Renee laid a hand on his arm and felt the muscles bunch. "I'm not saying there's anything wrong with your arrangement. What else can you do? Really. I didn't mean to upset you."

"I should have seen it." His hand caught her arm. "Why did you? And don't tell me it's a woman thing."

"I lived here on my father's sufferance."

"You didn't pay your way?"

"Sure I did." She made a face. "And then felt as if I had to explain where every other cent went."

"You know that staying here even when you felt that way is illogical as hell."

"Right." She smiled. "I'm crazy, remember?"

"Yeah." Head braced in his hands, Daniel studied her. His mouth had a sensuous curve, and his eyes were so blue, she couldn't look away. "Are you crazy about me?" he asked, low and rough.

Was he asking her to repeat her declaration? Or… Her breath caught. Was it possible he hadn't heard her? That he didn't *know* how she felt?

Did he have some of the same doubts and fears she had? But that would mean… No. He hadn't said he loved her, and why would he hesitate if he did?

Pure cowardice had her parrying, "If I weren't crazy about you, would I be willing to discuss your mother at a time like this?"

Something flickered in his eyes; he knew she was evading the question. But he chose not to press her. "Yeah, that's an uneasy mix, isn't it?" He grinned ruefully. "I've got a beautiful woman naked in bed with me, and I'm talking about my mother. Okay, now you've got me worried about myself."

"Well…" Astonished at her daring, Renee traced his lips with one fingertip. Hoping her tone was pro-vocative and not just silly, she suggested, "You could prove your masculine prowess and wipe this little lapse out of my mind."

His eyes darkened. "Yeah. I could do that." This smile was just plain wicked. "Maybe you could help me along. You wouldn't want my poor ego to suffer, now, would you?"

She might not be experienced, but even she could tell that Daniel wasn't going to have trouble proving anything to her. Still she arched her hips and squirmed a little, nibbled a few kisses on his neck, and trailed her fingernails down his chest.

"How am I doing?" she murmured.

A muscle along his jaw spasmed as her hand trailed lower. He cleared his throat. "Let me put it this way. You're on the right track."

"Oh, good." Giving as well as receiving could be an exhilarating experience, Renee decided. Even... erotic.

But, running her hand over his chest and belly was one thing; actually wrapping it around his erect penis was another. She took a breath and clumsily gripped him.

Daniel winced, and then groaned, "Don't stop," when she pulled away.

"I don't know what I'm doing."

"Then practice." His fingers tangled in her hair. "I'm all yours."

His choice of words clutched at her heart, half with pleasure, half with pain because he tossed them off so lightly. How many women had he said that to without really meaning it?

But she touched him again, at first gingerly, then with more confidence when she discovered how his muscles shivered and jumped because she stroked a certain way, or squeezed him, or teased with a feather-light touch. She sneaked a look at his face, to see that his head was tilted back so that cords stood out in his neck. His cheekbones and jaw stood out in sharp relief; his eyes were closed and his lips drawn back in a grimace of sheer pleasure. Another groan rumbled in his throat.

Suddenly his hands shot out and gripped her hips, lifting her on top of him. "You lied."

"What?"

"You know what you're doing just fine," he said hoarsely. "Too well."

"Oh." She wriggled a little. "Then…then why don't I know what to do now?"

"Here's an easy lesson." He urged her hips up, positioned himself, then pressed her down.

She sank onto him, her breath whistling out of her. "Daniel," she whispered. "Yes. Oh, Daniel."

His grin was fierce. "Now it's up to you, love."

Love. Delight—or was it desire?—spasmed in her belly. She gripped him with her knees and rose, higher, higher, until she was about to lose him, and then she sank onto him until he filled her.

She did it again and again, her pace quickening, his hips thrusting upward to speed her, to bury himself more deeply inside her. She rode him like a wild woman, and loved the exultation on his face. Cries spilled from her lips, guttural sounds from his. Something inside her tightened past the point of breaking; she thought she might die if release didn't come. But she almost dreaded it, too, because nothing ever in her life had been this glorious.

When it came suddenly, the tension snapping and flooding her with exquisite rivers of heat and pleasure, she thought for a moment that she *had* died. How could something feel so good you weren't sure you could survive it?

I love you, trembled on her lips, but she held the words back. Maybe this was just sex. How would she know, when Daniel was the first man she'd ever made love with? What if she said, *I love you,* and he broke it to her that love wasn't part of it?

Now *that,* Renee didn't think she could survive.

RENEE LAY on Daniel, utterly boneless, her head on his shoulder and her hair tickling his chin. He wrapped his arms securely around her and thought about how incredible it felt, having her breasts flattened on his chest, her toes curled against his calves, one long silky-smooth leg draped between his. He'd be happy if she never moved.

He'd no sooner had the thought than she stirred. "That was fun," she said breathlessly.

Fun? Daniel lifted his head in outrage, although he couldn't see her face. Didn't she know how rare what they'd just experienced was? He'd had other women, five or six maybe, and never felt anything close to this. Renee and he together had made the earth move, set off fireworks…hell, they'd pulled off every cliché he could think of.

And she thought it was *fun?*

Of course, she *hadn't* had five or six other men. Or even one. Maybe she did think this was everyday sex.

Or maybe she hadn't felt what he had. How did he know they'd been in sync?

"Yeah." He gritted his teeth. "It was fun."

"You didn't think so?" She lifted her head then,

giving him a wide-eyed look, her eyes lucid gray-green, bare of makeup and all the prettier because of it.

"I thought so," he growled.

Her smooth brow crinkled. "Then why are you grumpy?"

Grumpy? Goddamn it!

Get a grip! Daniel thought sharply. Don't blow it. He was thinking love and commitment and a walk down the aisle, but she was innocent, inexperienced. For her, he was a way of dipping her toe into the water, so to speak. She was a few years younger, too. Maybe not ready to settle down.

Not in love.

The thought was profoundly depressing, but it also steadied him. If he didn't scare her away, she might come around to his way of thinking. They'd only known each other a couple of weeks, kissed four or five times. Made love a few times. *Give her time,* he thought.

"I just don't think 'fun' covers it," he said. "That's a ride on a roller coaster. This was more like rocketing to the moon."

Her forehead smoothed. "It was, wasn't it?"

"Wanna do it again?"

Her mouth formed a surprised O. "Can we?"

"Uh…not yet," he admitted. Too bad. "Maybe later. If I stay all night." He paused, waiting for an objection, for a reason why he really should leave.

All she did was lay her head back down and snuggle into the curve of his neck. "If you don't mind the bed being so narrow."

He relaxed. "It means you can't get away from me. There are worse fates."

"But your feet must be hanging over."

Yeah. They were. He felt a cool draft on them. Small price to pay. "How about if we talk?" he suggested, partly to divert her.

With her forefinger, she drew a mysterious pattern on his chest. "What do you want to talk about?"

"You."

She poked him. "Unfair."

"Okay. Tit for tat."

"Um." She apparently thought it over. "I can go for that. Is there something special you want to know?"

"What's your favorite movie?"

"Oh, that's easy. Well, no, it isn't. I love *Dave* and *Sense and Sensibility* and *Bull Durham* and *Lethal Weapon* and *Titanic*…"

"Whoa!" He held up one hand. "I get the drift. You're a closet romantic."

"*Lethal Weapon* doesn't have a romance in it." She might have sounded dignified if she wasn't naked and sprawled all over him.

"No, but it has the noble hero willing to risk everything for a defenseless female."

"You always have to be right," Renee complained.

"Have to be? I *am* always right."

She nipped him. "So what are *your* favorite movies? Some blood-and-guts things?"

"I liked *Bull Durham,* too."

"Baseball. Figures."

"*The Hunt for Red October.*"

She made a rude noise. "Big weapons."

"*Fiddler on the Roof.*"

"Really?" she said in amazement.

"Hey, I'm a sensitive guy." He proved it by falling back in agony when she playfully punched him.

They talked for hours that night, sometimes serious, sometimes laughing. They made love twice more. By three in the morning, Daniel felt punchy and Renee giggled every time he looked at her.

"Time for bed," he decided, swinging his feet to the floor.

"You know, we're already *in* bed," she told him solemnly. "My bed, as a matter of fact."

He switched off the hall light and climbed back in with her. When he reached for the bedside lamp, she chopped at his arm.

"Don't! I like looking at you."

"I like looking at you, too, sweetheart." *I want to look at you for the rest of my life.* "But we need to sleep."

She pouted. "I'm having too much fun to sleep."

"We can have more fun tomorrow."

"Tomorrow I have to work." Her eyelids sank and the words began to slur. "Lots to do. If…if…what was his name? Oh, yeah. Bashter…" She frowned and enunciated more carefully, "*Baxter.* If he's not dead, who is?"

"Good question," Daniel murmured, but she didn't hear. She was sound asleep.

He kissed her gently, turned off the light and rolled onto his side facing her, pillowing Renee's head on his upper arm. Instinctively she reached for him. She fit just right, warm and slim and unexpectedly soft. He held her and she held him. The way it ought to be. Who'd want a king-size bed?

But before he slept, he couldn't help thinking about the last thing she'd said. *Lots to do.* And, *If he's not dead, who is?*

She hadn't given up, and worry stirred in him like an angina pain.

Did she care about her search more than she did anything—or anyone—else? *I have to do this,* she'd told him, letting him see that the decision hurt but making it nonetheless. Without accepting the losses in her life, was Renee capable of really loving a man?

Somewhere in there Daniel fell asleep, too, but only to dream of her. Some threads of his dream were happy: her laughter, her passion, her smile. Other threads were nightmarish: she was arresting his father—no, *him;* he was reaching for her even as she turned away, running toward an insubstantial figure he knew to be her mother. "Renee!" he cried, but she didn't hear him. She walked faster and faster, finally running, until she became as wispy and unreal as her mother.

Daniel awakened in a sweat. As if symbolically, Renee faced away from him now and he felt as though the heavy bar of his arm across her waist was imprisoning her. She made a ragged sound, a whimper, and then another, moving restlessly.

Carefully he eased back, leaving her alone in the bed. Under the hot stream of water in the shower, he washed away both sweat and the unpleasant residue of the dreams.

Why was he reading so much into her determination to solve a puzzle already begun? She was inquisitive, determined—qualities he admired and understood to be part of her. Of course she wouldn't quit! He didn't even know why he wanted her to.

No, that was a lie; he did know. He wanted her to be secure enough in herself to be able to love him wholeheartedly.

Or was it that, like a selfish child, he wanted to come first?

He looked back in at her, but she still slept. The clock radio said seven; he didn't suppose she'd set an alarm, and guessed she'd have to be getting up soon. He wanted to climb right back into bed with her, but something held him back.

Maybe it was the dreams. Or the waking uneasiness that had been their seed. Maybe just that she looked strangely peaceful, now that she was alone in the narrow, pristine twin bed.

Daniel propped one shoulder against the door frame. Before she fled into the night, had Renee's mother stood here, stealing a last memory of her middle daughter? Daniel couldn't recall how old Renee had been when her mother left. Did Renee remember at all what it felt like to have someone making her lunch, braiding her hair, singing lullabies, hiding an Easter basket? Or did she remember most the loneliness afterward?

He would have given anything to change her childhood, to make it loving as his had been, to bring back the lost mother and sister who had meant the world to her.

A private detective, Daniel thought. Maybe he could find Meg and surprise Renee.

But he knew Meg's presence now wasn't the point. Only Renee herself could either accept the loss or choose to find out the truth by hunting for her sister and mother. It was the deciding that would matter, not the finding. And that he couldn't do for her.

There must be something! he thought in frustration. If not something important, something small.

And then it came to him.

When he mounted the stairs half an hour later, he carried a tray. He set it on the floor beside her bed and gently shook her.

"Hey, Sleeping Beauty. Upsy daisy."

Renee grumbled and buried her face in the covers.

He massaged her neck under her silky fine hair. "Come on. Time to rise and shine."

She said something, muffled by the quilt.

He bent toward her. "What?"

"My mother used to say that."

The pang he felt was sharp, bittersweet. "Mine, too."

"I smell…" She peeked from her nest of covers. "Bacon?"

"And eggs. I hope you like them scrambled. And, uh, pancakes. And I mixed up some orange juice."

Her whole face appeared. "You made breakfast?" she asked as though she couldn't believe he'd done anything so bizarre.

Again his heart cramped. Had no one ever brought her breakfast in bed?

"I…" Renee raked her hair back from her face. "I must look awful."

"You look beautiful." He smiled with sensual intent. "Your cheeks are flushed…" With his knuckles he touched them, feeling the warmth. "Your hair is tousled. And that heavy-lidded look makes a man think about sex, you know. I'd kiss you, but then breakfast would get cold, and I worked hard on it."

"Oh!" Blushing even more fiercely, she jumped out of bed. "Let me…" The sentence trailed off as she fled.

He waited patiently. She came back with astonishing speed. Some women would have showered, put on makeup, styled their hair. Renee had brushed hers and tucked it behind her ears, washed her face and donned a robe.

"I'd forgotten I bought the bacon," she said, hopping

back into bed, tucking the pillow behind her and sitting cross-legged. She looked absurdly young and delighted at such a small treat.

"Milady—" he set the tray carefully in the middle of the bed "—breakfast is served."

The two plates were covered by mixing bowls to hold in the heat. Delicious smells wafted up.

"I'll never be able to eat all this," she said, even as she poured syrup onto her pancakes.

As they ate, she told him about yesterday's domestic violence case taken to an extreme. The sadness, the damage done to so many lives, the frustration for the police involved.

"You know she'll welcome him back, maybe even bail him out, and he'll hit her again, and she'll think that's the way life is. And *we'll* probably have to do this all over again, only next time he might shoot somebody, or get shot. Sometimes it seems easier to storm a hostage taker than to wait patiently until he wears down." She fell silent.

"So what's the answer?"

"There is no answer." Renee sighed. "Better education. Instant access to counseling, shelters, alcohol treatment… Would that make a difference, do you think?"

It seemed easier for a man to storm a woman's defenses than to wait patiently, too, Daniel thought. Male instincts called for action.

"I don't know," he admitted. If a woman's lot in life was exactly what she'd expected, would she ask for help no matter how readily available it was?

"I don't, either." Renee sighed again, then smiled a little wistfully as she set down her fork. "I can't eat another bite. Oh, Daniel. This was so sweet of you."

He moved uncomfortably. "I was hungry."

"Right." She leaned forward across the tray and kissed him on the lips. Now *that* was sweet.

"Want to ditch work today?" he asked on impulse. "Stay in bed all day?"

Longing shone briefly on her fine-boned face. "I wish," she said, wrinkling her nose. "But Jack was mad at me yesterday as it was. If I take a vacation day now, he'd never forgive me. Besides…"

A chill settled over him at the change in her voice. "Besides what?"

"I've been thinking about Les Greene again. And Gabe Rosler. Something isn't right there. While we wait for the fingerprint ID, I'm going to trace them."

His gut clenched. "You're obsessed."

Her gaze, startled and defensive, flew to his. "I'm curious. Is that so bad?"

He stood up and said harshly, "What you're really curious about is what happened to your mother. Why don't you look for *her?*"

She scrambled off the bed, too, stumbling over the hem of her robe. "Because if she can't bother to contact me, I don't want to find her! That's why!"

"Maybe she can't. Maybe she's dead."

"She shouldn't have left me!" Renee cried, tears shimmering in her eyes.

"You're an adult. Wouldn't it be better to find out why she left? Why she never called or wrote?" He leaned toward her. "Wouldn't you rather *know?*"

At the echo of her own words to him, she sucked in a sharp breath. "Why are you doing this?"

"Because I want you to grow up."

He felt sick at the sight of the shock and hurt in her

eyes. The cruel words weren't even true; what he wanted was for her to focus on *him,* not Les Greene or T. J. Baxter or Meg Patton.

He swore. "I didn't mean that."

"I think you did," she said quietly, her face pale. "Maybe you're right. Here I am in my father's house six months after he died. Totally inexperienced. That isn't very appealing, is it? I know you're right."

Daniel swore again and reached for her, but she shied away.

"I love you," he said, voice raw.

She shook her head hard. "Don't say that right now. Please. You don't mean it. Don't say it."

"I do! Renee…" In sheer terror, he took a step forward.

She took one back, still shaking her head. "Will you please go, Daniel? Thank you for breakfast."

Oh, God. How could he have been so stupid?

"Renee. I swear…"

"No!" she shouted, then clapped her hand over her mouth. Tears welled in her eyes. "Please…just…leave."

He closed his eyes for a moment, then backed clumsily away. "I'll call."

She said nothing.

He picked up the tray, carried it to the door. There he turned *back* for one last look at her.

"Just remember," he said, in a voice that scraped his throat. "I love you. I'm in love with you. I have every intention of marrying you."

She hadn't moved; still didn't speak. In her eyes was pain, not a leap of hope.

"Remember," he said, and left.

CHAPTER FOURTEEN

THE CLERK at the California Department of Motor Vehicle Registration was helpful and quick. On the basis of age, together she and Renee eliminated all but two of the Lester or Les Greenes who held driver's licenses in the state.

"I didn't catch that second address," Renee said. The woman repeated the information and Renee double-checked her notes.

"And not a single Gabe or Gabriel Rosler in the right age bracket."

"That's right, Lieutenant."

Renee thanked her profusely and hung up. Rubbing gritty eyes, she struggled to stay focused. If she let herself stop, she'd fall apart.

Keep busy. Don't think, was her mantra.

Okay. What had she learned?

Would Gabe have changed his name for some reason? A criminal record once he'd gone to California? Or was he lying to his parents in his annual Christmas letter about where he lived, because he didn't want them surprising him?

Heck, maybe he'd gone to Chicago, or Miami, or Enid, Oklahoma.

And maybe, with luck, Les Greene would know.

She dialed information and got the two phone

numbers. Chances were both men would be at work during the day, but she decided to give them a try anyway.

One lived in San Francisco, the other in Half Moon Bay, a small town half an hour south along the coast. She decided to go for the big city first.

The phone rang five times. She was about to hang up when she heard a clunk on the other end, a muffled curse, and finally the voice of someone wakened from a heavy sleep.

"Yeah?"

"May I speak to Les Greene?"

"That's me," the man said brusquely.

"I apologize if I woke you up."

"I work nights. Who are you?"

"Lieutenant Renee Patton. Elk Springs Police Department. I'm trying to locate a Les Greene who attended Elk Springs High School."

There was a long silence. The man sounded more alert when he said, "Is it my mother? Did she die?"

"Your mother's name?"

"Joanie. Joanie Greene. Unless she remarried."

"No," Renee said. "She didn't. Actually, I'm afraid your mother died three years ago. Cirrhosis of the liver."

Another silence. "Figures," Greene said. Then, "Maybe I should feel something, but I don't. She wasn't any kind of mother."

"So I understand."

"That's why you're calling?"

"No." Renee took a breath. "Actually, I'm trying to locate Gabe Rosler. I understand the two of you were good friends in high school."

"I haven't seen him since then. He took off before we graduated."

"And you left yourself a short time later."

"How did you know that?" he asked, suspicion coloring his voice.

"Gabe's mother reported you missing. I came across a police report on you."

"She reported me missing?" he repeated, sounding stunned.

"She was worried about you."

This silence was the longest yet. "I didn't think anybody would worry." Bitterly, "I knew my mother wouldn't. And with Gabe gone…"

"I was hoping you might have made contact with him after you left."

"I tried. We talked about places we'd go once we left home. S.F. sounded the coolest. I thought I might find him down here, but I didn't. I tried calling his house once, but his bastard of a father told me they didn't want to hear from me again. So—" Renee could almost hear the shrug "—I got a job and did okay. I figured maybe he'd gone home."

"I'm afraid he didn't." Renee hesitated. "May I ask you a very personal question?"

"I guess that depends," he said warily.

"Are you homosexual?"

"You want to know if Gabe was gay, too. Yeah. He was. I am. Why are you looking for Gabe, Officer? I mean, why now?"

She told him about the bones found on the neighboring ranch and her fruitless search for a name to go with them.

"I, um, actually checked your dental records, but, uh…"

"My teeth are still in my mouth."

"Exactly."

"Are you going to check Gabe's now?"

"Yes," she said slowly, "I think I am."

Another silence. "Will you call? After you've found out? I've always kinda wondered. You know?"

"Yes," she agreed. "Of course. I'll keep you informed. Um…one more question, Mr. Greene. If you don't mind. It's not important. I'm just curious."

"About what?"

"When you ran away, why did you leave your car? That's why Mrs. Rosler reported you missing, by the way. She couldn't imagine you would have left that car voluntarily."

He grunted, either with surprise or laughter. "Engine blew. The transmission wasn't so great, either. Do you know what my mother did with it?"

"Afraid not," she told him. "Doesn't sound like it was good for much but the junkyard."

"Yeah. I had some good years in that car, though." He sounded more nostalgic about it than he had about his mother. Who could blame him?

"Thank you, Mr. Greene. I'll be in touch."

Renee rose to her feet even as she hung up. *Keep busy. Don't think.* Time for another little talk with Marjorie Rosler.

As she drove, she did her best to blank from her mind the fact that this was also the route to the Triple B. To Daniel. Who had said, "I love you. I'm in love with you." But who had also seen through her facade to the terrified, lost little girl beneath and had no patience with her.

Don't think. Not about him.

Gabe Rosler, then.

How could those bones be his? Had his mother lied

about receiving those letters all these years? Were the pride and the grief false?

Or were the letters the kind anybody could have written? The "Dear Mom, I'm doing great, I'm an E.M.T. now" kind.

But why would somebody bother to write them?

Now she *was* chasing a will-o'-the-wisp. But something wouldn't let her turn back. *If not T. J. Baxter, who?*

She could wait for the fingerprint ID. But she had a cop's gut feeling that the charming ex-rodeo rider, arrogant enough to think he'd still have a job after raping the boss's wife, was going to turn out to have walked away from the Triple B with no more than a black eye and bloody nose.

What could it hurt to chase down one more lead? She'd already lost everything she had to lose.

She parked in front of the Roslers' white house and went to the door. Coming in answer to the knock, Marjorie peered through the screen, just like the last time.

"Officer." She didn't sound very happy. "Why, I didn't expect to see you again."

"May I come in? I have news about Les Greene."

"Oh. Oh!" She unlatched the screen door and pushed it open. "Please. That…that isn't him after all, is it?"

"No." Renee stepped inside. The house was as still as a graveyard. She'd have felt better if a soap opera had been playing in the background. "No, I actually spoke to him."

"You did?" Marjorie's tired face lit up. "He's all right?"

"Yes. He lives in the San Francisco area, although apparently he and Gabe never hooked up again. He didn't realize that Gabe was down there, too."

"But…but they were such good friends. I always thought…" She fumbled her way to the rose-pink recliner and sank down, distress coming from her in waves. "Why…why, that's too bad."

Here came the hard part. "Mrs. Rosler—"

The front door slammed. Blunt-featured face flushed with anger, Dick Rosler loomed in the arched opening to the living room.

"You're back out here."

Renee faced him, thinking again what an unlikely pair he and his pretty wife must have seemed when they walked down the aisle together. "Yes. I had some news I wanted to share with Mrs. Rosler. And a few more questions."

"What the hell kind of questions do you have for us? Look at her." He brushed past Renee, went to Marjorie and placed a heavy hand on her shoulder. He glowered at Renee. "You'd better have some mighty good reason for upsetting my wife this way."

In her husband's presence, quelled by his touch, Marjorie seemed to have shrunk. She stared down as if fascinated by her hands.

Resolve hardening, Renee said, "Mr. Rosler, do you have any reason to doubt that the letters you've received from your son are genuine?"

"What?" he exploded. "What kind of crap are you talking? Of course they're from our son! Who the hell else would write?"

That was the question, wasn't it?

"Could I see them?"

"They're none of your goddamned business!"

"I'd like to check his dental records. With your permission…"

"Which you're not going to get!"

Was it fear of what she might find out that turned his face purple and glittered in his eyes? Just because he and

Gabe had never gotten along didn't mean he didn't love his son. Did her suggestion confirm some deep-held suspicion that he hadn't wanted his wife to hear?

Had he wondered whether his son was dead? He wouldn't be the first to use anger to push back fear.

Only, if Gabe was dead, who wrote the letters?

"Mr. Rosler…"

"No!" he thundered. "I want you off our place! And don't come back. I'll be letting your superior know what kind of irresponsible accusations you're making."

Interesting, she thought, that he interpreted her request as an accusation. Did he think she was accusing him? Why would he assume that?

"Mrs. Rosler," Renee said.

Marjorie didn't move, didn't meet her eyes.

Feeling pity, Renee said gently, "I'm sorry to have bothered you. I hope you two will discuss this. If you change your mind…"

The rancher's fingers tightened on his wife's shoulder. "We won't," he said inflexibly.

Renee nodded. "I'll see myself out."

In her car, she sat looking up at the house for a minute. If only Dick hadn't heard her arrive! She just knew Marjorie would have given her permission, at least let her glance through her son's letters.

Now… Well, she'd done what she could without a warrant. Maybe she was wrong about the balance of power in the Rosler home. Dick Rosler wouldn't be the first man full of bluster who could be gently maneuvered by his wife. She might talk some sense into him.

Renee had to hope so, because she knew she didn't have enough justification to obtain a warrant. "I just have a feeling," wouldn't cut it with the judge.

The phone messages on her desk when she got back didn't include one from Marjorie Rosler. Abby had phoned, as had the owner of a local hardware store. Renee had had dealings with him only a few weeks before, when he discovered a clerk was stealing from him. He'd fired the thief, but decided not to press charges, which she'd considered a mistake.

She called him back first.

"Thanks, Lieutenant," he said. "You remember that kid I fired? Kyle Peterson? Well, shoot, this is probably nothing, but another young guy I have working for me says he's heard rumors that Peterson is talking big about killing me."

"Killing you?" Renee repeated, startled. "You let him off easy."

"That's what I figured, but I guess he doesn't see it that way. He actually had the gall to put me down for a reference—can you believe it? I told the fellow who called that I'd fired Peterson and why. So he didn't get the job and now I hear he's worked up about it. You know nothing'll come of it, but what with all you read in the newspapers these days, I thought I should report it."

"I'll go talk to him," Renee said. "I can dig out the file, but do you happen to have his address handy?"

"Isn't that just going to make him madder?"

"Scare some sense into him, is what I have in mind. As you say, it's probably talk, but he needs to learn not to shoot his mouth off like that. And if he's at all serious…well, I'll just feel better once I've had words with him."

Nervous, the owner reluctantly gave her the address and expressed confidence in her judgment.

On her way out to the house Kyle Peterson shared with three other young men, Renee took a call to a convenience store, where the chubby clerk waved a twenty dollar bill under Renee's nose.

"Look!" she said. "It's got to be fake. Jeez, I just know it's going to come out of my pocket. God. Counterfeit money. The manager says to watch out for it, but who thinks somebody is printing up funny money in Elk Springs?"

"They're probably not," Renee said. "The customer could have picked this up anywhere."

"How was I supposed to know?" the clerk said miserably.

Renee took the bill encased in plastic. It would be sent off to federal authorities, who took counterfeiting seriously.

As she walked out of the store, a blue pickup truck pulled in beside the gas pumps. Her heart jumped and she battled a desire to scurry back inside and hide in the ladies' rest room. Was it Daniel?

No. His didn't have a rifle rack in the back window. And the man who got out had a beard.

Renee's breath left her lungs with a whoosh. She collapsed in the driver's seat of her Bronco. She was shaking, she saw with a distant part of her attention. Drained, as if she'd just been shot at. All because she saw a pickup similar to Daniel's. All because she might conceivably have run into him.

I want you to grow up.

Could she?

She knew the streets of Elk Springs well enough to drive on automatic. Not until she pulled up in front of the ramshackle house shared by four guys in their early twenties did she regain awareness of her surroundings and the neighborhood, consisting mostly of small rentals.

Climbing out, Renee tsked mentally at the lawn that should have been mowed a last time before winter, at the torn, faded flannel sheets hung in the front window in place of blinds, at the loose board on the bare, splintered porch steps.

Her father would have said that you could judge a man—he always said a man, not a woman—by how he kept up his home. Of course, he hadn't made allowances for disabilities or for a single mother's struggle to survive or a landlord's refusal to pay for repairs. Still, she often found he was right.

Much as she hated to admit any such thing.

These guys weren't much more than teenagers, though, she reminded herself. Her impression was that a couple of them were ski bums, living hand-to-mouth in wait of powder snow. The other two, including Kyle Peterson, were local boys more interested in partying than taking on adult responsibilities.

She felt a brief spurt of anger at the comparison to herself. Not far separated in years from this quartet, she felt a century removed by how she lived her life. Damn it, they needed to grow up! How dare Daniel put her in the same category?

She climbed the porch steps gingerly, noting the recyling bin overflowing with beer cans. Tinny voices from a television set were muffled by the door. Her brisk knock brought a yelled, "Come in."

Wearing nothing but sweatpants, Kyle Peterson was sprawled on a shabby sofa. A pyramid of beer cans decorated the wood crate used as a coffee table. He couldn't seem to tear his gaze from the TV screen, where Steven Seagal debonairly kicked into submission several bad guys.

"Mr. Peterson," Renee said. "I'd like to talk to you."

"Who…?" He turned bleary eyes at her. At the sight of her uniform, alarm kicked in. "You're that woman cop."

"That's right. Lieutenant Patton."

He swung his feet to the floor and stood. The gray sweats sagged, exposing more of his groin than Renee wanted to see. "Do you have a warrant or something?"

"You invited me in."

"I didn't know—" He stopped. "Is this just some kind of follow-up?"

She planted her feet well apart. "What do you think?"

A scowl drew his brows together. "I don't know. You tell me."

"Would you please turn the television off." She didn't make it a question.

He wanted to refuse just to be a jerk, she could see it in his eyes, but abruptly he turned, grabbed a remote control and punched some buttons. The screen went dark and silence fell.

"Happy?"

"I am." Her hand rested on the butt of her gun. "I understand that you're not. I hear you're real unhappy about having lost your job."

Bitterness twisted his thin, unshaven face. "Shouldn't I be? I was good! The boss man said so himself. Next thing I know, I'm canned because some money is missing. Like he could prove it."

"He did prove it." Renee met his stare. "I urged him to file charges. He felt that firing you was enough to get the message through. Apparently he was wrong."

Wariness flickered in his eyes. "What's that supposed to mean?"

"You've been heard making threats."

"Bull!" he exploded, pacing a couple of agitated steps and then stopping. "I just want a job!"

"And you actually expected to get a good reference from a man you'd robbed."

"I'd have paid it back—" Belatedly, he put the brakes on. Then he swore and talked fast. "I just...I was really broke. You know? I couldn't make my share of the rent. The guys carried me one month, but they said they wouldn't another. I would've put it back as soon as I got paid. Really."

"But then where would you have come up with the next month's rent?"

"I'd have thought of something." He uttered an obscenity. "What am I telling you for?" He thrust out his hands. "Why don't you just put the handcuffs on right now?"

"That's very tempting," she said. "Let me think about it."

"Oh, God." He turned away and bumped his forehead against the wall, then stayed leaning against it, his eyes closed. "What am I going to do?"

She let no sympathy at all sound in her voice. "Lie around drinking beer and watching videos, apparently. Blame someone else."

He didn't react with renewed rage, which she figured was a good sign.

"How seriously should I take those threats against Mr. Carlton's life?" she asked.

"Oh, damn, damn, damn," Peterson muttered. "I didn't mean anything. I don't even own a gun, or... I was just... I was probably drunk. And pissed. You know? I can't believe somebody told the cops." Despair poured off him in waves, as powerful as the odor of beer.

Renee said abruptly, "I could talk to John Carlton about giving you a reference for a job where you had no access to money. He did say you were a good worker. He might consider coming through if you agree to make restitution in small monthly installments."

His head shot up. "Do you think…? Oh, damn. Why would he? I mean, I don't blame him for being really steamed. He *trusted* me."

She shrugged. "It's worth a try."

"I…" Peterson's Adam's apple bobbed. "If you mean it."

She went out to her car and leaned against the fender, dialing her cell phone. John Carlton, who had a heart as soft as spring snow, agreed immediately, as she'd guessed he would.

"Kyle's not a bad kid," he said. "Hell, who isn't impulsive at that age?"

Me, she wanted to say. *I never was.* She hadn't done an impulsive thing in her life until that night when she watched Daniel throw her father's recliner off the front porch. She'd been afraid to do anything without thinking it through ten ways to Sunday; afraid any change at all would upset the fragile balance that allowed her to cope. She almost envied Kyle Peterson, who could do something stupid and find redemption.

She went back up onto the porch to find that he'd pulled on a sweatshirt, stuck his feet in sneakers and combed his lanky hair. He cried when she told him the news, swore up and down and sideways that he'd pay Carlton back, pay *more* than he had to, mow John Carlton's lawn, paint his house, clean his toilet. Anything.

"All he's asking is for you to learn a lesson," Renee said. She tipped her hat. "Good day, Mr. Peterson."

Back at the station, she told Jack what she'd done, half expecting him to call her a sucker.

But he nodded from where he slouched in her office doorway. "My sister used to baby-sit Kyle Peterson. He wasn't a bad kid. I think he'll come through."

Renee sat down. "We'll see."

"Update me on the bones."

"Dick Rosler called you?"

Jack's gaze sharpened. "A week or so ago. Not recently, if that's what you mean."

"I know it'll be a while before we get an ID on those fingerprints, but… Oh, shoot. I'm getting this feeling those bones might be Gabe Rosler's. Dick is determined to keep me from finding out. I don't know whether that's because he doesn't want to know if they are, or because he already knows."

"That's a pretty wild statement," Jack said.

"No kidding." Even her wry smile took an effort. In less than twenty-four hours, she'd forgotten how to smile. "I can't even defend it. It's just a hunch."

He frowned at her without speaking for an uncomfortably long moment. Then he grimaced. "Your feelings are right on more often than I want to admit." He straightened. "It's five-thirty. You're not going to accomplish anything more. Why don't you go home?"

Her stomach took a panicky leap. She couldn't! Her house was too empty, too quiet. She wouldn't be able to help thinking. Remembering. She'd see him ripping up carpet, racing her for the bathroom, holding her close in her narrow bed.

The kitchen was about the only room where he hadn't spent much time, but she wasn't about to go back to huddling in there, hiding from life.

Grow up.

Maybe, she thought, with a flicker of hope, she was. Or maybe she already had and just didn't know it. Shoot, maybe Daniel Barnard was wrong, for once in his life.

Her phone rang. She snatched up the receiver. "Patton."

"Miss…that is, Officer Patton?" The voice was hesitant, just above a whisper.

"Yes?" Her heart took a different kind of leap. "Mrs. Rosler?"

"I didn't tell Dick I was calling." A pause. "He'd be upset, and he has that heart condition, you know. He's had a quadruple bypass."

"I didn't know that. I'm sorry," Renee said sincerely.

Marjorie begged for understanding. "He's just trying to protect me. He's always protected me."

"I'm sure he has." Renee twirled the cord around her finger. "Mrs. Rosler…"

"I mailed you one of Gabe's letters. Oh!" After a startled cry, she fell silent.

Renee sat bolt upright. "Mrs. Rosler? Is something wrong?"

Her voice came back, fainter than ever. "I thought I heard Dick coming, but I can see him down by the barn." She drew an audible breath. "He won't miss just one letter. And…and our dentist—we've all gone to him since Gabe was a little boy… Anyway, we go to Dr. Kauffman. Philip Kauffman."

Renee's mind raced. "I'll need your permission, Mrs. Rosler."

"I called and told them you could see Gabe's X rays. I pray it comes to nothing, but I need to know. I guess Dick would rather hope, but sometimes I think the way

Gabe left and never calls or anything is worse than having him dead."

"Yes," Renee said, and she wasn't thinking about Gabe Rosler. "I think you're right. It hurts worse."

"Your mama left, didn't she?"

Renee swallowed. "Yes. When I was eleven."

"So you know."

"I've hoped, over and over, that she was dead."

"Sometimes I did, too." Marjorie's tremulous voice shattered, then firmed. "Only, there were those letters."

"But now you wonder."

"Who could have written them?" The few words expressed a world of bewildered pain. "They would have had to know things!"

"Les Greene?"

"Maybe." She sounded doubtful. "I guess Gabe could have told him stories. Oh! I hear the front door."

A click sounded in Renee's ear. Thoughtfully, she hung up and opened her top drawer, taking out the phone book. In the Yellow Pages, she ran her finger down the list of dentists until she came to Kauffman, Philip, D.D.S.

A moment later, she listened incredulously to the recorded message telling her that Dr. Kauffman's office was closed for the day and he wouldn't be in until Monday. It seemed that Dr. Philip Kauffman worked only four days a week.

Renee said a word that hardly ever passed her lips and slammed down the phone. If she had to, she'd roust him out of the squash court or wherever he recreated to get in shape for ski season. The hell she'd wait until Monday!

The good dentist, however, was apparently out of town, she discovered after half a dozen more phone calls. His office manager said, no, *she* hadn't spoken to Mrs. Rosler and she couldn't possibly release those records without Dr. Kauffman's knowledge.

"He'll be in Monday morning at eight a.m.," she said crisply. "If this isn't a matter of life and death…"

Though more tempted to lie than she'd ever been in her life, Renee had to concede that it wasn't. She vented her frustration by slamming down the phone this time, too.

CHAPTER FIFTEEN

DR. KAUFFMAN'S VOICE creaked from age. Renee hoped his hands were steadier with a drill.

"Well, let me think." From the silence, he was apparently doing just that. He mused aloud, "I moved my office…oh, ten years ago. Records much earlier than that went into storage. It may take us a day or two to find the ones you want."

Renee gritted her teeth. Where had all her patience gone? "I'd appreciate anything you can do to expedite the hunt, Dr. Kauffman," she said as pleasantly as she could manage. "We're all hoping these remains don't turn out to be Gabe Rosler's, but, as you can imagine, his parents are terribly anxious. The sooner we can tell them one way or other, the better."

"Yes, yes, I can see that." He harrumphed. "Don't I remember Marjorie telling me news from Gabe's Christmas letter? I thought they heard from the boy regularly."

"There's some doubt now about those letters," Renee said.

"Ah. I see."

Plainly, he didn't, but who could blame him? The idea of a murderer writing his victim's mother for the next twenty years was a bizarre one. So bizarre, Renee had moments of wondering whether she hadn't gone off the deep end. Did she hate the idea of failure so much, she couldn't accept that she would never identify the bones? Besides T. J. Baxter, Gabe was her last possibility. After that, she might just as well close the file.

Which was probably what she should have done in the first place, she thought with a sigh. In her quest, she seemed to have trailed unhappiness behind her like Typhoid Mary. Her job was to serve and protect. Who was she serving?

Dr. Kauffman pulled her back from some heavy-duty brooding. "I'll tell you what. I'll send Cora over to the storage center right now to find those records. She's doing billing, but it can wait. I'll call the minute we find them."

"Thank you," she told him, probably scaring the man with how heartfelt she sounded.

After hanging up, she pushed her chair back, put her feet on her desk and looked around. Usually after two days off, she walked into her office and felt as if she hadn't been gone five minutes. Today she was so damned glad to be back after the longest weekend of her life, fond feelings enveloped her at the familiar squeak from her padded chair, at the sight of her gray steel desk and brown paper blotter, the green metal bookcase filled with law enforcement manuals and the black filing cabinets. Even the corkboard with Wanted bulletins looked positively decorative. This office was home more than her house was.

Though she'd finally realized she could change that if she wanted to. The only good part of her weekend had been the Saturday shopping expedition with Abby and Anne McWhirter. She'd chosen a denim couch, throw pillows made from blue-and-white quilt blocks, and white-painted cottage-style furniture. Thrilled at the size of her purchase, the store delivered Saturday afternoon.

Her TV now reposed in a white armoire; a vase of yellow and white carnations, bought on impulse, sat on the coffee table. A painting or two, and the living room would be complete. She loved it. And she wished Daniel could see it.

Not seeing or hearing from Daniel hurt so terribly, she'd been thrown back to her childhood, remembering the disappearance of her mother, the silence after Meg left. How could this be as bad? she kept asking herself, but in a different way, it was. She had always known that someday she would grow up and leave home; her mother and sister were part of her past, not her future. Daniel *was*—could have been—her future, her forever.

She couldn't bear it if he never came back, if he didn't mean those last things he'd said. She wanted so badly to be able to show him that she was a woman, not a scared child, but she didn't know how. She didn't even know how to convince herself. Face the past, or walk away from it?

Keep busy. Don't think.

She took a call at a rental business whose manager had just discovered their chain-link fence had been cut during the night and several expensive pieces of equipment had been stolen. Unfortunately, surrounding businesses had been closed, as well. The bar behind the rental yard was just opening; the bartender hadn't seen or heard anything, but he took Renee's card and promised to ask patrons, most of them were regulars.

A broken window at the five-and-dime down the block seemed to be the work of a vandal rather than a thief. The clerk hadn't noticed anything missing and the hole punched by a rock in the glass didn't appear to be large enough to allow ingress. Renee wrote up a report without any hope of finding the kid who'd probably done it.

She stopped for lunch and sat with a couple of other women, who asked her to speak at their monthly businesswomen's luncheon. Mildly pleased, she agreed. It was always good public relations, and she'd like to see more awareness of women in law enforcement. Their invitation spurred her to call the high school and ask the principal if she couldn't come there one day and talk.

"This isn't a career girls usually consider," she said. "I'd like to see that change."

As far as she could tell, he liked the idea and agreed to discuss with various teachers the best format for having her.

"I'll get back to you," he promised.

She hung up with a feeling of satisfaction and also the dip in her stomach that reminded her she needed to find something else to do.

Keep busy.

She was saved by the bell. Renee picked up her phone. "Elk Springs P.D. Lieutenant Patton."

"This is Phil Kauffman. Cora finally located that file, Lieutenant. You're welcome to bring the X rays you have on down and we'll compare them."

Her adrenaline kicked in. "I can't thank you enough, Dr. Kauffman. I'll be right over."

She grabbed the stiff manila envelope that held the X rays the coroner had taken of the maxilla, the upper jaw still intact on the skull.

Ten minutes, and she pulled into the parking lot at the side of the small brick building that housed Dr. Kauffman's dentistry clinic. A second name in smaller letters on the sign told her he'd taken in a partner; an heir apparent, presumably, given Kauffman's age.

The starchy woman behind the counter said, "Lieutenant Patton? Dr. Kauffman is expecting you. One moment, please."

Her nameplate said *Susan Ott*. Renee asked for the Cora who'd been so quick. A matronly woman appeared through the open door to a small office and accepted Renee's thanks.

"I know the Roslers," she said. "Poor Marjorie. I'll be praying for her."

"She'd appreciate that," Renee said.

The starchy office manager sent her on back then. Waiting for her in a cubicle with a light box, the gray-haired dentist held out a hand. "Phil Kauffman."

He was stronger and younger-looking than his voice had suggested. Keen blue eyes appraised her swiftly.

"Renee Patton," she said, shaking his hand. "Thank you for putting a rush on this."

"No problem. You have the X ray here?"

She handed him the envelope; he slipped it into one side of the light box. The other already held an X ray.

"This is Gabe Rosler's," he said absently, turning off the overhead light and peering at the two. "He had good teeth," he commented absently. "I reviewed his chart. Required very few fillings even in his baby teeth. Unusual, considering those were the days before mothers added fluoride to a baby's milk."

Renee looked from one X ray to the other. To her inexperienced eye, they were very similar. There was the filling in the back molar, and the other tiny one the coroner had spotted. The front tooth on both X rays was a little out of line—not so badly that parents would have seen the need for braces in those days, but sticking out just a little. When he smiled, it would have showed.

Renee saw in her mind's eye the photos of Gabe Rosler, the baby, the small boy, the teenager. In one picture he'd been grinning, and... Dear Lord. The small imperfection had given appeal to his too pretty face.

Phil Kauffman abruptly flipped on the light and faced Renee, his expression showing how disturbed he was.

"I'm afraid, Lieutenant, that you have a match. I couldn't believe..." He shook his head. "I still can't believe..."

"It's difficult, when you know the victim. I'm sorry to have had to ask you to do this, Dr. Kauffman."

"Oh, it isn't me! I just can't help thinking about Marjorie Rosler. A nicer lady, you couldn't find. And Gabe was her only child!"

"You have no doubt?" Renee felt compelled to ask.

He sighed. "None whatever. You're welcome, of course, to have the coroner look these over. You'll probably want to do that. But... No. I regret to say that I'm quite certain."

They shook hands. Renee took both X rays. Outside she saw how white the sky had turned. She shivered, feeling in the stillness and weight of the air the snow that would be falling soon. She hoped it held long enough for her to drive out to the Rosler ranch and make it back.

On the way, she analyzed how she felt. Now she knew, was even pretty sure who had murdered the teenager. She'd expected triumph when she found the elusive answer to the puzzle, but she'd come to know too many of the people involved. It wasn't a puzzle anymore; it was a tragedy.

Turning in the gates from the highway, Renee saw

flashing lights. Cinders crunching under her tires, she drove too fast up the lane. She rolled to a stop next to the ambulance and jumped out.

The attendants were just rolling a gurney out the front door. As it passed, Renee caught a glimpse of a face covered by an oxygen mask. The E.M.T.s were moving fast, urgency in their voices and hands. Behind them came Marjorie Rosler, wringing her hands.

She turned desperate, frightened eyes on Renee.

"What happened?" Renee asked.

"Dick." A sob escaped her and she looked back at the ambulance. "He… I think he had another heart attack. I think…" Tears began to fall. "I think it was my fault. I came into the room, and he had the letters in his hand. He turned around with this terrible look on his face, and then…" She shook all over. "And then he just collapsed. He must have discovered one was gone."

"I'm so sorry." Renee tentatively put an arm around the weeping woman, who stayed stiff in her embrace. "Do you have family? Have you called someone?"

"Yes. My sister."

The E.M.T.s folded up the wheels and boosted the gurney into the back of the ambulance.

Marjorie lifted her gaze to Renee, who had the sense that the older woman had just realized who she was, what her presence meant.

"You…you've found something out, haven't you?"

"Yes." Renee hesitated. "This isn't the time…"

"Tell me." Her mouth firmed, and her expression was suddenly fierce. "Gabe is dead, isn't he?"

One E.M.T. stayed crouched inside the back of the ambulance; the other hopped out. "Ma'am, if you're going to ride along, we need to go."

Renee felt helpless to comfort, to soften the blow. "Yes," she said again. "I'm afraid so."

"Sometimes I used to think Dick hated his own son," Marjorie said.

So she knew. Renee reached out a hand; Marjorie straightened, rejecting her touch.

"Ma'am," the ambulance attendant repeated more urgently.

"Your husband loves you," Renee said. "He went to a lot of trouble to send those letters."

"Oh, love." Grief, rage, bitterness, all tangled in her voice. "Is that love?"

She turned away then, and accepted the E.M.T.'s hand to help her into the ambulance. Just before the doors closed, she looked back. "Why? That's all I want to know. Why would he have killed his own boy?"

Renee could guess. What she couldn't decide was whether she should tell a grieving mother that her husband had probably found out his son was homosexual and murdered him out of rage and pride that wouldn't accept his neighbors knowing what his son was.

Renee watched the ambulance go, a lump in her throat.

Marjorie had said she'd rather know. Now she did, but this knowledge was grievous.

Staring after the ambulance until it disappeared toward town on the highway, Renee wondered again: who had she served?

SHE'D GO TO THE HOSPITAL. And hope, for the first time in her life, that a man died. If he survived, could she come up with enough evidence to convict him? She'd have to focus on the letters. Who had mailed them for him?

What would be gained from sending a sixty-year-old

man to jail for a murder committed so long ago? He wasn't a danger to society.

And yet, how could she let him go back to his life, a free man?

What kind of life would that be, now that his wife knew what he'd done?

Perhaps, Renee thought, Dick Rosler had chosen the time of his going.

Before she went to the hospital, she'd drive out to the Triple B. Although no one could be certain what had happened to T. J. Baxter until the fingerprint ID came back, they now knew the most important thing: the remains found on Barnard land were not his. Renee felt, after all she'd put her through, that she owed it to Shirley to tell her as soon as possible.

Renee swung the Bronco in a circle and headed for the R & R gates. This was something she needed to do.

Never mind that she might see Daniel.

She'd be just as glad if she didn't, she tried to convince herself. Seeing him would hurt. She'd hope he wasn't there, or didn't notice her arrival. The news would come better from his mother.

Which didn't explain why her heart was pounding so hard when she drove under the Triple B name burned into the gate arch.

But her luck was out. As she drove by the barns, Daniel stood talking with another man beside a strange pickup. A chill and then a flush washed over her face. Despite her dark mood, he looked so good to her in boots, dusty jeans and a denim jacket; a Stetson was pushed onto the back of his head.

She saw him, as if in a pantomime, turn to stare at her. The other guy, who appeared to have been talking, mimicked him exactly. Scarcely able to breathe, her heart was so constricted, Renee lifted a hand in greeting, and continued on to the white farmhouse. Without looking over her shoulder although she knew he would come, she went up the steps to the front door and rang.

"Just a minute!" Shirley called from inside. A moment later, she opened the door. She took a sharp breath when she saw Renee. "You…you have news."

"Yes." Better this time; easier to give.

"Come in." But Shirley didn't move. "No. Tell me now. Please. Was it Baxter who died?"

"We still don't know anything about T. J. Baxter," Renee said straight-out. "But I do know those bones aren't his."

Shirley sagged. Renee took a quick step forward across the threshold and grabbed her elbows.

"Do you need to sit down?"

"I'm just…" Her voice was a wisp and she trembled all over. "Dear Lord, I'm so relieved." She lifted a face already damp with tears. "That means…"

"Yes." For some absurd reason, Renee felt close to tears herself. "It's pretty unlikely a second body is lying out there somewhere. I think you can go back to believing your husband would never have done something so against his principles."

"I'm ashamed even to have been afraid…"

Neither woman had noticed Daniel's arrival until he said urgently, "Mom. What is it? Are you all right?"

It somehow felt natural to slip her arm around his mother's waist as Renee turned to face him.

His eyes, always bluer than she remembered, bored into hers even as his mother was the one to speak. Had to be the one to speak. Renee wasn't sure she could.

"The bones aren't that Baxter man's. Your father didn't kill him."

The intensity of his gaze didn't waver. "Then whose…" He stopped, his tone changed. "Not Gabe?"

Renee nodded dumbly, her tongue still paralyzed.

"Gabe?" his mother exclaimed. "The neighbor boy? Not Gabe Rosler!"

"Yes." At last she could talk. "I'm afraid it was. Is. I just told Mrs. Rosler. I would have rather put it off. Her husband has had a heart attack. I'm on my way to the hospital, but I wanted to let you know first."

"Oh, no! Poor Marjorie! Is there anything I can do, do you think? Does she have someone with her?"

"She'd called her sister, she said."

Shirley shook her head. "Dick had a heart attack…oh, three or four years ago, you know. He had bypass surgery, one of those triple or quadruple ones that makes it sound like his heart must be a maze now. And—oh!—another attack so soon."

"He didn't look good," Renee said.

"Oh, no! Well, you be sure to tell her to call on me for anything at all."

"I will." Renee could tell she meant it, which was a good thing. Marjorie was going to need all the help she could find to get through these next months, whether her husband lived or not.

Shirley looked at her son, then Renee, then back again. "Well," she said. "I'll let Daniel walk you out to your car. Bless you for coming today. I feel like I did after losing all that weight! Remember how plump I got?" she asked her son.

He didn't appear to have heard her. Gaze never

leaving Renee, he stood between her and the porch steps, just waiting, big and solid.

Shirley gently slipped away from Renee and gave her a slight push so that she had to step over the threshold onto the porch. Behind her, the door quietly closed, leaving her alone with Daniel.

"Renee," he said, voice low and gritty. "I was going to come by your place tonight. I figured this was long enough. That you'd know how you felt by now, one way or another."

Her heart was pounding so hard she could hardly hear herself. "I'm going to find my mother," she said, as if that were the most important thing she could offer.

"I don't care." He took a step closer. "Find her or not. Suit yourself. You're all that matters to me."

"But…" She searched his face. "No. Don't say it doesn't matter. It does! If only because I've been so self-righteous! Remember how I said you had to know about your father? Your mother had to face up to what had happened so that she'd *know*. And then Marjorie Rosler. Oh!" Renee said in shame. "*I* was so certain that everyone else should face reality. And all the time I couldn't face my own! How did you stand me?"

"But you were right." His mouth twisted, and for the first time he looked away. "What you were pushing us to do was have the guts to find the answers to questions that needed asking. That's not the same thing as you not wanting to know for sure why your mother walked out. Whether she's dead or still alive and just didn't give a damn. It'll hurt either way. What's the good of finding out?"

"Maybe…" Renee groped for an answer to this question. "Maybe if I did know why and what became of her after she left us, if I could understand, then maybe it *wouldn't* hurt as much. Do you see? Because I wouldn't be just a little kid who's lost her mommy anymore. I'd be a woman who could empathize. Maybe she had no choice. Maybe she did try to contact us. Maybe she even tried to take us, or fight for custody, or…" Renee's hands balled into fists as she shared her childhood dreams. "My father would have been careful not to let us find out. He never mentioned her." Her voice felt thick; her mouth worked. "Oh, damn. Now I'm going to cry."

"I love you." Daniel reached for her.

Renee backed away, holding her hands up, palms out. "No. Please. Let me finish. What I'm trying to say is, if the woman I am now could understand why my mother did what she did, then maybe the part of me that's still a scared little girl could be shown, too."

He made an inarticulate sound. Letting her finish wasn't easy on him; tension and frustration and anguish poured off him in waves. His blue eyes were almost black as he listened. But he did listen, which was the most loving thing anyone had ever done for her.

"What I'm trying to say is, you were right. I guess my development was kind of…arrested." She struggled to explain, knew she had to articulate how she'd felt. "It was like, if I stayed where I was, if I didn't grow up, I thought she'd come home and we could go on where we'd left off." She shook her head. "Oh, that sounds crazy!"

"But then, we're agreed that both of us are nuts." His voice was hoarse. "Remember?"

"Loco," she whispered.

He broke then. Swore, and hauled her into his arms.

Not to kiss her, although she hoped he'd do that sooner or later. He just squeezed her into an embrace that probably hurt, although she didn't care, because she was holding him just as tightly.

"I love you." His voice broke. "I wish I'd ripped my tongue out before I said what I did. All I really wanted was to be sure I mattered to you more than your mom and sister do."

"Well, of course you do!" She pulled back in astonishment, seeing for the first time how haggard he looked. The grooves in his cheeks had deepened; more lines feathered out from the corners of his eyes, which were puffy and tired. He had suffered, she saw. She liked the idea she wasn't alone in that, or in any other way.

Her future.

"If Mom and Meg were still at home," she told him, voice shaking with her need to convince him, "I wouldn't be planning to live with them forever, for Pete's sake! I mean, when a man… That is…" Her face flushed as she tried to take back a mighty big assumption. What if he still wasn't talking marriage? She'd given him plenty of reason to be cautious!

"But they're not still home," he said, with odd grimness. "Maybe them leaving hurt you in a way I can't heal. I guess that's what scares me."

"No," she said. "I mean, yes. Of course you can. You have! I'm going to sell the house and…and…"

"Marry me." Daniel framed her face with his big hands. "Come home with me."

"Yes. If you want me."

He gave a laugh that brought a lump to her throat, it held so much emotion. "You know the answer to that."

"Is it this simple?" she asked wistfully.

"Yup. This simple. If you love me." He swallowed. "You never have said you did, you know."

For one moment as he waited, Renee saw him again as others might, a plain, simple man who questioned whether he was worth loving, just as she questioned whether she was.

"Oh, yes," she said in a rush. "I love you. Oh, Daniel, I do love you!"

Heartfelt emotion made his eyes blue again, brought a slow smile to his face. It started out sweet, joyous, stealing her breath, slowly becoming a wicked, sensual grin.

"Then," he said, "let's go to my house."

"Yes." She tumbled back into his arms for a kiss that accelerated from gentle to hungry so fast, it buckled her knees.

Still kissing her, he scooped her up and started down from the porch, one fumbling step at a time. Her feet whammed into the newel post; she tugged at his hair and tangled her tongue with his.

"Oh, hell," he muttered suddenly. "You'll have to drive."

"Drive?" Her brain wasn't interested in anything so mundane, not when she could string kisses down his rough cheek, feel the pulse jump when she pressed her lips to his throat.

"If you don't want to have sex on my mother's front lawn," he groaned, "you need to drive."

Put that way… "Oh, all right," Renee conceded.

He let her slide down his body until her feet touched the ground. Feeling his thigh muscles and his erection with every nerve ending, she closed her eyes on a spasm of need only partly sexual.

Trying to make light of it, she said, "Oh, that really helped," but her whisper was husky and unnatural.

He opened the driver's side door to her Bronco and bundled her in without much finesse. Voices on the radio crackled, tugging her back from never-never land.

"Oh, no!" she said, as he jumped in the other side. "I can't come home with you. I have to go to the hospital."

"Why?"

"Because I told Marjorie Rosler…" Well, no, she hadn't, Renee remembered. She took a breath. "I think Dick killed Gabe. He's the only one who could have written those letters."

Shock and then understanding crossed Daniel's face. "Does Marjorie know?"

Renee bit her lip and nodded.

"Will he live?"

Recalling that glimpse of his face, blue and still, she said quietly, "No. I don't think so. I hope not."

"You being there might make it all worse for Marjorie."

Renee went still, thinking. "Maybe," she admitted. "But…"

"You can't let it go." His tone was carefully nonjudgmental; he wasn't expressing anger or disappointment or hurt, although Renee guessed he was feeling all of those.

She turned to look at him. Would he be waiting an hour or three hours from now, if she *didn't* let it go?

But all she had to do was look deep into his eyes to know that he would be. He would never issue her an ultimatum.

He wouldn't leave her.

Tears clogged her throat and burned her eyes. "I'll call the hospital," she said with a sniff. "You're right. Nobody there needs me."

"Somebody here does."

"I need to be here." She had one of those moments of profound understanding that came to her like a lightning bolt but, she suspected, would have seemed obvious to anyone not as dense about love and family. "I need that," Renee said steadily, "more than I've ever needed anything in my life."

Daniel's eyes closed; a muscle ticked in his cheek. Then he looked at her with stark vulnerability. "I will make up for everything you've ever missed," he vowed.

"I believe you will," she whispered. "But it won't be one-sided."

"No." He reached out a shaking hand, touched her damp cheek. "Let's go home," he said roughly. "I want to make love to my wife-to-be."

EPILOGUE

RENEE DID CALL the hospital that afternoon. Dick Rosler had died en route.

She attended his funeral, as she did his son's, a simple ceremony held two weeks after the father's. Besides Marjorie, Daniel was the only one Renee ever told about her suspicion that Gabe's father had killed him. She closed the file, noting that after so many intervening years the murder was unsolvable, and sent a copy to Marjorie Rosler.

Theon Josiah Harris, aka T. J. Baxter, turned out to be alive if not content, ensconced as he was in the Washington State Penitentiary in Walla Walla. He was serving a twelve-year sentence for rape as well as violation of parole for a previous conviction.

Shirley went through agonies of guilt, thinking she might have prevented at least one of the other rapes if she'd gone to the police, but with Anne McWhirter's help, she came to terms with the pain and helplessness of that night.

Renee's house was sold within weeks of the sign going up in the front yard. Abby was maid of honor at her wedding.

She did plan to institute a search for their mother, but after all these years, what was the hurry?

And then one day, Meg came home.

THE BABY AND THE BADGE

To all members of my writers' group,
all good friends and kind critics.

PROLOGUE

"JOHNNY!" Meg Patton protested. She batted at his hand, cupping her breast. "Stop! We don't have time."

And she had to talk to him. Talk, not…well, do *this*. She'd asked him specially to slip away from campus at lunchtime and come home with her. She had to be alone with him. To tell him.

"Come on," her boyfriend coaxed. "What's the big deal? So what if we're five minutes late to class? Like they're going to call our parents or something."

If he'd been intending to reassure her, he failed. She shuddered at the very idea. "No, really," she said, grabbing his wrist. "Besides, what if my dad came home and caught us?"

"In the middle of the day?" Johnny grinned, his warm brown eyes soft with desire for her. "You said yourself he never does."

"Yes, but…" She closed her eyes when he kissed her.

Oh, the way he kissed! His lips were needy, and the feel of his tongue inside her mouth always melted her knees. How could she help but kiss him back?

He peeled off her shirt, unhooked her bra.

"We should…at least…go up to my bedroom," she whispered, her head falling back as he nibbled on her neck. "In case…"

"In case what?" He sucked on her breast and held her up when her legs buckled.

"In case…" She couldn't think.

"Your dad's not coming home." He scooped up the hem of her little short skirt and whisked down her panties.

Oh, this wouldn't take long, Meg told herself. And it felt so good. She unbuttoned the fly of his jeans, feeling his weight bump against her. So good.

"Here," he said, depositing her on the couch. Johnny dropped to his knees in front of her.

Meg felt him nudging at her and closed her eyes. "Yes," she whispered. "Like this."

She heard something outside—a car door slamming?—but it didn't matter. Only this mattered. Not until footsteps sounded heavy on the porch, a key scraped the lock, did the fire of terror burn away the fog of sexual desire.

"Oh, my God!" she cried. "Johnny…!"

He'd heard, too. He was falling away from her, yanking his jeans up, when Meg's father walked into the living room.

In his uniform, with the wide black belt and the gun at his hip, he looked ten feet tall and near as wide, filling the living room with silent rage.

Meg pulled down her skirt and crossed her arms over her breasts. Her shirt, she saw with a frantic glance, was out of reach.

Johnny had gotten to his feet and was trying to button his jeans over his erection. Her father stared at it with violence in his eyes.

His gaze turned to her and she shrank back. "Get dressed."

She couldn't seem to move.

"Get dressed!" her father shouted. "I won't have a whore sitting here naked in my living room!"

"Sir, I..." Johnny's voice squeaked, broke. He was still fumbling with his fly. "It's not her fault. I..."

Her father crossed the room. His fist smashed into Johnny's face. Her boyfriend fell across the coffee table right in front of her. Blood splattered his face, and she screamed.

Her father went after him. His boot lashed out, and Meg heard Johnny's rib snap. He curled on the floor in a fetal position.

She was screaming still, screaming, screaming. Her father backhanded her, and pain exploded across her cheek.

"Get up!" he ordered. He kicked Johnny again. "Get up. Face me like a man."

Through her tears she saw Johnny push himself to his knees, then shakily rise to his feet. He wiped blood and tears from his face with his forearm.

"How do you feel about my daughter?" her father asked coldly.

"I..." Johnny swallowed. "I don't know."

Meg stared in disbelief, the pain in her cheek nothing compared to the agony in her chest.

"Are you ever going to touch her again?"

Johnny didn't look at her. "No, sir."

"Call her?"

Johnny shook his head.

"See her?"

His eye was almost swollen shut. He closed the other one. "No," he whispered.

Out of nowhere, her father punched him again, his

fist connecting with the swollen eye. Johnny screamed and went down again.

"What if she calls you?"

Johnny, her Johnny—the football player, the jock, whose swagger had every girl in school swooning—began crawling toward the front door.

Her father kicked him, his voice a crack like a rifle shot. "What if she calls you?"

"I'll hang up!"

One more kick. "Then get the hell out of here!" Ed Patton snarled.

Johnny staggered to his feet and ran, swaying. Meg heard the front door open and close, and a moment later the sound of a car engine, the screech of tires.

A sixteen-year-old girl, she was left alone to face her father, the man she hated and feared with every fiber of her being.

He must never know. Whatever she did, her father must never find out what she hadn't had time to tell Johnny.

She lifted her chin and waited for the first blow.

CHAPTER ONE

MEG HAD NEVER BEEN so scared in her life, not even facing down her father. Not even in boot camp, when she'd been sure she wouldn't make it through but had no idea how else she'd survive and support her infant son.

But he was fourteen now, and Meg would die before she'd let her son see her stark terror.

"Well." She gazed at the modern red-brick public safety building that stood across the snow-covered street from where she'd parked. An American flag fluttered on a pole in front. Leafless trees stood at attention like soldiers along the sidewalk, shoveled bare. "Here we are."

"Cool!" Her son unsnapped his seat belt. "Let's go in."

She wanted to sit here and think about this some more. Lots more. Maybe for half an hour. Maybe until it was time to get a hotel room for the night.

But she took a deep breath, reached for her purse and said, "Right behind you."

As she trailed him across the street, minding her footing so she didn't slip and fall, her heart was a knot of longing and fear, her stomach a ball of nausea. Oh, God, why was she doing this? She'd had a good life! After thirteen years in the Army, she'd been respected, well-established in her career, financially solvent. She was raising a terrific kid with no help, thank you. Why try to fix something that wasn't broken?

But she knew the answer perfectly well: because she thought about her sisters every day, wondered what kind of women they'd grown into, suffered guilt because she wasn't there to help them.

Because her son had the right to meet his father. For better or worse. But not, please God, today. She could face Renee, even if her sister hated her, but not Johnny, too.

Brass letters on brick above the double doors formed the words Elk Springs Police Department. No more old granite building; she'd gone there first, but it was an antique mall now. She'd have to check it out one of these days. After she and Will had gotten settled.

Settled. Her stomach took another dive. What if Renee and Abby didn't want her back in their lives? Meg wouldn't blame them.

Fresh panic roiled. She shouldn't have burned her bridges. She should have made this a visit, not a permanent move.

Too late.

Ahead of her, Will pushed open one of the doors, then remembered his manners long enough to hold it so that it didn't swing shut in her face. A true gentleman.

At fourteen, he was starting to look uncomfortably like a man. Just in the past few months, he'd begun to shave. Only once in a while, but the milestone had come nonetheless. She was used to his height—he'd passed her by the age of twelve—but now his shoulders were developing bulk, too, and his voice was deepening.

Scary.

Was this the worst of all times to make such a major change in their lives? Meg worried. Hormones were going to cause enough trouble without him being rejected by his father, too. Or what if…

His nudge jarred her back to the here and now. They were already inside the police station, looking around a lobby that could have belonged to a doctor's office: shining vinyl floor, rows of comfortable chairs, magazines strewn on low tables. A middle-age couple sat together, murmuring to each other; a sulky teenage girl slouched at the far end, staring down at her feet. Behind a long counter waited a uniformed officer.

"May I help you, ma'am?"

"Yes. I'm looking for Renee Patton."

"Renee?" His expression changed. "Hey, aren't you…?"

"Yes." She forced a smile. "I'm her sister."

"Well!" He looked pleased. "Isn't that something?"

Agonizing impatience warred with gratitude at the reprieve chatting with him gave her. "Yes," she agreed meaninglessly.

"Did you think she used her maiden name on the job?" he asked, resting his elbows comfortably on the counter.

Maiden name? That meant… She mentally gulped. Her scrawny little sister was *married?*

Meg gave her head a bemused shake. "Yes, I…" She backtracked, unwilling to admit she didn't know her own sister was married. Didn't know anything about her sister since she'd been fourteen years old, except that she'd become a cop. "Well, no. It was just…habit. We've been Pattons a long time."

He chuckled. "Yeah. I can see how that would happen."

Will stirred.

"Um…is she here?" Meg asked.

"What? Oh, yeah. Sure. Far as I know, she's in her office." He turned. "What the heck, here she comes now."

Forgetting to breathe, Meg stared. Absorbed in conversation, two police officers were coming down the long hall toward the lobby. One was so downy-cheeked he had to be a recruit. The other…

Even in uniform, Renee was beautiful and unmistakably a Patton. Her cheeks had fleshed out, her hips rounded, she had *breasts*. Meg had a flash, remembering her sister, the little kid, vowing never to get breasts.

"They're gross!" she'd proclaimed, scrunching up her face. "They bounce up and down, and you have to wear a stupid bra, and they stick out."

Rolling her eyes, Meg had told her, "You can't just decide something like that. I mean, you either get big ones or you don't."

"If I do, I'll…I'll bind them!" Renee had declared fiercely. "Like Deborah Sampson. You know, that girl who pretended to be a boy and fought in the Revolutionary war. I read about her the other day. She just wrapped this cloth around her chest." Renee demonstrated. "And *flattened* them."

"You do that," Meg had agreed, humoring her little sister. "Whatever makes you happy."

For a while there, Renee's resolve had seemed to work; she was still skinny and flat at fourteen when Meg ran away from home.

Well, Renee had breasts now, Meg observed, and immediately felt foolish. What, she thought her sister really would figure out how not to mature physically?

Renee still hadn't noticed her. Why should she? Meg reminded herself. Think how she must have changed, too!

"Is that Aunt Renee?" Will whispered.

Heart cramped, Meg couldn't have answered to save her life. She suddenly wanted to bolt. What if Renee recognized her and deliberately turned away? What if she didn't care, hadn't missed her big sister? What if anger was stronger than love?

Will said something. She didn't hear because Renee had spotted her.

Her sister stopped, just froze midstride. "Meg?"

Hot tears burned Meg's eyes. She didn't cry. She'd always figured she'd run out of tears, all those years ago when she'd used so many.

"Renee." Her voice choked, cracked.

"Meg." Renee couldn't seem to say anything else. She only stared, as Meg had done a moment before. And then she was crying, too.

They met at a waist-high swinging door at one end of the counter. They hugged so hard the door cut into Meg's stomach, but she didn't care. She was crying on her sister's uniform collar, but she didn't care about that, either.

Her skinny little sister was a woman now, but somehow she still felt the same. Smelled the same, a hint of vanilla that seemed to go with her white, white skin and pale blond hair.

"I've missed you so much," Meg mumbled.

"Have you?" Abruptly Renee pushed her away. Her face was soaked with tears, her eyes red, puffy. She gave an angry swipe at her wet cheeks. "Then why didn't you call? Write? Not even once? Why the hell did you…did you…" Her mouth worked, but she couldn't seem to finish. Fresh tears were pouring out.

"Desert you?"

Stilling the hands wiping her cheeks, her sister nodded.

"I… It's a long story." Understatement of the century. She glanced back to check on Will, who hadn't moved. "I need to blow my nose."

"Me, too." Renee sniffed. "Let's go back to my office. No… I'll just take the rest of the day off. You'll come home with me, won't you?"

"Home isn't still…" She hadn't driven by, however tempted. Her sisters first.

"No. I've gotten married and sold the house."

"Anybody I know?"

"Daniel Barnard. You went to school with him."

"I remember." She'd had a brief crush on him in about eighth grade. He'd been a foot taller than everyone else, so awkward he was always tripping over his own feet, but those eyes! So blue they looked like heaven. "He was nice," she said.

Her sister grinned. "Still is. He's cuter now, too." Her smile faded. "Are you married?"

"No, but…" Meg turned. "I have a son."

Renee's breath caught as her gaze followed Meg's. "Dear Lord," she whispered. "He could be Jack. You were *pregnant?*"

It wasn't so much a question as an exclamation, but Meg answered, anyway. "Yes. If Dad had known…"

Her sister gave her a single, horrified glance.

What she'd said finally caught up with Meg. "Why does he call himself Jack now?"

"I don't know. He has pretty much since you left. He was different after that." Renee shrugged helplessly. "I figured it had to do with you going. You did know he's the police chief, didn't you? I can check to see if he's in if you want…."

"No." Meg had to call on every grain of self-will she possessed not to bolt. "No. I knew he was police chief. But I'm not ready... I hoped we wouldn't run into him today. Eventually I'll have to tell him, but..."

Renee touched her arm. "It's okay. He won't come out here." A frown crinkled her brow. "But how did you know?"

"The same way I knew Dad was dead. I ran into Pete Branagh. I'd taken Will and some of his buddies to Disneyland. Can you believe it? Just out of the blue."

She still remembered the shock, her first instinct to pretend she wasn't Meg Patton, that he was mistaken. But the pharmacist—retired now—had been a nice guy, and there wasn't any reason to hide anymore. Nobody was going to take Will away from her. And so they'd talked about the old Elk Springs and the new.

"Are you going to introduce me to your son?"

Meg gave herself a shake. After a surreptitious glance toward that long hall—empty—she said, "I'm sorry. Of course I am. Will?"

He came to her side, his head ducked shyly.

"Meet your aunt Renee."

Across the counter, Renee extended her hand. "It's a pleasure, Will."

He took it, a flush running across his cheekbones.

Meg stole another glance at the hall.

Renee tore her bemused gaze from Will. "Let me check out and we'll go home. You can, um, see other old friends another time."

"Bless you," Meg said, meaning it. "Can we drive by the old place, or is that out of the way?"

"Not by much. You bet."

"I'll have to follow you. I'm not sure I could find it from here. This town has grown."

"Big time," her sister said. "You know about the new ski area?" Her expression changed. "Oh, my gosh. Abby. Shall I call her? Or do you want to do it yourself?"

"She's still here, too? In Elk Springs?" At Renee's nod, Meg felt more tears spring to her eyes. Will stared at her in astonishment. He'd think she'd morphed into some sitcom mother if she didn't watch out. She blinked, sniffed, came to a decision. "I'll do it. When I get to your place."

Renee leaned awkwardly over the counter, gave her another quick, hard hug, then retreated, looking embarrassed. "I'm parked out back—four-by-four with a rack of lights."

"Gotcha. Red Subaru station wagon," Meg said over her shoulder, steering Will toward the door. The hall behind them was still deserted; in her eagerness to make good her escape, she marched Will out double-time.

"But, Mom! *He* might be here." *His* identity was no secret. "Why do we have to go so quick?"

Because I'm not ready to run into your father. How did she explain that one? Will wanted more than anything in the world to meet his father. As far as he was concerned, Johnny Murray was why they'd come to Elk Springs.

"He doesn't know you exist. We shouldn't spring it on him in public. Especially in front of the people who work for him."

The look he gave her over the roof of the car told her he knew she was making excuses, but he waited until they were buckled in to say, "But he might be *here*."

The thought was enough to make Meg break out in

a cold sweat. She was all too aware that Johnny might be looking out one of those windows right now.

Take a deep breath. Don't hyperventilate, she told herself.

She met her son's eyes. "Will. Not yet. Please. Let me…let me find out what Renee and Abby think first. This is…a big step for me."

His outrage shifted into perplexity. "Aunt Renee was happy to see you."

"Maybe. But it won't be that easy." She swallowed. "I abandoned them. 'I'm sorry' won't be good enough. When they find out I'm trying to horn my way back in to the family, I may get the cold shoulder. That will…hurt."

"Here she comes," he said.

A Bronco topped with police lights pulled onto the street. Behind the wheel, Renee waved. Meg jockeyed out of the parking spot and fell in behind her.

"Mom." Will swallowed. "Aunt Renee will understand. I mean, she *loves* you."

Tears stung Meg's eyes again and she felt as if her heart might burst. She had him; that was enough.

But she hoped it wouldn't have to be. *He* needed more.

"Thank you," Meg said when she could. She blinked hard a couple of times and made herself look around at the new buildings on every side. Fancy stoplights had replaced signs at every intersection. "I don't know where anything is," she said, trying her best to sound like the mom he knew. "This was a little town. Now it looks like Southern California! There's an espresso stand on every corner, and a mall. A mall! Who the heck shops there?"

"Mom." Will gave her a look. "Elk Springs doesn't

look like L.A. Trust me. This is Podunk, U.S.A. I can't believe it didn't *have* a mall."

Meg hardly listened. "I knew they put in a ski area, but jeez!" Main Street used to have a Woolworth's and a Sears catalog store. Now… With her head swiveling she had to brake sharply when the light changed ahead, feeling the tires slip on the packed snow. Careless. She was too used to sunshine. But her thoughts reverted to the astonishing sight of her hometown.

"Art galleries," she muttered. "Designer clothes. And what's that?" With difficulty, she made out the script. "Holistic health!"

"Cool-looking bookstore," Will observed.

She hardly heard him. "And the restaurants! I can't believe it."

"You know," her son said, "it's been like, fifteen years since you've been here. Did you think you were time traveling or something?"

Wisdom from a teenager. One of life's little miracles.

"Okay, okay," she agreed, putting the Subaru in gear now that the light had turned green. "You're right. Time marches on. My waistline isn't quite what it was fifteen years ago, either. But still. This was an isolated ranching community. Suddenly, it's Aspen, Colorado, transported a few states west."

"Not suddenly."

"Are you trying to make me feel old?"

"You *are* old."

"Brat," she said amiably, and he grinned.

A right turn and they were crossing the Deschutes on a bridge she remembered. The thick concrete railing had been dated September 1939; the bridge was the work of WPA workers during the Depression.

How many times had she walked over that bridge on her way to town to hang out with friends or buy an ice cream cone or just get out of the house? She remembered how hot the rough concrete got under the summer sun as she rested her arms on it and dreamed, mesmerized by the slow, swirling current below. Just downstream the ducks and swans gathered at the park, hoping for handouts. There the willows dangled fingers of green in the water. She could smell it now, though it was January, the whole landscape snowy white and the car windows rolled up: the pines and grass, new-mown, and the river and the red volcanic dirt. Home. Her throat closed.

"Mom?"

She blinked.

"Are you crying again?"

"No." Meg cleared her throat. "Don't be silly. I was just…remembering something."

Will bounced in his seat like an impatient toddler. "Are we almost there?"

"Yep. We're almost there."

The neighborhood had changed hardly at all. The houses were still gracious, the yards well-groomed, the shade trees mature, though bare of leaf. Whoever shopped at the boutiques along Main Street, they didn't live here. These were old-time residents, people she might have known. Ones who probably didn't know what "holistic" meant and didn't care.

"There," she said, tension entering her voice. The brake lights flickered ahead as Renee slowed. "There's where I grew up."

Will turned his head as they passed, studying the white house with a wide porch, the picket fence and snowy sweep of yard, green in summer, that went right down to the riverbank. Now a tire swing hung from a huge old sycamore and a child's pink bike, spoke-deep in snow, blocked the paved walkway. A wooden sled leaned against the porch.

Her father must be rolling over in his grave, Meg thought with pleasure.

"It's not that big," Will said.

"Big?" she echoed, surprised.

"Well… You made it sound like some haunted house. You know. This huge dark place with lots of empty rooms where you had to tiptoe around because something might jump out at you. Boo! Like that."

In her memory, the house was bigger. But her father was the only one who'd jump out. They *had* tiptoed. Always. If Dad heard you… If Dad found out… If Dad even *guessed*…

"No, it's a perfectly ordinary house," Meg said to her son. Who never tiptoed. "A nice house. There are four bedrooms, but no family room. They didn't build 'em in those days. With different people living there, it could even be a cheerful house."

Giving it a last, lingering look in the rearview mirror, she thought maybe it *was* cheerful now, that it liked having a tire swing and a little girl's bike cluttering up the sidewalk.

And *she* liked the idea of her father forever restless in his grave.

Renee led them out of town down Butte Road toward the red volcanic cinder cone that held memories for every local teenager. She and Johnny had climbed and slid down, laughing hysterically. They'd parked there and necked and drank illicit beer, feeling like rebels, like grown-ups. While proving, she thought now, that they definitely weren't.

She remembered passing the gates of the Triple B, although she'd never been to Daniel Barnard's home. Renee's Bronco turned under the peeled pole arch with the ranch name burned into the crosspiece, the Subaru right behind it. A crushed cinder lane divided dry high-desert scrub: stunted junipers and sagebrush, everything gray-green but the dirt and the traces of snow. At a Y, Renee bore to the left and headed up a lava ridge to a gorgeous new Craftsman-style house commanding the ranch.

Meg parked beside her sister's vehicle and climbed out, looking below at the sprawling barns and green pastures. Mountains one direction, the working ranch and vast dry land beyond. She bet the sunrises and sunsets were really something here.

"Horses," Will said eagerly from beside her. "Do you think I could ride?"

Having joined them, Renee said without hesitation, "Are you kidding? Daniel—my husband—trains world-class cutting horses. He'll be thrilled if someone else in the family is interested."

"Cool!" Will said.

To Meg's relief, he'd apparently accepted the delay in meeting his father. His aunt and uncle were enough.

"Daniel's mother lives in the original house," Renee said, waving at the white clapboard place set among cottonwoods along a creek. "She's a sweetie. I'm lucky."

"I vaguely remember her from school." Meg frowned, thinking back. "She volunteered in the library, I think. I liked her better than the librarian."

As they started up the porch steps, Renee asked, "How long are you here for? We have plenty of room for you. You will stay, won't you?"

"Tonight we will," Meg agreed. "Actually…" Why was this so hard to say? "Well, we're here for good."

Renee stopped, staring with her mouth opening and closing like a puffer fish's. "For good? You're moving back here?"

"Yeah." Meg tried for nonchalance with her shrug, but defensiveness crept into her tone. "Why so surprised? Once I heard that Dad had died, I just…thought it was time to come home. This wasn't a bad place to raise a kid, you know."

"But…what will you *do?* For a living? There aren't that many good jobs here…"

Renee didn't want her here. Meg heard the truth, loud and clear. It hurt. Oh, God, it hurt.

"I already have a job." She was terribly conscious of the anxiety on Will's face. Of the burned bridges behind her. "I start Monday."

"You applied for a job here, and you didn't even call me?" Renee's expression closed and her voice chilled. "Well, it's your business. Don't feel you have to stay tonight if you've already rented a place."

"I was hoping you'd help me find a house," Meg said quietly. "I didn't come for an interview. They hired me sight unseen."

Her sister was unlocking the front door. "Oh?" she said distantly. "What will you be doing?"

"Law enforcement." As Renee turned back to her in shock, Meg smiled. "I'm a cop, too. Apparently, it runs in the family. I'll be a county sheriff's deputy. The guy who hired me knew Dad."

Renee looked as if a grenade had knocked her flat. Even so, she said, "But not like we did."

"No," Meg agreed, her smile twisting. "Not like we did."

Her little sister shook her head in dazed disbelief one more time before stepping into a slate-floored entry. Spreading her arms wide, she said, "My house is yours, and all that." At last, at last, her voice softened. "Welcome home, Meg."

AFTER DINNER Will went off to the barn with his newly discovered uncle Daniel, and the three sisters finally had time to talk.

Meg couldn't stop looking at them. Renee drinking coffee, Abby tea, they sat on opposite ends of the gorgeous, deep-cushioned leather sofa in the Barnard living room. Their postures mimicked each other; both had tucked their feet under them, lounging with the boneless comfort of two slender cats who were nonetheless aware of every sound, every movement.

It seemed fitting, Meg thought, that she was in the easy chair facing them, the coffee table a barrier symbolizing the years since she had seen them, the silence nobody wanted to talk about even now that they could.

How old had they been? Abby eleven and Renee fourteen when she left that terrible day. Girls. Skinny and blond and unfinished. Renee burying her anger, Abby so sweet even their father had been soft on her. *They would be all right,* she'd told herself, unable to let herself believe anything else. She couldn't stay, not pregnant, not once Johnny had betrayed her. Even if he hadn't, she recognized now, she wouldn't dare have stayed. For the baby she'd already carried, she had to go.

Would her sisters understand?

They gazed at her, Renee's eyes green-gold, Abby's sky-blue like Meg's, both curious but wary, as well. Their pleasure in seeing her was genuine, Meg thought, but they felt other emotions, too, that they couldn't yet articulate. Renee had asked just the once why Meg had never called or written; she had been careful since not to let the conversation wander close to the subject.

"I was only a girl," Meg said, startling them. "I didn't know what to do."

"What *did* you do?" asked Abby over the rim of her teacup.

"I packed." Meg looked at Renee. "You remember. You helped."

Her middle sister nodded.

"I stole money from Dad."

"Really?" Renee's eyes widened, as though the idea of doing so was unimaginable.

As it had once been for Meg. Only desperation so deep, she'd known there was no alternative, had sent her creeping into her father's bedroom. Hands shaking, she'd opened first the drawers in his nightstand, then his bureau. One had jammed, she remembered. She had battered it with her hands, her tears falling hot and wet on his undershirts. She could still see those splotches on the pristine white knit, and even though she was there to do something much worse, she'd been terrified at how angry he'd be that his shirts would have to be washed again.

In the bottom drawer, she'd found a gun, and the money.

"A thousand dollars," she said now. "Ten hundred-dollar bills in an envelope. I don't know why he kept so much in cash. It was between the folds of a shirt he never wore, not like he'd just been to the bank. This was hidden."

They exchanged unreadable glances, her sisters, then gazed back at her, still watchful, still expectant.

"And then you…hitchhiked? Took a bus?" Abby prodded.

"No." She looked back at them, feeling oddly detached. "I did take a bus, but first… After I made Renee go to her friend's house, I searched Dad's closet."

"Why?" Renee asked simply.

"Because I thought he might have something that would tell me where Mom had gone. So that I could find her."

Their expressions didn't change. "But he didn't," Renee said. "I went through all his stuff after he died."

Meg took a breath. "Then, he'd thrown away her letters. So you couldn't find them, too."

"Too?" they echoed in unison.

"You mean," Abby said, very carefully, "she wrote to him?"

"To us," Meg corrected. The box had sat on the shelf in the back corner of his closet. Inside, the flap ripped open, were the photographs of their mother the girls had hungered for. A wedding picture. An album filled with photos of her with first one baby, then a toddler and a second baby, and finally all three daughters. Dad must have snapped them himself, because he was never in any.

Though the letters were on top, Meg had looked at the pictures first, because Mom's face was already fading in her memory, first softening around the edges, then becoming fuzzy, until she couldn't bring it into focus at all. But here she was, blond and slender with

Renee's eyes, and a million memories rushed back, one image after another like old-fashioned cards that you flipped through to create animation.

At last she'd picked up the letters, all addressed to them. Abby and Renee and Meg. Dozens and dozens of envelopes, all unopened.

Why had he kept them? She would never know.

She had sat cross-legged on the floor, tearing them open, reading as many as she dared in the time she thought she had. The addresses neatly written in the upper left-hand corner of each envelope had changed as the years passed. The letters had come further and further apart, unless he hadn't kept them all. They had finally stopped a year before.

She'd taken that one, though she had also memorized the address in San Jose, California.

"So, you went looking for her. For Mom," Renee said in a voice like glass, as though she didn't quite believe it.

The dreaded moment had come, but Meg wouldn't let herself shirk.

"Yes," she said, meeting their eyes. Her sisters, who would never know their mother. "And I found her."

CHAPTER TWO

AS USUAL, he was the last one left in the vast dark lodge.

Scott McNeil flicked off his computer, stretching while the screen went dark. Nothing he'd been doing was particularly urgent; it could have waited. But why should it? His empty house didn't exactly beckon.

Frowning at the realization—not new—that he was hiding out in his office, Scott grabbed his parka, locked the door behind him and headed down the stairs.

The huge lodge was silent, the night lighting dim. During the day, ski boots thumped up and down the broad, battered wooden stairs. Goggles and parkas and gloves heaped the tables and floors as skiers ate chili or hamburgers from the café, warmed their hands on foam cups of cocoa or espresso, before hitting the slopes again.

Racks of clothing made hulking silhouettes in the ski shop, locked and dark but for the night-light. The banks of lockers were all closed.

Scott turned down a narrow hallway and went out an employee entrance into the cold. He rattled the door to be sure it locked. From a distance away, a flashlight was trained on him. Scott lifted a hand. "Good night."

Two security officers patrolled after-hours. The one who'd spotted him called, "'Night, Boss."

The path to the employee lot was trampled between banks of deep snow. A cloud veiled the moon, making the night pitch-black except for the sickly yellow glow from the sodium lights in the parking lot.

He was a hundred yards away when he saw that something pale sat beside the driver's door of his Jeep Grand Cherokee. He squinted, trying to make out the shape. Looked like a tall box. Strange. If somebody wanted to leave something for him, why hadn't they come by his office?

He'd covered half the distance when he identified the shape. A car seat. It was a baby's car seat, just resting upright on the packed snow where someone had set it. The back was to him as he approached.

There wouldn't be a kid in it. He didn't know why he felt his gut tightening. Somebody was junking a broken car seat. That's all. Nobody would set a kid down and forget him.

And then he heard…a whimper. Followed by a thin sad wail that lifted the hairs on the back of his neck.

"Oh, my God."

In a couple of running steps, he reached the child seat and dropped to his knees on the snow. Tiny mittened hands flapped and the cry increased in intensity. The baby was alive and well—couldn't have been out here long, because even earlier, in the sun of the afternoon, the mercury hadn't risen above freezing.

"It's okay," he murmured, rage whistling through him like an icy wind scouring the mountain summit. "We'll get you inside. We'll find your mommy or daddy."

Back to the lodge? But he had nothing there to feed this baby. If he called 9-1-1, it would take someone half an hour to get here, another half hour to turn around and head back to town. The ski resort was on Forest Service land, so no condos or inns clustered at the base of the mountain. The nearest private land was twenty miles down the road.

Making a decision, Scott scooped up the whole car seat and hurried to the passenger side of his Jeep. He buckled the child seat in, under the dome light finally able to see the baby better.

Six months old, give or take a few weeks. Nose and round cheeks red from the cold. Huge dark eyes staring at him, a fringe of brown hair beneath a knitted hat. A yellow hat, green snowsuit, orange mittens, which didn't help him guess gender. Nice clothes, as if someone had cared.

"Who left you?" Scott murmured. "Your mommy or daddy? Would they do something like that?"

The kid opened its mouth and screamed. Who could blame him/her?

Even so, Scott grabbed his flashlight from the glove compartment and took a minute to scan the area. No note he could see, nothing left but the baby.

God Almighty. He—she—couldn't be simply forgotten, as sometimes happened when parents got confused about who had which kid. Skiers would have had no business in this parking lot. Besides, the lifts had shut down hours ago. Anybody would have realized long since that the baby was missing.

He shone the light around for a moment more, then gave up. If there were tracks worth spotting, they'd still be here tomorrow, frozen solid. Snow wasn't expected tonight.

He backed out, then despite the ascending cry, took

a fast sweep through the area parking lots. Not a single vehicle was here that shouldn't be.

Why, in God's name, would you leave a baby sitting out in the cold? What if he'd decided to bunk down in the lodge, as he did occasionally?

At the very thought, fury and a kind of agony crushed his chest. How could anybody do something like this?

He'd had pleasanter drives. His passenger cried for the entire half hour, going from sad gulping sobs to window shattering screams. The kid could hit a hell of a high note. And sustain it. He'd forgotten…

Don't go there, he told himself on a clench of pain. Think about this baby. Not… But he didn't let the name form.

He passed his own road. A couple miles farther was a resort with condos, a classy restaurant, sporting goods, an ice skating rink and a small store where he sometimes picked up milk or a six-pack. Scott assumed guests must occasionally need baby formula.

He left the child in the car and hurried in. Thank God he was right; a selection of plastic bottles in neon colors, packages of nipples and three brands of formula shared a shelf. He chose some of each, plus a pacifier. Maybe he could plug that mouth temporarily. On the shelf below were diapers, which now seemed to come in girl and boy varieties, not to mention sizes. He grabbed the one package that wasn't gender specific.

The clerk rang it all up without comment.

Back in the car, Scott ripped open the packaging and popped that pacifier right in. After the smallest hesitation, the rosebud mouth closed around it and began sucking so hard, it rocked up and down like a fishing bob.

In the blessed near silence, Scott drove home. Feed

the baby, then call the cops, he figured. First things first.

By the time he rolled to a stop in his garage, the pacifier hurtled out hard enough to hit the dashboard and the siren began again.

"Not getting any milk, huh?" Garage door closed, Scott went around and unbuckled the baby, leaving the seat where it was. Expertly, he lifted the kid to his shoulder and jiggled. "Pretty frustrating, I know. Just give me a minute, and we can do something about it."

He spread a lap quilt on the leather couch, laid the baby on it, and began unpeeling layers of outerwear. Inside were cute pink overalls, soaking wet, and a tiny turtleneck with pink and yellow butterflies all over it. Lifting the little butt, he took off the overalls and the soggy diaper.

Definitely a girl. For reasons he didn't let himself analyze, that was a relief. No rash, so he didn't do anything but pat her dry and put on a clean diaper. That momentarily silenced her.

Formula warmed in the microwave, he tucked her in the crook of his arm and popped that nipple right in her mouth. She sucked with fierce concentration. He'd never seen the level in a bottle go down so quick.

Okay, she hadn't been out in the cold long, but she hadn't been fed in hours.

The whole thing didn't make sense. Where were her parents? Had she been snatched, and then the kidnapper panicked?

About the time she hit the bottom of the bottle, her eyelids got heavy. He rocked gently, murmuring a nearly forgotten song. At last the nipple fell from her slack mouth and he'd have sworn a tiny snore emerged.

Moving as carefully as if he were traversing an avalanche slope, Scott eased down the hall, grabbing some blankets from the linen closet on the way. In his bedroom, he set her on the bed, then pulled a drawer from his bureau and dumped its contents on the floor. Putting it down beside the bed, he padded it carefully, nestled her on her back inside it and tucked a quilt around her. Exhausted, she didn't even stir.

Babies slept as wholeheartedly as they did everything else. He'd forgotten. Nate had always frowned...

Scott bit off an obscenity and retreated, switching off the light as he went. Outside the bedroom, he stopped, then swore again and went back. Light from the hall fell in a band across the floor, touching her with pale grace.

He crouched beside the drawer and watched, waiting for her to puff out a breath, move, do *something* to show life. Her face was still, soft and pale. Tension rose in him until he couldn't bear it and had to lift the quilt. Her small chest rose and fell, rose and fell, and his anxiety quieted. He gently tucked the bedding back around her and slipped out of the room.

In the kitchen he went straight to the telephone, dialed 9-1-1 and told the dispatcher, "I found a baby."

MEG DISCOVERED how much of a coward she really was when the end of her shift neared and, instead of groaning, she was relieved to have to go out on a call. Relieved, so she didn't have to go home.

Because if she went home, Will would want her to phone Jack.

Her son wasn't alone in his opinion. Renee would probably call—again—to nag.

"You *have* to do it," she'd said yesterday evening.

"He knows you're back. What if somebody mentions Will? Even if nobody says anything about the resemblance, once Jack finds out Will's age, he'll know. Wouldn't you rather tell him?"

"Yes," Meg had agreed meekly. "Of course you're right. I know I have to. I just thought it'd be nice to get settled in first."

"You *are* settled in," Renee said crisply. "Tell him about Will. Soon. You've got me slinking around the police station hoping I don't see him, because he'll ask me about you, and something might slip out, or he might be able to tell I'm hiding something… For Pete's sake, I did *traffic* duty yesterday, just to be sure Jack couldn't corner me."

"Tomorrow, when I get home from work," Meg had promised. And she'd meant it.

But now, if she was lucky, this would take a while, and by the time she got home and had something to eat and listened to Will talk about his day, it would be too late to call Jack.

The duty officer had given her the option of going home. It was, after all, her first day as a Butte County sheriff's deputy and her shift was over. Meg had been hired, however, to work part-time in Investigations and part-time as a "youth" officer. Juvenile crime was rising; the sheriff's department was being asked to go into the schools for preventive programs and to crack down on drug use and fighting. Child abuse and neglect was an increasing problem in rural areas of the county as well as in Elk Springs itself. It so happened that the high school was outside the Elk Springs city limits, making it a county sheriff's department problem. When the sheriff got funding for one new officer, he'd chosen to have one who'd specialize in kids. That one was Meg.

So there she was, about to walk out the door, and a call comes in from a guy who says he's found a baby. How could she say, "Oh, just let a patrolman handle it"?

Trouble was, she'd never been good at deceiving herself. And she knew perfectly well she would have seized any excuse that came her way to procrastinate for one more day.

The address was on a dead-end road off the mountain loop highway. The road itself hadn't existed fifteen years ago. Meg hadn't been up that way yet, but she'd heard about the fancy houses that were springing up like seeds scattered by the ski area. This must be one of them. It wouldn't be hard to find, even in the dark.

She gave Will a quick call, squelched his protests and set out. The sheriff's office was out in the flat desert scrub east of town. Tonight she passed within a few blocks of her old neighborhood and crossed the Deschutes River on that Depression era concrete bridge where she had once dreamed.

About Jack.

Meg scowled. *Okay, be honest,* she told herself. She'd come home partly so that Will could know his father. So why the foot-dragging?

Maybe because she could handle only one emotional issue at a time. And the one that mattered to her right now was reconciling with her sisters.

After Meg had dropped her bombshell that first evening, Renee had stared at her for a long moment, face blank with shock, and then leaped to her feet. Unnoticed, her mug tilted and spilled coffee down the leather arm of the sofa.

"You never told us? You let us think she was *dead?*" Her voice quivered with a sense of betrayal. "How could you do that, Meg?"

Meg bit her lip so hard she tasted blood. "Mom *is* dead. She was dying when I found her. She'd had breast cancer, and apparently when she had the lumpectomy they didn't get it all, because it came back a year later. And then it was in her lymph nodes, and..." She stopped.

"But we could have seen her," Renee wailed with the distress of a child. "Said goodbye."

"Would we have wanted to?" Abby blurted out unexpectedly. "She never said goodbye to us!"

Renee whirled on her sister. "But she wrote! You heard Meg."

"She could have done more." Abby's tone was unforgiving. "Say what you want about Dad, but at least he was *there.* He fed us and raised us and came to school stuff. He didn't just walk away and never come back."

"Mom knew he'd never let go of anything that was *his,*" Renee countered bitterly. "Whatever he felt, it wasn't love."

"How do you know?" Abby snapped. "Maybe he just didn't know how to express what he felt! Maybe his parents were jerks. Maybe he did the best he could."

"Oh, yeah, he always was the softest on you," Renee jeered. "It figures you'd defend him."

"Guys..." Meg began.

Both sisters turned. Abby was the one to speak. "But we should have had the choice of whether we wanted to see Mom again. Why didn't you give us that choice, Meg? You, of all people. You knew how much we wondered about her. How much not having her hurt. How could you be just like him?"

Meg tried to explain. Mom had begged her not to tell the younger girls. It was better if they were angry at her, she'd said. Anything was better than her daughters remembering her as a frail extension of the machines that gave her a semblance of life.

"Later, sometime, tell them that I know I was a coward. I should have fought for you. All of you. But I was being crushed." Her eyes were huge, pathetic, pleading. "Sometimes I couldn't breathe. It was like… like running from an avalanche. Your body says run and you do, and then afterwards you worry about the people you were with. Only then it's too late."

Once she was a parent herself, Meg had remembered and tried to imagine herself running from that avalanche and leaving a child behind. Responding to instinct that said, *Go!* And she had concluded with fierce certainty that a stronger instinct would have had her frantically hunting for her son, throwing her body over his to save him from the crushing weight of snow. She had run once, but to save him; she would never have run if it had meant leaving him.

But she wasn't her mother. Perhaps, for the strength that Jolene Patton had lacked, Meg, Abby and Renee had their father to thank.

Oh, how she hated to be grateful to him for anything.

Meg had tried to convey some of what she knew and felt, but she sensed that her sisters didn't really hear any of it, didn't want to hear it. She was no longer to be trusted. In their opinion, who was she to pass judgment on their mother? Or perhaps they just didn't want to believe that their sainted mother had been flawed.

Renee had calmed down enough to notice the

spilled coffee and grab a dish towel from the kitchen to wipe it up.

Then she sat. "Okay, you honored your promise to Mom." Her tone was hard, unforgiving. "How about later? Couldn't you have let us know after the funeral? Told us she was dead? You were okay? Would one phone call have been so tough?"

Meg gazed back at them and remembered herself, eight months' pregnant, walking across the springy grass at the cemetery, leaving behind her mother's open grave. She had let the symbolic handful of dirt trickle from her fingers onto the shiny casket, listened across the vast distance of the open hole in the ground to the minister who had not even known her mother as he mouthed the traditional send-off. She was alone. Completely alone. She wanted desperately to pick up a phone, hear her sisters' voices, even her father's. She wanted to buy a bus ticket and go home. She could not bear to be so alone and so frightened.

But inside Will had somersaulted and poked her as if to say, *Don't forget me,* and she had known she couldn't go home. Like it or not, she wasn't really alone. She had a child. Although barely seventeen years old, *she* was the mom now.

If she called her sisters, they would dump their fear, their grief, their longing on her, and her own was almost overwhelming.

Now, facing them after the passage of so many years, she closed her eyes, which felt gritty. If only she could cry. In a voice that felt like shattered glass, she said, "One phone call might have killed me. If you'd begged me to come home…"

"We would have understood," Renee said.

"Would you?" She looked from one to the other, and

found no understanding now. How could she have hoped for it then, when they were children? "Think back. What if I'd called and said, 'I found Mom, I just buried her, and I can't come home? If Dad hits you…well, deal.' Would that have comforted you?"

"You could have called regularly." Renee stared at her with dislike. Hatred? "Checked on us. Let us know you were all right."

"I had to cope on my own. Every phone call home would have left me feeling guilty all over again because I couldn't help you. I had to focus everything I had on going forward."

Abby spoke for both. "But we were the ones you left behind."

What more was there to say? What more would there ever be to say? She'd come home fifteen years too late. She'd saved her son by abandoning her sisters. No wonder they couldn't forgive her.

Oh, they were adult enough to lay a veneer over the raw emotion, to pretend that they still loved her, but conversations since that first night had been rocky ground where each foot had to be placed with exquisite care so as not to slice skin and draw blood.

Toward Will, Renee and Abby were warm and welcoming. Daniel Barnard's sister was coming soon for a visit with her young son, which made Will feel as if he even had a cousin.

But he did have first cousins, Meg knew; Renee had told her. Jack's older brother was married. He had two girls, nine and eleven. Jack's mother nudged him often toward marriage, telling him he had to give her grandchildren, too, according to Renee. How would she feel about Will?

Assuming Jack ever told her about the son he hadn't known about.

And that, Meg thought ruefully, was assuming *she* ever told him about the son he *still* didn't know he had.

Which she'd be doing right now if she weren't driving up the mountain loop highway in the dark, instead slowing every time she saw a road turnoff so that she could peer at the small street signs. The highway itself was plowed bare, although snow still lay under the ponderosa pines that became denser as the elevation rose.

She passed the Sunrise Resort, where she could see a lighted ice-skating rink and the aqua glow of a swimming pool with steam rising into the cold night air above it. Another half mile and she at last spotted Sumac Drive. Making a left, Meg followed the road past half a dozen driveways to the end. The number on the mailbox was right.

The driveway curved between pines and manzanita. She drove carefully, following the tracks other vehicles had made. In front of the garage, she set her parking brake and turned off the ignition.

The house was sharp angles and steep roof, glass and window boxes. It reminded her of Alpine villages, although she could see none of the cute shutters or gingerbread that characterized the Swiss chalets. A porch light was on.

She got out, crunched through the snow, and gingerly climbed the steps, shoveled bare but still icy. After ringing the doorbell, Meg didn't have long to wait. The house was too well-insulated for her to hear footsteps; the first she knew was the click of a dead bolt being released. Then the door opened and a large man filled the opening.

He wore cords and a turtleneck; his dark auburn hair was cut severely short. And he was built—six foot two or three, broad-shouldered, with the easy grace of a natural athlete. But it was his face that made her heart give a peculiar little bump. Handsome, she could have resisted. Handsome, she wouldn't have trusted. But, no, his face was like his house, all angles and planes, so bony it might have been homely if the lines weren't so clean and strong. His eyes were light blue or gray, she couldn't tell; tiny white creases beside them betrayed how often he must squint against the sun.

"Mr. McNeil?" she inquired.

"That's me," he agreed, voice low, deep. He was studying her with as much interest as she was him. Or so she thought, until he said brusquely, "Come in. You're here about the baby?"

"Yes. A little girl, I'm told?"

"That's right." As she stepped across the threshold, he said, "I assume you were told I found her up at Juanita Butte. Right next to my Jeep, as if she'd been left for me. Have you sent anyone up there yet?"

"I'd like to see the baby first," she said levelly. "If you don't mind."

Irritation flickered in his eyes. "And your name is…?"

Embarrassed, she said, "I'm sorry. Deputy Patton. Margaret Patton."

"Patton," he mused. "Any relation to Abby Patton? A firefighter, I think?"

What was this? Twenty questions? Was he dawdling for some reason? "Yes. She's my sister."

"Ah." He frowned at her, seeming to brood over something.

Waiting, Meg felt the stir of an uncomfortable, edgy awareness of him and of their isolation.

McNeil appeared to make up his mind. His decision did nothing to soothe her disquiet.

He nodded into the depths of the dimly lit house. "The baby's in my bedroom."

Come in, said the spider to the fly.

Meg hesitated only a second, then followed at a wary distance.

CHAPTER THREE

LEADING THE WAY across the tiled entry, Scott was disconcerted by the second odd turn his evening had taken.

She was damned pretty, this policewoman. Pretty, hell. She was sexy. Blond, blue-eyed, with a rich, full mouth. Long legs beneath an olive-green county sheriff's department parka that hid her curves. His first reaction to her had been an uncomfortable one.

Good God, Scott thought in horror. He wasn't a horny adolescent anymore. He *never* got turned on like this, at first sight.

It was having a baby in the house, he told himself. That had taken him back to another time, another life. A time when he'd had a pretty, blond wife and thought it would last forever. What he was having now was…hell, a flashback was a good way to think of it. This woman just reminded him of Penny.

He glanced back as he switched on the hall light, only to have his theory blown to smithereens. Except for the superficial resemblance because of coloring, the policewoman didn't really look like his ex-wife. Her face was more interesting than sweet, her eyes too guarded.

He saw that she was keeping a wary distance, which riled him plenty. You called a cop, and they immediately assumed you were some kind of crazed murderer?

The door stood ajar. He pushed it open farther, until the ribbon of light fell across the maple floor and touched the sleeping infant.

"Smart place to put her," the officer murmured, and brushed past him, crouching as he had to look down at the little girl. After a moment she rose and came back to his side, nodding.

He eased the door partially shut again and led her to the living room. "Here's her clothes. There's nothing to identify her, but if you want to look…"

She did. She examined each piece thoroughly, probing pockets on the snowsuit and overalls, even running her finger inside the mittens.

"Okay," she said at last. "Where's the car seat?"

"I'll get it." He straightened from where he'd been half sitting on the arm of the couch. "It's still buckled in my Jeep."

"I hope you had on gloves when you handled it."

Fingerprints. Now, there was an idea. "Yeah. I'll put them on again."

"Don't touch it anywhere you normally would."

"Yeah, I get it," he agreed.

Her head was still bent over the clothes when he returned. Barely glancing up, she asked, "This was all she was wearing?"

"She still has on a turtleneck and undershirt. And little booties." He rubbed his jaw as he envisioned the layers as he'd removed them. "Knit by hand, I think. Uh…mittens. But you saw them."

"Diaper?"

"Paper. Pink. Sopping wet. She hadn't been changed for hours, it looked like. Diaper's still in the kitchen garbage, if you want to see it."

Her sharp glance told him she recognized a dig when she heard it. "Thank you, but that's not necessary."

After he'd set down the car seat, she went over it as carefully, tipping it forward with one finger on an edge, but it had no name on the back, no phone number, no convenient note saying, "Return to 313 Main Street."

Finally sinking back on her heels, she stared into space for a long moment. "Odd," she concluded.

"No kidding."

"A doctor should look at her. She might have frostbite."

He shook his head. "No. She's fine. I'll bet she hadn't been out there five minutes."

"If you're not a medical expert…"

"I manage the ski area. We know frostbite when we see it."

She dipped her head, conceding the point. "All right. Tell me exactly where you found her."

He described the spot, telling her he'd taken a quick detour through the mile-long parking lot that bordered the highway. "I've already called my security people to tell them what happened, have them keep an eye out for anything unusual."

"I'll drive on up there, anyway," she said. "It may be hard to tell much before daylight, but I might as well try, just in case it snows."

"It won't."

She opened her mouth, then closed it, evidently realizing that he had better sources than the daily paper with its little drawings of sunshine, clouds and snowflakes.

"It's damned cold out there," he said, the words just coming. "Sometimes I spend the night at the lodge. I have a cot. If I hadn't decided to come home…"

Their eyes met in mutual horror.

"How could somebody just leave her?" Deputy Patton said. Asked. But she wasn't really asking; no one with any conscience could have given a reasonable answer.

Unless…

"She was safer there than wherever her mother or father was going," Scott said slowly.

Her nostrils flared, like an animal catching an alarming scent. "How many people work at the ski area?"

"You're suggesting one of them deserted his kid?" Instinctively he shook his head. "I can't imagine…"

"Somebody did. You said yourself it was as if she'd been left for you. Your employees seem likeliest to assume you'd come out and find her."

He felt sick at the idea. How could somebody have taken that kind of chance?

Making himself consider it, Scott said, "There are two lodges. Eleven lifts. A ski shop. Rental shop. Food services. Instructors, snow removal, mechanical… Over a thousand people work at Juanita Butte. This is Monday, our slowest. No night skiing. Maybe half of those wouldn't have been working. Almost everyone had gone home a couple hours before I did."

Surprise showed in her eyes; she hadn't realized skiing was quite that big a business.

"You're sure you've never seen this child before?"

"Positive."

"Do you know anyone with one this age? Maybe someone who's showed you pictures, talked about her…?" She spread her hands.

"I don't think so." He'd have tuned out if someone had. Pretended to look at the picture. But he didn't remember having to do that recently.

"Okay," she said, rising to her feet. "It's somewhere to start. I'm going to head on up there now. I hope you don't mind waiting up for me. I'll collect her—" she nodded in the direction of the bedroom "—on my way back down."

Voice rough, he said, "Drive carefully. The road's slippery tonight. I'll put on some coffee."

"I can taste it already." She gave him a quick, rueful smile. "I'm not used to this climate yet."

He hoped she was used to driving snowy roads.

More waiting. He'd never been very good at it. He was a man who preferred to take charge. Not being able to do anything useful drove him crazy.

He had another look-in at the baby, as sound asleep as ever. He put on the coffee. Paced. Went back to the newspaper but found he didn't give a damn about the high school basketball team or the city council's debate about zoning. Half an hour passed. Forty-five minutes.

Finally, in desperation, Scott grabbed a pencil and went to work on the crossword puzzle. He was three-quarters done, his scrawl near illegible, when the doorbell rang.

The policewoman didn't wait for an invitation this time. She scooted in, shivering, her cheeks rosy red.

"I need new long johns!"

"It's only January. In this country, that means a lot of winter left."

"I just came from Southern California."

"Ah." He wanted to ask her personal questions, but a driving need overcame his casual curiosity. "Did you find out anything?"

She shook her head. "Met your security people. Neither of them saw anything, which isn't surprising because they weren't around."

"Not around?" Scott echoed sharply.

"One had been down at the other lodge during the half hour before you left tonight, and the other was inside warming up."

He grunted.

"We're not going to be able to isolate any tire tracks with the parking lot frozen so solid," she continued, reaching for her zipper. "That coffee ready?"

"Sure. Hang up your jacket." A Danish oil-finished coat tree stood in the slate-floored entry. A couple of jackets were already heaped on it.

He left her shrugging out of her parka and went into the kitchen. By the time she got there he'd taken cream from the refrigerator and a sugar bowl from the cupboard.

She used both. He took his coffee black. She perched on a wrought-iron stool pulled up to the eating bar, he leaned back against the counter. They looked at each other in silence that shivered with awareness having nothing to do with the baby in the bedroom.

Okay, he thought. *Why not?*

"What's your name?" Scott asked. "I mean, what do friends call you? Margaret?"

"Meg." A faint smile. "No shortcut to Scott, is there?"

"Nope." He didn't want to talk about himself. "Why were you in Southern California?"

"I was career Army. An MP." She looked down at her steaming mug. "I just hung it up, came home to Elk Springs."

"How long ago?"

This smile was wry. "Thursday. Today was my first day of work." On her easily read face, the collage of expressions was amusing. "Which isn't to say," she added, "that I don't know what I'm doing. I was hired because of my experience."

"I assumed that." He kept his voice grave. "I don't suppose policing an Army base is any different than doing the same thing here."

"Not much." The policewoman—Meg—shrugged. "In fact, I get the impression things are tamer here. Some of the Army bases are pretty tough territory. I investigated an ugly series of rapes last year."

"Why'd you come home?"

Those crystalline-blue eyes contemplated him. "You're nosy."

He could think of a couple of ways to answer that. Chose one. "Are you curious about me?"

She nibbled on that luscious lower lip. "Maybe," she conceded.

"So?"

Her answer was blunt. "I heard my father was dead. He was why I'd stayed away."

"Ed Patton?"

"Yep."

Scott made a noncommittal noise in the back of his throat. Interesting. Already he wanted to know more, but he was reasonably sure she wouldn't answer right now. Not yet.

"Married?" he asked.

"No." Her gaze challenged him. "You?"

"Divorced. Kids?"

"I have a teenage son. You?"

"None." He'd gotten used to saying that as if it were the entire truth, as if the emptiness of it didn't matter.

"But you knew what to buy for her." Meg nodded toward the bedroom.

He looked away. "How hard is it?"

She accepted his nonanswer, but he was aware of speculation in her eyes. She was a cop, all right, with the sixth sense to let her know he was hiding something.

Well, let her wonder.

"What will you do now?" he asked. "About locating her parents?"

"Check into missing babies." She anticipated his questions. "There aren't any locally. Believe me, we'd be looking hard if there were. But, shoot, someone could have driven over from Portland, or down from Washington…"

"And then dumped her at night up on the mountain?"

"I didn't say it made sense."

"No." He scrubbed a hand over his face in frustration. "Have you found a place for her yet?"

"Not my department." She sipped her coffee. "Don't worry. They'll come up with a receiving home."

"I wasn't worried." The idea of the poor kid being dragged back out into the night disturbed him. "I don't mind having her here. My housekeeper is coming in the morning to take care of her."

He'd called Marjorie right after talking to the police dispatcher earlier. Shocked and indignant when he explained how he'd found the baby, she professed delight at coming to his rescue. Or at the idea of playing grandma for the day, he wasn't sure which.

"I'll call if they take her away before then," he'd said. "I just thought, since she's comfortable now, and I've read that they never have enough foster homes…" Feeling like an idiot, he'd trailed off. If he babbled on, Marjorie would be thinking he wanted to keep this baby.

"Well, we'll take good care of her," his fiftyish

housekeeper had said firmly. "Until they find her mother."

Assuming they did. Or that it wasn't her mother— or father—who'd left her out there in the dark parking lot on a freezing-cold night.

Meg Patton looked thoughtful. "We're pretty short of receiving homes right now, I'm told. Did you read about that mess over in Milton?"

"Mess?"

"This couple had been featured nationally for providing a home to so many unwanted children. They just kept adopting them. I'm told an allegation of abuse was received six weeks or so ago. Last Wednesday, the children were all taken away from the adoptive parents. Twelve of them were under three. Our system isn't designed to take that kind of onslaught."

"I did read about it." But skimming was all he'd let himself do. Had the parents really been well-meaning? he'd wondered. The children in diapers had rashes so bad they looked like bedsores, according to an anonymous source. Scott didn't like reading about things like that. How could you be lucky enough to have a little boy or girl who trusted you, then be so neglectful? The article had concluded that the county was going to be pressed for foster homes to accommodate these children, ranging in age from three months to twelve years. That article was where he'd gotten the idea, he realized now.

"You know," he said, "she's fine here. I mean it. She can stay for a while."

"You'd have to get licensed."

"I don't mind." Was he nuts? he wondered incredulously. How would a baby fit into his twelve-fifteen-hour workdays? Marjorie wouldn't be able to stay that long; she had a husband and a home of her own.

"Well, then," Meg said, setting down her empty coffee cup, "a social worker will be contacting you in the morning. They'll want to interview you and your housekeeper. If you've changed your mind by then, we'll find someplace for her."

He saw her to the door, watched her bundle up and take the child's seat in an awkward grip presumably meant to avoid smudging any prints. "Will I see you in the morning, too?"

"Yep. I'm going to want to talk to employees. Starting with supervisory personnel. I assume I should get up there well before the lifts open?"

"You might want to go as early as seven."

Thanks to his big mouth, *he* would be home baby-sitting. Damn it, he ought to be there; those were his people, the ski area was his responsibility. The little girl was not.

Trouble was, he seemed to have been elected.

Meg nodded at the time he'd suggested. "If I see any reason, I might co-opt the ski patrol to mount a search."

"That's what they're there for." That, and reining in stupidity. He held open the door for her.

She hesitated, finally coming out with, "Good night, Mr. McNeil."

His surname almost stuck in her throat. Well, good. That meant she'd wanted to call him by his first name.

"I'll see you tomorrow, Deputy Patton." He emphasized her title. "Take care."

"I *can* drive." The note of acerbity in her voice was probably not aroused by anything he'd actually said.

"I'm sure you can," he soothed.

Heading out the door and down the porch steps, she chose not to respond. He watched her go without pushing for a dinner date or any other kind of step toward a personal relationship he wasn't sure he wanted, however intriguing and appealing a woman she was.

Time for him to get to bed. He needed his rest in preparation for those middle-of-the-night feedings he had a strong forboding were going to be his lot.

He could see it now: just him and the baby, a still, dark house around them, and memories of other nights, of another trusting, warm child, long since cold in the frozen ground.

Scott's face contorted and he swore softly. He was a goddamned fool, setting himself up like this.

But he would still comfort her when she awakened, cuddle her close, walk with her if he had to, sing lullabies.

And he would not cry when he laid her back to sleep.

"SIX-MONTH-OLD BABY." The ski area Chief of Operations frowned. "Nobody that I know of has one." He sounded unapologetic. "The kids that sign on here are too young."

Meg had borrowed Scott McNeil's office today—after all, *he* hadn't needed it this morning—and interviewed dozens of employees, mostly supervisors, but also a random selection of lift operators, mechanics, ski instructors and cooks.

Five minutes ago, Mark Robillard had stuck his head in and said, "You wanted to see me?"

He hadn't offered anything she hadn't heard a dozen times already.

Although his manner thus far had been dour, enthusiasm sparked when she asked if he had children of his own. "You bet," he agreed, whipping out his wallet and displaying school pictures of a second-grade girl and a boy in fourth, both well-scrubbed, cheerful and earnest. The boy could have been Will or any of his friends at that age. Those annual fall school portraits had a sameness that was strangely reassuring.

Meg repressed a sigh, asked further about the people who worked directly under Mark at Juanita Butte, and then thanked him for his time.

He wished her luck and left, one of the rare workers here—underling or supervisory—who wasn't a tanned Nordic god or goddess. Medium height, whipcord lean, Mark Robillard did have the weathered look of a man who spent time out of doors. She'd have thought him harsh and verging on uncooperative if he hadn't warmed at the mention of his children. Or, heck, maybe the man was just too busy to waste time gossiping about a young woman he wouldn't have had any reason to know well.

Frustrated, Meg picked up her list and leaned back in the desk chair, studying it.

She hadn't learned a thing. Not from the head honchos like Mark Robillard, not from the random selection of underlings she'd chosen. Just before him, she'd talked to a fresh-faced, nineteen-year-old girl who worked in the rental shop.

Neither of them knew any more than did the…fifty-two other people she'd interviewed, which included the heads of food services, building maintenance, snow removal and marketing. Nobody had an infant daughter or knew anything about anyone who did. Which would seem highly improbable, except for the fact that about ninety percent of the workers here were in their early twenties and unmarried. They worked so they could ski, she had heard. Over and over. They didn't mind the seasonal nature of the work. Summers, some of them headed for the beach, surfed, lifeguarded; others stayed around town, waiting tables or working the dude ranch or river-rafting gigs waiting for snow to fall.

These were not people ready to settle down and have children.

Suppose, Meg thought, staring into space, one of these young women had gotten pregnant and had the baby—say, because of moral objections to abortion. Or the mother of the baby had dumped it on one of the guys who lived this nomadic existence. The change in life-style would have been drastic. So drastic he or she would have abandoned the baby?

At the moment this particular scenario was Meg's front runner. In part she liked it because of Scott McNeil's involvement. He seemed solid and trustworthy, a man you knew would take care of any problem. Leaving the baby next to his car made sense.

Meg muttered a mild profanity, all she allowed herself so that she didn't slip in front of Will.

Leaving the kid there made sense—except for one little problem. Scott claimed everyone who worked at Juanita Butte knew he bunked down in the lodge sometimes. Once or twice a week, he said. He'd thought about it last night.

Whoever had left the baby had taken an enormous chance.

Unless he—or she—had been lurking to make sure Scott did find her.

But then, why hadn't he spotted another vehicle? Why hadn't the security men seen anyone?

This was a big place, Meg reminded herself. Forest Service roads ran like spiderwebs through these woods, used by logging trucks, hikers and fishermen in the summer. None of them was plowed during the winter, but that didn't seem to stop what looked like regular traffic from the tracks she'd noticed on her way up the mountain that morning. Cross-country skiers drove in half a mile, parked and skied into the silent wilderness. Families who just wanted to take the kids sledding did the same. Snowmobilers had their favorite roads.

Whoever abandoned the baby could have headed down the mountain, turned into the first logging road and waited for Scott's Jeep to pass. If it didn't, he or she could go back.

Okay, that worked, Meg told herself. It was cold-blooded as all get-out, but it worked. Now all she had to do was figure out which of these tanned youths with gleaming white teeth and an aura of joy had done such a thing.

She rubbed the back of her neck, then rotated her head a few times. Maybe she'd forget it for the day; after not getting much sleep last night, she'd been here since seven this morning, and her butt and her mind were both going numb. Overwork induced paranoia, which might be why this crawly feeling of apprehension kept raising goose bumps on her arms. She smelled something worse than child abandonment in this case, something…evil.

Meg made a disgusted sound. For crying out loud! Yeah, cops were given to hunches. But only some of them turned out to be right. She had nothing to go on, no reason to think that baby's mother was in trouble or dead.

Nothing but the way a shiver walked down her spine.

To distract herself, she glanced around. The office was remarkably spare, with one window overlooking the ski area, the only personal touch an extraordinary Northwest Coast Indian mask depicting a bear with its mouth open in a snarl. Beyond that, the walls were bare but for an enormous whiteboard calendar covered with scrawled notes. The piles of paperwork were meticulously organized in cubbies and the computer desk was clean. Meg wrinkled her nose, comparing it to what her own desk would look like once she'd occupied it for more than a few weeks.

But if you were going to run a business on the scale of this ski area, maybe you couldn't afford to misplace notes or file something wrong.

Truthfully, she'd had no idea a ski area was a huge operation. Juanita Butte was now officially the largest single employer in Butte County, she'd learned. When Scott came in to work at ten or so that morning, she'd asked a few questions.

Looking faintly amused, he had answered willingly enough. She'd known they groomed the slopes, but not that the grooming machines cost between 170,000 and 200,000 each. And a heck of a lot besides skiing and boarding went on here. Building maintenance alone was a big department. The mechanics department had to keep more than sixty vehicles running. Marketing, strategic planning, ticket sales, rentals… For Pete's sake, they employed two hundred instructors alone!

The numbers boggled the mind. But the one that had really stuck was liability insurance: 400,000 a year.

"Mostly," Scott had growled, "because we get too many reckless fools on the slopes. They ski too fast, they won't stay inside the marked areas, they get drunk, they try to do jumps or flips because they saw it on TV and they figure it's easy…" He shook his head. "They break their idiot necks or they clobber some poor woman stemming her way down the hill. Or they disappear over the ridge and we have to mount a two-day search and bring the poor bastard in with frostbite and a broken leg."

Although she sympathized—she felt the same way about idiot drivers—she couldn't resist challenging him. "Come on, didn't you get into this because you were a skier? You can't tell me you came down the hill like an old lady when you were eighteen and cocky."

"What makes you think I was ever either?"

She'd grinned. "It's a natural progression."

It was the first time she'd seen him smile. His mouth didn't do that much, just twitched at one corner, deepening a groove in that cheek. The smile was all in his eyes, which held a world of laughter and kindness and mischief.

He'd taken her breath away.

Again.

By the time she'd left his place last night, she'd caught herself mumbling an incoherent prayer that this incredibly sexy man not be a criminal. Or involved with a woman, please.

This from someone with no interest whatsoever in becoming involved herself. A new man, a new job and a teenage son didn't mix.

And then there was her reluctant admission to herself that she seemed able to handle only one emotional issue at a time. She couldn't even deal with calling Johnny Murray. She sure as heck wasn't going to start dating.

However tempting Scott McNeil's smile, however honestly he'd expressed an interest in her last night.

She just wished she could be sure there wasn't too good a reason that he'd been the one to find that baby.

Like, for example, he was her father.

But why would he have called 9-1-1 if the baby was his, even if he didn't want to be saddled with her?

Another part that didn't make sense. Meg sighed and stretched again. When someone knocked on the door, she called, "It's open."

"Hi." Abby stuck her head inside. "I heard you were here. Busy?"

Taken by surprise, Meg quit scrabbling for her notes. "No. Not right now. Just thinking. What on earth are you doing here?"

Her sister slipped in and closed the door behind her. "Skiing. What else?"

Sexy in a stretchy bodysuit, she wore her shoulder-length blond hair in a perky ponytail. The bulky boots just made her legs look longer and slimmer than ever. Cheeks pink from the cold, eyes sparkling, she'd stepped right out of an ad for the sport.

Meg felt old just looking at her little sister.

"But don't you have to work?" Meg asked.

Abby slouched bonelessly in the extra chair. "We've gone to ten-hour shifts at the fire department. I work Sunday/Monday and Wednesday/Thursday. Leaves me lots of time to ski." Her smile was catlike in its smugness.

"I can see that it would," Meg said wryly. "Jeez, you look just like everyone else up here."

"Meaning?"

"Young, tanned, fit, irresponsible."

Her sister arched a brow. "I could take offense at that."

"None intended." Meg grimaced. "You know why I'm here?"

Abby propped one booted foot on the other. "Nope. You've got everyone buzzing out there. A cop's here, she's asking everyone about babies. Can you tell me what it's about?"

Why not? From Scott's discovery of the baby to Meg's ungrounded disquiet took about five minutes.

Abby gave her a disconcertingly sharp look. "You just don't want to think anyone could abandon their own kid."

So, they were going to get personal. "No," Meg said evenly, "I didn't say that. Babies are abandoned all the time. But usually not under such dangerous circumstances."

"I read just the other day about a newborn someone had tried to bury alive."

"Newborns are a different story." How did you explain instinctive understanding to someone who'd never had a child of her own? "Those are usually left by young girls who panic. The baby isn't real to them. It's just a disaster. They think if they can get rid of it, they can go on as if the whole thing never happened."

Abby's expression was exaggeratedly patient. "Isn't that what probably happened here?"

"It's different with kids even a few weeks old. People care, at least enough to abandon the child somewhere safe. At Grandma's, at the baby-sitter's, at a neighbor's. Sometimes they have to work their way up to the complete severing of ties. They'll leave the child for a few days, then come back. Do it again, maybe stay away longer. Until finally one time they don't come back."

"You're saying no parent ever dumps a kid someplace that might not be completely safe?" Abby didn't bother hiding her skepticism.

"I didn't say 'never.' Just rarely. This time doesn't settle with me."

Abby gave an unconcerned shrug. "What I'm saying is, don't let your personal feelings about a parent walking out on her kids warp your perception."

Annoyance edged Meg's voice. "What makes you think I am? You and Renee are the ones still hot and bothered by Mom leaving us."

Abby should have been ticked. Meg was vaguely shocked when she only gave another of those bored, nonchalant shrugs. "Renee is. I'm not. I hardly remember Mom. And Dad wasn't that bad. Renee rubbed him the wrong way. I swear she *tried*."

Meg said cautiously, "But you were mad the other night, too."

"I was mad at *you*. You should have let us in on the secret. That's all." She sounded so indifferent. As if Meg's disclosures had been mildly interesting, possibly a little irritating, but basically no big deal.

Now Meg had something else to feel unsettled about.

"Do you miss Dad?" she asked.

"Miss him?" Abby sounded surprised. "Not especially. It wasn't like we were buddies. I got along with him okay, that's all. I mean, you just had to know how to get around him. I'd try to tell Renee, but she wouldn't listen."

"Maybe she had too much pride to 'get around him.'"

"Oh, pride." Abby rose lithely. "Why make life rougher than it has to be?"

"Because he was a bastard," Meg said harshly. "Because I'd rather feel the back of his hand any day than knuckle under."

"I thought we were talking about Renee."

"She and I have something in common."

"Yeah, you're both bullheaded." Malicious amusement glinted in Abby's eyes. "Maybe you got that from him."

Meg began hotly, "I didn't get anything from…" Remembering yesterday's meditations, she had to stop. Bullheadedness and pride and strength of character all went hand in hand. Their mother hadn't possessed a one of them. Once again, Meg had to overcome her revulsion to concede that maybe she did have something to thank Ed Patton for.

Her sister watched her mockingly. Meg couldn't help thinking that, despite the loss of their mother early, life had come too easily to Abby, the baby of the family. With her looks and brains, her run of luck might continue. But it was also possible that one of these days she'd butt up against someone who couldn't be wound around her little finger, and then she might discover pride was a more reliable prop than tears or wheedling smiles.

Meg was ashamed to discover that she almost hoped so.

"Well, I'll leave you to your business," Abby said. Her eyes met Meg's, and for a moment they held genuine caring. "I hope you're wrong. About the baby's mother. I hope the little girl was kidnapped, and someone is dying to welcome her home."

Meg tried to smile. "Yeah. I hope so, too."

But when her sister was gone, Meg couldn't help wishing Abby had chosen a better turn of phrase. Someone dying was exactly what had Meg worried.

CHAPTER FOUR

WILL WAS ONE OF THE FIRST to burst out the front door of the school after the bell rang. *He* had nothing to hang around for.

He'd been okay with the idea of the move; hey, he'd moved every few years all his life. Everyone he knew did. What was different this time was that the other kids in this school weren't used to newcomers. It wasn't like a high school near a base, where three-quarters of the students were Army brats.

Most of the other freshman boys were just ignoring him. A bunch of the girls weren't, and he almost wished they would. He liked looking, but he wasn't ready to go out with one. He'd rather hang with his buddies. If he had any.

"Hey, Will!" a girl called from behind him.

He pretended he didn't hear. Jenna Marsh and that dinky friend of hers—Erika, yeah, that was it—they just didn't get the message.

Shoving his hands into the pockets of his parka, Will thought, *and I don't like the cold, either.* He walked faster, hearing some giggles behind him. School had let out at 2:20, and yesterday he'd gone straight home. Today he had other plans.

Will gave a hunted look over his shoulder. It wasn't

just Jenna and Erika; a whole pack of girls trailed him, and they were getting closer.

Reaching the corner, he turned and broke into a run. He hit the next corner and went around it before they appeared. After that he slowed down. He was pretty sure they wouldn't go so far as to track him; they had to pretend whichever way he went was the way they were really going.

What he'd decided to do was visit Aunt Renee at the police station. He wouldn't talk to his father or anything, because that would make Mom mad, but she hadn't said he couldn't go there at all. Like, to see Aunt Renee's office, ask if she'd let him ride along with her sometime. And if he just happened to catch a glimpse of his father… Well, it wasn't like he'd know who Will was, anyway.

Mom said she needed to talk to Will's father first. Only, she kept saying that, but she didn't do it. She had all kinds of excuses, but they'd been in Elk Springs practically a week, and she *still* hadn't called him. All Will wanted was just to *see* his dad. Just to know what he looked like.

Will stopped across the street from the red-brick public safety building. His father was probably inside it. Weird.

The red Don't Walk hand stopped him, even though there was no traffic.

He had trouble believing he was going to meet his own, real father. Aunt Renee said they looked alike. Most kids were used to people saying they looked like their mom or dad. But Will had never gotten that, because nobody would even guess he and Mom were related. He'd always thought maybe he'd inherited his dark hair and eyes and the shape of his face from his grandfather or grandmother. Mom didn't have any pictures of her father. But Aunt Renee did, and now he could see that nothing about him was from the Pattons.

He was a Murray.

Aunt Renee knew Jack Murray really well. She said his mom and dad were still alive, and that he had a brother who had two girls. But Will's father wasn't married, and he didn't have any other kids.

Will had tried to hide how he felt when Renee said that, about his dad not being married. Had he been, like, waiting for Will's mom all these years? *She* hadn't married anyone else, either.

But Will didn't let himself think too far ahead.

Instead he wondered: once his father knew about Will, would he tell his family? Will tried to convince himself he didn't care that much; he and Mom were fine by themselves, weren't they? But he knew the truth. He did care. It would feel really crummy to have his own father not want to bother with him. And those were the only grandparents he'd ever have.

The light turned green. Again. Will didn't move.

Maybe this was a dumb idea. Maybe he should wait, the way Mom wanted him to.

But what could it hurt, just to see what his father looked like? Aunt Renee would understand.

His feet were moving, he discovered, even though the Walk sign had been replaced again by the red hand. Nobody was going to run out of the police station to ticket him. With the snowy streets, what cars were out were driving real slow.

He walked in the front doors and asked the desk sergeant if Aunt Renee was in. The guy sent him back.

"Third door on the right," he said, holding open that swinging gate at the end of the counter.

Will went. He passed a couple uniformed cops and stole peeks in the offices he passed. Nobody looked like his father.

"Will!" Aunt Renee said when he appeared. She tapped a key and her computer screen went dark. "Is something wrong?"

"Nah." He shrugged, trying to look cool. "I just thought I'd stop by. See where you work. I don't have any friends to hang with yet. It's kinda boring with Mom working. You know?"

She rose to her feet. "Yes, but I'm not sure this is the best place for you. Your mom hasn't called Jack yet, has she?"

"She didn't get home till really late last night," he said. "Somebody found a baby, and she went to check it out. And then she left even before me this morning."

Single-minded, Aunt Renee stuck to the point. "I just think your father should have some warning before he comes face-to-face with you."

"I didn't think he'd even be here."

The lift of her eyebrow told him she knew a fib when she heard one. "He's here," she said, sounding grim. "It's not that I mind having you visit. Normally that would be great. But let's wait until the fireworks are over, okay?"

"But why would he even know who I am?" Will said stubbornly.

"Oh, he'll know." She gripped his arm and steered him out of the office. "Go home, Will."

Another woman cop hailed them in the hall. "Renee! Is this your nephew?" Her voice seemed awfully loud.

"Yes," Aunt Renee said tightly. "But he has to go home now. I'll give him the grand tour another day."

Behind her another uniformed officer appeared in a doorway. A big, dark man, his eyes met Will's, and Will felt icy cold and then hot like when he'd had the flu. On the man's face was pure shock. The moment seemed to stretch on forever. Will was vaguely conscious of Aunt Renee turning, of curious looks from the other woman, but all he really clearly saw was his father, who backed up and quietly closed his office door.

"Oh, jeez," Aunt Renee whispered.

Will swallowed. "I gotta go," he blurted, and stumbled backward.

"Here." Aunt Renee took his arm again. "You can go out this way."

He let her propel him toward the back. The hall took a turn and ended up at a gray steel door that led out to a plowed parking lot where some police cars were parked in a line.

"I'm sorry," he said, giving his aunt a desperate look.

He expected her to be mad, but her smile comforted him. "Don't worry. I wouldn't have chosen to do it this way, but your mother shouldn't have procrastinated, either. Jack's a nice guy. Really. It'll be all right."

He felt shaky, dizzy. He knew he'd done something terrible. "I wish I hadn't come."

"Don't worry," she said again. "Just go home. I'll lie and tell your mom it was my fault."

He couldn't let her do that. "No. She already thinks you're mad at her. I'll tell her the truth."

Aunt Renee got a quizzical expression on her face, but he was walking away backward. "I gotta go," he said again, and turned around.

Her voice floated after him. "'Bye, Will."

When he heard the steel door shut, he stopped and closed his eyes, trying to slow his racing heartbeat. Mom was going to be so ticked. And his father...his father would *hate* him! Surprising him in front of other people had been so stupid!

It must have been a minute or more before he calmed himself enough to start trudging across the parking lot. Gol, Mom was going to kill him. He was dumb, dumb, dumb...

The back door of the police station opened again, and his heart jerked. He really, really, didn't want to look, even though it wouldn't be—couldn't be...

"Will." Only a cop could make one word—a name—into a command. The voice was deep, male.

Will stopped, cheeks flushing again. He swallowed, turned... And faced the total stranger who happened to be his biological father.

"You didn't have to run away."

Without thinking, Will blurted the truth. "Mom'll be mad at me."

The eyes narrowed a flicker. "She wants you to stay away from me?"

"She said she should talk to you first." His voice squeaked in the middle, making Will angry. Just when he needed to act cool.

"I see." Unreadably, the man continued to study him. "But you didn't agree."

Will hunched his shoulders, feeling his cheeks burn. "I was just curious. And I wanted to visit Aunt Renee."

Jack Murray bent his head in acknowledgment. "I'll wait to hear from your mother." He didn't sound as if he was going to be especially friendly to her.

"Why did you come out?" Will asked daringly.

"Maybe I was curious, too." His father scrutinized him. "What's she told you about me?"

"That you're my father. That you never knew she was pregnant."

"Did she say why…" He stopped, shaking his head. "Never mind. That's between your mother and me."

Will answered anyway. "She said you were just kids. That you couldn't have helped her. And she was scared of her father."

A muscle jerked in Jack Murray's cheek. "I won't argue about any of that. Except the part about not helping. I wouldn't have abandoned her."

Will didn't know what to say.

"How do you feel about this?"

"I just wanted to know what you were like. That's all."

He wished that were the truth, but it wasn't. He had all these dumb dreams of having a father who took him fishing and came to his basketball games and talked to him about girls. He'd seen some of his friends with their dads. But those fathers had been there all along. They weren't men whose girlfriends had never told them they even had a son.

"Fair enough," Jack Murray said.

What did that mean? Will swallowed. "You believe I'm your son?"

His father got this weird expression on his face. "All I had to do was set eyes on you."

Will nodded. It was true. He wondered why Mom had never told him. He hadn't believed her when she said she'd forgotten what his father looked like. How could you? Unless you tried really hard to forget.

And why would she do that? It was one of the mysteries Will was determined to solve.

"It's cold out here. You'd better get on home."

Will shoved his hands into his pockets. "Um. I shouldn't have come today. I mean, like this." He struggled for words. "So you had to find out about me in front of other people. I'm…well, I'm sorry."

His father half smiled. "Your mom and I'll talk soon."

"Do you need my phone number?" Will began eagerly, starting back.

A lifted hand stopped him. "I'll get it from Renee. Now, scoot."

Will backed up. "Okay. Uh…'bye."

His father waved and went back inside. Will turned and ran, part of him scared at what he'd done, part feeling as high as if he'd sunk a three-pointer to win a championship game.

Maybe he didn't have that dream father. But at least he did *have* a father. He didn't seem like that bad a guy.

And he wasn't married.

Will leaped into the air and slam-dunked an invisible basketball. This might turn out cool. Really cool.

MEG'S NEXT VISITOR was Scott McNeil.

"Wanting your office back?" she asked.

He sat on the corner of the desk, and she couldn't resist a quick peek at the way the stretch fabric of his ski pants outlined the long, powerful muscles in his thigh.

When her gaze lifted, his eyebrows had a quirk that suggested he'd seen her looking. "Find out anything?" he asked.

She chose to assume he was talking about her investigation and not her perusal of his physique.

"No." Meg sighed. "They're all so…young."

The twitch of his mouth quickened her pulse. "You must have had your son when you were at least that young."

"Seventeen," Meg admitted.

"Tough," he said without expression.

"Yes, it was." She had a flash of memory, herself hardly more than a child yet so fiercely protective of the vulnerable baby she held.

The little girl he'd found had been dressed with such loving care. Would a woman do that, and then just leave her tiny daughter in a frozen parking lot on a bitterly cold night? Would a father do that any more than a mother?

The squirrelly sensation drove her to her feet, set her to moving restlessly. "I have a bad feeling about this," she said. "The ski patrol did the sweep I requested?"

"And didn't find a thing." He followed her to the window.

Volcanic in origin, Juanita Butte was smaller than Bachelor or Mt. Hood, but shared their conical form, ideal for skiing. Four lifts started here, and another three half a mile away by the East Lodge. Above them, still others rose toward the summit. From here, Meg could see the ticket booths, people heading down toward the parking lots, the lift lines—short on a Tuesday afternoon—and skiers and snowboarders enjoying the meticulously groomed slopes above. It was all innocent and fun.

If you didn't think about that massive liability insurance. Or the baby abandoned last night.

"What did you expect them to find?" Scott asked.

Meg started. She'd almost forgotten he stood at her shoulder.

"Expect is too strong a word," she said reluctantly. "I just can't help wondering…"

"What do you *wonder* if you'll find?"

"The baby's mother." She turned to face him. "Dead."

His expression was first surprised, then perturbed. "What makes you think that?"

"The baby's clothes. Everything was clean, reasonably new, cute. Coordinated. She looked…loved."

"Nice clothes don't equal love."

"No, I know that. I just…" She focused on the scene outside the window abruptly, alarm quickening her voice. "Did I just see a snowflake?"

He stared out, too. Another tiny white flake floated past the window. Then another. "I'm afraid so. We're expecting four or five inches tonight."

"If there are tracks anywhere, they'll be gone."

"We've looked." He faced her. "What do you have in mind?"

"I was just thinking about those Forest Service roads." Grabbing her list and notes, she headed for the door. "I'm checking some of them out."

"Do you have experience driving under that kind of condition? Those roads aren't plowed."

"I'll manage," she snapped.

"You could get stuck."

Impatient, she whirled back. "Well, what do you suggest? They'll be buried by tomorrow."

Buried. Another unfortunate choice of words.

"If a woman was dumped, too, she's dead," he said quietly. "You know how cold it was last night."

"If she was dressed warmly enough…"

"Then why not leave her in the parking lot, too?"

"Because she could have called for help." *Weak.*

His huff of breath might have been a snort.

"I'm going to look. I have snow tires and four-wheel drive."

"Will you let me come?"

"You mean, drive?"

He didn't say anything, just waited.

She thought quickly. His presence might compromise a crime scene. She worried about his motives in wanting to go with her. On the other hand, Meg wasn't anxious to find herself stranded a mile up a deserted logging road with snow falling and night coming.

Yeah, Meg mocked herself, *you'd rather be stranded with him, wouldn't you?*

"Fine," she said ungraciously, then tried to improve on it. "Thank you."

They took his Jeep Cherokee. "Which way?" he asked as he backed out.

"Towards town," she decided. "Isn't the road closed for the winter a few miles farther on? Would he have wanted to backtrack?"

"Maybe not, but there'd have been less chance of being seen coming out…" Scott shook his auburn head impatiently. "Hell, it was dark. With no night skiing, there wasn't any traffic, anyway. East it is."

They traveled close to ten miles before coming to the first turnoff that appeared driveable. Logging roads higher on the mountain had vanished for the winter under twenty feet of snow. But the size of the snowbanks beside the road dropped with the altitude.

Scott slowed, then stepped on the gas again. "Nobody's been up there since the last snowfall."

The second one showed several recent sets of tire tracks. A green sign peeked above the snow: Lake Martha Trailhead, 1 Mile.

Scott turned. "I'll look to the left, you to the right," he suggested.

Cars had gone as far as the trailhead, where a nice little slope was obviously a favorite with sledders. Snowmobile tracks vanished into the trees, their deep green the only color in this white landscape. Even down here snowflakes drifted from a pale sky in silent, slow motion.

"If he had a snowmobile…"

"Murder is usually committed on impulse," Meg said. "Even murder in the first degree is rarely planned way ahead."

He grunted. "Shall we look around?"

"Yeah."

They followed half a dozen tracks made by feet rather than skis or sleds. Most ended abruptly and returned to the parking lot. A couple yellow spots in the snow signaled the reason for the trek.

At last she said, "Let's go."

They got nowhere with the next wilderness road, either. The snow was falling harder, making a white veil. Meg glanced at her watch—three-thirty in the afternoon. Darkness wasn't that far away. Common sense told her this was a wild-goose chase. That itch, that certainty something was *wrong,* kept her quiet.

Maybe it was contagious. Scott, driving more slowly as the visibility worsened, didn't suggest giving up. His face was tight, frowning, as he peered ahead. Tension hummed through him. Meg didn't know if the source was him or her. She was glad, suddenly, not to be alone.

"Crap," he muttered, braking. "Forgot this one was here."

The Jeep fishtailed and came to a near stop. He

wrestled with the wheel and they swung onto another Forest Service road.

"I didn't see a sign…"

"Must've been buried. This is the Puma Lake trail-head."

The name triggered memories: wildflowers and murmuring brooks running over the stony trail. The blue-green lake water, so astonishingly clear that she could lie on her stomach on a big rock that stuck out and watch the shadows of trout ten feet down. Her sisters' high girlish voices pierced the mountain quiet. Her mother was part of those memories, laying out the picnic lunch as Meg's father cast his line for the fish. Meg would feel the sun hot on her back and drowsily hope he didn't catch any. Mom had brought plenty to eat without, and Meg didn't like watching her father bash in the trouts' heads after he'd pulled them flopping onto the shore.

His hand would be a blur, and she'd hear the crunch, see the rock come away smeared with blood…

She shivered.

Scott gave her a sharp look. "Ghost tap you on the shoulder?"

"Something like that." She didn't elaborate.

This parking lot had been used less heavily. With no good sledding hill, families on a Sunday outing didn't come here in winter. Through the falling snow Meg couldn't see tire tracks at all.

"Let's get out and circle," she suggested.

Ski tracks led up the trail and disappeared. Meg blinked away the snowflakes sticking to her lashes and peered into the woods. Pine branches were weighted from the last snowfall. Wells around each trunk were deep enough that scrambling out would have been difficult. She'd heard of skiers off the marked runs falling into one and dying, unable to escape by themselves.

"Meg!" Scott called. He'd gotten fifteen or twenty feet ahead while she meditated.

Feet sinking deep with each step, she hurried to his side. He pointed. Two sets of tracks disappeared into the trees, the individual footsteps oddly jumbled and smeared. Several places, a compression in the snow suggested someone had fallen.

Only one set of footprints came back.

Instincts kicking into high, Meg said, "We'll circle wide. Stay right behind me."

Once under the trees, the snowfall thinned, the tiny flakes floating individually to the forest floor. Meg walked parallel to the tracks, which continued a couple hundred feet into the woods. Except for the squeak and scrunch of the snow beneath their feet, the puff of Scott's breath, all was completely still and silent. Her own breath came out in visible clouds, the cold biting at her cheeks and nose.

The tracks ended at a well circling a huge ponderosa pine.

Moving carefully, Meg closed in on it. A few feet away, she saw the first blood splatters, the vivid scarlet already muted by the fine coating of fresh snow.

Scott made a sound.

"Stay back," Meg said harshly.

The last few steps, and she sucked in an icy lungful of air. A woman lay in a broken heap against the rough tree trunk. Blood was frozen beneath her like a cherry snow cone. Lividity had settled in the cheek that rested on the snow, but her face was tragically young and pretty.

A strangled obscenity brought Meg whipping around. Scott had followed her and was staring down at the girl.

"Oh, my God," he said hoarsely. "I know her."

CHAPTER FIVE

"I'M SORRY." The cold plastic of the cell phone to her ear, Meg glanced over her shoulder at the floodlights and the half dozen police cars, the medic units, the yellow tape and the huddled officers. "I'll be another couple hours," she told Will. "Are you okay?"

"Mo-om!"

"I'm doing my best. You know I always do." She was freezing her butt off and she had a dead girl not that many years older than her son lying in the snow with a bullet through the head. Meg was not in the mood for anyone's whining but her own.

"I saw my dad today."

Not just the words but the defiance in his voice snapped her out of her self-pity. "You *what?*"

"I mean…" Will gulped. "I was bored, you know. So I went to see Aunt Renee. For something to do. Only he saw me, and he recognized me, and…"

Her stomach did a somersault so tight she was suddenly nauseated.

"I can't believe you went to the police station when Jack didn't even know you existed yet."

"Yeah, but he never would have known if I'd left it up to you."

Snotty, but possibly true.

"The thing is, he wants to talk to you."

Meg just bet he did.

"I made it sound like you'd call tonight," her son continued. "And now you're not going to be here."

"I wish I were." Little as she wanted to talk to Jack, she meant it. Lord, how she meant it. "I found a body, Will. I can't simply come home because it's five o'clock."

"Yeah, I know, but…"

"If Jack calls, tell him I'm sorry but I'll have to talk to him tomorrow," she said firmly. "Now, I've got to go. I'll be home as quick as I can." She hung up before he had a chance to protest further.

Stowing her phone back in its case, she crunched through the snow toward where the body still lay. Tugging her fleece hat back over her now icy ear, she tried to bury her chin inside the collar of her parka. Damn, it was cold!

Her mind was the only part of her warm enough to be working at top speed: annoyingly, on several levels at once.

Jack had talked to Will. What did that mean? Would he acknowledge him? Try to spend some time with her—no, *their*—son? Or had Will put him on the spot and he hadn't wanted to say, "Leave me alone, kid"?

At the same time as she worried about Will, she was aware of the scene ahead, canopied in blue plastic, brilliantly lit by a floodlight set up under the dark looming pines. Several police officers stood in a clump ahead, staring downward. The falling snow made a filmy curtain that isolated her from the activity ahead and behind.

She imagined herself as the victim, falling, begging, pleading, the snow sucking at each foot and keeping her from running. Just as important, she tried to see what had happened through the murderer's eyes, and found herself consumed by anger but also preternaturally alert, listening for the sound of a car engine, a snowmobile, the whisper of skis—anything to warn of the arrival of a witness. Her imaginary replays were so real, so personal, she was shaken. Sometimes she wished her imagination wasn't quite so vivid.

Just as Meg arrived at the murder scene, Ben Shea, a detective from the investigations unit, gave a hand to the coroner and boosted him out of the well surrounding the tree. Meg hadn't handled enough murders to get over her squeamishness, if anyone ever did. She tried not to look at the body, concentrating on the coroner's face.

"No surprises," he said briskly. "It's hard as hell to see much, but she's been shot in the head twice, close quarters. I'd guess eighteen to twenty-four inches away. She was probably standing. Small caliber. There's one exit wound. You might look for the bullet."

"We already have." Meg pointed at the fresh hole torn in the tree trunk. "At least, we think so. We'll dig it out once we're done with the scene."

The coroner glanced, made some mental calculations, then nodded with satisfaction. "Height looks about right if she was standing when she was shot, which seems likely. I'll tell you more after the autopsy."

Meg had met Bobby Sanchez, the elected county coroner, for the first time tonight. She wasn't sure she'd recognize him if they met face-to-face tomorrow. Not much but his eyes and nose showed between his blood—no, strawberry—red wool hat and the plaid muffler tucked under the collar of his bulky parka. They knew how to dress in this country; she was probably the only one here who had to clench her jaw to keep her teeth from chattering. At two degrees, the cold sank into her bones.

Long underwear, she reminded herself. A muffler. Or would one of those face masks be even better? Definitely new wool socks. Maybe silk gloves to add another layer.

How could she have forgotten how cold winters were in central Oregon? Or how long? Her father used to say that in Elk Springs, winters lasted nine months and summer took up the other three. But she was sure there'd been a spring. Please God, let there be a spring.

"Patton?" Ben Shea's voice penetrated her misery. "What do you think?"

"Think?"

Not much of his face showed, either, but she saw one eyebrow lift sardonically. "Shall we go ahead and move the body?"

"Uh…" It was unavoidable at last. Meg, too, turned and gazed at the dead girl. "Did we get enough pictures?"

She *had* gotten to know the evidence technicians tonight, and been pleasantly surprised at their efficiency and knowledge. They'd measured, photographed and searched under her direction for any evidence dropped along the trail of footprints.

Hansel and Gretel, she had thought. *We should be so lucky.* Of course, they hadn't been.

"Sheila says yes," Ben told her. "She could do better in daylight, but with snow coming down this heavy, I don't know if we want to leave it out here all night."

Meg tried to hide her shudder. "No. We don't. Is this your case now?"

"Nope. I'm just here to back you up."

Did everyone have to sound so cheerful?

"Yeah, okay," she said. "Well, let's take a look."

They had, of course, already studied the body and surroundings, planning a search pattern just in case the murderer had thrown the gun into the woods, figuring it would stay buried in snow until spring. But now, with the coroner's okay, they'd take a more detailed look at the body itself and ready it for transportation to the morgue where Sanchez would do an autopsy.

Fighting her repugnance, Meg slid down into the well and heard Ben doing the same. Both crouched over the dead woman.

Meg checked pockets. Nothing. She unzipped the parka. Beneath was a waist-pack. Inside it she found a wallet and keys attached to a fuzzy ball. Lipstick. Comb. Hairclip.

Each item went into a separate paper evidence bag held out by Ben, who swore under his breath as he awkwardly jotted the whats, wheres, and whens on tags. Meg sympathized; she wasn't sure she'd be able to read her own notes tomorrow. Writing with ski gloves on was a challenge.

Meg patted down the girl's jean pockets, then struggled to roll her. She hated this stage. Between rigor mortis and the freezing temperature, the body was so stiff that moving it was like trying to wrestle a one hundred and twenty pound store mannequin.

Nothing in the back pockets, nothing beneath her. Meg glanced up. Ron Wczniewski, the head of the crime-scene techs, stood waiting.

"Let's shovel up this top inch or two of snow and dirt," Meg ordered. "We can let it melt, then check for trace evidence."

"Up here, too?" He nodded toward the jumbled footsteps where first victim and then murderer had stood.

"Definitely there."

"Shelly Lange." Ben was flipping through the wallet. "That the name you were told?"

"Yep."

"Nineteen years old."

Pity and anger churning in her belly, Meg rose to her feet. "That's what McNeil guessed," she agreed. "Shelly lived next door to him years ago. When she was thirteen or fourteen."

"And he remembered her well enough to recognize her now? Looking like this?" Skepticism edged Ben's gravelly voice.

"She worked at the ski area last year, too."

"And he just happened to lead you to her body."

"It wasn't like that." Oh, hell. She sounded as if she was being defensive. Maybe she was. She didn't want to think of Scott McNeil as a suspect. She'd have to, of course; why *had* he remembered a neighbor's teenage daughter so well? Tomorrow she'd ask him. But she didn't believe he was a murderer. Damn it, she'd seen too much tenderness on his face when he talked about the baby, too much anger and abhorrence when he speculated on who might have left her out there in the cold. And she'd seen his shock and horror this afternoon when he saw the dead woman's face. She would be willing to swear in a court of law that he hadn't known what they would find at the end of the jumbled trail.

Unless he was a heck of an actor. Some of the worst serial murderers were.

What she really meant, Meg thought wryly, was that

she didn't want to believe she could be attracted to a man capable of such a brutal crime.

Good thing Ben would be with her tomorrow when she interviewed Scott. Obviously, she needed help staying dispassionate.

But still… She kept her voice even, unemotional. "Checking out these back roads was my idea. He drove because he was convinced that on my own I'd end up in a snowbank and somebody would find me out here come June."

"He might have a point. You don't have that much experience in snow country, do you?"

"I was stationed in Germany for three years."

He grunted. "Here's a picture of a baby girl."

Meg looked at the pretty, smiling baby wearing a red velvet dress trimmed with white lace. She felt a squeeze of pain and grief. "That's her."

"Good enough." Ben nodded toward the body. "We done here?"

He was prodding more than asking, she guessed. Meg waved her agreement and took a hand proferred by one of the other cops to boost her out of the well. She was a little surprised when Ben did the same. She'd barely met him the other day but had the impression that he was the macho type, not much for admitting that he needed help.

But then, she was going on appearances, and she knew better.

She and Ben stood back and watched as the body was bagged and hoisted out of the tree well, then loaded onto a gurney and carried toward the ambulance back in the parking lot. Taking a last look at the blood soaking the dark frozen earth and the snow, Meg ignored a fresh surge of nausea.

Pulling a trigger…now, that was nice and quick and almost impersonal. Anyone might be able to do it, given the right motivation. But making the victim come out into the woods, with her knowing the whole way that she was going to die… What could be crueler?

The murderer wouldn't have seen it that way. It certainly had been faster, more efficient, to force Shelly Lange to walk to her grave. Footsteps, assuming they were spotted before January snows filled them in, weren't likely to excite attention if a snowmobiler happened to notice them, but marks left by a bloody body dragged through the snow would be. Conceivably the murderer had even been angry enough to enjoy her terror.

"We'll search the perimeter in daylight," Meg said.

Nods all around.

"Have we made casts of the footprints yet?"

"We're working on it," Ron said.

"Any hope?" she asked.

"Damn straight." The twenty-something evidence technician became animated as he described how he'd prepared the best couple impressions by sifting layers of powdered plaster in, reinforcing them with sticks and then slowly soaking the plaster with water. "Works better in snow than the usual shellac solution and talc," he insisted.

On being asked, Sheila agreed that she'd taken photographs of every tire track in the parking lot. She didn't sound optimistic. The falling snow had blurred any clear definition, and it looked as though half a dozen vehicles had been in here within the past ten hours.

Scott had long since gone. Meg's impression had been that he was pretty shaken up, although like any man he tried to hide it. Knowing that securing the scene would drag into hours, Meg had insisted that he leave. Tomorrow would be soon enough to talk to him further.

Now she followed Ben Shea back to the parking lot and had the unwelcome realization that she had no car.

"Can you give me a ride back up to the ski area?" she asked.

"Sure. I'm parked over here." He jerked his head. When she fell into step beside him, Ben asked, "We going to talk to the parents next?"

"I don't see how we can put it off." However much she would have liked to.

During the drive up the winding, snowbanked highway, she asked whether Ben knew the Langes. "Or aren't you a local?"

"Nah, I come from Portland." A dark, intense man, he had to be younger than she was, but seemed to have nothing in common with the rootless twenty-five-year-olds she'd talked to that morning at Juanita Butte. "I asked around," he continued. "Ron thinks the victim's old man is a member of some crazy religious sect. They were in the news a while back for beating a kid bloody when he fainted during Wednesday prayer meeting. Around about the third hour of being on his knees."

All Meg could think was, good thing her own father hadn't gotten religion. That would have been his brand of it.

Ben dropped her beside her Bronco in the Juanita Butte parking lot. Tonight there was night skiing; the hill blazed surreally white, skiers and boarders riding the chairlift up and coming down as if it were noon instead of 10:00 p.m.

Shaking her head—in some ways Meg had to admit to being a conservative—she backed out and accelerated carefully. Incredible to think she'd arrived at seven this morning. Fifteen hours ago. She was tired, but too wired to fall asleep even if she had the chance. Too wired to be hungry, either.

Ben's headlights stayed in her rearview mirror all the way down the mountain. Receiving confirmation on the police radio that Kenneth and Alice Lange resided on 12th Street, Scott's old neighborhood, Meg was able to drive straight there even though she couldn't make out street signs through the falling snow. She knew this part of town on a level deeper than memory. It was part of her, one of the reasons Elk Springs would forever be *home*.

But once she'd pulled up at the curb in front of the brick house blurred by the snow, Meg didn't get out immediately. She hated looking at bodies, but she'd take that any day over having to tell a mother and father their daughter was dead.

She couldn't procrastinate forever, though; Ben waited on the sidewalk, a dark, patient figure hunched against the weather.

Meg joined him. "I hate doing this."

Both picked their way carefully up the walk, icy pavement beneath the fresh inches of snow. Meg had a sudden picture of Shelly Lange's father out here shovelling tomorrow, working despite his grief. Or perhaps because of it.

"I can tell them," Ben offered, his glance unreadable.

Tempting, but she couldn't take him up on it. She'd feel like a coward. And, new as Meg was in the department, she didn't dare appear weak. Women cops had to be stronger than the men in ways that had nothing to do with muscle mass.

"I found her." Stepping onto the small porch, Meg pressed the doorbell. "But thank you."

The porch light came on, and she faced the door as it opened. Scowling at her was a short, husky man with a receding hairline, still dressed as if he'd just stepped in the door from work in an office—he hadn't even loosened his tie. "Do you know how late it is?" he was growling before he saw who stood on his doorstep.

"Mr. Lange?" she asked.

Wariness replaced his irritation. "That's right."

"We're police officers." She showed her ID. "We need to talk to you."

He continued to block the opening. Behind him a television set murmured and a woman asked whether something was wrong. The man ignored her. "What's this about?"

"Your daughter."

"I don't have a daughter." He started to shut the door.

Quicker than Meg, Ben inserted a foot.

"Mr. Lange," Meg said bluntly, "your daughter is dead."

Through the crack she saw no visible reaction on his face. He said nothing.

"We do need to speak to you and your wife."

For a moment he still made no move, although a muscle jumped along his jaw. At last he grunted and stood back. "Come in, then. If you insist."

Meg and Ben trailed him across a small entry into a dark living room. As they entered, a woman leaped to her feet and scurried behind one of a pair of recliners. Only one lamp at the far end of the room was on; the television set glowed a hypnotic blue-white. Out of the corner of her eye, Meg noticed that it was tuned to an evening soap opera aimed at older teens and notorious for sex and scandal.

Kenneth Lange went to the TV and switched it off. "Trash," he muttered. "I'm watching for the good of the youth in my church."

"Right," Ben breathed in Meg's ear.

She poked him with an elbow. "May I turn on this light, Mr. Lange?"

He mumbled what she took as assent. The illumination from the second lamp let Meg really see the woman hovering to one side, her hands clasped and her entire body language radiating anxiety.

Alice Lange would have been a pretty woman still if she'd worn makeup and been more relaxed. But tiny lines etched beside her eyes and mouth looked as if they'd been formed by a lifetime of worries, like earth worn down by trickles of water rather than torrents. Her face was bare, her uncolored brown hair graying in streaks accentuated by the tight bun. Her housedress was shapeless and faded.

"What is it?" she asked timidly.

"Mrs. Lange," Meg focused on her alone, "I'm afraid your daughter Shelly is dead."

Shock made Alice Lange's face go blank; agony crumpled it a second later. She sucked in a breath that was also a moan.

Her husband didn't even look at her. "We've already said our goodbyes," he said brusquely. "Whatever she's gotten herself into has nothing to do with us."

Ben stirred. "What makes you think she's 'gotten herself into' anything?"

Uncertainty flickered in Lange's eyes. "Why…your attitude. Coming here like this. Confronting us. Instead of just bringing word."

"As it happens," Ben said coldly, "you're right. She was murdered."

Shelly's mother let out a keening sound that made Meg ache to comfort her. But she couldn't. Not in these circumstances, not with this odd reaction to news that should have brought pain to both parents.

"How long has it been since you've seen your daughter?" Meg asked, looking at Kenneth Lange.

"A year." His mouth puckered, as though even so much of an answer tasted sour. "She defiled my name. She made her own bed."

Meg imagined the young woman being forced to walk through snow, falling into the tree well, trying to scramble out, begging for her life, the crack of the gun, the bullet shattering her skull....

"Not this one." Her own tone was harsh. "Nobody deserved this one."

A muscle tic below his eye betrayed some emotion. "What do you want from us?"

"You know she had a child?"

Mrs. Lange stared wildly. "She's dead? Not her, too?"

"No. Your granddaughter is alive and well. Thanks to Shelly." Of course, Meg knew nothing of the kind, but it was a reasonable assumption, and as much comfort as she could give. "She's in a foster home."

"We have no granddaughter."

His wife gave a small gasp through her silent tears.

Meg faced him. "She's a baby. Six months old at the most. She didn't shame you."

"She's the wages of sin. A bastard." He seemed to savor the word.

Meg looked at Alice Lange. Grief and hot tears filled

her eyes, but she said nothing. Didn't dare say anything, Meg guessed. Perhaps it didn't even occur to her to protest.

Meg took another step forward. "Mr. Lange, I have to ask you where you were yesterday evening."

He stared at her, uncomprehending for five seconds, ten. Then he got it. Rage twisted his face. "You may be a police officer, but you have no right to come to my house and accuse me of something like that! I won't have it! Do you hear me?"

"We both hear you," Ben said. He stepped to her side, dropping the pretense of being her shadow. With his size, he wordlessly expressed an implicit threat of force in a way she couldn't. "But, given the conflict between your daughter and yourself, we must insist that you answer."

A different time, a different place, Meg would have called him to heel, like a good dog. This was her interview. She would never have interfered if Ben had been in her place. Every new partner, she had to start over again. Why did they all assume that she, a mere woman, couldn't stand up to an angry man?

Quelling her irritation, Meg told herself he'd learn. He was trying to be helpful. She'd proved herself too many times to get her feelings hurt.

Ben and Kenneth Lange were glaring at each other in a typically masculine game of chicken. Meg put her money on her new partner. He did that narrow-eyed, cold stare so well. And he carried a gun and the law on his side.

"Ken," Mrs. Lange whispered, her frightened gaze going from one man to the other. "Just tell him."

He looked away first. His face soured, and his voice was bitter with humiliation. "Home. My wife can tell you."

"That's right. He came right home from work," she said quickly. Too quickly, given the tears she was wiping from her face with the back of her hand? "We had dinner and prayed. The bishop called, didn't he? You spoke to him while I cleaned the kitchen and did laundry. I got the ink stains out of Kenneth's shirt…" She stopped, finished lamely, "That's all. And then we went to bed."

Meg switched gears. "What is the baby's name?"

"We have had no contact with our daughter."

At least he admitted he had one.

"She did write." The whites of Alice Lange's eyes showed as she realized that she was contradicting her husband. "Kenneth didn't read them."

"But you did." Meg was immediately sorry she'd spoken; Kenneth Lange's wife would pay for any disobedience, just as his daughter had. Just as Meg's mother had; as she herself had.

"Oh, no," Mrs. Lange whispered. "I wouldn't… Not when Kenneth said…" Her eyes filled with fresh tears. "How was she killed?"

"She was shot," Ben said.

Mrs. Lange put a hand to her mouth and backed up blindly. Suddenly a strangled sound came from her. She whirled and ran from the room. Meg made a move, then stopped. Her comfort wouldn't be welcome. Alice Lange wanted what she was unlikely to get: her husband's.

Another assumption. Irritated at herself now, Meg turned back to the man she had just realized she acutely disliked because he reminded her of her father. Okay, Kenneth Lange was a sanctimonious jerk who had disowned his daughter—*and* his infant granddaughter. He wasn't showing any sign of regret or grief at the news of Shelly's murder.

On the other hand, Meg didn't yet know what Shelly had done to anger him. And plenty of men hid pain because they thought they were supposed to.

Wait, she told herself. *Be sure. Then I can hate the SOB.*

"Your wife needs you," she said flatly. "We'll undoubtedly have questions another time. Good night, Mr. Lange."

He said nothing, only followed the police officers to the door.

On the porch, Meg turned. "One last question. Who is the father of Shelly's baby?"

For the first time, she saw pain on his face—pain and bitterness. "I doubt she knew herself. She was a whore." He closed the door; the porch light went out.

"Nice guy," Ben muttered.

"I wonder," Meg mused, turning up her collar against the snow and starting down the steps, "if anything she did ever pleased him."

Ben, just ahead of her, shook his head. "All I know is, she sure did figure out how to tick him off royally."

As, Meg thought suddenly, she had done with her own father. She sometimes speculated that she had wanted him to walk in on her that day with Johnny. She had wanted to hurt him, and what better way?

It was sad—no, pathetic—that young women had to feel so powerless. Sex seemed the only way for them to deal mortal wounds. What they didn't understand was that they, too, would be hurt.

Meg stopped beside her car. "Question is," she said, dealing with the present, "whether he was ticked off enough to kill her."

"Yep," Ben agreed. "That is definitely the question."

CHAPTER SIX

WHETHER KENNETH LANGE had hated his daughter enough to kill her was not the only question worth asking, of course. It might be interesting to know, for example, whether in his opinion real promiscuity was required to make a woman a "whore"—or whether any premarital sex at all was enough to qualify poor Shelly.

Also high on Meg's "to learn" list was discovering the identity of the father of Shelly Lange's baby.

At first sight, her studio apartment offered no clue.

It was above a detached garage, facing an alley. The older couple who had rented out the apartment to Shelly admitted to knowing little about her. She could come and go without their seeing her, the husband told Ben apologetically. She *seemed* nice. She paid her rent on time. The baby was always well-dressed and appeared happy. They did know that Shelly attended the junior college and worked part-time in the library there. She'd told them that she was enrolled in a program for young women on welfare, and that daycare for Emily was free. Is she all right? they asked, and cried when Ben told them.

Emily. Meg savored the name, picturing the little girl with soft brown hair and round cheeks. It was a lovely name, just right. Had Shelly chosen it herself, or with Emily's father?

Ben and Meg briefly looked over Shelly's car, a ten-year-old Honda Civic with duct tape holding together the upholstery, but otherwise scrupulously tidy inside. A backpack on the passenger seat held textbooks and school notes. In the trunk was a jack and spare tire, as well as tire chains for heavy snow. A red plastic rattle lay on the floor in front of the back seat. She'd been careful, Meg thought, and buckled her daughter in the back, even though it would have been easier to put her in the front, since the Civic was a two-door.

The one-room apartment had come furnished. Shelly had added a crib, painted white, and a plastic folding playpen. Ben and Meg looked around without opening drawers or the medicine cabinet. Tomorrow the apartment would have to be dusted for fingerprints. Tonight was merely a reconnaissance, but not a successful one. No silver-framed photograph of a handsome man sat on the end table; no uncashed check for child support lay on the kitchen counter.

"Done?" Ben asked.

Meg took another lingering look around and felt a stab of pity for the girl, so young, who had done everything she could to make a cheerful home for her baby.

No assumptions, she reminded herself. It would be all too easy to see herself in Shelly. If she looked in the mirror, she'd see a reflection, not the true picture.

"Yeah," she agreed. "I'm done."

They sealed the apartment with police tape and parted ways. Midnight, and Meg was finally able to go home.

Will was long since—she hoped—asleep. No matter how late she got home, Meg always slipped into his bedroom and kissed him good-night. How lucky she'd been, she thought, from such a hard start to end up with such a neat kid. Even if Jack chose not to play a role in his son's life, Will would do fine.

Why hadn't Shelly been as lucky?

The question hung in Meg's mind like a foul-smelling wisp of air, but she ignored it. Tomorrow was soon enough to investigate its origin—to track down the garbage that needed taking out. Tonight she would kiss her son's cheek, close her eyes and breathe in his essence.

And go to bed herself, to dream of something besides blood-red snow.

"COFFEE?" Scott asked, jiggling baby Emily against his shoulder as he stepped aside to let the two police officers into his house. He patted Emily's back and she let out an unladylike belch.

"No, thank you," Meg Patton said. She avoided meeting his eyes.

The other cop echoed her refusal. Both were being straight-faced and formal, even stiff. With a flash of anger, Scott wondered whether, if it weren't for Emily, he'd have been slapped in handcuffs and read his rights. Only once had Meg softened, and that was earlier when she'd phoned to warn him they were coming and to tell him Emily's name.

"Isn't it pretty?" she had said. Even over the phone, he could hear the sweetness as she sampled it again. "Emily."

The name had been on the list Penny and he had made when she was pregnant. If the baby had been a girl, she would have been Emily, Sarah or Elizabeth. He wondered if Shelly knew that, if his wife, chattering, had shared every possibility as the neighbor teenager helped her refinish the chest of drawers for the nursery or paint the walls. Could her choice of name be coincidence?

Shelly Lange. God. Pretty, bright-faced Shelly, dead with a bullet in her head. He shied away from the too vivid picture he had from yesterday of the blood and the corpse frozen like meat in a locker.

When he made himself remember Shelly alive, it was the thirteen-year-old girl he saw, not the young woman he'd known more recently. Emily's influence, he thought again; he had this vision from his other life, of turning back just as he and Penny were going out the door, seeing Shelly cuddling Nate, making faces until he gurgled in delight.

A little girl herself, brutally murdered.

He gave his head a baffled shake, then realized both police officers were looking at him as if waiting for a response. "What?" Scott asked.

"Mr. McNeil," Detective Shea said woodenly, "I believe your doorbell rang."

"Doorbell?" Good God, he was losing it. "I'm sorry. I'm…" What? Lost in the past? Too tired to function normally? Busy burping a baby? "Excuse me," he said just as unemotionally. "That must be my housekeeper."

Marjorie bustled in, freed herself from her winter trappings, and delightedly took charge of little Emily. Leaving Scott, unfortunately, to face the police officers without her leavening presence.

"You're sure you don't want coffee?" he repeated, going back to the entry. Damn it, he sounded as if he were begging. The concept was so primitive. *Accept my hospitality; prove that you trust me.*

"No, Mr. McNeil," Meg said, gaze expressionless. "We'd prefer to get right to our questions."

He didn't like having Meg Patton look at him as if he were bacteria growing in a petri dish. He knew her; they'd spent hours together. For God's sake, he'd helped find Shelly Lange's body! And for that he was being treated like a suspect.

Hell, why beat around the bush? He *was* a suspect, clearly.

"Fine," Scott said, as if unaware of the undercurrents. He nodded toward the arched opening into the living room. "Let's sit down. You're sure Emily is Shelly's daughter?"

Stupid question. Or phrased stupidly. Emily wouldn't be Emily if she weren't Shelly's baby girl. She'd be…who knows. Susan. Samantha. Lisa.

"Ms. Lange did have a photo, taken at Christmas, in her wallet," Meg said. "I have no doubt this is the same child."

"Good." He heard himself and thought, *Good? Why good?*

They all sat, Scott in the leather chair where he often read, Meg at one of the couches and Detective Shea in the other chair. Scott had been flanked, which made him edgy.

"Mr. McNeil," Meg said, "please tell us what you know of Shelly Lange."

"Uh…" He wanted to leap up and pace. He moved his shoulders restlessly, but made himself stay sitting. "As I told you, she lived two doors down from the house my then wife and I bought when we came to Elk Springs. I was involved with developing the ski area from the beginning," he added as an aside. "Shelly was…just a kid. Twelve, thirteen. The moving truck had barely parked at the curb and she was over knocking at our door. She was always friendly, bubbly, liked being around people."

They were making notes, both of them. Scott felt more than ever like a lab subject.

"And so you established a...friendship with this girl?" The faint pause midsentence made it clear where Detective Shea was going.

Scott's jaw muscles locked and his fingers tightened on the arms of the chair, but he was familiar enough with adversarial tactics to keep his voice civil. "No. My wife, who was home days, enjoyed Shelly's company. The girl seemed to like to hang out at our house, but mainly after school. I actually saw very little of her. Until..." His throat tightened.

"Until?" Meg prodded.

"We had a baby." His voice was as raw as bare skin scraping gravel. He was careful not to look at Meg. "Shelly baby-sat for us. Probably a dozen times. She was...really good with my son."

"Did you fire her?" Shea asked.

Scott didn't rise to the bait. "My wife and I got a divorce. We sold the house. I bought this one, she went back to Seattle to be near her parents." The truth, but not the whole truth. "I didn't see Shelly again until she applied for a job at Juanita Butte. I recognized her. Barely."

"Was she qualified for the job, or did you offer it to her because of your...past?"

Another one of those goddamn pauses raised Scott's hackles. "She knew how to work a cash register. She dressed with style and she was friendly. That made her plenty qualified to work in the ski shop."

"Did you see much of her after she hired on?" Meg asked, tone neutral.

"No," he said shortly. "I glanced in the shop now and again. That's all."

"What did she say when she quit?"

"She gave notice to her supervisor. I didn't know anything about it until later. She told Carol she was going back to school. It was about the time when winter quarter started. I don't know whether she really did."

"And did you call her later?" Every damn word Shea said held an undertone of doubt, even sarcasm.

Scott had too much self-control to show how irritated he was. "No. Why would I?"

One dark eyebrow slid up in unspoken answer. *Because you had something going with her.*

Meg gave her partner a warning glance, then focused on Scott. "Did she have a boyfriend that you were aware of? Did you see her with anyone? Did her supervisor mention a relationship?"

He rarely paid much attention to that kind of thing. People talked, which meant he knew more than he usually acknowledged. But in this case…

"I saw her with someone. Surprised them once in an empty part of the lodge."

The passionate embrace might not have stuck in his memory if the two participants hadn't looked so startled and fearful. *Not fearful, embarrassed,* he'd told himself at the time, unable to understand why they'd be anything more. Surely they hadn't believed they'd lose their jobs because they were necking in an out-of-the-way part of the lodge.

"I presume," Detective Shea said with that heavy note of irony, "you recall who that 'someone' was."

Was this a good cop/bad cop game? Scott was getting seriously annoyed. What's more, he felt like a crud, throwing this poor kid to the wolves. But did he have a choice?

"One of the young guys who works in Mechanical." He frowned. "Tony. Uh…Tony Rieger."

"Mechanical," Meg repeated, making a note. When she looked up, her eyes met Scott's. "You understand that we'll need to interview a number of your employees. Anybody who knew Shelly."

"Yes, I understand."

"Then I believe that's all we'll need from you for now." She rose, closing her notebook.

Detective Shea followed suit.

They were going to walk out, just like that? Without telling him anything about what was going on?

"Wait just a minute." The crack of authority brought startled expressions to both their faces. Good. "Did you talk to Shelly's parents?"

"Yes, we did." Comprehension showed in Meg's eyes and she sank back to the couch. "I'm sorry. You want to know about Emily's status. Yes, we did see her parents. Mr. Lange apparently disowned Shelly—a year ago, he says. Since her baby was born out of wedlock, he considers her the 'wages of sin.' Quote unquote. He has no interest in custody. I didn't get the impression his wife is willing to defy him, even if she feels differently. So at the moment, if you're doing okay with Emily…"

Bad sign that he was so relieved. Emily wasn't his. She was a guest. He couldn't let himself get attached.

"She's fine." A reluctant smile caught the corner of his mouth when a happy squeal drifted from the bedroom wing. "Obviously."

Ben Shea almost smiled. Meg did. Forming dimples,

the flash of merriment transformed the grim-faced law enforcement officer into a woman he could imagine kissing.

About the furthest thing from her mind, Scott thought ruefully, considering he was currently a murder suspect. The devil of it was, he had no easy way of taking himself off her short list. Scott had been alone in the lodge for the couple hours before Emily was abandoned. The security officers wouldn't be able to swear he hadn't left for an hour.

Unless Shelly had been killed substantially earlier, he wasn't off the hook.

And how could he prove that he'd never had a sexual relationship with Shelly? All he could do was hope like hell that Meg believed him. He was in his mid-thirties; to him, Shelly had been a kid. He didn't go to bed with teenagers.

Meg started to rise again, then sat back. "Any chance you have a list of ski area personnel here at home? Names, jobs, phone numbers?"

"You seriously think somebody at Juanita Butte did this?" He looked from her to Ben and back. "Most of Shelly's life had nothing to do with the ski area! She only worked there for five months, and that was a year ago."

"It's just a starting point. Emily was left in the area parking lot. Why were they there? And the murderer almost had to know that country. Unless he'd killed and dumped Shelly hours earlier while it was still daylight—and then why abandon Emily when and where he did?—he'd have been turning into the Puma Lake road in the dark. Would he have dared if he hadn't driven it in winter conditions before? If he didn't know it was used regularly by cross-country skiers and snow-mobilers? He sure as heck couldn't afford to get stuck."

"Patton..." her partner growled in clear warning.

Meg waved him off. "It's just common sense. Mr. McNeil can figure this much out himself."

Shea still didn't like it. Standing, he said stiffly, "We'd better be on our way. We need to talk to Forest Service people. And reporters."

"Why don't you do that while I get the information from Mr. McNeil?" she suggested. "I can meet you at the office in...say, an hour and a half?"

He scowled at Scott and conceded grudgingly, "Yeah, okay."

Scott let her walk her partner to the door. He heard the murmur of their voices for several minutes before she returned.

The other man gone, Scott offered coffee again. This time she took him up on it. Perching on one of the bar stools in the kitchen, she watched him pour.

"You don't want to think anyone who works for you could commit murder," she observed.

Glass damn near cracked as he whacked the coffeepot back down. "Would you? No. I don't. If I hired somebody who could do this, that makes me responsible. And a bad judge of character."

She tilted her head to one side and regarded him gravely. "You've heard the saying that anybody could commit murder in the right circumstances."

"Yeah." His mouth twisted. "The right circumstances for most of us involve protecting our wives or children. Or self-defense. That I could understand."

"How do you know this murderer *didn't* have one of those motives?"

"What?" He looked incredulously at her, sitting so calmly in his kitchen, gun on her hip, talking about rational reasons for killing.

"Shelly's father implied that she was promiscuous. What if one of those affairs was with a married man? What if she was blackmailing him? Isn't that a threat to the security of his family?"

"Not the same kind of thing," Scott argued.

"Not to you or me." Meg stirred cream into her coffee. "But to the man who murdered her, it might have seemed that way."

"And maybe he just enjoys killing."

"Maybe," she agreed. "But we haven't had a serial killer working around here. And someone wandering through Butte County wouldn't have known about the Puma Lake road."

"He might have stumbled on it," Scott said stubbornly. "Taken a chance."

"Why would he? Why not kill her and dump her body out between here and Medford somewhere? Lower elevation, lots of deserted roads, not much snow…" She shrugged. "Which is not to say we won't consider every possibility."

"Did you find any fingerprints on the car seat?"

"Only glove prints."

He grunted, disappointed.

She sipped coffee, watching him over the rim. Speaking abruptly, she asked, "Why did you tell me you didn't have any children?"

He'd been waiting for the question. Scott looked around the kitchen, done in pale natural maple with a rust-brown tile countertop, and tried to ground himself.

This was a long way from the past; he could recite the bare facts without tapping into the emotion.

"It's not something I like to talk about." Even to his own ears, his voice was robotic, mechanization without soul. "My wife and I had a son. Nathaniel. Nate. He died of Sudden Infant Death Syndrome when he was five and a half months old."

"Ohh," came out on a soft, pitying breath. Startling Scott, Meg laid a hand over his and gripped with fierce strength. "I'm sorry. Sorry for your loss, and sorry I asked."

He turned his hand; palm met palm. "You had to," he said roughly, telling himself the burning in his sinuses wasn't tears. "Now you know."

"Is that what happened to your marriage?"

"Yeah." He cleared his throat, swallowed hard, blinked a couple of times. "We couldn't get past the grief. And the blame."

"Blame?"

She had kind eyes, soft and blue like a summer sky. Now, after that first moment, he didn't sense pity coming from her so much as compassion. Scott still didn't want to lay bare his pain, but somewhat to his surprise he did feel a compulsion to finish the story.

"I put Nate to bed that night. Penny believed I'd done something wrong. She could never decide what, but something." He swallowed. "She was right, as things have turned out. If I'd laid him on his back…"

Meg's fingernails bit into his hand. "You didn't know. You *couldn't* know. Not even the doctors did."

Now his eyes burned. "But I still can't help thinking. That one night, if I'd just put him down on his back…"

"You couldn't know," she repeated.

She might as well not have spoken.

The present had vanished but for the anchor of her hand on his. He was seeing the past, the soft darkness of the nursery, the golden glow from the Pooh night-light. Hearing the swish, swish as the rocker slowed and stopped when he rose to gently lay his sleeping son in his crib.

Nate sighed and pulled his knees up under him so that his diapered bottom stuck up. Scott was once again tucking the blankets over the small figure, his hands lingering, feeling the warmth. Slowly backing away from the crib, trying not to wake the sleeping baby.

He was trying to remember if, after that sigh, he'd heard his son take another breath.

"Scott."

He tasted blood, his jaw clenched so hard.

"Scott, you couldn't know." She took his coffee mug from him, held both of his hands, looked deep into his eyes. "It happened. It might have happened no matter what."

He bowed his head and fought for control. "That's not the worst part," he said rawly.

"What is?" Meg's voice was aloe on a burn, soothing, liquid.

"I blamed Penny, too. I told her so. I couldn't have hurt her more if I'd tried. Hell, I probably was trying! I could see in her eyes that she thought I was right. She'll live with that forever."

"Why did you blame her?"

He freed one of his hands to rub it across his face. Usually he'd have been embarrassed by the dampness. Today the fact that he'd cried seemed…unimportant. Natural. How long had it been since he'd had a woman's comfort?

"She smoked when she was pregnant. Just couldn't quit. Nate was born two weeks early, a couple ounces under six pounds. The doctors had warned her."

"And birth weight seems to have a connection to SIDS."

"Yeah." He scrubbed his face again.

"But most babies born to mothers who smoke don't die."

"No." Now his eyes were so dry they felt wind-burned. "Penny tried. She cut down. She did her best. If only I'd kept my mouth shut…"

"But she must have been thinking the same thing. That's why she wanted to blame you."

"Yeah, and I wanted to blame her." He uttered a short, gruff laugh that held absolutely no humor. "Hell of a note. Feel guilty? Must be someone else's fault. Make sure they know it."

"And it wasn't anyone's fault."

His eyes met hers. "Maybe. But I'm not sure I'll ever believe that."

"I think," she said softly, not looking away from his pain, "that someday you will. Or at least that you'll find peace."

Enough self-pity. Scott let go of her hand and stepped back, physically as well as emotionally. "I've learned to live with it. That'll do."

Her blue eyes seemed suddenly clear rather than soft, and disconcertingly perceptive. "Most of the time, it has to," she said.

"I'll go get my company directory."

Nodding, she accepted his retreat. "Thank you."

Twenty minutes later she was gone and Scott prepared himself to head up the mountain to break the bad news to people who'd known and worked with Shelly Lange.

He only hoped they were more upset by her death than by the fact that every one of them was now a murder suspect.

CHAPTER SEVEN

THE DESK OFFICER on duty at the Elk Springs P.D. told her Chief Murray was in. "I'll take you on back," she said, eyes full of curiosity.

Meg had hoped that this time she'd be just another county sheriff's deputy here to see the police chief. Yeah, right. People had been talking. The unexpected reappearance of Renee's sister had been worth a good gossip or two.

"Is Renee here?" Meg asked.

That question earned a more probing glance. "I think she's on a call. Shall I check?"

"No, thanks. I'll catch her at home." Meg waited a few steps down the hall while the young woman officer stopped in an open doorway.

"Chief, Deputy Patton's here to see you."

Apparently he agreed to see her—Meg didn't hear his voice—but the officer waved her in.

Oh, God—oh, God—oh, God. Fifteen years and one big secret later, she was about to see Johnny Murray again. Her heart was trying to bounce out of her chest.

She had a horrible feeling that Renee was right; however much she'd dreaded telling Johnny—Jack—about Will, it was worse facing him now that he'd already discovered the secret.

Taking a good firm grip on her pride, Meg sauntered into that office as if she'd been here a million times. She wasn't about to give away the fact that she was pumping out adrenaline as if she were entering a deserted building after an armed felon.

Meg looked everywhere but at Jack, but he might as well have been strung with blinking lights. She saw him through her pores, even though she made herself take her time and glance around.

The office was modern and spacious but institutional, with pale gray linoleum tile, cream-colored walls and gray blinds at the window. He hadn't bothered to personalize it with artwork, but had managed to make it his own all the same with the heaps of files that sat on every surface, the file cabinet drawers that were open, the uniform coat hung haphazardly over a chair back.

"Well," Meg said brazenly, "your mother tried."

Jack's eyes narrowed. "You want to explain that?"

"You haven't gotten any neater."

He shook his head. "And you're as mouthy as ever."

"That's what you liked about me." She turned a chair around and straddled it with her arms crossed on the back. And she looked, finally and thoroughly.

He'd changed so much he wasn't Johnny anymore. And yet he was. Oh, she knew that face, lean and stubborn. Those eyes, the color of melting chocolate. That straight dark hair, which had once grazed his collar and fallen over his forehead. As if it was yesterday, she saw him pushing it impatiently back before making a point with some emphatic gesture.

Only then…then he'd been skinnier, not so muscular. His feet and hands had been too big even for his lanky body. His walk had been gawky. He'd tended to hunch his shoulders and slump in his seat, not hold himself with pride and patience. His face had been more open, too, happier, she thought.

He'd been a boy, not a man.

He'd looked like her son.

He still did.

He waited out her scrutiny, or didn't notice it because he was busy looking her over, too.

"Actually," he said at last, his gaze flicking lower, "I'm not so sure that is why I liked you. You had other qualities that attracted me."

She made a face, conceding the point. "We were young, weren't we?"

Did his eyes soften? "Yeah. Kids."

Meg looked around again. "Was this my father's office?"

"Yep." Jack leaned back in his desk chair and clasped his hands behind his head. The uniform fabric pulled tight over impressive muscles.

Meg didn't feel a twitch of interest.

She looked pointedly at the file spilling its contents onto the floor. "He must be rolling over in his grave."

Jack raised an eyebrow. "Maybe I hope so. Could be that's why I'm tossing files all over the place."

"Hoo boy." She congratulated him. "Quite a revenge."

Anger flickered in his eyes and he sat up abruptly enough to make his chair squeal. "Your father and I made our peace. I can't help it if you didn't do the same with him."

"He never would have given me any peace." Meg held up a hand. "Let's drop it. There's no point in our quarreling. Too many years under the bridge. You said it. We were kids. How about if we leave it at that?"

His mouth thinned. "How can we, considering?"

"You mean Will."

"How could you not tell me?"

"I didn't dare."

His jaw muscles spasmed. "If I'd known you were pregnant, I wouldn't have left that day."

He looked as if he believed it. Who was she to disillusion him?

"I'm here today for official reasons," she said.

His face went stony, expressionless. "All right."

"You've heard about the body we found at the Puma Lake trailhead?"

Jack inclined his head.

"The victim lived in Elk Springs. So do her parents. She attended the junior college. Just wanted you to know we'll be conducting interviews."

He didn't blink. "As always, we'll be happy to cooperate in any way."

"And we'll keep you informed."

"Fine," he said curtly.

Oh, good. They were off on the right foot. Suddenly ashamed, Meg was glad Will couldn't know how she'd set about this interview.

She hesitated. "Will told me about coming here."

"Apparently your edicts didn't cover visiting Aunt Renee. He looked pretty shocked when he saw that I recognized him."

She found herself smiling ruefully. "It's hard to be specific enough to cover everything. He thinks creatively."

"Like his mom." Jack wasn't exactly smiling, but his mouth had definitely relaxed. "You always were too smart for your own good."

"That depends on your point of view." She went solemn again. "He's your son, Jack."

"I can't deny it. He's the spitting image of me in that high school graduation picture my mom keeps on the mantel at home."

"Will wants to know you."

His face hardened again. "Then why didn't you give him that chance fourteen years ago?"

"You know why."

His gaze didn't waver. "No, I don't."

"You saw my father."

"If I had a daughter and I walked in on some guy on top of her with his pants down, I don't know how I'd react."

"Do you remember when I had a black eye?"

A nerve spasmed below his eye. "The time you said you'd poked it with the handle of the mop?"

"I lied." She swallowed. "The broken jaw?"

Jack closed his eyes. "Why didn't you tell me?"

"I was ashamed." She studied him. "Why don't *you* sound surprised?"

"A couple months ago Renee told me your father was abusive. I think maybe I wasn't surprised even then, but I wanted to be."

With genuine curiosity, Meg asked, "Why would you want to think well of Ed Patton?"

Jack swore and ran a hand over his face. "He was good to me. After I came on the force. Sometimes I wondered if he recognized me. I never reminded him and he never said."

"I don't remember you having any interest in being a cop." That was phrasing it tactfully, Meg congratulated herself; actually, he'd talked about medical school or biology or becoming an astronaut, none of which she'd figured would amount to anything, Jack being Jack. Probably, she had thought, he would drift into taking over his father's appliance store.

He met her eyes as if with difficulty and said, "You're not the only one who was ashamed."

Meg blinked. "What are you saying? You had to prove something to Dad? You decided to make a man of yourself?"

His mouth thinned. "Is that so bad?"

She made a sound. "The bad part is that your idea of a man was anything like my father's."

"You're a funny one to talk." He nodded toward the badge pinned to her uniform. "You seem to have walked in his footprints, too."

Was that shame or anger heating her cheeks? "It was all I knew. College wasn't an option."

His lip curled. "Come on. You must have had other choices in the military. Why aren't you an electrician? A computer programmer? A journalist?"

She didn't like being sneered at. Her instant, hot defensiveness was, ironically, the answer to his question.

"I needed to feel strong."

Jack didn't say anything. Didn't have to. He just lifted one dark brow in that speaking way he had.

Meg made a face. "Yeah, okay. So maybe it makes sense you went the same route. That means you do understand that I was scared of my father."

"So scared you had to disappear for fifteen years?"

"He'd have taken Will away from me if he'd known he existed. He always wanted a son. And he'd have done anything to hurt me."

"You could have told me," he said stubbornly.

"When I took off, didn't he come looking for you?"

"Yeah..." He swore. "I wouldn't have told him."

"Are you sure?"

"Of course I'm sure!" he snapped, but she saw in his eyes the truth: he didn't know.

"He was a bad man," she said. "So full of anger he couldn't hold it in. I don't think he ever loved anybody, or ever thought about anybody else's feelings."

"Renee tells me you found your mother. Why did she marry him in the first place?"

Meg sighed and rested her chin on her forearm, squeezing her eyes shut for a moment. She saw her mother in the hospital bed where she died, wan and thin and attached to life by needles and tubes.

"He said the right things. And when he told her what crap she was, she believed him. Why not? Her father had told her the same things."

Jack shook his head. "But you never believed your father. Why's that?"

"Are you so sure I didn't?" Voice flat, Meg pushed herself to her feet. "I'm not in the mood to be psycho-analyzed. I shouldn't have started this. I just wanted you to know that I'll be glad for whatever you can give Will. And I wanted to say I'm sorry for not sharing him. I was afraid. I don't know if that's enough excuse or not."

"Too late to improve on it." Jack clearly wasn't in the mood to say, "Sure it is. You're forgiven." She couldn't blame him.

Meg sighed. "Don't take out your anger at me on Will."

He swore. "Goddamn it, Meg! Do you really think I'd do that?"

She bowed her head and swallowed the lump in her

throat. "No," she said inaudibly. "The other day…it sounds like you were nice to him. He was excited. It must have been a shock. I *am* sorry about that."

"Were you planning to keep him hidden for the next four years?" Jack studied her with genuine curiosity.

"No." She grimaced. "I kept chickening out. Some things I'm brave about, but I guess telling you the truth wasn't one of them. I really am…"

"Sorry. Yeah, yeah." Jack frowned. "I won't make any promises."

"No." She met his eyes with naked hope. "Just give him…"

"What I can." He finished her sentence again. "I heard you the first time."

Meg held herself straight. "I love my son. Don't hurt him."

Another flicker of anger narrowed his eyes. "Some things can't be helped. But I won't on purpose. That's the best I can do."

Meg hesitated, gave an abrupt nod and left. She couldn't ask any more of him. If Will got hurt, it was her doing, not Jack's. She had made the decisions that counted, long ago.

She refused to regret them.

SHELLY LANGE'S APARTMENT had little to tell Ben and Meg, though poignancy aplenty lurked to tap them on the shoulders.

Textbooks and a binder full of notes testified that she was, indeed, a community college student. Meg thumbed through the binder. Math 103—pretty basic, it must not have been one of her strengths. English 202—report writing. Child Development. That one made Meg shiver. Shelly's reason for taking it was likely personal. Ceramics. Aerobics. A reasonably full schedule. No hint at her major, if she'd settled on one yet.

No computer; she must have used the computer lab on campus. Both her wardrobe and Emily's were fairly extensive, which surprised Meg given Shelly's limited income. Without any real hope of finding anything interesting, Meg flipped through the miniature corduroy overalls and cute printed turtlenecks in the dresser drawers stenciled with bunnies. In the bottom, she found a grocery sack. Interested, Meg sank back on her heels.

These were larger sizes—eighteen months, two years. Cute stuff, but used. She found the receipt from the Salvation Army store. All these clothes had cost 13.78. A flyer mentioned a red tag sale.

Shelly had been a careful shopper.

"Damn it, no address book," Ben said behind her.

"Figures," Meg muttered. "Did you look in the phone book?"

He grunted. "The only numbers she'd noted were for the Pizza Palace and the women's center at the community college."

"Any reason Scott McNeil can't come get the crib and Emily's clothes?"

Ben sent her a sharp glance. "You've talked to him?"

"He called this morning to ask." Meg made a point of turning away so her partner didn't see the blush she feared might belie her casual tone. She wasn't about to tell Ben about the fifteen-minute conversation covering a little bit of this and some of that—the kind you had with someone when words came easily, when you both wanted to share the small happenings of your day. Scott hadn't asked questions about the investigation; she hadn't asked any more about his wife and baby. They'd just…talked.

She'd hung up the phone reluctantly. And blocked out the voice of conscience that whispered, *He could have been sleeping with Shelly. He could have killed her and then called 9-1-1.*

Brushing aside that particular wisp of memory, Meg continued, "He's rented a crib and bought a couple of outfits for her, but he's going to have to do some major shopping if we don't free this stuff up."

"It's all a mess."

Meg followed his gaze. The fingerprint techs had already been in. Powder dusted the rails of the crib and grayed the cheerful yellow ducks printed on the sheet. The handles of the white-painted dresser that held Emily's clothes were smudged. The clothes themselves would all have to be washed.

"He has a housekeeper," she said dryly.

"True." Ben shrugged. "I don't see why he can't take the kid's things once we've looked 'em over."

Looking Shelly's possessions over didn't take long. She had so little. No photo albums. The only picture was a framed eight-by-ten version of the one in Shelly's wallet, sitting atop Emily's dresser.

The couch pulled out into a bed. Dishes and utensils were minimal, food sparse in the tiny kitchenette. Shelly had apparently eaten fruit and microwave dinners; her beverage of choice was Pepsi. A twelve-pack was unopened on top of the small refrigerator; four were cold in the fridge. One cupboard held rows of baby-food jars, a box of Gerber's oatmeal, and several cans of formula.

The lack of possessions suggested she'd left home in the clothes she stood up in. No chance to pack stuffed animals or photos of friends or high school yearbooks. She'd started from scratch, which for a pregnant nineteen-year-old girl meant she'd begged, borrowed and stolen food and shelter. Meg knew.

It looked to her as if Shelly had done darn well for herself—and for Emily—under the circumstances. She was lucky or smart. Maybe both.

But however smart, she'd gotten into a car with a man who'd intended to murder her. Meg's job was to figure out why Shelly had gone. If he'd forced her, how? If she'd gone willingly, why did she think she could trust this man?

Or woman, Meg amended silently, although she was reasonably sure the perp was a man on two counts: first, the crime didn't have the stamp of a woman; and second, the footprints returning alone to the parking lot were way bigger than Shelly's.

"We need to take a look at Shelly's bedroom at her parents' house," she said aloud.

"Her father's the kind I can see burning everything she owned after he booted her out," Ben said.

"Maybe," Meg agreed doubtfully. Her own father had shut her bedroom door, shrugged and not bothered. She knew; she'd asked Renee. But then, he hadn't cared, not really. What Meg hadn't figured out yet was whether Kenneth Lange did care underneath the bluster.

They went by the Lange's quiet brick house, but no one came in answer to the doorbell.

"The college?" Ben suggested.

Meg glanced at her watch and nodded. "Students should still be around."

They picked up Shelly's schedule at the Admin office after listening to expressions of regret from staff who obviously hadn't known her well enough to be of any use to the investigation.

The Child Development class would be letting out in ten minutes. Shelly would normally have taken math that morning at nine and aerobics at three. English and ceramics were Monday/Wednesday classes, but the secretary marked a map of the campus so Meg and Ben could find the professors' offices.

The Child Development instructor was a woman, fortyish, who stopped midsentence when Meg eased open the classroom door and she and Ben slipped into the back.

Behind the podium, Clara Simpson said, "Yes? May I help you?"

Students turned in their seats, pulled into a semicircle.

Meg hesitated, then stepped forward. "I apologize for interrupting. I'm Deputy Margaret Patton. This is Detective Ben Shea." She looked from face to face. "I imagine you've all heard that one of your fellow students, Shelly Lange, was murdered three days ago. We're the investigating officers. We'd like to talk to each of you privately for a moment before you go to your next class."

The instructor said briskly, "Why don't you get started now? We discussed the tragedy earlier and would like to do everything we can to help."

Meg nodded her thanks. "Would you mind waiting, too, Professor Simpson?"

Clara Simpson wore Birkenstocks and a flowery broomstick skirt, her graying blond hair in a loose knot on her head. She had a no-nonsense air and kind eyes.

"Certainly," she agreed. "Class, let's continue our

discussion while the officers take you aside one at a time. Jennifer, we were discussing separation anxiety in the eight-month-old child. You had a comment?"

"Yeah," the young woman said. "My older sister, see, she has a baby, and he's always crawling after her and crying if she shuts, like, even the bathroom door. He's like, like some kind of *leech. She* doesn't mind, but…eww." She gave a delicate shiver.

Meg tuned her out. She and Ben each chose a student and summoned them out into the hall.

Twenty minutes later they'd released the last of them. Some of the girls weren't even sure who Shelly Lange was. The guys did; Shelly had been really hot, as one put it. Several had known her from high school, and talked about a party girl who got okay grades but didn't try very hard.

"She really liked…" That boy flushed.

"Drugs?" Meg supplied. "Sex?"

"Um…" He shifted. "I don't know about sex. But boys, yeah. She always had…kind of a crowd around her. You know?"

Neither he nor any of the others knew who Shelly had dated her senior year of high school or the summer and fall after graduation.

Clara Simpson didn't have much to contribute, either. "I'm sorry," she said. "This is the first time I've had her in a class. She was doing very well—she contributed to discussions, turned her work in on time, and seemed quite involved. I'm told she's a young mother, however, so her interest is understandable."

Meg left a card, just in case Professor Simpson heard anything or thought of any insight into Shelly's behavior. "We're trying to get to know her, of course,"

Meg said, "but I'm also very interested in finding out about any men she might have been involved with. We have no idea who the father of her baby is."

"I'm afraid we had no personal interaction," Clara Simpson said apologetically, "but I'll certainly keep an ear out."

The aerobics class was even less helpful, not surprisingly. Ninety percent of the students were female. A few knew Shelly had had a baby, and they were awed that she had gone through pregnancy so recently but still had such a great bod.

"I mean, she didn't even have any stretch marks," one named Liza said in awe.

"Yeah, she was really fit," chimed in a second.

A quiet, thin girl said, "It's so sad. What's going to happen to her baby? Does she have, like, parents or something?"

"Yes, she does." Meg chose to leave it at that.

Her pager beeped, and Meg glanced down at the read-out. "Coroner," she told Ben.

The aerobics instructor took them to her office where Meg used the phone. The autopsy was over, Bobby Sanchez told her. He'd assisted Dr. Myron Bart, a pathologist at St. Anne's Hospital. No surprises. The bullet wound had killed Shelly Lange instantly. She wasn't pregnant, and apparently hadn't had sexual relations in the twenty-four hours preceding her death.

"Toxicology screen is back," he continued. "No drugs or alcohol. She was a good girl."

"According to one of the students here at the college, Shelly was still nursing."

"Yeah, that's in the report."

"Emily seems to have come first," Meg commented to Ben as they returned to their car. "The party girl did nothing that would endanger her child. Which makes the timing of the murder odd. Did she start a new relationship? Her landlord and his wife didn't think so. She doesn't seem to have done anything lately that would have set her father off."

"We don't know that," Ben reminded her.

"No," she admitted. "Shelly must have some real friends. Somebody who can tell us what was happening in her life. Whether she'd approached her father. Was seeing a man."

"What I'd like to know is what she lived on." Ben unlocked the passenger side door. "Whether she was paying her bills."

They decided to split up for the rest of the day. Ben would go to the Women's Center to find out what help they'd given Shelly. From there he'd stop by the bank, see what a credit check turned up, and again interview the elderly couple who owned Shelly's apartment.

Meg would drive up to Juanita Butte.

Cars with skis in racks on top streamed down from the mountain. A few wended upward, but the smaller crowd that would take advantage of the night skiing would show later. By the time Meg parked behind the lodge, the lots were two-thirds empty.

The perfect time, she figured, to catch some of the employees.

Upstairs in the lodge, she poked her head into the office where Scott's secretary reigned. Trish Lord was thirty-one years old and pregnant. After racing at Mt. Hood as a kid, she'd started at Juanita Butte operating a lift, eventually taking secretarial and computer classes during the off season at the college. All she'd wanted to do was ski, she'd confessed to Meg the other day. And now the obstetrician said not while she was pregnant.

"As if I have time, anyway," she added, making a face. "My husband's started his own contracting business, and I do the bookkeeping at night. And, you know—" she'd gently touched her swelling belly "—I don't especially miss it."

"To everything, there is a season," Meg had said softly, and seen the agreement in the other woman's eyes. Trish was comforting proof that even ski bums did grow up eventually.

Today, when Trish saw Meg, she said, "Scott told me about Shelly Lange. How horrible! Are you looking for him? He's out taking a few runs, but I can page him if you need him."

"Heavens, no! I wouldn't want to ruin his fun."

"Work," the secretary corrected her, going stiff. "He's General Manager. How can he know whether the lift attendants are doing their job, or how long lines are, or whether complaints about grooming on Sunset are right on, if he doesn't get out there?"

Meg held up her hands. "You're right. He couldn't, any more than cops can do their job from the station. Conditions look good today, though. Unless you groomed away all the fresh snow…"

Trish's quick grin lit her face. "Are you kidding? That's not just snow, it's powder! Light as air. People come here for it. I'd rather be out on the hill, too." She glanced ruefully down at her stomach, bumped up against the desk.

They discussed how hard it would be to ski pregnant, given the different center of gravity. Then Meg said, "I want to talk to the security guys when they come on. But I wonder… Did you know Shelly Lange?"

Trish tapped a few keys and her screen went dark. "To talk to," she said willingly. "She didn't work here that long. And somehow she wasn't…a woman's woman. Know what I mean?"

"Just because she was so pretty?"

"No. I mean, she was, but…" Trish thought. "It was like other women were invisible. The only people she saw were men. She wasn't exactly rude—I even kind of liked her—but I had the feeling that…oh, she *needed* to be noticed by men. You know?" Trish appealed again.

"Mmm-hmm." In basic training, Meg had known a woman just like that. She was cordially disliked by anyone not male, but Meg had finally decided that Shannon Colter's problem wasn't so much that she loved men as that she needed them. She was an extension of whatever man she was with. Maybe she was invisible to herself without a man around, as if she could see herself only as the shadow cast by his sun. Meg outlined her theory to Trish, who nodded immediately.

"Yeah, she was like that. Not rude on purpose, but always looking over your shoulder at some guy coming into the room. Even if she didn't move a muscle, you could feel her quivering to attention. Like my science teacher said, everything magnetic in the earth points toward the pole."

"Did she like, uh…all men equally?"

Trish blinked, hesitated, then said candidly, "Nope. She had a boyfriend, but *he* became invisible when someone more important came in. And older. I'm not sure which part attracted her."

"Like Scott," Meg said thoughtfully.

"Yeah, but he would never have looked twice at her. So I think she, well, *settled*."

Meg snapped to attention. "As in, she had an affair with someone here? Besides the boyfriend?"

Trish physically shrank back in her chair, her expression becoming wary for the first time. "I didn't say that. I don't *know*." She drew out that last word.

Meg pounced on it. "But you suspect."

"Once, I saw…" She stopped. "But I probably misunderstood totally. He's…well, not that kind of guy."

"Trish," Meg said quietly, "I'm not heading up a lynch mob. I can be discreet. So long as this man had nothing to do with her death, I'll keep my mouth shut."

Trish gazed into space without focus. "I'll think about it," she said finally, and after that she clammed up.

Meg conceded temporary defeat and headed down the stairs to the security office. It was bare bones, reminding her of her home-away-from-home, the police station. Here, on the mountain, the public generally turned to the ski patrol for help, although they'd send for a security officer if a crime had been committed.

Her timing was perfect. Len Howard and Jerome Baker, the two security men who'd been on duty Monday night, had just arrived and were having coffee and doughnuts before beginning their shift.

Len spread a map of the ski area on the gray steel desk and outlined their movements from five o'clock—nightfall—until Scott had left the lodge at eight-thirty and discovered the baby.

They were confident, within narrow windows of time, about when other employees had left. They claimed that one or the other had seen the employee parking lot every half hour at least.

"We have a dozen vehicles parked there," Jerome explained. "Unless they're in the shop for repairs, that's where we keep the dozers we use on the parking lots, see. And the half-pipe grinder. That kind of equipment doesn't come cheap."

The half-pipe grinder was a grooming machine, she knew, to create the chutes for snowboarders. From what Scott said, definitely a big expense.

"No," Meg agreed, weighing how she could ask her next question. She couldn't see any way of disguising what she really wanted to know. Would they be outraged?

"Okay," she said, pretending to think. "From seven on, the general manager's Jeep was the only employee vehicle left in the parking lot."

"Except for Jerome's Bronco," Len contributed. "He gave me a lift."

"Right." She took a breath. "Would you have noticed if Mr. McNeil's Jeep was gone?"

"Yeah, sure." He frowned. "But he was there. I mean, he was the one who found the kid."

"Yes, but could he have left for a while and come back?"

His eyes met hers. Len Howard was no dummy. "Maybe for twenty minutes," he said. "I guess twenty-five, if he timed it perfectly."

"You're positive you'd have noticed if his Jeep was gone." She looked from one man to the other.

"I'd have noticed," Len said.

"I did." Jerome had been twirling a toothpick in his mouth. Now he plucked it out. "He never left. I remember thinking how he was probably going to bunk down up here. And how he oughta have somebody to go home to. All he does is work."

She couldn't shake them. Scott McNeil couldn't have been gone for long enough to take Shelly Lange to the Puma Lake trailhead, murder her and come back to park in exactly the same spot. Even assuming Meg could figure how Shelly and Emily had been magically transported to the Juanita Butte parking lot where he would have had to meet up with them.

Nope. Scott McNeil was definitely, officially, off the hook. Which didn't surprise Meg, but did relieve her.

Maybe a cop here and there had been careless enough to fall for a murder suspect. For the first time, she understood how it could happen. Had even felt it happening.

Which meant Scott McNeil wasn't the only one off the hook.

She was, too.

CHAPTER EIGHT

MEG WAS IGNORING traffic outside the glass front of the ski shop where she'd been asking questions until a sixth sense made her turn her head. There was Scott. Sunglasses pushed atop his black ski hat, he was unzipping his parka as he stopped to talk to someone she couldn't see. Which didn't matter, because for those seconds while she stared, no one else existed. Only him.

The salesclerk kept talking, but Meg didn't hear. She'd tried very hard not to let herself notice how damned sexy Scott was, which left her staggered now that she did. Now that she *could*.

Above the bulky ski boots, unbuckled, plain black ski pants made the most of long, powerful legs. A red sweater under the black parka stretched across his broad chest. His face was lean, craggy, intense; his mouth interesting, crooked, sensuous without being full. His chin bristled with pinpricks of a red more fiery than the thick tousled auburn color of his hair.

She felt a quick, tender squeeze of amusement. He hadn't had time to shave this morning. Emily must have been cranky.

He yanked his gloves off as he talked, then slapped them against his thigh. A moment later he lifted a hand in farewell and started to walk away. But his head turned as he went, his sweeping gaze taking in everything around him.

Including, through the glass, Meg.

His stride checked. Without looking away, he pushed open the door and came into the shop. From behind the counter, one of the two clerks said, "Mr. McNeil. Is there a problem?"

"No problem." His eyes never wavered from Meg's. "Are you done in here?"

"For now." She did manage to bestow a vague smile toward the two young women. "Thanks. If you think of anything…"

"Sure. I didn't know her, but I wish I could help," the one assured her naively, eyes wide.

As the glass door closed behind her and Scott, Meg muttered, "You hiring 'em before they even graduate from high school?"

He was behind her, but she heard the faint smile in his voice. "That's…uh, Melody something. She did graduate. Last May. She's smarter than she looks, or so I'm told."

"Wouldn't be hard," Meg muttered, before guilt stabbed her. "I'm not being nice. There's nothing wrong with being young and innocent."

He was kind enough not to ask, as she had the other day, whether she ever had been.

Instead he asked tactfully, "Learn anything useful?"

They'd reached the hallway outside his office. "Just that you couldn't have killed Shelly," Meg said, blunt to the end.

Only in his eyes did she see his anger. "And you thought I did?"

"Nope." Since he wasn't moving, she walked past him into his office. "Just thought I should be sure."

"Well, good." Irony hung like icicles from his tone. "And how did you satisfy yourself that I couldn't have pulled it off?"

She told him and watched as he mulled it over.

"I'd rather," he said, "that you'd just had faith in my character."

She made a production out of inspecting the painted mask that hung on the wall. "I don't know you that well."

Scott stayed by the door. "Did you seriously think I might have done it?"

"No." Meg pressed her lips together, then faced him. "No. But I've been wrong. Every cop has. The worst serial murderers can be charming. The kind you want to trust."

Emotion flickered in his eyes, the gray of a California fog. "Am I charming?"

To heck with the social niceties. "No," Meg said again. "I don't like charming men. You're…forceful. Straight with people."

His mouth had a wry look. "You make me sound irresistible."

"You're also kind underneath that occasional gruffness. Otherwise you would have shaved this morning."

"Shaved?" His hand went to his chin, and he grimaced. "What if I said I'd forgotten?"

"I'd know you were lying. You're not a man who forgets anything."

A muscle twitched in his cheek. "Even when I wish I could."

"I'm sorry…"

"No." He pushed himself away from the door frame. "You're right. Emily was fussy this morning. I figured—" ruefully he scraped a palm across his jaw again "—nobody would notice."

"Ah," Meg said softly, "but I notice everything."

"So I see." Now his eyes held a smile. "About me, anyway."

"Gave myself away." She tried to sound light, to make a joke out of it, but her mocking smile trembled around the edges.

"Will you have dinner with me tonight?" Scott asked.

"Dinner?" How had they gotten here?

"Yeah. As in a date." His voice changed subtly. "Or am I misreading you?"

Crunch time. The coward in her wanted to begin evasive maneuvers; the woman wanted to charge into the barrage of fire, the certainty of pain bedamned. It had been a long time since she'd let herself be a woman, not a cop, a military officer, a mother.

"No," she said quietly. "You're not."

Light flared in his eyes. "Then?"

"I can't tonight." Was that regret or relief she felt? At her age, she was discovering, it was scary to think about falling in love. What had once been joy, whispers to her friends, notes and corsages was now a serious business. "I need to talk to Will—my son," she explained. "Besides, I'm in the middle of a murder investigation. I can't just…just drop it so I can get dressed up and go out to dinner."

He lifted his hand and touched her cheek, just a brush of his knuckles that raised goose bumps down to her toes.

"All right. What about tomorrow night?"

"The investigation…"

"You must eat."

"Actually, I forget a lot of the time."

"We can make it quick." His eyes were grave, intent.

He knew this was serious business, too. "But…let's make a start."

"A start." Meg swallowed. "I…" There was the battle line again, the temptation to retreat. She wouldn't let fear rule her life. She never had, and she wouldn't start now. "Fine," she said, voice completely steady. "Why don't I come by your place. Seven o'clock?"

The faintest of smiles softened his mouth. "Deal."

"Now, tell me where to find Tony Rieger."

"I'll take you."

"No," she said quickly. "I don't want to be associated in his mind with you. You're his boss, with a capital B. He might tell me things he wouldn't want you to know."

Scott frowned, mulled it over, then agreed and gave her directions.

Outside, the sun had sunk behind the mountain, leaving the ski area in the shadow of oncoming dusk. The air was noticeably colder. She shivered, thought again about going shopping for warmer clothes, and hurried past a copse of trees screening the guts of the area from the public. Big metal buildings housed the mechanical department, whose job was to keep grooming equipment, dozers, 4x4s and snowmobiles running.

Tony Rieger was taking a break in a small office with a computer and a space heater. It wasn't all that different from one in a gas station: the only window looked out at the shop and greasy fingerprints discolored the computer keyboard and the corners of paperwork stacked on the desk. Nothing fancy here.

Tall, with curly dark hair, brown eyes and cleft chin, Tony was not happy to see a uniformed officer. He was young and inexperienced enough to show it.

"Yeah," he agreed sulkily. "That's my name."

"You've heard about Shelly Lange's death."

A spasm of emotion twisted his face. "Yeah. I heard."

"I understand the two of you dated."

His dark eyes flashed up. "Who told you that?"

"Does it matter?"

"Yeah, it matters!" He sounded belligerent. "Like, somebody's trying to get me in trouble, and I'm not supposed to care?"

"Why would the fact that you dated Shelly mean you're in trouble?" Meg asked.

"She was murdered, wasn't she?" He moved jerkily around the office, finally ending at the door. His back to Meg, he splayed both hands on the metal door and bowed his head. His mechanics' jumpsuit badly needed a wash. "Jeez, I can't believe…I mean, Shelly! Of all people…"

"Why 'of all people'?"

"She was so…pretty. Everyone liked her."

Everyone male, Meg thought, unsurprised that he hadn't noticed Shelly's admirers didn't include any female friends.

Meg perched on a stool and flipped open the notebook that sometimes felt like an extension of her arm. "Tell me about your relationship."

He turned, his eyes baffled and red-rimmed. "We just…saw each other for…I don't know. A couple of months."

"Who broke it off?"

"She did… Well, I guess I did, because I didn't like sharing her."

"Sharing?" Meg repeated. She pretended to make a note, watching him.

"Before me, she'd been seeing some other guy.

Someone here. I don't know who. She was scared of him. He was, like, possessive. You know? We had to be really careful that nobody saw us together. You see? That's why I wanted to know who told you."

"Let me get this straight. She'd broken up with this other guy, but she was still scared enough of him that she didn't want to be seen with you in public."

"Yeah." His Adam's apple bobbed. "At least, that's what I thought. But then after a while I figured out that she was still seeing him, too. I was, like, backup. She admitted he was married, so I guess he was busy a lot of the time, and that's what she wanted me for."

His pride, if not his heart, had been hurt. Meg wondered why he'd admitted so readily to something so humiliating. He hadn't even made her prod.

Heck, maybe he was just a good citizen. Believed in law and order. Cared enough about Shelly to want her murderer brought to justice.

Or was scared of the man who might have killed her.

"What else did she tell you about this guy? You're sure he worked here?"

"Yeah. I think he was older, had more money. I tried to get her to tell me who he was. I was going to make him back off. I guess she knew that. Maybe that's why she never said who he was."

"Okay." Meg doodled in her notebook. "Please tell me where you were Monday."

"This guy who works with me—Jeff Drake—he got married Sunday. Over in Eugene." Tony was eager to tell her. "A bunch of us went. We stayed over until Monday, since that's the slow day here. We got home maybe eleven? I just crashed the minute I walked in the door."

He directed her to two of the guys with whom he'd driven to Eugene and back. When they clambered out of the engine of one of the huge grooming machines, they confirmed his story. Unless the three had colluded to murder Shelly Lange—very unlikely—Tony Rieger had had nothing to do with her death.

As Meg walked back past the office, Tony stopped her.

"You know she took classes at the community college?"

She agreed that she did.

"Well, see, I've been taking some evening classes, too." He talked fast. "Anyway, I know this girl who's taking English 202 with Shelly. Kari says Shelly had something going with the prof. They were really obvious, Kari says. And Shelly got an *A,* but she didn't deserve one. I just thought you should know."

The English professor was the only one Meg and Ben hadn't yet talked to. Meg scribbled down the full name and phone number of Tony's friend and thanked him for the additional information. She wasn't quite sure what had prompted it: resentment, a genuine desire to be helpful, or fear that she still suspected him. But a chat with this Kari would be interesting indeed.

Meg went straight to her squad car, radioed in and headed down the mountain.

"TOMORROW NIGHT? Uh, yeah. Thanks. That would be cool. Um…" Will hesitated, his hand feeling sweaty on the phone. "Who'll be there?"

"Just my parents." His father paused. "Your grandparents."

Oh, wow. Grandparents. Unreal.

"They know about me?"

"I told them today. They're eager to meet you."

His heart was beating like crazy. Will swallowed. "I'll have to ask Mom. About dinner, I mean."

"She's not home?" his father asked.

"No…" Will heard the garage door. "Wait a minute. I think that's her now."

"Well, you just call me back. Okay?"

"Yeah. Sure." Will hung up before he realized he didn't know his father's phone number. This was all too strange for him.

Mom came in the door from the garage.

"What's for dinner?" Will asked.

She groaned.

He looked in the cupboard. Bare. "We could order a pizza."

"What did you have last night?"

"Pizza. Hey." He brightened. "I have some left. You want me to put it in the microwave?"

"I can do better than that." Mom kissed him on the cheek and headed for her bedroom.

Will trailed her, stopping out in the hall where he couldn't see her shedding her gun and uniform. He raised his voice. "Dad called."

"Did he tell you I talked to him today?"

"Yeah." Will stared at the framed photo of his mom and her two sisters together as little girls that hung on the wall. They all looked back at him, their faces so solemn, he'd asked Mom once if they'd been unhappy when it was taken and she'd said, Yes, that day their dad had yelled at them right before the picture was snapped. That's why they weren't smiling. Why didn't she hang up one where they looked happy? he'd asked. Because we weren't, she'd answered, never really totally, but see—she'd touched the little girls in the picture—see how close they'd stood, their arms around each other? See how much they trusted each other? How they were one against the world? Will didn't say, *But you left.* He could tell Mom was thinking it. That her sisters shouldn't have trusted her.

"What did Jack say?" his mom called from the bedroom, her voice more distant, muffled. She was either in the bathroom or had her head stuck in the closet.

"He asked me to dinner tomorrow night. To meet his parents." *My grandparents.* "Can I go?"

He worried she'd ask if she had been invited. Because she hadn't been. Will guessed that his father's parents remembered her from when she was their son's girlfriend. But they hadn't wanted her to come to dinner.

She appeared in her bedroom doorway wearing jeans and a long baggy sweater. "Don't be silly." Her smile was wavery, like it had been when she let him go to Oregon for two weeks with a buddy when he was eight. As if she knew she had to say goodbye but didn't want to. "Of course you can go," Mom said. "Isn't that what we're here for?"

"What if they don't like me?" Will blurted. That shaky smile of hers had made him feel like crying. Not that he would, but suddenly he was scared. What if these grandparents hated him? What if his dad didn't like him that much?

What if Mom was letting him get to know his father because she didn't want him anymore?

Will knew immediately that wasn't right.

Okay, what if she knew she was dying, like his other grandma had, and she wanted to be sure he had family before she was gone?

But she looked awfully healthy.

Mom had always said they should be honest. So he asked, almost nonchalantly, "You wouldn't want me to live with Dad, would you?"

Fire entered her eyes. "Did he ask you?"

"No…"

"You've got it right. No. Not on your life!"

"Dad didn't ask," Will said in a rush. "I just…well, wondered. If you were hoping maybe he would. I mean, I know it's hard having me all the time when it's just you…"

His mother framed his face with her hands and lifted his chin so he couldn't look away. "It is *not* hard having you. I love you. Period. You're stuck with me until you leave for college, okay? Maybe you won't even get rid of me then. I might come along. They hire housemothers for the dorms, you know. My police experience should be a plus."

"Yeah, right." He wriggled free of her hands, although he wouldn't have minded a hug if she'd insisted.

She didn't. Instead she tucked her hand in the crook of his arm and pulled him into the kitchen.

"Actually," she said, "I'm glad Jack asked you tomorrow night. I have plans, too."

"Plans?" He watched her open the refrigerator.

She gave him a grin. "Unbelievable as it may be, your very own mother has been asked out by a man."

"Asked out?" Will repeated in shock. His mother hardly ever dated. She said she didn't have time. Why did she suddenly have time, when she was never home?

"Scott McNeil. He's the general manager of the ski area."

"The guy who found the baby."

"That's right. I forgot I told you. He's…interesting."

He stared at her incredulously. What did she mean? Did "interesting" mean she had the hots for this guy? His *mother?*

Besides, he'd had this secret dream ever since Mom announced they were moving back to Elk Springs. In the dream, his mother and his father realized they still loved each other. They got married, and his dad was there to take Will fishing and let Will whup his butt on the basketball hoop he'd install at their home. Maybe he'd even put a small one-on-one asphalt court beside the garage, like Silas Norden's dad had. They'd be a family, Mom and Will and his then faceless father.

Okay, it was probably a dumb dream—he'd recognized that from the start. But now he thought it might not be impossible. Jack Murray wasn't married. He seemed like an okay guy, and he looked like the jock type women would go for. So why not Mom? And Mom was still pretty, for her age. Think how perfect it would be!

"Are you, like, interrogating him?" Will asked hopefully.

"Scott?" She set a head of lettuce on the counter. "If I had to interrogate him, I wouldn't date him. No. He's definitely in the clear on this case."

Will slouched against the island. "But you don't know him that well. What if you don't like him?"

"Then I won't go out with him again." She produced a green pepper, cauliflower and two carrots from the vegetable drawer. "That's why you date. So you can get to know each other."

She wouldn't like him, Will decided. She was just flattered, because she didn't get asked often. And she always said the guys her age who were single were creeps. This one wasn't that bad, so she'd figured, what the hey.

But she must be thinking about Will's dad a lot. Here they'd had *sex,* and now they were seeing each other for the first time in all those years. How could she not be thinking about him?

In fact, it might not be a bad thing that tomorrow night Will could say, just casually, "Mom went out to dinner with some guy." Dad might not like the idea. He might be spurred to making a move faster than he would have otherwise.

Yeah, Will decided, his dream might not be as dumb as he'd originally thought. Now that he'd met his father, Will could see it coming true. He wasn't going to worry about this McNeil guy. How could he compete with Jack Murray?

"Have fun," Will said with a shrug, and grabbed the carrot stick she tossed him.

WEARING A HOUSEDRESS, Alice Lange blocked the doorway, just as her husband had the other time. The hand that gripped the door was dry and flaky; the fingernails were short and unpainted. In the light of day, her face looked colorless.

"Why would you want to see Shelly's bedroom?"

"I'm really just hoping to get to know her," Meg explained. "We can get a warrant if you insist, Mrs. Lange. But your cooperation would be preferable."

Anxiety hung around her like a cloud of gnats. "My husband…"

"I'll wait while you call him, if you'd like."

She agonized, the indecision deepening every line on her face. "I'm not supposed to bother him at work."

"Why would he object to my looking at Shelly's bedroom?" Meg asked reasonably.

"He won't like you being here," Mrs. Lange worried aloud.

Once she must have been as pretty as her daughter, Meg thought again. Had she ever had Shelly's spirit? It was hard to imagine in this woman who didn't care for herself physically, who deferred to her husband even to the point of rejecting her own child.

"Why?" Meg asked again, though she knew. Or thought she did.

"He says we don't have anything to do with whatever Shelly got herself mixed up in. Maybe drugs or organized crime or whatever." The words came out by rote, clearly not hers. "It upset him, you asking where he was that night, like he might hurt his own daughter."

"He said he didn't have a daughter. He'd disowned her."

"That was hard, but she had it coming. A father should be obeyed, don't you think?" Alice Lange looked at Meg as if she expected understanding.

"It depends what the father asks of his children," Meg said flatly. "He's there to love and guide, not rule."

"The Bible says a man should be the master in his own home." It was a fact, no argument. But grief...oh, yes, she could wish it might be otherwise.

"Mrs. Lange," Meg said gently, "can you tell me why your husband and daughter clashed?"

She clutched the door frame, her knuckles white. "It was men. Shelly really liked the boys, even when she was twelve or thirteen. She always wanted her daddy to spend more time with her—she just couldn't understand that he had to work and that the Lord had called him to counsel others. Well, after she discovered boys, she didn't care anymore whether her daddy was there or not. They fought all the time. He wanted what was best for her. That's all. Sometimes I thought maybe she had a disease. You know, that one where a woman wants…" She swallowed convulsively. "Men. That way. You know."

Meg was glad Ben wasn't with her. Mrs. Lange wouldn't have been even this forthcoming if it hadn't been between two women.

"May I come in?" she asked. "So you're not letting the heat out?"

"Oh!" She blinked several times. "Oh. Yes. Please do come in, Officer. I'm afraid I don't remember your name."

Meg introduced herself again. They sat in the living room, Meg on a couch that might have been there when Shelly was a little girl. She could see it, the doilies protecting the arms, Shelly forbidden to put her feet on the olive-green fabric.

Alice Lange faced her, sitting on the recliner but with her spine so straight it didn't touch the back of the chair.

In answer to Meg's question about whether she knew the names of any of the men with whom Shelly had been involved, Mrs. Lange said, "Oh, there were always boys from school. Why, she'd sneak out her bedroom window at night to meet them! But at school, she had such a crush on a teacher, he called us in to ask us to talk to her. She was following him around and making excuses to hug him and such."

"Was that in high school?" Meg asked, making notes.

"No, seventh grade, I think. Or was it eighth?" Mrs. Lange closed her eyes, squeezing out tears that made damp tracks on her cheeks. "Shelly was such a sweet little girl. That's why I think it might have been a disease. She was still sweet. It was just men. Always men."

Meg couldn't help thinking that if Kenneth Lange had given his daughter the attention she craved, Shelly might never have been so desperate for a different kind of attention from any and all men.

Or was that too easy an answer, one seen through Meg's experience, not Shelly's at all?

"Mrs. Lange." Meg waited until the other woman opened her eyes, sniffed, wiped away the tears. "I have to ask this. Is there any possibility your husband made sexual advances on your daughter?"

"My husband?" Astonishing for this day and age, it took a minute for Alice Lange to understand. When she did, she sucked in a breath. "How can you even ask…"

"Because it happens," Meg said bluntly. "More often than you'd think. As I said, I have to ask."

"My husband lives in a godly way, Officer." Her cheeks flushed with outrage. "He has even suffered doubts over whether a man should have such relations with his wife when procreation is not the goal. He would never think of his own daughter in such an obscene way."

"I'm sorry I had to suggest it."

"You've met my husband." Alice Lange quivered with such emotion, the recliner creaked. "Surely you could see what kind of man he is!"

Too tactful to say, *Yep, sure could,* Meg only repeated, "I'm sorry. I had to ask."

"Look at her room." Mrs. Lange stood. "And then leave, please."

Behind the closed door, Shelly's bedroom had been sterilized. It was perfect, the room of a preteen. Stuffed animals slumped in too tidy a row against the pillow on her twin bed. The spread was ruffly, as were the curtains; the books on the one shelf were titles like *Alice in Wonderland* and *The Secret Garden,* worn and well-loved, but surely not by the eighteen-year-old Shelly. Porcelain dolls stood stiffly behind glass in a case. The only thing of interest Meg found were the high school yearbooks, in which Shelly was pictured as a bubbly, glamorous, popular girl—a homecoming princess, cheerleader, and "Most likely to marry well," according to her peers.

Shelly's parents hadn't preserved their daughter in this room. Nor had they stripped it to wipe out any evidence of her existence. Instead, they had selectively discarded what they didn't like, as if they could create a different reality.

The disturbing part was that, along with posters of rock stars, her parents had discarded Shelly herself, the living, breathing young woman their daughter had grown into.

Meg had thought Shelly's mother might feel differently than her husband. She'd been wrong. He'd spoken for both of them: they had already said their goodbyes. The real Shelly's death didn't touch them; they didn't know her. Didn't want to know her.

Meg drove back to the station feeling grateful, most of all, that the Langes weren't seeking custody of little Emily.

FINGERING THE PINK SLIP of paper with the message— Renee called—Meg dialed her sister's phone number.

"Patton, here." The voice was brisk, businesslike, a cop.

Two peas out of the same pod, Meg thought wryly. She put her feet up on her desk. "Hey. Meg, here."

"Meg." Her sister's voice changed. "At last. Do you know how tough you are to catch? Anyway, is everything okay with Jack and Will? I, uh, wanted to say I'm sorry for my part. I was trying to hustle him out…"

"Hustle?" Meg got it. "You mean, when Will came to see you? Oh, I know my son too well to blame you. And, yeah, things are fine. I should have listened to you and not procrastinated. My fault. But Jack took it better than I deserved. Will's going there for dinner night."

Renee expressed pleasure; they chatted idly. Ben knocked on the glass insert in Meg's door and jerked his thumb toward the parking lot. She waved him off, but opened her mouth to say, *I've got to go.*

What came out instead took her by surprise. "Have you ever had an investigation that got really personal for you? I mean, either the crime hit too close to home, or the people involved made you think about stuff in your own life?"

Renee was quiet for a moment. "Yeah," she said at last. "I had one like that."

"What was it?"

"Daniel's dog brought home a human skull. I spent a few weeks following up on missing people. I'd lay awake nights thinking about you and Mom."

I'm sorry. Meg didn't say it, not again. Apologetic words were like table manners, something your upbringing made easy or hard, but good or bad they said nothing deep about your true state of regret or repentance.

"How did you handle the investigation?" Meg asked. "I mean, how did you keep your feelings out of it?"

Again there was a small pause before Renee said brusquely, "My feelings weren't a problem. I did my job. That's all."

Subject closed. Or maybe Renee had chosen a simple way of saying, *I decided I could do fine without the mom and sister who chose to go missing. And I'm still doing fine without them. Without you.*

Whatever, she didn't want to talk. It hurt, but Meg had to respect that. Choices made couldn't be unmade. Love and trust once lost couldn't be restored.

Right this minute, Meg was glad Jack was holding out welcoming arms to Will, because otherwise she'd think she had made a big mistake.

"Okay," she said to her sister, her voice as uncaring as she could make it. "Listen, I've got to go. I'll see you later." She hung up without listening to Renee's polite promise to call.

A big mistake, Meg thought again, pressing a fist to her left breast as if she could stifle the heartache. Or maybe she should think of it as a lesson.

You can't go home again.

CHAPTER NINE

A SEXY WOMAN was on his doorstep, and Scott had to say sheepishly, "I, uh, couldn't find a baby-sitter. Do you mind if I bring Emily?"

Meg Patton smiled, making him immediately regret the loss of the evening he'd planned. Did you kiss a woman for the first time in front of a baby?

"Oh, yeah," she said, "entertaining a baby in a restaurant is so much fun. How about if I go pick up some takeout?"

She'd changed out of her uniform, which he took as a good sign—maybe she planned to do more than eat and run. Or should he say, *had* planned, before she discovered her date had become a threesome?

Below the parka, her pants were black, the fabric something plushy. Corduroy? Velvet? He didn't know, only that it was softer and dressier than denim. On the other hand, the black boots beneath them didn't make it look as though she expected to be taken to Chez Marie, which was a relief.

"Can I admit something?" he asked.

"If you invite me in."

Feeling like an idiot, Scott stood back. Busy imagining her without so many clothes on, he hadn't even noticed the freezing air rushing in.

"Just my way of making you welcome."

"Ah." Inside, she didn't unzip her parka. "Confession?" she nudged.

"My housekeeper couldn't stay tonight, but I asked her to make dinner. A lasagna is ready to go in the oven. Unless you'd be uncomfortable here," he added scrupulously.

Her smile deepened. "Let me get this straight. You've been scheming to keep me locked in your house."

"Uh…" He hadn't actually tried very hard to find a baby-sitter once Marjorie had turned him down. "I guess you could look at it that way. The truth is, I didn't like the idea of leaving Emily with some fourteen-year-old who'd spend the whole evening on the phone with her bosom friends giggling about boys."

"Is that what Shelly did?"

The question was a zinger, pulling a double punch: he had a sudden memory of coming home with Penny and finding Shelly curled up on the couch asleep, looking almost as young as Nate; superimposed was the image of Shelly's crumpled body.

"Is that why you came tonight? To ask more questions?"

He saw a flash of hurt in her eyes. "No. You're right. I'm sorry."

Scott swore. "No. I'm the one who's sorry. I don't like to think about Shelly alive because she's all tied up with Nate in my mind, and I don't much like remembering her dead, either."

Meg gave a small nod, left it there. "Where *is* Emily?"

At a distant clang, his mouth tilted up. "Kitchen. She's emptying the pans out of a cupboard."

Meg shed her outer garments and followed him and the clatter of metal. They found Emily's pink corduroy rear end poking out of the cupboard. A delighted squeal was followed by a lid that came shooting out to roll across the kitchen floor. Scott winced.

"You might want to try keeping plastic storage dishes in the bottom instead," Meg suggested.

"Ah, she's not hurting anything." He bent over and patted that round, diapered bottom. "Right, Emily?"

Wham! A sauce pan crashed into his shins. Scott jumped back. "You've got a mean arm on you, kid."

Meg's chuckle was almost as delighted as Emily's. They were both easy to please, he thought in amusement.

"So," he said, "what's it going to be? Lasagna, or takeout?"

"Oh, there's a toughie." She gave him a look. "I'll bet your housekeeper can cook."

"Yep. Why do you think I hired her?"

"Pop it in." With the ease of a child, Meg sat cross-legged on the floor so she could peer in at Emily.

As he turned the oven on to preheat and got the foil-covered casserole dish out of the fridge, Scott listened to her talking to the baby.

"Hi, Emily. I'm Meg. You know, you're missing a good bet here." She rose to her knees and opened two drawers before she found what she wanted: a wooden spoon. Back down at baby level, she showed it to Emily, who sank back on her rear end on the floor. "See? You bang it on the pan. Like this."

Emily got the idea. A thunderous metal drumming vibrated Scott's eardrums.

"Thanks!" he called.

Meg gave him a wicked grin. "You're welcome."

Emily wasn't crawling yet, although she was learning to scoot along on her tummy like an eel wriggling through the water. Mostly she was content when he plopped her down in a sitting position, as long as she had something to entertain herself with.

"She eating solids yet?" Meg asked.

"Cereal. She likes to play with Cheerios and slices of banana. She's getting the hang of it."

Emily's soft dark hair stuck straight up, as if the ceiling called to it. Her brown eyes were wide and gleeful, her cheeks plump and pink. Meg was making faces at her, and Emily laughed until her belly quivered. All the while she banged pots and lids and finally the cupboard door with her spoon/drumstick.

Finally he couldn't take it anymore. "All right, pipsqueak," Scott said. "Let's find something quiet for you to do."

Emily didn't want to do quiet. She screeched and then burst into tears when he scooped her up. Meg rose, too.

"Can I hold her? I haven't had an armful of baby in a long time." Immediately, she looked appalled. "I'm sorry. I know you…"

Scott shook his head and handed over the sobbing little girl. "Don't worry. It's hard not to talk about babies with her here."

They finally got her settled in the living room, where the softer dhurrie rug in front of the couch was strewn with her toys: stacking bright-colored rings, foam cloth-covered blocks and a plastic noisemaker that whinnied and mooed and baaed when she punched buttons or turned knobs or moved levers. The sight of Meg sitting on the floor playing with the baby tweaked a few uncomfortable emotions in his chest.

Since Emily had come, memories thinly disguised as dreams haunted his nights. They didn't bother with disguises during the day, just trooped around after him like ducklings who thought he was mama, pecking at his heels.

So far they'd mostly been of Nate, with Penny present only by necessity. One night he'd lived again seeing his son born: the vivid colors, Penny's grunts and wails, the slick head crowning, the rush with which he'd come out, his rasping cry and the sight of him suckling on his mother's breast. Scott had never known such euphoria, such awe.

He'd awakened—or had he ever been asleep?—and read for a while, some thriller that was supposed to be great but failed to grip him. Eventually he'd slept again, only to find himself in a movie theater, with Nate's funeral playing on the big screen.

Scott would have been the star if he'd displayed any emotion, but as it was he walked through the part looking blank, numb, a man in a dark suit with dry eyes and a sobbing wife on his arm. Jesus, the sound of the casket dropping the last inches into the ground, the clunk of dirt striking the shiny top, the minister's speech about God's will, the guilt clawing at him—was this somehow his fault? Had he done something wrong? Hurt his son laying him in the crib? Committed a sin that demanded repayment?—all of it filled the screen and crashed over his head in Dolby sound.

But watching Meg sit there on the floor playing with Emily, apparently completely absorbed in the baby's chortles and wonder, brought back Penny, too.

In retrospect Scott realized they had married too young, that even then a silence had been growing between them, one they'd needed a child to fill. Nate had been fresh glue to their relationship. He'd allowed Scott to see his wife anew. She'd been a wonderful mother: soft, gentle, patient, content to wrap her life around their son. In a primitive, male way, Scott had found appealing the idea that he and their son were her whole world.

One morning, on a thin cry of terror and grief, her world was torn in two.

"Penny had other children," he said suddenly, earning a startled look from Meg. "Later, I mean. She remarried. A boy and a girl, according to my mother. The oldest must be almost ready for school now."

Understanding softened Meg's eyes. "Does it bother you that she had more?"

"No." He shook his head. "No, I was glad for her. After Nate…after he was gone, I had work, a life. Penny didn't have anything."

"Did you really have that much of a life?" Meg asked gently. "Or were you kidding yourself because you didn't want to admit how much you'd lost?"

A week ago he'd have scoffed at the idea. Now he made a sound in his throat. "I was kidding myself, of course."

Her mouth curved. "Honesty."

"Emily coming along hasn't been a bad thing for me," Scott admitted.

"How like a man." A dimple flickered in her cheek. "Not 'she's been good for me,' but she 'hasn't been a bad thing.' For starters, she's not a *thing*."

Probably by accident, Emily had stacked blue and red rings onto the central rod. Not in the right order, of course, but they were both on there. She looked so damned cute, with her downy hair that refused to lie flat and small plump hands and a smile that lit a room. She made him think about Nate, but she wasn't Nate; he had no confusion there. Emily Lange was her own determined self.

And he was having a harder and harder time imagining the day when he handed her over to some eager adoptive parents.

When that day came, he wasn't so sure he'd still think she had been good for him.

Scott let out a gruff laugh. "This has been a hell of a dinner date. Now you know why I have women lining up."

Meg's smile was pure delight, too. "I have a suspicion you do."

Pleased despite himself, Scott countered, "Not so's I've ever noticed."

She gave him a long slow look that raised his blood pressure. "Come on, you're a sexy man. Maybe you just haven't been ready to start noticing."

"Oh, I'm ready," he said. He'd gone right on past "noticing" to Step No. 2. He was already savoring the idea of kissing Deputy Margaret Patton. He had always liked tart better than sweet.

Scott didn't let himself contemplate the question of why, then, he'd married such a sweet woman.

Emily flung a ring away and let out a screech, then kicked the whole toy away in a fit of rage.

"Did it get the better of you?" Meg asked, scooting toward her. Meg's hair, loose tonight, streamed like a ribbon of moonlight over one shoulder and breast. It was all Scott could do to tear his attention from her slender, creamy neck and his fantasies of kissing his way down to her shoulder and breasts.

Emily helped by letting out a bellow and looked tearfully at Scott at the same time as she lifted her arms. Forget food or sex as a way to a man's heart. This little girl already knew the secret.

He stood and picked her up in one movement. "Hey, getting hungry, pip-squeak?"

Her lower lip trembled and tears shimmered on her lashes.

"Yep, I'd say so," Scott murmured. He looked apologetically at Meg. "Why don't you come pour us some wine while I warm Emily's formula? I can smell the lasagna. I'll throw a salad together as soon as I put her down for the night."

"A salad I can do," Meg said firmly.

Emily snuffled until the microwave beeped and he pulled out her yellow plastic bottle. Then she grabbed for it and began to suck furiously.

"Why don't you take her out into the living room?" Meg suggested. She was already hauling things out of the refrigerator. "I'll just putter here."

THE BABY NODDED OFF just as she finished her bottle. Scott had to wake her up to change her diaper and wriggle her out of the overalls and into a sleeper, but when he settled her on her back in the rented crib and gently pulled a flannel comforter over her, Emily closed her eyes and stuck her thumb in her mouth. Scott slipped out of the room, taking only one quick peek back in.

He was getting better at this.

He returned to the kitchen to find the table there set with quilted place mats and matching napkins folded into small fans.

"I rooted around," Meg said. "I hope you don't mind."

"Don't be ridiculous." He couldn't remember the last time he'd bothered to do more than hook a leg over a stool and shovel his microwaved food in his mouth while he read the newspaper. He guessed he'd needed a woman's company.

"Next time we'll go out," Scott promised.

Meg gave him a quick, absentminded smile as she shredded lettuce. "I like this better, anyway."

Emily wasn't the only one who knew her way to a man's heart. "Your son's a lucky kid. Does he know that?"

"Most of the time." Meg picked up the peeler and started in on the carrots. "Right now, Emily's lucky to have you."

Right now. Two innocent words reminded him of the ache ever-present under his breastbone.

"You'd have found some place for her."

Another quick glance made him wonder if she didn't see more than he'd like. "But not all places feel like home to a child."

He was a man generally suspicious of compliments. She had a way of slipping them under his guard. He said abruptly, "This place didn't feel much like home until she came along. I barely slept here."

"It's a beautiful house." Meg touched the leaf pattern in the tile backsplash. "Did you design it?"

"With the builder. Gave me something to think about."

"Did your wife ever live here?"

"No." He didn't want to talk about Penny, and could think of only one out. "You found Rieger okay yesterday?"

"Mmm." She set the salad bowl on the table and watched him take the lasagna from the oven. "Yum, garlic bread, too."

"Let's hope Emily doesn't wake up just as we sit down. It wouldn't be the first time."

Over dinner they talked about the investigation. He frowned at her recap of Tony Rieger's story. "He thinks Shelly was afraid of someone who works at Juanita Butte?"

"Well, he didn't make it sound as if she feared for life and limb. More that she was seeing someone who was possessive. Although…" Meg frowned, her fork halfway to her mouth. "I wondered if he wasn't so forthcoming because *he* was afraid. If this guy killed her because she was messing around with other men…"

"But Tony was old news, from what you say."

"Yeah, the guy'd have to become a serial murderer if he decides to knock off every man Shelly dated. She got around."

"She was a nice kid." And he sounded defensive, for no reason he could figure.

Meg didn't seem to notice.

"Her father's a jerk." Her voice held some indefinable tension. "If I can indulge in a little pop psychology, I'd say she was trying to find herself a new daddy. Hard to tell if sex was ever really the point with all these men."

"I barely met Lange." Scott chewed thoughtfully. "I'm trying to remember Shelly's mother and coming up short."

"That's because there's not much to notice. Her entire purpose in life seems to be keeping her husband happy. No, that sounds too active. Trying *not* to make him unhappy."

"She's afraid of him?"

"Yes, but also genuinely of the opinion that the man

should be lord and master in his home. Her role in life is to smooth his way."

Scott growled a profanity.

Meg touched his hand, sending a shockwave up it. "I think we can assume Kenneth Lange never gave his daughter her bottle or changed her diaper or tucked her in."

"Then he's an idiot."

"That, too," she agreed serenely.

Something he'd been wondering. "Is your son home alone tonight?"

Her head was bent as she stripped the crust off a piece of garlic bread, but he felt her hesitation. "No," she said then, voice too even, too careful. "He's with his father. He lives here in Elk Springs."

Scott was uncomfortable to discover that he didn't like the idea of her seeing her ex—on a regular basis. Chatting about the good old days with him. Smiling. Sharing the boy they'd made together.

What in hell was wrong with him?

In the face of his silence, Meg continued. "I have family here in town, too, you know."

Scott asked about her sisters, but he felt restraint there, as well.

"You're not close to them?" he asked, and was stunned when she flinched.

"No, I guess you could say we're not." She continued shredding the bread. "My fault."

"Why?"

She told him a story then, about a pregnant, sixteen-year-old girl who ran away from home in terror of what her father would do to the child she carried.

"Did you ever meet my father?" At Scott's shake of

the head, Meg continued. "He was cold. Except when he was angry, which was too much of the time. Abby and Renee and I were disappointments to him. He wanted a son. Well, look at us! In our own ways, we tried to meet his expectation. How else to explain two daughters who are cops and the third who's a fire-fighter? But, you see, whatever we did was never enough. He'd have punished me for getting pregnant, and the worst thing he could have done was sue me for custody. Once he found out I'd had a son…" She shud-dered, this fearless woman.

"And if he'd raised your boy…"

"Will would either be a juvenile delinquent, or he'd be just like my father."

"Sounds as if you did the only thing you could do." Scott frowned. "So what's the problem with your sisters?"

"I should have found a way to rescue them, too. I should at least have called regularly and *listened* to them. Instead I just—" now she was stabbing her lasagna with her fork "—took the course of least resis-tance. I didn't do anything. I convinced myself they'd be fine. They didn't need me." Meg looked up at last, torment in her eyes. "You know what I had the gall to say to them just last week?" When he wordlessly shook his head, she said in a tone of self-loathing, "I told them, my own sisters, that for Will's sake I'd felt I had to think about the future, not the past. Well, they were in my past and I let them down."

"You can only do what you can do." Scott grimaced. "I'm sorry. That's pat. But also true. You were sixteen, not even an adult yourself. And it seems like Will's father wasn't helping you."

Her gaze shied away from his again; she didn't want

to talk about Will's father. "Okay, I was sixteen." She poked that poor lasagna again, as if she were trying to maim it. "A kid. I'm excused. So why didn't I call when I was eighteen? Or twenty-one? Or whenever 'adult-hood' struck?"

"Because it was too late," he said bluntly, "and you knew it."

She stared at him in shock, then gave a laugh that held not a grain of amusement. "You understand, don't you?"

Scott swore. "We're all cowards sometime. Why should you be any different?"

"Because I'm the big sister and I'm supposed to be perfect." Humor did light this smile. "Big sisters can never admit they're wrong. Didn't you know that?"

"Yeah, I had a pretty good idea," he agreed, cracking a smile of his own. "Big brothers hold to the same belief."

"You're one?"

"I have a little brother." Six two and two hundred pounds, but "little" forever more to Scott. "He's a park ranger at Bryce in Utah."

Meg asked, so he told her some about growing up with a father who worked nine-to-five Monday through Friday but packed the family up every weekend and vacation to head for the mountains.

"We backpacked, camped, skied… The farther away from civilization, the happier he was."

"Past tense?"

"He died three years ago. Stroke." A late-night phone call from his mother had set Scott to frantic efforts to get plane reservations. His mother had called back ten minutes later. Dad was dead. Just like that. Scott rubbed the back of his neck. "It was sudden, at least. He'd have hated a long stay in a nursing home."

"And your mother?"

"Doing fine. Her idea of a vacation these days is a Caribbean cruise."

They talked about nothing and everything after that: family, childhood, movies and pets. He told her about the first few days with Emily, when she would cry and cry and nothing he did was right, because he wasn't her mother; about the gradual change, the sense that they were connecting, her increasing trust.

Emily didn't wake up, and Meg didn't rush off to interview a murder suspect. Just as she'd been content earlier to play with the baby, now she seemed happy to sit at his dining room table, sip wine and talk.

The further the evening wore on, the more Scott thought about the end of it. The idea of kissing her, now that was a spice to flavor any topic.

Funny thing, though. He wasn't sure their conversation needed any jazzing up. He thought of himself as someone who went straight to the point, not given to meaningless chitchat.

So maybe this wasn't meaningless.

Which meant he liked her. No more, no less. *Don't get carried away,* he told himself. *Remember the Emily factor.* Having a baby in the house was making him soft, too inclined to feel domestic.

The argumentative side of him countered, *Yeah, but if that's all you feel, a tart-tongued lady cop busy investigating a murder is a damned unlikely choice for romantic fantasies.*

Sexual ones, maybe. Domestic, no.

Stick to thinking about a kiss, he advised himself.

Not hard, given that luscious mouth and the way a tiny dimple flickered in her cheek when she smiled.

Right now, the dimple vanished and he realized she was waiting politely for…what?

"Uh, excuse me?" he stammered, feeling like a sixteen-year-old with a tight zipper.

"I just said that I'd better be getting home." She made getting-up motions. "I've got an early morning tomorrow."

The reminder of her job made Scott feel all grown-up again suddenly, and not in a good way. Memories of Shelly and the maybe-married man she'd feared— someone Scott knew and trusted—got in the way of fantasies of any kind.

"Can I help you load the dishwasher?" Meg asked, starting to pick up her coffee cup and saucer.

"I'll get it." Scott rose to his feet, too. "I'm glad you took this evening off."

Her blue eyes met his directly. "My pleasure."

No, his. Definitely his.

On the way to the front door, Scott asked, "Working a murder like this, can you ever get it out of your mind? Or do you keep seeing her…"

"Dead?" Meg stopped by the front door, faced him. "No. I guess I have compartments. You have to. Otherwise the scumbags you deal with would leave you feeling dirty all the time. Or you'd get to be scared, not wanting your kid to drive, because after all he might end up like the teenagers in that four-car pile-up out on Highway 2." She shook herself, as if shedding unpleasant memories. "No. Life outside work is one thing, enforcing the law another. Once in a while the two trip over each other, and it's not comfortable."

"You mean, you have to arrest someone you know?"

"Well, I guess that could happen, but no, I was thinking of this case, actually." She wrinkled her nose.

"Shelly and I have a lot in common. She wanted her father's attention and love so much. I haven't figured out whether she hated him, too, the way I hated my father. I have to keep telling myself, 'She's not me. Don't assume you know what she was thinking.'"

He'd been itching all evening to slip his fingers into her hair. Now he did, smoothing it back from her face. "She's making you remember things you'd rather not, just like Emily does for me."

"Except I might have been remembering, anyway." Meg closed her eyes and turned her face toward his hand. Her voice sank to a murmur. "Coming home does that."

Blood roared in his ears. Her hair felt as shimmery and insubstantial as it looked, so delicate it was an illusion that might vanish when he took his hand away. Her breath, warm against his wrist, shook him to the core.

"Meg," he said roughly.

She lifted her face as naturally as if they'd kissed a thousand times. He found that more breathtaking than shyness or surprises.

He bent his head, touched his lips to hers, felt her tremble. They tasted, eased back, came together again. All so softly, so tenderly. Her shoulders felt fragile. He kissed his way across her cheek to the pulse that beat beneath her jaw. Her breath caught; she gave a ragged gasp when his mouth trailed to her throat.

And when he captured her mouth again, it was with a ferocity and intent that surprised both of them, although after the first start Meg only gripped him and held on, kissing him back with a strange mix of innocence and knowing that was her and her alone.

When he finally lifted his head, they stared at each other, first in shock and then wariness.

Too much, too soon. He thought it; could see she did, too.

A first kiss was supposed to be clumsy, tentative, not all that satisfying. It wasn't supposed to feel as perfect as pouring the foundation for a house an architect had worked on for months. A man might feel randy, or disappointed, or hopeful. But he shouldn't feel his guts turning over because the woman he'd kissed was going to say a casual good-night and walk out the door.

She was opening her mouth to do it when he cut in. "Meg, I enjoyed this. If I promise to get a baby-sitter next time, will you have dinner with me again? I'd suggest tomorrow night, but I know you'd say no. Sunday night?"

Her smile was like dawn in the high mountain country, pure, sweet and mysterious. "You're right. I would've said no. I'm too fond of my son. But I would love to do this again Sunday, whether you get a baby-sitter or not."

A moment later she was gone, and Scott felt a kind of anticipation he hadn't known in years. Since seeing his son's cold body, he had learned he could get through any one day, as long as he never thought of having to get through tomorrow, too. He had, for him, a rare poetic image: the days were like stepping stones through a tangled garden. To endure, he'd had to concentrate on each one, refusing to let himself know that it wasn't a single stone, but instead the beginning of a path that would lay itself unceasingly before him. *Today* was flat, hard, sometimes rounded, sometimes sharp-edged. He didn't give a damn what tomorrow's stone looked like.

He didn't know how to go on and on anymore; didn't care what was around the curve.

Hadn't known how. Hadn't cared.

Suddenly, thanks to Emily with her big brown eyes and Meg with her too perceptive questions, Scott found he did care. Sunday was beyond the next curve of the path, and he wanted to get there as much as he'd ever wanted anything.

He wanted to live.

CHAPTER TEN

JEFFERSON ROBB, Shelly's English professor, proved hard to nail down. He was sick; his colleagues had to take over his classes. But he wasn't answering his phone or his doorbell at home, and he wasn't in the hospital.

"Bastard's hiding out," was Ben's opinion.

And Meg's. But, in fairness, she felt compelled to say, "He might have been feeling too crummy to answer the phone. Or he could have been visiting family when he got sick…"

Ben sneered. She gave up.

"Okay. You want to scale the back wall of his house and peer in his bedroom window?"

He growled something she took as an admission that no, doing so would be stupid.

"Do you really think he killed Shelly?" she asked.

They were on their way to Robb's place again, Ben driving—when they were together, she'd conceded to his male need for control and usually became the passenger. Meg figured with her behind the wheel, sooner or later they'd have an accident when she was distracted by him squirming and slamming his foot down on an imaginary brake when he wasn't offering helpful comments on approaching traffic.

"Who better to have killed her?" he asked.

"I don't know." Meg sighed. "Her lover at the ski area."

"The one nobody seems to know anything about?"

"Except Tony."

"You have only Tony's word for it."

"Why would he lie?" she asked.

Ben didn't answer. He didn't *have* an answer. She knew, because they'd had this conversation before. Several times.

A phone rang, and both Meg and her partner reached for their cell phones. "Mine," she said, and pushed Send. "Patton, here."

"Meg, this is Jack Murray."

Her heart raced. "Jack. Is something wrong with Will?"

"Why would you think that? I haven't seen him today. I'm just wondering…well, if you'd have dinner with me tonight."

She was speechless for a moment. "Dinner? You mean, like a date?"

She'd seen Scott again last night. This time per his request she'd dressed to the nines and they'd had an elegant candlelit French dinner at Maximillian's, after which he'd kissed her on her doorstep. Kissed her very nicely, thank you.

Scott McNeil was plenty to handle at one time.

Sounding uncomfortable, Jack said, "I just thought we should talk. About Will. How he feels about all this, what kind of time I'm going to spend with him. But if you're busy…"

"No." She glared at Ben Shea, who was quirking one of his thick dark brows interestedly her way. "Dinner sounds fine. Seven? Sure." She disconnected.

"Was that Police Chief Jack Murray hisself?" the detective asked, tone mocking.

"None of your business."

His face went expressionless.

"Yes." Her mouth clamped shut. She made herself add, "He's…uh, Will's father."

"So I've heard."

"You listen to gossip?"

"Don't you?"

"Sometimes," she admitted reluctantly.

Ben pulled into the driveway of Jefferson Robb's modest house in old town Elk Springs. Gray clapboard with white and black trim, the little bungalow wasn't that different from the house Shelly had grown up in. Or Meg, for that matter. She should have felt at home.

Instead, she was in a bad mood. She didn't want to have dinner with Jack tonight. They'd argue again about the past; he'd try to twist the way she remembered it, convince her he'd been capable of self-sacrifice at seventeen, which she doubted. She'd be jealous because Will took her for granted and was infatuated with his father.

And she'd wish she was with Scott instead.

"Coming?" Ben stood with his hand on his car door, preparatory to slamming it.

Meg went.

Professor Jefferson Robb answered the doorbell so fast, he had to have seen them coming up his cracked concrete walkway.

"Officers?" he asked, pretending to look puzzled.

Meg didn't buy it for a second.

She showed her badge. "We need to speak to you about a student of yours. Shelly Lange."

"I heard about her death. Tragic." He shook his head, dark wavy hair going silver at the temples. "By all means. Come right in. I won't get too close to you. I've had a nasty flu. Probably past being contagious now, but you never know."

The front door led right into the living room, which even to her less-than-critical housekeeping eye was untidy. Newspapers littered the floor, books and dirty dishes heaped the coffee table and end tables. At least two cats fled the room at the sight of visitors. If Meg wasn't mistaken, their unseen litter box could use a change.

"Mr. Robb—"

"Doctor," he interrupted, then chuckled. "Not that it matters. But 'mister' makes me want to turn my head and see if someone else is behind me."

I'll just bet, she thought uncharitably. Jefferson Robb was a tall, strongly built man, clean shaven with finely chiseled features, a rich voice, and just a little paunch above the waistband of his trousers. She noticed only because he tugged his sweater-vest down self-consciously.

"Dr. Robb," she corrected herself, "tell us about Shelly. Was she a good student? Conscientious?"

He waved them to the sofa and said patronizingly, "Oh, not capable of great depth of thought. But willing and smart enough. Turned in her work on time. I detected an eagerness in her that I hope I encouraged."

"You had her in your class last semester, as well?"

Yes, indeed he had. Oh, yes, her *B* first quarter had risen to an *A* second quarter, and he credited himself with inspiring her to greater effort.

"Dr. Robb." Meg paused for effect. "We've received an allegation that the *A* you gave Shelly was in fact payment for physical favors from her."

"What?" he spluttered. "Ridiculous! Who told you that?"

"Actually, other students have since substantiated the story. Your…body language toward her was apparently quite revealing."

Sweat beaded on his high forehead. "What you're suggesting would destroy my career! Are you reporting to the college administration?"

"No." She gentled her voice. "Dr. Robb, we're trying to get at the truth about her death. Your professional ethics are not our concern."

"Oh, God."

With melodramatic suddenness, he buried his face in his hands. Those hands were long-fingered, elegant. She imagined him on stage, but doubted he was pretending.

"Dr. Robb," she prodded, her tone neutral now.

"My wife left me because of her." He lifted a distraught face. "I had to cleanse my conscience. I told Jeanette. She wouldn't listen when I told her it was over. That it wasn't about Shelly. I just…lately I've been overwhelmed by everything." He flung out an arm, compelling Meg to look around at the modest living room, the trappings of small-town middle-class life.

Not an irrelevancy, she guessed, but the crux, for him. He wouldn't be the first man his age to have a midlife crisis. Most people had to come to terms at some point with where life had taken them. Robb had a Ph.D., apparently. Had he dreamed of full professorship at Harvard? Yale? Regular publications in literary digests?

Instead, he found himself teaching at a two-year college, which even Meg knew was the bottom rung of the academic ladder. He'd probably never written a great novel. This house was the most he could afford.

"She was so beautiful," he mumbled, and she realized he was actually crying now. "She admired me, flattered me. I did inspire her, she claimed. How could I resist?"

"Seducing her?" Ben asked in disgust.

Jefferson Robb looked up wildly. "She seduced me! She kept coming to my office, sitting on the edge of my desk, touching me... Oh, God," he said again. "I've lost Jeanette."

They untangled his story, which erupted from him in angry, fearful and grieving bursts. Shelly *had* earned the A, he insisted; she'd worked hard for it, whatever other jealous students insisted. He'd seen dramatic improvement in her work.

They'd had sex only three or four times, always in his office, with the door locked. Staring, remembering, he said, "Right on my desk. She just sat there, and lifted her skirt, and she didn't have any underwear on. Not that first time." The stare swung blindly until it encountered Meg, focused with difficulty. "You see? It was her. But I should have resisted. I admit it."

He'd been going to end the affair, but hadn't had a chance. After the Christmas break, Shelly had appeared to lose interest. She didn't come by his office, and he could hardly say anything to her in class. His hints that she wait afterward were ignored.

He'd been relieved, her professor claimed, but Meg had her doubts. Why had he wanted Shelly to stay after class if he didn't want to continue sexual relations?

Two weeks ago he'd apparently talked in his sleep. His wife probed, and he confessed. She immediately packed up and left him. Except for a few trips to the grocery store, he'd been holed up here ever since.

When asked, he said that Jeanette Robb had gone to

her sister's in Redding, California. He knew she was there, because he heard her voice in the background when he called, saying that she didn't want to talk to him.

Anguished eyes lifted again to Meg. "She would never…*kill* someone!" He said it with such astonishment. An impossibility. "Not Jeanette. She carries spiders outside rather than step on them. You can't seriously think…"

No, Meg didn't. If events had occurred that Monday evening as she imagined, Shelly had driven around with her murderer for some time, persuaded him to leave her daughter behind, perhaps sat there without running while he unbuckled the car seat and set it on the icy ground. She had struggled, fallen, tried to escape once they had parked at the Puma Lake trailhead and he led her into the woods. She had known then, if she hadn't sooner. Another woman might have shot Shelly as she fled through the heavy snow, but could she have yanked Shelly to her feet, shoved her on, dominated her physically? No.

Jefferson Robb, however, could have done all of that.

And yet, why would he have? He'd already confessed to his wife. What more did he have to lose?

His job, Meg reminded herself. Would Shelly have tried blackmail?

And murder, of course, was not a crime of logic. When he saw his world crumpling, he might have turned his rage on Shelly, the seductress. He might have decided it was all her fault, that she should pay, that her death would absolve him.

"Dr. Robb, where were you last Monday evening?"

"Monday?" He looked around as if for enlightenment. "Was that when she… Oh. I was here, of course. I told you. I haven't gone any place."

"Did you speak to anyone on the phone?" Meg asked patiently.

"Monday." With a shaking hand, he reached for a mug of coffee that sat beside his chair. He stared into it and then set it down without sipping. "I called Jeanette. Spoke to her sister."

"And do you have a cell phone?"

"Yes, but I didn't use it. Why would I? The phone's right over there."

He didn't seem to realize that, as far as Meg was concerned, he could have used the cell phone without anyone ever knowing. He could have called from the Puma Lake trailhead. "Dr. Robb," Meg asked, "when did you meet Shelly Lange for the first time?"

"When?" He stared, understanding coming only slowly. "Why, September. When she enrolled in my course."

"So, she already had her daughter."

"Yes. That is, I didn't know she had one, until…" His fingers clenched on the arms of the chair. "When we were making love, I found that she…that she was nursing. I hadn't known…"

"Very well." Meg closed her notebook and rose to her feet. "Dr. Robb, please don't leave town. We may well have further questions."

He didn't see them out, his bonhomie gone like his wife.

"YOU'RE NOT GOING to wear that, are you?" her son, the critic, asked the moment Meg stepped out of her bedroom.

She glanced down involuntarily. The slacks were the same ones she'd worn to Scott's, and she liked the crocheted linen vest over the untucked white silk shirt. "What's wrong with this?"

"It's…" He shaped something formless with his hands. "It's *baggy*."

"Yeah? So?"

"Don't you want to look pretty?"

Well! She'd actually been rather pleased by what the mirror showed her. Under the hurt pride, however, suspicion niggled.

"Why would I want to look pretty?" Meg's eyes narrowed. "William Patton, you aren't getting ideas, are you? Your father and I are old history. We are *not* getting back together."

His chin thrust out, but he backed into the living room. "I didn't say that."

"But you were thinking it, weren't you?" An observant parent would have seen this coming, she scolded herself. One not working twelve-hour days and trying to conduct a romance, too.

Flinging himself onto the couch, her son said sulkily, "I just thought…when he asked you out…"

"We're going to talk about *you*. About his visitation rights. For Pete's sake, Jack probably has a girlfriend. *I'm* dating someone, in case you hadn't noticed."

"Yeah, like *twice*." He sneered. "You're not exactly married, you know."

"No, I'm not, but I won't be marrying your father, either. So forget it." She waited until he met her eyes. "All right?"

He rolled his eyes and shrugged. "Yeah. Whatever."

This was the first major teenage attitude she'd gotten from Will, but she let it go. She'd made herself clear; message sent and received. She could even sympathize;

from his point of view, think how great it would be to have newfound father marry his mother, forming the great American family.

The phone rang. Will rolled from the couch and bounded for the kitchen. Meg stared after him in astonishment. Back before they'd come to Elk Springs, that behavior had been typical of him. Nobody, he seemed to believe, would bother to call his mother; ergo, the phone must be for him. He'd always seemed so disbelieving when he had to hand it over to her. But so far he apparently hadn't made any friends in town, and usually couldn't be bothered to pick up the phone even when she was in the shower.

She heard the murmur of conversation from the kitchen, then he bellowed, "Mom! It's Aunt Renee!"

"My eardrums," Renee groaned when Meg took the phone.

Meg grinned. "They thicken once you have kids. Kind of like developing callouses."

"It's called 'going deaf.'"

"Well, yeah, now that you mention it."

"What I called for," her sister said, "is that we thought it might be fun to have a potluck tomorrow. Abby's coming."

"I can't take the day off…"

"Dinner at seven," Renee said persuasively. "Will tells me you're dating someone. You can bring him. And his kids, if he has any."

"Come on." Meg leaned a hip against the counter and watched her son pretend an interest in the contents of the freezer. Frosty air poured out. "Surely Will told you every gory detail."

"Well, he did say that you were out with the guy who

found the baby. Scott McNeil, the general manager of the ski area."

"And Abby gave you the rundown on his looks, career prospects and general character."

"Hunky, excellent, and she doesn't know him well enough to say for sure."

"What a family." Meg shook her head. "I'll ask him. He may not want to declare himself that far. Coming to meet the family... I don't know."

"Family," her sister mused. "Somehow, it was hard to think of us that way, with just Abby and me. Now, with Daniel, too, and you and Will..."

"I didn't forfeit my right to be included?" Meg asked, tone light although the question wasn't.

"What are you talking about?" Renee sounded outraged.

"I was kidding."

"You weren't."

The doorbell rang. Meg covered the phone. "Will, can you get that?"

Dumb question. He was already gone.

"I'm sorry," Meg said to her sister. "I'm having dinner with Jack, and he's here."

"Dinner?"

"You mean, he didn't tell you?" Meg asked wryly. "There's something you don't already know?"

"I guess not." Renee sounded awed. "Jack?"

"Don't you get ideas, either," Meg warned. "We're discussing visitation."

"Uh-huh."

Argh. "I'll ask Scott. If he's home."

"Okeydoke," her sister said cheerily. "You can have Will call me."

Meg hung up and poked her head into the living room. Will was going through the motions of sinking a basketball shot and Jack was laughing, head thrown back and teeth white. Shirt open at the throat, he wore slacks and a sportscoat that hung the way it was meant to from his broad shoulders.

Shoulders *she* had once gripped as he kissed her, she thought, with that sense of disorientation earned by visiting the past.

If it weren't for Scott, would she be thinking like Will?

"Hi, Jack. I've got to make a quick call."

His gaze swept over her. "No problem."

Scott answered at home on the second ring. "McNeil, here."

"Hi." Glancing at the door to be sure neither Jack nor Will had followed her, she spoke softly. "This is Meg."

Scott's voice warmed. "I was just going to call. Any chance you and Will would like to go out for pizza?"

"I'm sorry." She was, despite the handsome man waiting out in the living room. "Will's dad is here. We need to talk. You know. About visitation and stuff." Meg was immediately annoyed with herself. Why hadn't she just said, 'I'm having dinner with him?' But no, now she felt as if she'd lied.

Scott seemed to sense that, because his tone became expressionless. "Oh? No problem."

"Any chance you're free tomorrow evening? Renee is having a potluck. I mean, you don't need to bring anything. I will. But I thought it would be fun if you and Emily could come."

"You sound like you're suggesting a fate worse than death," he said, amusement coming through.

Meg took a deep breath and laughed at herself. "It's

just that there's something about inviting a guy to come meet the family. I thought *you* might think…"

"I didn't think," he interrupted her. "I'd like to come. Are you sure your sisters won't mind if I bring Emily?"

"Are you kidding? You'll have to pry her away at the end of the evening. I think Renee is starting to get ideas."

"Ah." That gravelly note of amusement still lingered in his voice. "I'd better tell Emily to be on her best behavior, then. Wouldn't want her to scare your sister off. Be responsible for her never having children."

They set a time, Meg called Renee back and then returned to the living room. Jack half sat on the back of the sofa while Will chattered. Meg felt a pang that was becoming familiar. Ever since the move, he hadn't talked to her like that. Her inquiries about how school was going were returned with a grunted, "Fine." If she asked whether he'd made friends, she got a shrug and, "Not really." He didn't become animated, not the way he was right now.

Did he resent the hours she was working? Her dating when she didn't have time for him as it was? Or was he just reaching an age when he needed a father more than a mother?

Jack saw her and smiled the crooked, slow grin that had turned her stomach into knots when she was sixteen. "Ready?"

"Ready," she agreed.

She felt guilty as all get-out when they left Will standing alone in the living room, even though he looked far from unhappy. In fact, his expression as he waved goodbye was irritatingly smug.

Sitting in the car, she waited until Jack slid in behind

the wheel. "Maybe we should invite him. Make it a family outing."

Buckling his seat belt, he shot her an unreadable glance. "I was hoping to talk to you alone."

What did he have to say? Meg worried. "Oh. Okay," she agreed. As he backed out of the driveway, she saw Will standing in the front window watching them go.

On the way, Jack asked about the Lange murder. He was familiar with the father's oddball church.

"They're narrow-minded," he said. "I think they're folks who came together because they share the same intolerance and desire to punish themselves and everyone else in the name of the Lord, but they're not one of those nutty sects with some messiah, either. Making a kid pray until he faints and then punishing him is one thing, but I think they're sincere in their belief in the Bible and the Ten Commandments. You getting any hint Lange sexually abused his daughter? Is that what you're driving at?"

"The thought crossed my mind," Meg admitted. "But we've talked to other members of the church who believe Kenneth Lange is a good Christian who wanted what was best for his daughter. The bishop told Ben Shea he spoke to Lange at about nine o'clock, like the wife said. They claim not to have a cell phone. While my guess is that she'd lie for him about some things, I think even she'd balk at having her husband bedding her daughter."

"And nine o'clock lets him out?"

"Looks like it," Meg said.

He pulled into the parking lot of Maximillian's. "This okay?"

"Fine," she said brightly. Like she was going to admit she'd been here last night.

The maître d' arched a brow at her, but was far too tactful to comment about her succession of men. Meg pretended to peruse the all too familiar menu, then ordered beef bourguignonne, a change from last night's duckling Rouennaise. She might as well enjoy. Hey, how often did men want to wine and dine her at a place this fancy?

The waiter brought wine, uncorked it and waited for Jack to sip the first glass and nod his approval. He and Meg chatted for a while. Meg was pleasantly surprised by Jack's intelligent, open-minded views. Yet, as they compared anecdotes from their police work, she sensed in him the violence and intolerance learned from her father.

The conversation reached a lull; Meg toyed with her food, feeling the increased intensity in Jack's dark gaze. She was braced for his abrupt decision to finally get to the point.

"My parents liked Will."

She met his eyes squarely. "He's a nice boy."

"That's to your credit."

"How nice of you to say so." Meg tried valiantly to keep the sarcasm from her voice.

"Was he okay with the visit?"

"His exact words, I believe, were, 'They're cool.' Said with enthusiasm. He's never had grandparents, you know."

"He could have had them."

She closed her eyes. "Do we have to do this again?"

Jack continued ruthlessly. "Why didn't you tell me you were pregnant?"

"I was going to." Her mouth twisted. "When I got done panicking. I was trying to talk to you that day. Only, instead…"

He finished, "We made love."

"I don't know about the love part," Meg said flatly.

The waiter appeared, to be sure they didn't need anything; Jack curtly expressed their satisfaction.

The moment the man was out of earshot, Jack said in a hard voice, "I guess it wasn't love, or you wouldn't have walked away without a word, would you?"

Her temper began to rise. "How many times do I have to say it? I wasn't walking away from you."

"I think you were." Lines deepened on his face. "Your dad scared the hell out of me. What kind of man did I look like?"

She wanted to tell him that wasn't it, but in all honesty couldn't. If he'd stood up to her father, maybe she would have decided to trust him. Maybe she'd have turned to him and his parents, or at least stayed in touch.

"You were a teenager, not a man." They both needed to remember that.

"I had no business getting you pregnant if I couldn't take care of you and the baby."

"Maybe so," she said wearily, "but neither of us had the sense to be careful. Any more than teenagers in general have the sense to drive within the speed limit, not take pills some other kid hands them..." Meg gestured helplessly. "Jack, don't beat yourself up forever over something that happened when you were in high school."

"What makes you think I'm beating myself up?" He glowered. "I'm just asking why you let one incident change both our lives. Why you didn't give me a chance."

"Because I didn't dare." She lifted her hands, let them fall. "Jack, I wasn't thinking about you. That sounds awful, but remember, *I* wasn't even seventeen.

I'd just finished hearing you tell my father you'd never call me again. What was I supposed to do?"

A muscle in his jaw worked. "I never forgave myself for crawling away from him. Leaving you to face him alone. And then, when you were just gone the next day…"

"You were mad at me?"

Jack swore. "No. Only at myself. But I didn't know you were pregnant. To go all these years and never tell me…" He shook his head.

"I thought you'd probably be married, have other children…" Meg gave a small shrug. "I wasn't so sure you'd welcome the news that you had a son."

"It's taking some getting used to." He took a long swallow of wine. "But he's a good kid. I can see myself in him. The best part. Will's no coward."

She tried again to convince him that he hadn't been, either. Only outmatched. Her father had been a big, powerful, angry man; Jack, a gangly teenage boy who'd never dealt with anyone like Ed Patton before. He hadn't grown into it, the way she had.

And she realized, in retrospect, that he had attracted her in the first place because he was so different from her father: laid-back, uncritical, a good athlete but not competitive enough to be a great one. She had loved him because of his nature, and yet that very nature meant he would never be able to stand up to her father.

She couldn't say any of this, however, because her impression was that the Johnny Murray she had loved as a teenager had set out to change in himself the very qualities that had made him loveable to her. And now it was too late; Jack Murray wasn't her father, but he had certainly learned harshness from her father. Or perhaps he had learned it on his own; self-contempt was a sharp prod.

They resolved nothing; how could they? Jack paid the bill and left a generous tip. He opened the passenger door for her, closed it when she was settled in the car. He went around, climbed in behind the wheel and shoved the key into the ignition.

But to her disquiet, he didn't turn it. Instead he looked at her, his face etched in lines of torment by the inner fire she hadn't—couldn't—quench.

"I loved you. I would have married you."

She swallowed. "We were too young."

"Maybe." He let out a ragged breath. "I don't know whether to be glad you brought Will home, or wish you'd stayed away."

"I needed...closure."

Jack gave a humorless laugh. "You sound like some damned pop psychology book."

"I think you need it, too."

"Great," he growled. "Give it to me."

"I can't," she breathed, unable to look away from his dark eyes.

"Yes. You can."

Just like that, he reached for her, his hands gentle despite his mood as he tipped her face up and kissed her.

Meg stayed passive, let him claim her mouth, but she didn't respond. On the heels of Scott's kiss the night before, this was a strange experience. Their mouths touched, pressed, moved; Jack's shaven jaw scraped her cheek. But that's all it was: she felt more emotion when she hugged her sisters.

As suddenly, Jack broke off the embrace, releasing her. They stared at each other.

He cleared his throat. "Well. That was more fun fifteen years ago."

"It was, wasn't it?"

He actually laughed. "I figured it was worth a try. You have to admit, the two of us together would have been convenient."

"For Will," Meg agreed.

"Ah, well." He started the car, laid an arm on the back of her seat as he looked over his shoulder to back out. "You don't mind my seeing him regularly, do you? Maybe take him camping when summer rolls around?"

"Of course not. He's got a huge crush on you, you know. He can't believe he has a father. Just…deserve him, okay?"

Jack shifted into gear. In the diffused lighting from the street lamp and dashboard, his expression was dead serious. "I didn't deserve you. I won't make the same mistake with our son."

CHAPTER ELEVEN

UNDERCURRENTS TWISTED and sucked beneath the surface of this family gathering. The most powerful and obvious to Scott was the fact that Meg's son hated his guts. Heck, it wasn't even an undercurrent; white rapids ripping over jagged rocks was closer to the truth.

He felt obligated to keep trying with the kid, although he wasn't getting anywhere. At the moment, they were beside each other dishing up from the array of offerings on Daniel and Renee Barnard's dining table.

"Your mom tells me you're quite a basketball player," he said.

The boy's shrug was the essence of youthful sulkiness. "I used to be okay."

Scott pushed the potato salad on his plate aside to allow room for Boston baked beans. "You're not playing this year?"

"The season was half over when we got here." *You must be stupid not to know that,* was clearly implied.

"Yeah? So? Did you ask to join the team?"

"It's full." Sullenly.

In other words: no.

They'd reached the end of the table and Scott's plate was overflowing. "Well," he said, with an effort at friendliness, "from what your mother tells me, it's their loss."

Ignoring him, the kid added two rolls to the mountain on his plate. He looked too stringy to put that kind of food away, but Scott seemed to remember being hungry all the time at that age.

Will gave him a dirty look, then slouched away. Daniel Barnard's big yellow Labrador retriever clicked after him, apparently choosing him as the best bet for handouts.

Scott caught Meg's eye. She'd already dished up and was sitting on the couch. Patting the spot beside her, she smiled invitingly. He glanced around for Emily, who was being entertained by Meg's two sisters.

The fact that they were on one side of the big living room and Meg on the other was the surface ripple from another of those undercurrents Scott sensed. The three women were polite enough to each other—everyone had been all smiles when he, Meg and Will arrived—but none of them was totally comfortable, not the way family should be. Too quickly, Meg had ended up talking to Daniel Barnard, Renee and Abby cuddling Emily.

Scott paused above the two women, his hands full with food and a can of soda pop. "Let me set this down and I can take her over now."

Neither of them even bothered to look up. Renee cooed at the little girl, who grinned back. Abby dangled a ribbon with bells until Emily's plump hand seized it and shoved one end into her mouth.

Rescuing the ribbon, Abby said, "You can't have her. We're having too much fun."

Renee bent forward and kissed the fuzzy corkscrew curl on top of Emily's head. "Eat. Take a break. Abby's right. You can't have her back yet."

Shaking his head, Scott joined Meg and Daniel, who

sat with his plate balanced on his knee, watching his wife and sister-in-law.

"You were right," Scott told Meg. "I think they wanted Emily, not me."

Saved from homeliness by friendly blue eyes, the big rancher chuckled. "Renee's getting ideas. I can tell. Well, hell," he said in an easy voice. "She's the one who wanted to wait, not me. I'm all for populating the Triple B with little Barnards."

"Being a cop and a mother at the same time isn't always easy," Meg remarked between bites of fruit salad.

"Yeah, that's why she wasn't in any hurry." Daniel shrugged. "Maybe she still isn't."

The three looked in unison at Renee, who was now holding the baby. Emily grabbed Renee's nose and gave a deep belly laugh. Renee pinched her nose in return and laughed just as joyously.

"Yeah?" Scott said. "Don't count on it."

"Where's Will?" Meg asked, craning her neck to see as far as the dining room.

"I saw him go into the family room. I figured maybe he was going to turn the TV on." Daniel downed some beer. "He's not in a good mood."

Get it in the open, Scott decided. "I'm afraid it's me."

Meg's hesitation was brief but noticeable. She must have realized she'd given herself away, because she made a face and said in a low voice, "Yep. In a manner of speaking. He just doesn't seem to like me dating. I'm afraid he has visions of me marrying his father."

"Jack Murray?" The rancher almost choked on his roll. "What would make Will think anything like that?"

"It's a common fantasy for a kid with a single parent." Meg sounded wry, resigned. "If the parents have divorced, they're going to get back together. If the father has never been around, he's going to sweep in, romance mom, become the perfect dad. Here's Will getting to know his for the first time…" She made a face. "It'd probably be surprising if the idea didn't occur to him."

Scott watched her narrowly. How did *she* feel about the idea? She and Jack Murray had gotten together for dinner; was there more to it than she'd said? He'd had the feeling she wasn't saying something yesterday, but told himself he was imagining it. She'd kissed him like she meant it Sunday night; she'd invited him today, hadn't she?

And why the hell was a fourteen-year-old kid barely getting to know his father? What was wrong with Jack Murray? Scott would have given anything to watch his son grow up, and Murray had thrown the chance away.

"He'll get over it," Daniel said comfortably, digging into his food.

Meg looked at Scott, her eyes troubled. "I know you're right," she said, but she didn't sound as if she believed it.

Too harshly, Scott said, "If Murray didn't bother to take any part in raising his son, why does Will give him the time of day now? Much less want you to marry him?"

Barnard looked startled, and Meg's eyes widened. Hastily she said, "It was…complicated. Not all Jack's fault." Looking at her brother-in-law, she gave her head a small shake, and Scott couldn't help wondering what she was warning him about.

"Not *all* his fault?" he echoed.

"I'm the one who took off." She stared down at her plate, voice stifled.

Belatedly, Scott realized this wasn't the time or place to say what a bastard he thought Jack Murray was for not helping his girlfriend raise their son. Bastard? The word hardly did him justice. Scott made a sound in his throat.

"I'd better check on Emily," he said abruptly.

Meg raised her head and gave a twisted smile. "She's happy. Look."

Scott didn't even have to turn his head; Emily's giggle wafted across the big room.

Playing host, Daniel asked Scott how he'd gotten into the business of ski areas, and he let other worries go to concentrate on a fine meal and the kind of casual conversation that built friendships.

"I was a ski bum," he admitted. "My dad hooked us on wilderness life, though he didn't like lifts and grooming equipment and the necessity of logging mountainsides to open the ski runs. He cross-country skied, but me—once I discovered speed and moguls, hell, I was an addict. I went to the University of Vermont so I could ski and get an education at the same time. After that—well, I'd been a lift operator and run the groomers while I was a student. I went into public relations, financial…" He shrugged. "What you don't realize is that pretty soon you won't have time to ski."

"Do you mind?" Meg asked.

He smiled faintly. "Skiing turned into work. For maybe five minutes a day, when we have some new powder snow or the skis carve right, I remember. Most of the time, I'm too busy checking out the job the workers are doing, watching for reckless kids on boards or blindspots to get any pleasure from going down the hill."

"Would you go back if you could?" she asked softly. "Do something else, so skiing was still fun?"

Scott shook his head. "I'm lucky enough to do what I love for a living. Sometimes it's not as much fun as it was when it was just a hobby, but I remember often enough. I consider myself a lucky man."

"Amen," the rancher murmured, and their gazes met for a brief moment of communion.

As soon as he'd finished eating, Scott insisted on taking Emily upstairs for a diaper change and a try at getting her down to sleep. She'd be cranky in no time and wear out the welcome for both of them if her routine got too messed up.

It took half an hour of rocking and turning country-western tunes into lullabies, but the house was well enough insulated that he couldn't hear voices from downstairs and Emily finally nodded off.

Renee had blown up an air mattress on the floor. Scott swaddled the baby in the afghans his hostess had left neatly piled, then checked to be sure Emily couldn't get into anything if she woke up and he didn't hear her right away.

Downstairs he found that Meg had disappeared.

"She's talking to Will," her youngest sister said airily. "So, what's this I hear about a new lift at Juanita Butte dropping over the ridge past Outback?"

He lounged in an easy chair and pretended that he didn't wish like hell he could hear what was going on between Meg and her son.

"You know all the environmental laws," he said. "We are thinking about it. The studies and permits will take a year or more, though."

He'd already known Abby Patton, even wondered a

little about her. She was a beautiful woman, slim and strong and vibrant, eyes as blue as a Siamese cat's. Her pale gold hair was thicker than her sisters', just long enough to shimmer like aspen leaves in a breeze when she shook her head, to provide her something to brush back with a deliberate slow movement, drawing attention to a lush mouth and delicate jaw and a dimple that came more readily than Meg's.

Abby was too young to interest Scott no matter what, but she wouldn't have, anyway. She was too conscious of her beauty and its effect; everything she did and said was too deliberate. Her playing with Emily was the first time he'd seen her let go and act silly, laugh like a girl instead of with throaty, sensual intent. She was cool, this woman, her real emotions held back. A man too blunt to play games, Scott was wary of Meg's youngest sister.

He liked Renee better, felt at ease with her. She and Meg were more alike, he thought; strong women with soft hearts and sharp minds. The middle sister, Renee had hazel eyes and the same straight, fine hair as Meg, but somehow their similar features had made two distinctly different women. An occasional gesture or smile, a turn of the head, and he saw the other, but for reasons that puzzled Scott, Renee would never have been sexually attractive to him while every time he saw Meg he imagined her long legs bare and wrapped around his, her breasts freed for his mouth and hands to explore.

Funny thing, the trigger that turned a man on. Once he saw Daniel looking at his wife, and he knew that even after a few months of marriage the rancher was thinking the same things Scott was about Meg.

In the middle of that thought, Meg wandered back

into the living room, but some tension around her eyes derailed his idle fantasies. His muscles tightened as he prepared to stand, but just then Renee called from the dining room, "Meg, is that you? Come on. We haven't talked yet. Let's put the food away and catch up at the same time."

The three adults left behind chatted idly. Daniel explained that his mother was over in Portland visiting his sister Mary.

"She likes playing grandma," he said with a smile.

Scott glanced around with pleasure at the big, spare room. He liked the texture of the Berber carpet and the soft leather couch and chairs, the bird's-eye maple of the coffee table, the few paintings and drawings against white walls. He didn't like clutter. This room—this house—suited him fine.

After a bit he slipped upstairs to check on Emily, who still slept soundly. She was mostly a noisy sleeper, today being no exception. She slurped on her fist, grunted, wriggled, then relaxed again. He could never resist taking a minute to watch her sleep, face round and dimpled, unmarked by the trauma she didn't know she'd experienced.

Tenderness bumped up against him, as tangible as Emily's solid little body when she slept on his shoulder. She hadn't been with him that long—just over a week, but already she felt rooted in his heart, as if she were his.

The past few days he'd been wondering if maybe she could be. The adoption agency probably had a long list of ideal couples just waiting for a baby. Did the fact that Emily already knew him and lived with him count for anything, or would she be handed over to whoever had been waiting longest? Heck, maybe they'd turn him down anyway because he was a single man who worked long hours.

And maybe one of those perfect couples would be better for Emily. But he loved her, and that mattered most, didn't it? Scott hadn't gotten past thinking; nobody was worrying about Emily's final placement yet anyway. For one thing, they might find her father.

If he wasn't a murderer, it could be that he'd want his daughter, and then Scott would have no choice but to hand her over.

As he came down the stairs, he heard Renee's voice from the kitchen.

"Do you remember what you asked me the other day? About whether I'd ever had a case that was so personal it gave me trouble?"

Meg murmured assent.

"Well, I lied." Meg's younger sister spoke abruptly, with a hint of defiance. "Yes, I solved it, but not before I'd met Daniel, fallen in love, trashed most of Dad's stuff and realized I was wasting my life waiting for you or Mom to come home."

Silence fell briefly; even the clink of dishes stilled. Then Meg fixed on one part of that list.

"You trashed Dad's stuff?"

Scott stopped where he was on the stairs, knowing he shouldn't be listening but unable to help himself. Meg Patton was taking root in his heart, too, just as quickly as Emily had. Her place there scared him as much as Emily's, maybe more. At least Emily herself was uncomplicated. If the state agency let her, she would happily stay with him and love him. Meg, now—he didn't have the slightest idea how serious she was about him.

Whoa! he told himself. *You've dated twice. Kissed twice. You don't even know if* you're *serious. Don't get ahead of yourself.*

"Yeah," he heard Renee say, "it just all got to me one night. I was living in that damned house as if Dad were still walking in the door every day at five-thirty demanding dinner. I didn't change anything. I was afraid to. I couldn't even bring myself to sit in his chair. A few times I'd swear I saw it rock out of the corner of my eye. I moved the TV out into the kitchen, hurried through the living room when I had to. I was just…existing. One night Daniel decided to exorcise Dad. He threw his recliner off the front porch. When it crunched and splintered, I wanted to scream with joy. I didn't see any reason to stop there. Everything went. I even pulled up the carpet. When I was done, it seemed like there was nothing left of him."

"Good for you." Meg's voice was slightly muffled, and Scott guessed that she was hugging her sister. "I used to wish he'd die. That someone would shoot him in the line of duty. I don't know what I thought would happen to us, but at least *he* wouldn't be part of it."

"You, too?" Renee asked. "I felt so guilty for thinking of him dead! For wishing…"

"What about Abby? How'd she feel?"

"I don't know." Renee sounded worried. "He was easier on her. Mostly, she had him wrapped around her little finger. I don't think she loved him, but she didn't seem to hate him, either. Do you think that's healthy, not to be passionate one way or the other? I mean, this was her *father!* The only parent she remembers."

"I've wondered…"

Increasingly conscious of what they'd think if they

caught him hovering up here, Scott started down the last few steps. On the way up he'd noticed the basket sitting there, but he'd forgotten and managed to kick it. A hairbrush and a bottle of fingernail polish clattered onto the floor.

Both sisters appeared in the doorway to the kitchen.

"Sorry," he muttered. "I wasn't paying attention."

"Did you put Emily down?"

"Yeah, I was just checking on her. She's out like a light."

"Why don't you come in the kitchen?" Renee suggested, as if he hadn't interrupted anything. "I was just telling Meg about how I met Daniel. His dog brought home a human skull."

The grotesque image made him curious enough to intrude. "That would make you sit up and take notice," he said, following them. "What can I do?"

Renee handed him a dish towel. "Why don't you dry as I wash the pans?"

Behind him, Meg puttered around the kitchen putting food away in the refrigerator and wiping counters. As they worked, Renee told the story.

Daniel had thought the skull belonged to his senile grandfather, who had wandered away one snowy night and was never found. But Lotto, the dog, had brought home other bones, as well, and taken together the coroner could tell that the skeleton was that of a young man—and one who had been murdered ten to twenty years before.

"But he didn't seem to be anybody who'd been reported missing." Renee went still for a moment, hands in the dishwater, unfocused eyes meditative. "That ate away at me. Nobody caring enough to report him missing. I started wondering if first Mom and then you, Meg, had really left and just never bothered to call or write, or whether you weren't dead somewhere in an unmarked grave. Jack kept wanting me to drop the case—it's not like we aren't always busy enough that he needs every officer, and it was an old crime. But I just couldn't let it go.

"Daniel didn't like me too much at first, because I was out here bugging his mother all the time. With his dad dead, she was the only one who'd remember ten, fifteen years before. Thank goodness she's forgiven me—we're just about best friends now. I finally figured out that the dead man was Gabe Rosler, the son of the neighboring ranchers. You might remember him, Meg."

She paused in the act of putting tin foil around a pile of ham. "Was he a year or two younger than me? Kind of a strange kid? Yeah, I think so."

"His father killed him," Renee concluded. Her voice sounded odd. "Pretty well my worst nightmare."

"I'm sorry." Meg went to her in a rush, and they hugged, wet hands and all. "I should have called. I know I should have called."

Feeling as out of place and about as comfortable as a skier after his first lesson suddenly stranded on a forty-five degree hill, Daniel grabbed another pot and pretended not to notice the two women's damp eyes.

They murmured a few watery *sorries,* and *It's okays,* then apparently remembered his presence and backed awkwardly away, returning to their tasks. He saw Meg tangle some cling wrap, wipe away a tear and then start over. Renee swished around in the dishwater without accomplishing anything for a minute.

Finally she asked, "Are you getting anywhere with finding out who killed Emily's mother?"

"Well, we've eliminated some people. Shelly's parents, for one. Aside from a phone conversation at a critical time, his feet aren't big enough."

Scott swung around to stare at her. "You didn't say anything. Did you get any kind of decent casts of those footprints?"

"Better than you might think." She gave him a warning look. "This is just between us and the wall. Okay? But, yeah. The print isn't clear enough to tell brand of boot, but we can eliminate some. The last time I went to the Langes', I saw his slippers. Size nine. He's not a big man. Those weren't his tracks."

"So now what?" he asked.

"So now I keep digging." Meg closed the refrigerator door. "I hope you'll make it clear to your people that you want them to cooperate with the investigation. At least one person has hinted to me that she knows something she isn't saying."

He frowned. "I'll have her into my office. Who is it?"

"Let me approach her again, not send you crashing down on her."

That stung. "You think I'm a tyrant?"

She squeezed his arm, a light comforting touch, as she passed him on her way back to the kitchen table. "No, but you're the boss. No one doubts that for a second. Telling tales on another employee is awkward, you have to admit."

Scott grunted reluctant agreement.

"I'm going back up there tomorrow," Meg continued. "If I talk to enough people and I'm persistent enough, something will give. It always does."

Then why did so many murder cases remain unsolved? he wanted to ask, but guessed the answer might be—because a Patton wasn't investigating them. These two sisters had that in common: they were dogged once they started on something.

"I worry," Meg said then, out of the blue, "that I'm identifying too much with Shelly Lange. That's why I asked whether you'd gotten too personal about any case, Renee."

"You're identifying with the victim?" her cop sister echoed. "Why more than usual?"

"Oh, it's all mixed up. Partly me having just come home, which set me to thinking about Dad and our childhood." Meg took a dried pan from Scott's hand and absentmindedly hung it on a wrought-iron rack over the kitchen island. "Partly it's Shelly's relationship with her father. It seems to be the key to her behavior. She never got his attention or approval, so she's been looking for both from other men ever since. But, see, that's where I start wondering... Am I reading something into the choices she made that isn't there, because I figure she must have felt about her father the way I did about mine?"

Soapy water was gurgling down the drain. Renee turned her back on it to face her sister. Drying her hands on a dish towel, she said, "But you didn't go looking for approval from other men." Sudden uncertainty gave a hitch to her voice, uneasiness to her sidelong glance at Scott. "Did you?"

Meg looked from one to the other of them, then laughed. "You ought to see your faces! Do you think I'm going to admit that I was wildly promiscuous after I ran away from home?"

Scott decided then and there that he wouldn't let it

matter if she had been; God knows he'd done and—
most of all—said things of which he was ashamed. Meg
was who she was now, not what she'd been at seventeen, trying to care for a baby and scrape up the money
for rent and food.

Renee gave it a moment's thought, then a brisk,
knowing nod. "No. Of course not. You would have been
promiscuous in high school if you were hunting for a
sugar daddy." Her amused gaze slanted toward Scott
again. "Sorry, Scott. I don't suppose your relationship
was quite ready for this."

"Oh, I don't know," he drawled, lifting a brow at
Meg. "I'm a man. It's never too early for sex. Isn't that
the stereotype?"

"You wouldn't be here today if I thought you were
a stereotype," Meg snapped.

Renee flung the dish towel at her sister. "Hey, give
him a break! I set him up."

Turning away with a sniff, Meg said, "Well, I'll tell
you what. I can't figure out how Shelly found the
time for men."

"Maybe there weren't any," Scott heard himself
saying. "Maybe her image was all smoke and shadow."

Meg stuck out her lower lip while she thought. Scott
wanted to kiss her.

"I don't think it was faked, not totally," was her conclusion. "Everyone seems to agree that she lit up for
men. In her world, women were just…there. Wallpaper.
Even though she was vibrant and beautiful herself, the
reality she grew up with is that men are dominant,
women are important only as they relate to a man. Alice
Lange as good as admitted to me that she exists only to
support her husband. Just for a minute, when we told

them what happened to Shelly, I saw some fire, but it was dead ten minutes later when she was more anxious to alibi Lange than she was to mourn her daughter."

"I still can't remember Shelly's mother," Scott admitted, "and I lived next door to the Langes for two years."

"Exactly." Meg pulled out a stool and perched on it, knees boyishly apart although she wore a long swirly skirt and a skimpy top with spaghetti straps under a white cotton shirt.

Knowing she wore no bra under there might be why his imagination wasn't having any trouble undressing her.

Renee boosted herself up onto the counter and sat with feet swinging. "Okay. So your theory is, Shelly had to be like Mama and find a man to worship and obey?"

"Something like that." Meg sounded troubled more than eager. "Maybe she'd have been okay if her father had ever validated her by spending time with her and expressing pride in her, but he didn't. So she's been looking for a substitute ever since. Maybe she loved sex. Maybe it was just the price she paid. But boys her own age wouldn't do. She needed a man who was older, in a position of authority. A guy her own age was better than nothing, which is why she had boyfriends, but as one woman told me, Shelly was always looking over their shoulders for someone more important. The professor was worth going for aggressively. Question is, who else was?" She leaned forward, voice going quiet, intense. "And who satisfied her drive enough that she chose to get pregnant by him?"

"You think it was a choice?" Scott asked.

"On some level."

Renee was nodding. "Yeah. I agree. Don't you think *you* made a choice with Jack?"

"I'd have denied it then, but now…" Meg made a face. "Sure. You're more likely to be careless when you're ambivalent about the outcome."

"But there's no sign of the baby's father in Shelly's life?" Renee said. "No child support? Photos? Nothing?"

"Not that we've found so far. Certainly no financial support."

Scott had been brooding about something else entirely. "She really liked Penny," he said. Seeing Renee's puzzlement, he added, "My ex-wife. Shelly used to hang out at our house. She'd get all excited and giggle when I came home—flutter her eyelashes at me, talk loudly, get me to admire her nail polish. That kind of thing. But she spent time with Penny. If it weren't for Nate, if Penny and I had stayed put, I wonder if Shelly's life would have come out different."

Compassion made the blue in Meg's eyes so vivid they seemed bottomless. "Shelly wasn't your responsibility."

"No. Of course not." Absorbed in their grief, neither he nor Penny had given a thought to the neighbor girl who seemed to have too much time to spend at their house. They had abandoned her from the moment they laid their son to rest. Why hadn't they wondered about Shelly's life in that house where a mother was home, but seemingly not present? Could they have made a difference?

Oh, hell, Scott thought. There was no way now of knowing whether Penny had meant anything to Shelly. After the move to Elk Springs, his wife had been a housewife, just like Shelly's mom; maybe that put her in the same category—dependent on a man. But Shelly had seen Penny argue with him, tease him, defy him. Maybe…

He swore silently. All he needed was one more burden of guilt.

Meg let out an exasperated huff of breath and for a wild moment he thought she'd been reading his thoughts. But, no, she was looking past him at the doorway.

"I suppose I should go see what my oh-so-charming son is up to. And here I thought I was raising the one teenager who would never suffer this kind of ridiculous angst."

Her sister hooted. "You would! Meg, Superwoman! You always did think you could do anything." But her laughter was affectionate, running deeper and quieter than the studied politeness earlier.

Meg seemed to recognize that, because she only gave a Big Sister look and said, "Wait'll you have kids."

"Go." Renee hopped down from the counter and flapped a hand. "I'll finish up in here."

"I'd better check on Emily," Scott said guiltily. Except as an abstraction, he hadn't thought of her in half an hour or more. What if she was screaming upstairs, scared at waking in a strange place, without the familiar white-painted crib?

He'd have sworn she had slept better once he'd picked up her very own crib from Shelly's apartment; Emily was more likely to be cooing and cheerful when she woke up than she had been those first days in the rented crib. Once, he'd come in to find her chatting to the yellow and pink ducks stenciled on the headboard, her bright eyes fastened on them as if they'd come to life. "Your mama painted those," he'd murmured as he picked her up. "Aren't they pretty?"

But Emily left Scott's mind again the minute he followed Meg and realized they were briefly alone in the hall. Behind them, dishes clinked in the kitchen;

ahead, lazy voices drifted from the living room. But nobody could see them here.

Meg had—he hoped—the same thought, because she turned to face him.

"Scott, I'm sorry," she said in a rush. "Will's a great kid. He's not usually…"

"It's okay." Scott wrapped a hand around her nape, under the silky fall of hair. "He's a teenager. They're entitled. He's used to just the two of you. Of course he resents me."

She turned her head enough to kiss the bare skin on his forearm. "If it weren't for Jack…"

"Why are you even giving Murray a chance now? You must have come back to Elk Springs just to make fatherhood convenient for him. Is knowing him that important to Will?"

Some emotion flitted across her face. *Guilt?* he thought, then couldn't believe it. Resentment, maybe.

"I'm the one who didn't give Jack a chance." She said it apologetically, without her usual conviction. She didn't even believe herself. "I've lived all over the world, you know. I should have made it my business to get home to Elk Springs sometimes, but… My father was here, and… Life gets complicated."

Why should she have had to do all the work? Scott had heard good things about Jack Murray, but did people know he had a son he hadn't made any great effort to see? Scott growled in the back of his throat.

"You've had to do too much alone," he said.

"No!" She stiffened under his hand, and that elusive emotion ghosted through her eyes again. "It's been all joy. I wouldn't have wanted to lose Will every summer, the way some single mothers do."

"*All* joy?" His voice had gone husky. He kneaded her neck, feeling the delicacy and strength both. He wasn't troubling to bank the fire anymore. "There weren't times you would have liked a helping hand?"

"How could Jack have helped me?" Meg fired back, eyes hot with—what? Then the expression on her face changed, blazed with hunger. "Let's not talk about it. Kiss me good-night now. While we have the chance."

To hell with Jack Murray. Fool that he was, he'd lost not only a son, but this incredible woman, too.

"With pleasure," Scott murmured, and captured her mouth with his.

Quivering with tension, she rushed into the embrace as if she'd been waiting forever for it. Her lips parted, her tongue met his, her arms came fiercely around his neck.

Desire slammed into him. Scott backed her into the corner by the stairs. One hand tangled in her hair while the other gripped her buttocks and lifted her against him. The tenderness of those other kisses was missing; flat-out *wanting* had shoved it aside.

And he wasn't alone. She was sobbing for breath and rubbing against him, as lost in the need as he was.

But he couldn't quite forget where they were. God Almighty, if Will came on them—saw his mother taking a man's hand and laying it on her breast...

A groan tore its way from Scott's chest and he weighed her small breast in his palm with pleasure and regret.

"Sweetheart," he said, low and rough against her neck.

"Kiss me," Meg demanded raggedly.

One of the hardest things he'd ever done was lift his hand from her high, firm breast and smooth her hair back from her face. "Meg, anyone could come along. Including your boy."

Her eyes had gone cloudy with wanting; the focusing came slowly, as reluctantly as he called her back.

"Oh, my God," she said. "Will."

"We'll take this up another time." Scott kissed her smooth forehead, intending to let her go. But, oh, the way her face tilted up! Somehow his lips found the bridge of her nose, her closed eyelids, her cheekbone, her earlobe…

"Scott," she whispered. "Emily is crying."

"What?" Then he heard it, the thin frightened wail. He swore under his breath, rested his forehead against Meg's. "Yeah. Okay."

"And there's Will. I should find him."

"I know, I know."

"I wish…" she barely breathed, not finishing.

"I wish, too." He kissed her, quick, hard, then made himself retreat a step. "Someday we'll be alone."

"You think?" She backed away.

"I don't think. I know," Scott promised.

She must be visible to the people in the living room now. "I'll hold you to it," Meg said, so softly Scott just heard her. And then she disappeared to find her son.

All he could think about as he headed up the stairs was how soon they could be alone.

And that Jack Murray was an even bigger fool than he'd thought.

CHAPTER TWELVE

FINDING TIME to be alone wasn't as easy as it should have been. Between work and kids, Meg and Scott couldn't manage it.

Dinner, yes—Scott brought Emily over to Meg's condo and they talked in the kitchen while she cooked and Will hunched over the computer in the next room playing some grisly game. The clash of metal occasionally resulted in blood-curdling screams. Will was currently hooked on this game, and Meg had carefully *not* looked at it; she knew she'd hate it. And she knew, too, that he was playing right then so that he could chaperon Mom. He wasn't about to go to his bedroom and leave her even briefly alone with Scott.

A quick lunch in Scott's office on Thursday—that one was too short to be satisfying, especially since his secretary interrupted twice. A lift had broken down, skiers were stranded on the chairs. The Chief of Operations, Mark Robillard, just wanted Scott to know. They were working on it. About the time Scott started getting restless, Trish stuck her head back in.

"Up and running, Mark says. Folks were cheering."

"I'll bet they were," he muttered. "But give 'em an hour or two to stew, and they'll be down here demanding ticket refunds."

"Will you give them?" Meg asked.

"Probably." He grimaced. "They weren't up there more than half an hour, but... We want them back."

"Said as a good businessman," she teased.

"That's what I am."

He'd been working on a new brochure. Layouts were spread across his desk. By this time she recognized the dark decisive handwriting in every margin. The sketches, however...

"Well, you're definitely not an artist." She tapped one. "Is this a Christmas decoration?"

"A tram." A smile tugged at his mouth. "Don't be insulting."

She sighed and stretched. "You're right. Otherwise you'll start speculating aloud on why I'm not better at *my* job."

He stood, too, and wrapped big hands around her waist. "Hadn't occurred to me. Has somebody been on your case?"

"Mmm." Meg kissed Scott's hard, scratchy jaw. His hands tightened; a rumble started in his chest. It was like making a cat purr, she thought with amusement and the stirrings of the hunger that cramped in her womb every time she saw him.

"Who?" He nibbled on her earlobe.

Brain fogging, knees weakening, Meg had to think. "The sheriff himself. He wants results. The high school is having problems with gangs—can you believe it, in Elk Springs? Anyway, they want me there. He didn't cut us off yet, but he will if we don't make an arrest soon."

"That's ridiculous," Scott began.

"No." She laid a hand on his cheek. "If a murder is solved at all, it's usually right away. We wouldn't file this one yet, anyway, but I don't want to make it a part-time pursuit. Ben may have to. There was a shooting at the truck stop last night. One dead, one in critical condition. The witnesses don't agree on how it started or who pulled a weapon first."

His phone rang; she felt his muscles jerk in reaction, but he made no move to reach for it.

"Answer it." Meg gave him a gentle push. "I've got things to do, too. Places to go, people to see."

Scott hesitated, then grabbed the phone. "Yeah? Can you hold on a minute?" He covered the mouthpiece, stopping Meg before she went out the door. "I'm having a staff meeting at three. You want to stop by? Say a few words?"

Look for a murderer? she thought, but only nodded. "Sounds good."

On the way out, Meg told herself it didn't matter that she hadn't yet told him that Jack had never known about Will. A chance would come, but she wanted to be alone with him, have some uninterrupted time. Her decisions weren't ones he'd accept without question; she knew that. He felt too much anguish at the loss of his son.

She'd never meant to lie. He'd misunderstood her, and she hadn't corrected him, and then suddenly she *was* lying. Doing so didn't come naturally to her, and now the consciousness of the lie dogged her as insidiously as her fear in the early days that her father would find her anytime. But what could she do about it? This wasn't the kind of thing you just blurted out.

Or was that simply an excuse, because she was afraid he'd hate her for what she'd stolen from another man?

In the outside office, Trish was talking on the phone at the same time as she worked on the computer; two

Hold buttons flashed. She didn't even notice Meg, who told herself to put aside personal problems. She had a job to do.

And Trish could wait. Meg went looking for other fish to fry.

So far as she could determine, the community college had been a bust. Shelly had been a model student. Her boyfriend had been no more than casual, another Tony Rieger. Jefferson Robb had been Shelly's only handsome male instructor; the others were either female or edging toward retirement.

Robb didn't work in Meg's mind as the murderer. Yeah, on the surface he blamed Shelly for the seduction, but it was his own weakness in succumbing that tormented him. He'd already lost his wife a week or more before Shelly's murder. Revenge as a motive never satisfied Meg.

People were more likely to kill to protect something—or someone—precious to them.

His job? In a fog of despair over losing his wife, would Robb have cared enough about his tenure at the college to kill? Had Shelly threatened it in any way? Would a woman hungry for a man's approval have dared blackmail him?

Maybe. But Meg didn't think so, although Ben Shea didn't agree. He'd taken an acute dislike to Jefferson Robb.

Portland police had interviewed Robb's wife and her sister, plus some neighbors. The wife had definitely arrived several days before Shelly's murder and had stayed put. The neighbors were sure. And the sister agreed that he had phoned on the night in question; he phoned every evening at more or less the same time. She was getting tired of it. She'd never believed in answering machines, but she was about to go buy one.

No, Meg still thought the answer lay here, at Juanita Butte. Where Shelly had worked when she got pregnant; where she had been afraid of someone.

Meg stopped by the ski shop this morning, but she'd already talked to the three employees working. Rental shop—ditto. At the ski instructors' hut, she hit the first pay dirt of the day.

A young woman she'd never seen before said, "Shelly Lange? Oh, sure. I remember her. She was really murdered? I mean, it's so scary!"

"That's one way of putting it," Meg said dryly. "Do you have time for a few questions?"

She had a lesson to teach at two; until then, she was all Meg's. The instructors' hut wasn't very big. At a counter in the front room, new students could sign up for lessons. In back, wet gloves made ragged lines on the plywood floor in front of a potbellied wood stove. A couple of sagging couches were good enough for breaks; right now, several guys who didn't look a heck of a lot older than Will seemed to be amiably arguing about a Lakers basketball game.

Meg and the young woman—Rhonda Buchanan—chose to go outside. The day was hazy but warmer than it had been—twenty degrees instead of eight. Meg pulled on her gloves and tucked her chin inside the collar of her olive-green parka.

The area was relatively quiet today—it was Thursday, over a week since Shelly's murder. Lift lines were almost nonexistent; a few clusters up the hill suggested ski classes. A couple came laughing out of the lodge and unlocked their skis, stamping into them not far from Meg and Rhonda.

Watching with a trace of envy as they skated toward

the roped-off entry to the chairlift, Meg said, "I'll have to get up here skiing."

"What?"

"Nothing." She sighed and sat on a bench. Her butt was immediately cold. "Were you friends with Shelly?"

Rhonda had given her a few lessons; Shelly hadn't skied all that much before she took the job here. "Can you imagine?" Rhonda marveled. "She said her dad wouldn't spend the money."

"I don't think the Langes are well-to-do."

"But *everyone* around here skis!"

"Not everyone. I grew up in Elk Springs, you know." And her father wouldn't pay for lessons or lift tickets, either. *God damn waste of time,* he'd called the sport.

"Well...most people."

"I'll give you that." Meg didn't want to argue. "So, did you and Shelly talk?"

"Oh, yeah!" About lots of things, Rhonda insisted. Books, politics, environmental issues. "Not just makeup and who was hot," she said earnestly.

But she wasn't disappointed to find out that what Meg most wanted to know was who Shelly had thought was "hot."

"Mr. McNeil," she said, blushing enough that Meg guessed she felt the same. "Mr. Robillard—she liked the older guys. Oh, and I saw her one time hanging all over Evan Hannah. He's the head of the ski patrol. I mean, I could see her point there."

"Anyone else?"

There were a few others—all cases of Shelly admiring from afar, Rhonda thought. "And that guy from Mechanical, you know about him, don't you? Tony something?"

"Tony Rieger. I've talked to him."

"Well." Rhonda ruminated. "I can't think of anybody else."

"The only one you actually saw Shelly with was Evan Hannah?" Meg asked, to be sure.

"Besides Tony."

"Right. Besides Tony."

With two o'clock looming, Rhonda left Meg to her meditations. She'd beard Hannah now, she finally decided, then Trish. Bottom numb, she trudged awkwardly back to the main lodge. The ski patrol was on the bottom floor.

Another of those tanned, blond gods with flashing white teeth was behind the counter. "Evan? Oh, jeez. I don't know where he is. Can I help you?"

"No, I have a question specifically for him," Meg said patiently.

"Well, I know he's coming down from the mountain for some kind of meeting with the general manager. McNeil," he added helpfully.

"I'll catch him before then," Meg said.

To fill the time, she went back up to turn the screws on Scott's secretary. Trish had her hands on the computer keyboard, but no phone receiver crooked between her ear and her shoulder. Hearing Meg's footstep she glanced up, looking instantly wary at the sight of the uniform.

"Deputy Patton. Scott says he suggested you stop by for the meeting at three. That'll be at the end of the hall in the…"

"I wanted to talk to you first."

The secretary sighed and let her hands fall from the keyboard to her swollen belly. "About who I saw Shelly with, right?"

"Yep."

Trish squirmed. "It just feels…"

"Like tattling?"

"Yeah, I guess so."

Meg pulled a rolling secretarial chair over and sat gingerly. No feeling in the nether regions yet.

"Trish, I need to find out who Emily's father is. If he didn't kill Shelly—great. But why hasn't he come forward?"

"Maybe he doesn't know he's a father."

"Maybe. But this is a small town. Wouldn't you think he'd have followed up to see why she quit working here?"

"Not if they weren't seeing each other anymore," Trish said stubbornly.

"But everyone in Elk Springs knows now. Shelly was killed and she left a six-month-old baby. An honorable man would have come forward and said, 'I was having sex with her. The baby might be mine.'"

"Unless…" Trish nibbled on her lip, her eyes worried. "Unless he's married."

"If he's married," Meg pointed out, "he may well have an alibi for the time Shelly was murdered. We won't have to tell his wife anything. I promise. Adultery is his business." She paused, then added with quiet force, "Murder is mine."

The secretary heaved a breath. "Okay. I know you're right. And what I saw…it may not have meant anything. I mean…he's not that kind of guy. He *is* married, and he's always calling his wife and bragging about his kids."

Meg hid her impatience. "He?"

"Mark. Mark Robillard. Chief of Operations."

"Ah."

Trish eyed her suspiciously. "You don't sound surprised."

"Someone else mentioned his name. Also…" she spread her hands. "He fits the profile."

"You mean…he's the kind Shelly liked?"

No, what Meg had really meant was that Mark Robillard had the motive to kill if Shelly had threatened his secure family and job in some way. Blackmail? An insistence on resuming the relationship? A half tearful, half spiteful threat to tell the whole world how he'd slighted her?

It didn't matter *how* Shelly had threatened him, only that she had. And that his family was precious to him.

Under questioning, Trish told her about seeing the two of them in front of a convenience store at the High Mountain Resort, ten miles south of town. Mark was putting Shelly into a car and kissing her.

"He was supposed to be out of town," Trish said unhappily. "And…oh, it was just chance that I was there. I was meeting a friend…they have some really great boutiques there, you know—well, maybe you don't since you're new around here."

Ski season hadn't opened yet, Trish remembered. Shelly had been working at the shop from early summer; this had been just after Labor Day weekend.

"You don't think…" she asked doubtfully.

Damn right she did, Meg thought, her hunting instincts sharpened. But she reassured Trish, left her momentarily confident she'd done the right thing in talking.

Robillard might not be the only one who fits the profile, Meg reminded herself. *Evan Hannah might, too. Remember, he was seen with Shelly, as well. There might yet be an unknown who had the same motive. Don't jump to conclusions.*

She went straight to the staff meeting. Both Robillard and Hannah were present, along with a half dozen others, all department heads. Advertising, Financial—the one woman, Mechanical, Snow Removal, Parking… The list went on: an attorney headed the legal department, security, ticket sales and lift operation fell under the Chief of Operations. Scott oversaw and approved all their work.

The group listened attentively as Scott stood at the head of the lone table in the bare-bones conference room and reminded them that the police required their cooperation.

"Deputy Patton has found a few employees reluctant to be frank with her. Please urge everyone to help her in any way they can. Assure them that their jobs will not be put in jeopardy because they pass on either substantiated evidence or rumor."

"Thank you," Meg said, when her turn came. She let her gaze run down the table. "Most of you I've met. Mr…Hannah, is it?"

Perhaps forty, he was dark-haired, deeply tanned and fit. It struck her how attractive all these men were, given that they were essentially corporate executives. A daily game of racquetball wasn't required to keep any of them in shape. If they didn't ski as part of the job, they did for pleasure.

"Mr. Hannah, could I speak to you afterward?" Meg asked. "Since we didn't have a chance earlier?"

"Sure, no problem," he said easily.

After giving a basic rundown on the progress of the investigation, she excused herself and waited outside. The meeting continued for another fifteen minutes. At last the door opened and they filed out, each nodding as he—or she—passed.

Meg saw nothing different in Mark Robillard's manner. Not that he was easy to read. A dour expression must keep his underlings intimidated.

"Evan's waiting for you," Scott said in a low voice as he followed Robillard out. "Did Trish get the message to you that Will called?"

"Did he say…"

"Not an emergency. Trish discovered that much. He said he guessed it could wait until you got home tonight."

"Oh." How strange. Meg glanced at her watch. School was out for the day. Would he have called for permission to go to a new friend's house?

Would he ever *make* a new friend?

"I'll use your phone after I talk to Mr. Hannah, if you don't mind."

"Of course not." He didn't touch her, not with the attorney and the chief financial officer apparently waiting for him.

Hannah sat with his big brown hands clasped behind his head. He started to rise when she entered the conference room, but Meg waved him back.

Liking his twinkling eyes and rakish smile, she decided to take the most direct route.

"Mr. Hannah, are you married?"

His eyebrows shot up, but he answered after a barely discernible pause. "Yes. I am."

"Children?"

"Teenagers." One corner of his mouth lifted in a rueful smile. "I've recently become an idiot."

She almost rose to that, admitted to being the parent of a fourteen-year-old, but she kept her face impassive.

"Mr. Hannah, did you know Shelly Lange?"

He sounded cautious now. "By sight."

"Not feel?"

Hannah flattened his hands on the table and shot to his feet, his eyes narrowing in quick anger. "What the hell does that mean?"

Meg didn't alter her pleasant expression. "I've been told that you were seen with Shelly. She was 'hanging all over you,' according to the witness."

He swore. "I usually think of myself as a gentleman, but I'm going to be straight with you here—Shelly Lange 'hung all over' anything in pants. I wouldn't have had her working for me! She had a way of backing me into corners. She imagined that I was battling secret lust for her, Deputy Patton."

"She was a beautiful young woman."

He made a disgusted sound and abruptly sat back down. The chair legs screeched across the floor. "Do you know how many beautiful young women work here? Women make up half the ski patrol. Some of them look goddamn nice in their stretch pants. Do I notice? I'm a man. Sure I do. Would I act on it? Nah. See, I've got something better at home. I have a gutsy broad who knows everything about me. I've got two kids who won't turn out to be worth crap if I don't set an example for them. You think I'm going to blow the things that really count for some hot young thing?" He glowered. "Let me put it this way. My kids may think I'm an idiot right now, but they're going to figure out one of these days that they're wrong."

Meg had to suppress a smile. "Mr. Hannah, where were you on the evening of Monday, January 14?"

"You should have asked that in the first place." He'd

relaxed again; his eyes even held a hint of that twinkle. "I was coaching a freshman girl's basketball squad at the high school. We had a game. Beat Medford 24-18. Went for pizza afterward."

"I'll need to confirm that."

"Well, I can't say I'm thrilled at the idea of you asking questions about me, making the folks at the school wonder."

"I'll do it discreetly," she assured him.

He grimaced. "That it, then?"

"That's it." She allowed herself a smile. "Thank you, Mr. Hannah. By the way, we have something in common. I have a fourteen-year-old son."

"Yeah?" He frowned. "Patton. My daughter's a freshman. That name rings a bell."

"We just moved here a couple of weeks ago. His name is Will."

A flash of recognition was followed by a broad grin. "Big dark-haired kid? Yeah, yeah. I saw him shooting some hoops the other day. My daughter says he's 'hot.'"

"I don't think Will's of an age to appreciate that," Meg told him. As they scraped their chairs back and walked out of the conference room she got the particulars on who his daughter was so that she could ask Will later.

Upstairs she called Will from Trish's desk. All he wanted was permission to take the school rooter bus to a basketball tournament Friday evening.

Except, of course, he was already backpedaling. "If you want me to stay home, I don't have to go…"

"Why were you thinking about it in the first place?" Meg interrupted. "Considering you haven't been to a single game since we moved here?"

She could see him shrugging as well as if he were here. "I played a pick-up game with a couple guys today. One of 'em was the big star forward. A junior." He was trying to sound sarcastic, indifferent to the importance of these other boys, but she heard the pleased undertone. "They said I should be on the team next year. I just figured I should watch them play once, see if they're any good or if they're crap."

"Yeah, I think you should," she agreed. "Then why the hesitation? You never seem to have that much homework."

"Well, if you want to do something…" Even he knew that was lame. His voice trailed off.

It came to her in a blinding flash: he didn't want her to be alone with Scott.

Followed by: she could *be* alone with Scott. A whole evening. She could do something with a man she hadn't done in…well, years. So long that the whole idea scared her even as she felt a cramping of pleasure and excitement in her belly.

"Go," she said in the no-nonsense voice she used when she meant what she was saying, no argument allowed. "You know, you might even get to know some of the other kids."

The rolled eyes came through as well as the shrug had earlier. "Mom, I don't need a social director."

"Well, then, get a life," she said unsympathetically. Before he could hang up and go off to sulk, she had an idea. "Do you know a Marie Hannah? Your age?"

"Why?" Nobody could be as suspicious as a teenager.

"I hear her dad coaches the freshman girl's basketball team. I just want confirmation that he really was at a game on January 14, and that when they went out for pizza afterward he was with them. Can you casually ask around and find out for sure?"

"Oh, yeah. Sure," Will sneered. "Casually."

"Don't be a brat. Can you or can't you?"

Heavy sigh. "I'll try."

"Good. See you in a couple of hours. Put the mani-cotti in the oven at five-thirty—375 degrees."

Her son grumbled agreement.

Scott wasn't in his office; Meg didn't know whether to be disappointed or relieved. She left a note on his spindle. *Dinner tomorrow night? No Will. Meg.* Summed it up nicely, she thought.

Mark Robillard had just left, his secretary a floor down told Meg. There was some problem up on the Sugar Bowl lift. But Meg could catch him if she hurried.

She hurried.

In front of the lodge, Robillard was just dropping his skis to the snow and was talking on—not a cell phone, a walkie-talkie, she thought. He held it in a gloved hand. Meg noted the glove: black leather, comfortably shaped to his hand.

"Mr. Robillard."

His eyes focused on her. Looking less than pleased, he said into the walkie-talkie, "Gotta go, Clint." Brief pause. "Yeah. Do your best. I'll be up in a minute." With a practiced flick, he stowed the antenna and shoved the walkie-talkie into an inside pocket on his parka. All deftly done, considering that most people were awkward wearing gloves. "More questions, Detective?"

Tension around his eyes; he didn't like her here. But then, most people didn't like cops asking questions. And she was probably fouling up his busy day.

"I hear you had a lift shut down earlier."

He shrugged. "It happens."

"People error, or mechanical?"

"Mechanical. Usually is."

He spoke dismissively; she didn't really care about the answer, had merely wanted to establish a conversational tone.

The nearby lift growled and clanked as chairs swung along the cable, empty on the way down and around the pole at the bottom, a few filled for the ride up.

Somebody bumped Meg from behind. "Oops!" a young guy said. "Sorry!" His snowboard was propped casually on his shoulder as he dodged skiers and other boarders coming down from the hill.

She lifted a hand. "It's okay." Concentrating on the man waiting silently, she said, "Mr. Robillard, can you give me a minute?"

He shot a look at his watch. "I'm here, aren't I?"

She'd been going to suggest they talk somewhere more private. Irritation drove her to the point. "You were seen kissing Shelly Lange. When you were supposed to be out of town for the weekend."

For a moment he stared at her without any change of expression. Then a nerve twitched below his eye; he swallowed. "My wife," he said hoarsely. "I don't want my wife to know."

"Will you tell me about it?"

He looked around blindly, goggles shoved up on his head, his poles planted in the snow to each side of him. His lips, cracked and dry, had the look of a man who'd been out in the weather too much. His dark hair grayed at the temples. The five o'clock shadow on his cheeks glinted gray mixed with the darker beard growth. A handsome man, but one edging into his forties.

"She… It didn't last long. A few weeks." His Adam's apple bobbed again, but with every word spoken, Robillard collected himself, overriding the distress. "My wife and I'd had a rough patch. Oh, hell. I was flattered. Shelly was young and pretty. I didn't know then that she was cheap." He said it with contempt, this man who had cheated on his wife, lied to his children. "If he wore pants, she'd spread her legs for him."

"You're saying you weren't alone?" Meg asked neutrally.

"Alone?" The Chief of Operations gave a harsh laugh. "Every time I saw her she was coming on to some other man. Ask around, Deputy Patton. I'm telling the truth."

"Did you see her with another man while the two of you were…dating?" How delicately put, Meg congratulated herself.

His jaw muscles flexed and anger was dark in his eyes. "Damn right, and she had a pack of lies! Apparently she thought I was stupid."

"Did you end the relationship?"

"Yes."

"Because?"

"I don't share."

"Not because of your wife and children?" *Who had to share?* she thought but didn't add.

His eyes narrowed; his gloved hands locked around his poles. "I don't make a habit of this."

She chose to ignore that. "Given the timing of your affair with Shelly Lange, has it occurred to you that her daughter, Emily, could well be yours?"

"She could be anybody's."

"Did Ms. Lange ever tell you that she was pregnant with your baby? Did she claim Emily was yours? Did she ask for child support?"

"No. No to all three questions." His hard, cold facade was back, if she had ever truly cracked it. "I never saw her again after she quit working here."

"Would you submit to DNA testing to determine paternity?"

He made a harsh sound; now she had shaken him, at least a little. "How can I, without my wife finding out? What the hell would I do about it if the kid was mine?"

"Are you aware that Shelly Lange's parents have no interest in adopting the baby?"

His jaw worked. "No."

"She will grow up with no biological family if her father is not found."

"I…can't." Voice raw, Robillard forced out each separate word.

"Mr. Robillard," Meg said formally, "do you want to reconsider your account of your activities on the evening of Monday, January 14?"

Pure fury boiled in his eyes. "No! I was home with my wife. She'll tell you. Now, if you have no more questions?"

"Not at the moment," Meg said, standing back. "Please don't leave Elk Springs without informing me."

His head bent; he stamped into one binding and then the other. Meg waited where she was until he looked up, the tic jerking beneath his eye.

"Don't tell my wife." Now, finally, torment made the plea sound real. "Please don't tell my wife."

Without a trace of emotion, Meg said, "I can promise

you only that, if you didn't kill Shelly Lange, I'll do my best to keep what I know from your wife."

He squeezed his eyes shut briefly. "That'll have to do, won't it?"

She watched him push himself forward with his poles, take a few skating steps, quick-step around the barrier that, on busier days, would keep the lift line orderly. His movements were as natural as if he were walking down a street.

An important man here at Juanita Butte, Meg thought again. An attractive man, but outwardly cold, unlikely to be attentive, charming, to a young woman. Not easily won even by pretty Shelly Lange, and therefore a satisfying emotional surrogate for the father whose attention she had never won.

Yes, Meg mused, she could easily see Shelly trying to hold Mark Robillard by having his baby.

Unfortunately for her, Meg was beginning to suspect that he was also a man who would kill rather than lose what he had.

Now all she had to do was prove it.

CHAPTER THIRTEEN

"ROBILLARD? What was it, two months ago? Yeah, sure," agreed the woman patrol officer who stood in Meg's office doorway. "I went out on the call. I remember it. Second domestic disturbance at that address, wasn't it? Has there been trouble again?"

"I'm investigating a murder," Meg said. "Mark Robillard's name came up. I ran a background check, and guess what."

Patricia Barr nodded. "Amazing, isn't it? House like that, nice family… Last thing you'd expect."

"I haven't seen the house yet." Meg waved at a chair. "Got a minute?"

Already she had to move a stack to allow the other cop to sit down. These—she glanced at the top notes ruefully—were contacts she'd meant to make as the new Youth Services Officer. Before she'd found something else to do.

The stack went on top of her filing cabinet.

"Okay, I read your report," Meg said, settling back in her office chair, "but I see no charges were filed. With the change in laws, that's unusual. I wondered about your impressions."

The other woman was about Meg's age, plain but for thick dark hair and warm eyes. "Husband and wife met me at the door together. He's handsome, smiling. She's all made-up though it was late evening, smiling, bustling around, wanting my partner and me to take a cup of coffee, a cookie—it was like we were making a social call. They have a little girl, who came in blushing to tell me that Mommy and Daddy were having a fight and Mommy got mad and threw her hairbrush at the wall and it scared her. She thought something bad was happening, maybe some stranger was in there with Mommy and Daddy, so she remembered what they said at school and dialed 9-1-1.

"The parents had a story about what they were arguing about—something silly, but the kind of thing you do get mad at your husband about. They pretended to be proud of their daughter, even though they were embarrassed, too. I noticed the wife was cradling one arm when she thought I wasn't watching, so I got her aside, but she looked me right in the eye and insisted everything was fine. On the surface, it looked like a genuine mistake, even though it was the second call. The first one hadn't panned out, either."

That time nobody had been home by the time the responding officers arrived. A neighbor had called; she'd heard crashes, a man bellowing, a woman's scream. But the house was dark and deserted when the unit got there; the Robillards claimed the next day that they'd been out all evening. Maybe a young couple had parked out front and had a fight? they'd asked. Or some teenagers were having a beer party?

"Tell me your gut feeling," Meg said now.

Patricia Barr's expression hardened. "That the bastard had been hitting her, and the kid panicked. Maybe he'd scared the hell out of her by the time we arrived; more likely, he fooled her into thinking she hadn't seen what she thought she'd seen. But I'd bet my next paycheck Robillard is abusing his wife. They were all smiling, but let me tell you, the tension in that house raised the hair on my arms."

"That's what I wanted to know," Meg said, thanking her.

Her blood sang with a kind of fierce pleasure. She was closing in. Not someone who ever would have enjoyed hunting animals, Meg thought nothing on earth gave the satisfaction her job did. When she wound up a case like this, it was a puzzle coming together, a scumbag off the street, emotional healing for the victims—a rush of adrenaline for her. The good kind.

Today it had a sexual edge. She and Scott would be alone tonight. They'd planned the time to do something that should be impulsive, hot-blooded, the furthest thing from deliberate. She'd made love—no, had sex—with only two other men since Johnny Murray. Both times she'd been dating them for a while—longer, she thought, than she'd known Scott McNeil. In neither case had she made a decision—*I care enough about this man, I want him enough*—to go to bed with him. They had simply been kissing, her blood had heated—she was a healthy young woman, for all that she was the mother of a kindergartener, then a fifth grader. She'd found herself naked, grappling with the man.

And in each case, she had shortly thereafter broken off with him. Sexually, the experiences had been reasonably satisfying. And yet…and yet they left her feeling naked in ways she didn't want to examine. She had made herself too vulnerable. Sex wasn't enough, on its own; Meg was old-fashioned, maybe, but she wanted more, thought it ought to *mean* more. Like forever. And she couldn't trust herself and Will to either of those men.

Any more than she had been able to trust Johnny.

Meg wasn't a fool; she knew she both hungered for a man's love and distrusted it because of her father. And yet she'd grown up with love: her mother's, her sisters'. She rather thought she was a good mother.

She was convinced that somehow, someday, there would be a man she could trust. She'd always worried about how she would know.

And now she did.

Breathtaking, but true.

She'd only known Scott a couple of weeks; they had dated—what?—five or six times. And here she was, deciding in cold blood to bare herself emotionally and physically. To trust that he was steady, loving, faithful; that he would listen to her, talk to her, feel the same fire for her that she did for him.

All this, so quickly, Meg thought in awe.

The next second, a wave of panic struck. Dear Lord, what if she was wrong? What if he wasn't ready to love anyone again? He was a man; just because he kissed her like that didn't mean he was handing over his heart and soul.

What if, when the moment came, she couldn't take that leap of faith? What if she chickened out? Or did it, and felt herself freezing inside just as she had the other times?

What if she wanted Scott to be that man, and he wasn't?

The phone rang. Meg took a breath to steady herself, to shove the fear back down, and answered.

"Butte County Sheriff's Department. Patton here."

"We still on for dinner?" Scott asked.

"Oh, yeah," she said, and felt her deep-down certainty tumble like desire through her veins.

THANK HEAVEN she hadn't suggested cooking for him again; a nice sit-down dinner in a restaurant was an interlude, a sort of airlock between job and intimacy, between the hunt for a killer and the acceptance of falling in love. Meg needed this in-between, to be sure she wasn't letting on-the-job adrenaline push her into anything foolish.

But before the conversation got entirely personal, she had some questions to ask him.

They'd gone Mexican tonight, the restaurant small and stuccoed, the waiters and owner all family with strong accents. Scott ordered the chicken fajita, Meg a chimichanga. They sipped margaritas—she would allow herself only one; tomorrow, she didn't want to be able to blame alcohol for her decision, either.

Only herself.

Business first, Meg reminded herself.

"Scott, I'm assuming you were wearing gloves when you found Emily. That you had them on when you picked up her car seat and buckled it in."

Not what he'd expected, clearly, but he showed only a flicker of surprise. "That's right. Remember, it was a cold night."

"What kind of gloves?"

His brow rose.

"I mean…leather? Gore-Tex? Some other synthetic?"

Scott didn't even have to think. "Synthetic. I keep that pair in the pocket of my parka. They're black, nothing special. They're in the car."

"Definitely not leather. You're sure."

"Positive. Are you going to tell me why you're asking?"

She had to, before she could ask him to do something for her. "We lifted some prints from Emily's car seat. No…" Meg stopped him before he could speak. "Not fingerprints. Glove prints." She went on to explain that leather had patterns as distinctive as did human skin. "They're not something we can run through an FBI computer, obviously, but once we have a suspect, they can be used to convict him."

"But you don't have a suspect…" Scott stopped.

"Yes," Meg said quietly. "I do."

Their waiter set their dinners in front of them. "Hot plates," he warned them. "More margarita?"

"No. Thank you." Gaze never leaving Meg's, Scott covered his glass with his hand; Meg shook her head. The waiter went away, leaving them alone at their corner booth with the one fat candle flickering inside amber glass.

As soon as she was sure she wouldn't be heard, Meg said, "I've got to tell you, this is a gut feeling as much as anything."

Will had eliminated Evan Hannah as a suspect; he'd called from school at lunchtime today to tell her that "this girl he knew" said that Hannah was at the game and the party afterward. "He's so cool!" she'd told him, a pronouncement that Will had wickedly mimicked.

Now, Scott waited, not touching his meal. "Who?"

"Mark Robillard."

Almost any other man she'd ever known would have been bent on denying her answer. Would have been angry that she'd even presented it.

But Scott was too smart, and too controlled. "I've worked with Mark for seven years. He's a friend. No, not a friend, but close enough." His eyes bored into her, giving her the feeling of being turned inside out. "Why?" he asked simply.

"Why did he kill her? Or why do I think he's the one who did?"

"Both."

She told him both whys. Robillard had had an affair with Shelly Lange; she had been afraid of him, had broken it off, had been wary enough to stay clear of him for a while. But then she had done something—asked for child support, perhaps. And he would not let anyone, much less a young woman, threaten him. For that's how he'd seen it.

"He admitted to having had an affair with her. He isn't interested in finding out whether Emily is his," Meg said. "My guess is, he knows quite well that she is. His wife has taken a lot from him, and probably blamed herself the whole time for upsetting him, but even he must know that this would be the last straw. She might leave him, take the children. And what if he lost his job when you found out he'd slept with an employee? He couldn't let any of that happen. So he killed Shelly."

Scott rubbed a hand across his face. After a minute he asked, in a voice stripped of emotion, "And how are you going to prove that he did?"

"I need you to do something for me."

She saw him weighing it, deciding. "What?"

"He carries a walkie-talkie."

Scott took a swallow of his margarita as though he needed it. "Yeah?"

"Yesterday Robillard wore black leather gloves. And he was handling the walkie-talkie. The plastic should take a print well."

"He may have other gloves."

"He may," Meg agreed. *Please, no, or else he'll walk.* "Do you?"

"I usually stick to one pair for a few months."

She leaned forward. "I want you to lift that walkie-talkie without him knowing. If he sees you or guesses, he may get rid of the gloves."

"You could take them…"

"Not without a warrant. And I can't get that without something solid. Like a match on the prints. If I don't get the warrant, the evidence can't be used in court."

He jerked his head; rubbed the back of his neck. "Yeah, okay. I see. I'll do it."

"I'm sorry," Meg said softly.

"If he did it, there's nothing to be sorry for." He sounded cold, distant, but the look in his eyes betrayed how he really felt.

Meg began eating. After a minute, Scott did, too. The silence lasted several minutes.

Meg broke it. "Where's Emily tonight?"

"Um?" Scott looked up. "With Marjorie. My house-keeper. I'm not ready yet…"

"To leave her with a teenager?" She didn't give him time to think about pretty, bouncy Shelly. "I don't blame you. Will's a smart kid. Really. But he does the dumbest things." She told tales on her son, then. About the time he'd had a friend dangle him by the ankles from a hotel balcony so he could scare the cheerleaders staying in the room below his; about Will sneaking a buddy onto the base without a pass; about him refusing to turn in a single assignment for an entire quarter in one class because the teacher had ticked him off.

"And then there's this thing with Jack…" *Nice segué,*

she told herself. Now all she had to do was say, *Oh, by the way, I've been fibbing to you. I cheated Jack out of fourteen years of his son's life.*

"Will came up with it by himself?"

She looked sharply at Scott, alerted by something in his tone. Was he jealous? "Darn straight he did." Incurable honesty jabbed at her. "He might have had help from Jack. I'm not sure. Jack took me to dinner one night. He even kissed me." *Do you have to be* that *honest?* Meg asked herself. Answer: *Yes. And you can't stop here.* "No fireworks went off. As Jack said, the two of us together again would have been convenient. For Will."

Scott didn't react in any predictable way. He didn't ask *when* she'd kissed Jack. She saw no sign that his male ego was injured, or that he was ready to rev the engine, so to speak, with Jack in the car beside his. Maybe, she thought in amazement, he was that rare man who drove more or less within the speed limit, who didn't want to punch every jerk who challenged him...

"Why did the two of you break up in the first place?" he asked, his gaze resting thoughtfully on her face.

"I got pregnant." Now was the time to tell him. It wouldn't have been so hard if she'd been sure in her heart that she'd done the right thing back then. But she'd taken to wondering: had she hugged Will to herself entirely out of fear? Or because she was mad at Jack and she didn't want to share?

"The moment of truth," Scott murmured. Paused. "People around here respect him."

Meg was supremely conscious of the irony. The moment of truth was still ahead of her.

Edge into it, she told herself.

"We were both afraid of my father," Meg admitted. "We were kids. Too young to have a baby. No sixteen-year-old wants to tell her parents. But this was different. I was afraid my dad would kill me. I always wondered if he hadn't murdered my mother."

Scott swore. "You're serious."

She told him more about her childhood, about the mother who left without a trace—thanks, it turned out, to Chief Patton, who'd had the mail delivered to a post office box so he could intercept his ex-wife's letters. Scott needed to know all this, or he couldn't understand why she'd done what she'd done.

"And yet," Meg mused, "as Abby pointed out one day, our father provided a home, he went to parent nights at school, he even took me shopping for my first bra…" After telling her she ought to be ashamed of herself, not covering up any better than that.

"Do you think he loved you?"

"I truly don't know." She tried to smile and failed. "He was so full of hate and anger, there wasn't room for much else. If he felt affection, he hadn't a clue how to show it."

"That's a sad epitaph."

"No kidding," she said on a spasm of pain that surprised her. She had thought she'd come to terms with her father's memory.

Taking a deep breath, she said, "Scott…"

But he wasn't looking at her. He'd spotted the waiter and lifted his hand to signal for the bill. He came, smiling, to the table. The moment was lost.

Scott paid and before Meg knew it, they were walking out. Panic knotted her stomach. She still hadn't told him. On the drive home…

But in his Jeep it was dark, and she wanted to be able to see his face.

Another excuse.

When we get there, she decided, and let the conversation stay desultory.

Emily had slept through the night finally. A critical step had been taken toward construction of the new lift at Juanita Butte. Small subjects. Nothing either of them wanted to linger over. Just words to fill the dark car, to let Meg, at least, think about something besides the solid bulk of the man beside her, about what she was going to do.

He pulled into her driveway and turned off the engine. In the silence both sat still for a moment, looking straight ahead. She couldn't do it, not now. It wasn't that important; it could wait. He'd understand.

Scott spoke first. "Can I come in, Meg?"

"Yes." What had happened to her voice? "Yes. Please."

He hadn't moved; both his hands were curled around the steering wheel. He sounded just as odd as she had. "I'm falling in love with you."

"I…hoped you were."

His head turned; in the dim light from the street lamp and her porch, he looked searchingly at her. "What about you?"

"Yes." Oh, Lord, she was actually blushing. "I mean, I feel the same. It's fast, but…right."

What little he could see must have satisfied him, because he nodded. "Just so we both know what we're getting into."

She swallowed and nodded, too.

Scott took the key from the ignition and got out. Meg followed. He took her arm and steered her up to her own front door, as if she wouldn't make it alone. He waited while she unlocked, let her open the door, step inside, set her purse down on the small hall table.

Then he said in a hoarse voice, "Meg?" And when she turned and saw the look on his face, she stumbled into his arms.

Those first kisses were pure, raw emotion. She hadn't had to take off her clothes to offer herself up. The comforting part was that he was doing the same. This wasn't sex; oh, no. It was lovemaking from the start.

His hands were powerful, lifting her, holding her against the hard, muscled length of his body. Meg kissed him back with what felt like unpracticed fervor, but otherwise all she could do was hold on. Her knees were threatening to buckle; her whole body had gone weak, pliable.

She should have hated the contrast with him, the difference in strength, the aggressive way he took what he wanted from her, while she—the woman—gave. Maybe that's what she'd resented before, not understood, not wanted to be part of.

But this—it wasn't like that. She saw that, just as Scott lifted her in his arms.

"Which bedroom is yours?" he asked, voice guttural, eyes molten silver. Mercury.

She kissed his throat and felt him shudder. The reaction made her happy, so she did it again, this time licking his skin, tasting skin and salt and something that stung. Aftershave, maybe. An interesting and erotic combination. Meg rather liked it, so she kept kissing him, nibbling her way up to his ear.

Scott was groaning as he shouldered open her door, carried her across the room and lowered her to the bed.

"I want you," he said just before his mouth ravaged hers.

And that, Meg thought dreamily, as his big body bore her down, was why she didn't mind being outmatched, in a sense. Need meant vulnerability, even weakness.

And miraculously, Scott McNeil wanted her, needed her, was maybe just as scared by what he felt as she was. His muscles tightened under her hands; his skin shivered; he took a ragged breath. He was vulnerable. To *her*.

She quit thinking after that. Maybe for the first time in her life, Meg let herself be swept away. No wariness, no part of herself one step removed. She just felt, touched, cried out, and said his name. Over and over.

When she closed her eyes, images were burned onto her eyelids: his hands, big and dark on her breasts. His body, so beautifully muscled. The fiery chestnut of the soft hair that curled on his chest, down his belly. His mouth, suckling her nipples, kissing her belly button. His face, skin stretched tight, the sweet smile coupled with the fierce need in his eyes as he entered her.

It was a dance. Music: two flutes, achingly high, teasing notes around each other. No, a symphony, the final movements crashing around her with inescapable power and glory. Or perhaps it was a battle, hot, sweaty, needy, each trying to master the other.

If so, she won; she lost. All Meg knew was that her body reached for the glory, and found it.

Afterward, she settled against Scott's side, her head pillowed on his shoulder, and she had no regrets.

IF HE'D KNOWN it could be like that, he wouldn't have wasted half a lifetime existing when he could have been searching for Deputy Margaret Patton.

Thinking that way felt ridiculously adolescent, but right this minute he didn't give a damn. He was too happy.

She lay cuddled up to him, her head nestled on his shoulder, her satin sheet of pale hair flowing over his chest. They'd made love twice now. The clock was ticking, and he had to go soon. He just didn't want to.

Meg began drawing some mysterious picture on his chest with one finger. She was smiling as she did it. Scott kissed her head and with startling suddenness she rolled on top of him.

Her grin was all joy. "What do you say, big guy? I'm game if you are…" Until she saw the clock. "Oh, no! Will."

"Don't we have half an hour before you have to pick him up?"

"But I have to get dressed. And I don't want to be late." She sighed and eased down in Scott's arms, settling for a long sweet kiss.

He slapped her bottom, dumped her off him and jackknifed to a sitting position. "How am I going to convince your son I'm not so bad?"

She scrambled off the bed, too, and went to her dresser. "Just be yourself. He'll see."

God, she was beautiful! Long legs, tiny waist, an elegant stretch of back and hair that had slid through his fingers like water. He forgot about getting dressed himself and just watched her, until she'd squirmed into a pair of panties and then jeans and tugged a sweatshirt over her head.

Turning, she smiled at him, face soft. You'd figure she was a teenager in those tight jeans and bare feet until you looked at her eyes, smart and sensuous.

"You planning to shock my son?" she asked, with a tilt to her head.

"What?" He looked down. "Oh. Yeah."

He'd never wanted less to get dressed; staying here right now would be good, maybe making love with her one more time before they fell asleep, waking in the night to the weight of her against him, seeing her eyes heavy with dreams in the morning before she remembered her responsibilities and worries.

Instead, he got dressed and followed Meg into the kitchen, where she poured them both coffee. Scott had barely taken his first sip when they heard a key in the front door. "Did Will get a ride?" he asked.

"He doesn't know anybody." She eased toward the door, moving like a cop.

The door slammed. "Mom?"

"Will."

Scott could just see her from where he stood, the tension in her body visibly gone although she didn't move. Her voice was easy.

"Somebody gave you a lift?"

"Yeah. We got back early. Jason—you know, that junior I told you about? He doesn't drive yet, but his dad was already there."

"How'd it go? The team any good?"

"Actually, not that bad. They won…" The boy reached the doorway and saw Scott. He was too young to hide his displeasure. "*He's* here."

She laid a hand on her son's shoulder, her fingers tightening. "That's right. Scott's here."

Will took a longer, harder look at his mom, whose mouth was swollen from kisses, whose cheeks were rosy red, whose feet were bare and who didn't wear a bra beneath the sweatshirt. Anger and hurt sparked in his eyes.

"Dad wanted to see you again," he said loudly.

Her apologetic gaze met Scott's. "Your father and I said what we had to say. It's you he comes to see."

The kid oozed out from under his mother's grip and slouched into a chair across the table from Scott. "Maybe because *he's* always around," he said rudely.

"Will Patton." Meg's voice cracked, and the kid's spine straightened in automatic response. "That's enough out of you. Apologize. Now."

His chin jutted. "I didn't say anything!"

"It's okay," Scott began, until one razor-sharp glance from her shut him up.

"Now," she commanded.

"You never listen to me!" he cried.

Her eyes closed briefly, but her voice didn't soften. "An apology, please."

In an abrupt, violent movement, he grabbed the napkin holder and flung it. Made of teak, it cracked and skidded across the kitchen floor. His voice rose; cracked just like the wood, like the little boy he didn't want to be. "You've never given Dad a chance! If you'd ever told him about me, we could have been together all along!"

In the stunned silence, Meg shot another lightning glance at Scott. "You don't know anything about it," she finally said icily. "Now, apologize."

The boy's face worked. "I'm sorry, Mr. McNeil." Rising to his feet, he knocked the chair back. "But I do know what I'm talking about! You always said—"

"Later. Not in front of company. Go to your room."

A sob wrenched him. "You're…you're just like *your* father!" he exclaimed, and rushed from the room.

Meg sagged into a chair. Tears glittered in her eyes. She tried to wipe them away.

"I'm sorry. I—I don't know where that came from. We…we used to be such good friends."

He seemed to be watching her from some great distance, as if through binoculars. His heart was being squeezed in a fist.

"What did he mean?" He sounded strange to his ears, his tone so…unemotional. "When he said, 'If you'd ever told him about me'?"

Tears spilled over as she stared at him, stricken. Abruptly she buried her face in her hands. Watching her cry, Scott knew he should go to her, hold her, comfort her. But he couldn't seem to move.

"He never knew you were pregnant, did he?" That same dispassionate tone reflected the peculiar flattening of his emotions.

"No." Slowly she looked up, eyes red and puffy, her nose running. "He—my father caught us together. He beat up Johnny—Jack. Jack left me alone to face Dad. After…after he was done with me, I packed up, stole money from him, and ran away."

"When did you tell him?"

"I…"

"When?"

She took a shuddering breath. "Two weeks ago. When I found out my father was dead and came home to Elk Springs."

"My God." Disgust—no, rage—roughened his voice. "For fourteen years, Jack Murray didn't know he had a son."

"I—I was afraid." She was pleading. "Of my father."

Scott shoved himself to his feet. "Do you have any idea how much you took from him?"

Now her mouth trembled. "It's not like with you. Jack wasn't ready to be a father. He would have told mine. I might have lost Will!"

The sense of betrayal damn near swallowed him. "I thought you were courageous. Beautiful. Generous. I'm having trouble believing you'd rob a man of his son, but I guess it goes to show that I don't know you very well."

Meg rose, shaking, crying, to her feet. "Scott, I've been trying to make you understand. Listen to me! Please!"

"No!" Throat raw, he moderated his voice. "Maybe another time, but not now. God. If I'd lost Nate because a woman had been so petty…"

"It wasn't like that," she said again, but he could see that even she didn't believe it. "Scott…"

"No." He took one last look at her face, the delicate bones, the shimmering blue eyes, the moonlight-pale hair, and groaned. "If you'd told me yourself… But you knew what I'd think, didn't you? I've lived all these years with my chest cut open because I lost my son. And you did that to a man. Knowing." He shook his head, staggered, blundered toward the door.

He heard a cry behind him, but he kept going.

How could he have been so wrong?

CHAPTER FOURTEEN

WILL'S CEREAL sat untouched in front of him, probably getting soggy. He watched Meg sit down with her toast and coffee across the table from him.

"Mom, I…" He gulped. "I mean, I…" Whatever it was, he couldn't get it out. All he did was stare at her like a dog waiting to be hit.

Any other day in her life, Meg would have been hurt that he would ever in a million years look at her that way. She would ache for him, as any parent would. Today… Today her emotions were as arid as desert sand. She'd cried them out last night; they'd seeped into her pillow and out of her soul. Once before, she'd thought she had cried every tear she would ever cry. Now she knew she had been wrong, but she also knew it might be years before she could summon another tear.

But she also knew none of this was Will's fault. It was hers. Hers for long-past mistakes, hers for ones just made.

"Eat your breakfast," she said gently.

"Mom, I didn't mean…"

"I know you didn't."

"*How* do you know?" he wailed like the little boy he'd once been, the one who didn't understand why his best friend's dad wasn't coming home from Kuwait.

"Because..." Well, how did she? "Because you're you."

To her shock and discomfort, this big tough teenager was actually crying now. "But I've been a jerk lately!"

She didn't have the energy for this, for him, but she had to find it somehow. "Yes, but it's understandable. This move...finding your dad...family...me working so much..." Meg sighed. "I would have wondered what was wrong with you if you'd taken it all in stride. You're a kid. And you know what makes kids act the way they do sometimes?"

By rote he said, "Hormones."

"Right. You've found your dad, he's really cool, you suddenly think we could be like Colin's family. But we can't, Will. I don't know how to tell you any better than that, but we can't."

He wiped away the tears and lifted his chin, his red-rimmed eyes steady on hers. "But I'm not really a kid anymore. It's not like I'm going to...to hate Dad or anything if he...well, did something bad. Back then. So why won't you tell me?"

She had talked about his father when Will was growing up. Funny things he'd done, his interest in living creatures too small for the naked eye to see, the way he threw the football. She'd wanted her son to be able to grow up knowing his father was a good man; to know that the part of himself that came from his father was worth having and valuing.

Maybe that was another of her mistakes. Maybe she'd created a perfect father in Will's mind, Michelangelo's *David* on a pedestal. And now she was refusing to love that perfect man, which made her seem either foolish or perverse. Perhaps it *was* time for him to know that Jack had feet of clay, too.

"All right." She sat back in her chair and looked her son in the eye. "Your dad let me down badly. I know now that he *couldn't* stand up to my father; he was only a few years older than you are. But then…then all I knew was that he didn't. He promised my father never to call me again, to cross the street if he saw me coming. He abandoned me to my father's anger and brutality."

She saw by the shock in Will's eyes that he'd expected something else, something more easily explained away.

Meg got up from the breakfast table and went around to his side just to kiss his cheek. He gripped her suddenly in a strong, awkward hug, his face momentarily buried in her stomach. She stroked his hair and closed her eyes, but although they burned, no tears came.

"I know," she said, when Will looked up, "that you want your dad to be everything that's noble, courageous…good. What you have to understand is that nobody is born that way. He's changed. Some of the change came about because of that terrible scene with my father, and because I ran away and Jack knew that I'd needed him and he'd let me down. If I'd had more faith in him, I might have waited to see if he *would* change. But because I was pregnant with you and scared of my father, I didn't think I had that luxury. And, of course, I was mad and hurt and melodramatic about it all. After all, I was a teenager. And you know what that means."

He grimaced. "Hormones."

She held Will's shoulders. "So, maybe I should have

given him a chance. For his sake as much as mine. But I didn't, and we can't go back. Neither of us will ever know if he would have come through back then, when I needed him. And though I can see now that he's not the same man, I can't ever forget he let me down, and he can't ever forget it, either. We're working on coming to peace with what happened, but it's not something you forget." Meg searched her son's face. "Do you understand?"

"I—I think so." The desperate need for reassurance made him look so young, but the way he let her words sink in, accepted them—in that, she saw his growing maturity. "I wish you'd told me," he said gruffly.

"I wish I had, too." She kissed his head again, closing her eyes to breathe in his essence. *My little boy.* "But maybe neither of us was ready."

"Yeah. Mom." He looked up again, his eyes stricken. "What are you going to do? About…about Mr. McNeil?"

"I don't know." Her approximation of a smile hurt them both. "I just don't know."

"I GOT THE WALKIE-TALKIE," Scott said without preamble the moment she'd identified herself after answering the telephone.

Meg closed her eyes, grateful he couldn't see her. "I didn't know if you'd still do it."

"Shelly Lange's murder has nothing to do with you and me." He sounded cold, indifferent. "I want to know who killed her."

"Then…thank you. I'll head up there right now."

"I'm on my way to town, anyway. Shall I bring it by the station?"

"No." She gave him directions to the crime lab shared by city and county.

"Then I'll see you shortly," he said, still as if he were speaking to a total stranger. "I hope like hell you're wrong."

"I hope I'm wrong, too," she said, but knew herself to be lying.

She had looked into Mark Robillard's eyes.

SCOTT SET DOWN HIS CUP of bad coffee when Ben Shea and Meg turned expectantly. The three had been waiting in the lobby for the fingerprint tech to do his stuff.

He'd lifted the expected jumble from the black plastic walkie-talkie, he announced.

"Some fingerprints, mostly gloved," he told Meg and Ben Shea.

Scott stood grimly behind them, listening, but also bitterly conscious of Meg Patton, who was acting as if they'd barely met, as if last night had meant nothing. She'd agreed with obvious reluctance to let him wait with them.

"You'll need expert corroboration," the fingerprint guy continued, "but in my opinion they definitely match those we took from the car seat."

If anything could have knocked memories of last night off the front burner, that was it. *The glove prints matched.* Scott let out a harsh breath.

This had to be a nightmare. He'd worked with Mark Robillard for the past seven years, since Juanita Butte was nothing but a scar on the mountainside. He'd had dinner with Mark and his wife; Robillard had stood beside Nate's grave. He'd offered gruff sympathy when Penny walked out.

People you knew didn't kill.

"Crooks in books and on TV always wear gloves so they *don't* leave a fingerprint," he said, knowing his voice was too loud but not giving a damn. "How can you be so sure?"

The fingerprint tech glanced at him with one of those looks that said, "Who is this guy?" but he answered. Hell, he was probably thrilled to get to explain his job.

"If you want to commit a crime," he said, "wear latex. You know, the kind doctors wear. Just be careful not to rip them. There've been cases where the perp did tear one and left a partial…" He seemed to realize he was wandering from the point. "The thing is, leather is organic. It's skin, just like our fingertips. It's distinctive. Now, a glove print isn't proof that a particular pair of hands was wearing the gloves on that one occasion, but what's this guy going to claim? He lent them to someone? He misplaced them, but found them the next day lying in the parking lot?"

"Anything you can tell me about the hand?" Meg asked thoughtfully. "Would they be different if someone different was wearing those gloves?"

"Depends." The tech rattled on at some length, but the gist was that he'd bet on the same hands. A smaller hand would have gripped at a different point on the leather finger of the glove. Ditto a bigger one, squeezed into the gloves. He grabbed Detective Shea's hand and held it next to his own, showing how the size of the pads varied, the strength, the way they closed on an object. "Like I said, we've got a dandy match here," he said. "Whether it'll stand up in court… I hear it can go either way."

Meg and her partner huddled over how to handle the next step and finally decided to leave it until morning.

"He's not going anywhere," Scott heard her telling Shea. "I shook him for a minute the other day, but he's used to controlling people. He was sure he had me convinced. I'd put money on it."

Scott muttered an oath. "I can't believe it."

Both turned to look at him. "That's because he's good. We ran a background check on him," Shea said. "There have been two domestic disturbance calls to his house. Both times he walked. The cops weren't convinced, but the wife was charming, they were apologetic, once they even had one of the kids take the blame."

"You're sure." He was numb.

For the first time, Meg spoke directly to him. "That he murdered Shelly? One hundred percent. No. Am I sure in my own mind? Yeah. We found where Robillard had been taking Shelly last summer. I tracked down the people who own the neighboring cabin—they live in Springfield, so they'd never read about the murder. We faxed photos, they remember Shelly and Mark Robillard. They saw them looking happy, but she had bruises a couple times, too. They thought she was scared of him."

Scott's jaws clenched. "Then why wait until tomorrow?"

Ben Shea spoke up again. "We need to sell it to a judge. Get a search warrant." He glanced at his watch. "It's after hours now. No reason to rouse Her Honor at home."

"So you do nothing?"

"We'll put it together in the morning."

Scott wondered distantly if Shea knew there was trouble between his partner and Scott. Detective Shea was a hell of a lot more chatty than usual, picking up the conversation before silences had a chance to congeal.

From the minute Scott arrived, Meg had been civil, cool, willing to look him in the eye. He couldn't tell if she felt a thing.

She had to. However collected and apparently serene she was today, yesterday she had sobbed out his name, first in passion and then hurt. He didn't like thinking of that last sight of her face, eyes huge, tear-drenched and full of pleading. He wondered if Meg Patton had pleaded for anything since she was five years old and wanted an ice cream cone. Scott could see her, a gawky twelve or thirteen-year-old, gazing at her father with cool reproach and disdain when he wanted her to cry. From things she'd said, Scott guessed her father had hit her, and he could just see it, her lifting her head with stubborn pride no matter what the bastard did.

It took you to make her cry. You to make her beg, his inner voice observed with disgust. *You couldn't even listen.*

And why should he? She'd done the unthinkable, denied the boy's father the most precious part of both of their lives. What she'd taken could never be restored. It might be defensible if Jack Murray had abused her or been a drunkard or a druggie.

Yeah, that insidious voice retorted, *but you don't know what he* did *do. You didn't listen to her side.*

She lied, he thought harshly.

Did she? Or was it just none of your business until you started kissing her? And then when it was you wouldn't listen.

"Goddamn it!" Scott exclaimed, and then felt like a fool when the two cops stopped walking and turned around to stare at him.

For just a second, he saw something human in Meg's

eyes. Sympathy, maybe. Understanding. She thought he was mourning the loss of a friend—the discovery that a man he'd thought he knew was evil. But the moment was brief. Walls slid into place; her gaze was cool, inquiring.

"Never mind," Scott muttered.

They'd reached the parking lot, where he had parked right next to the Butte County squad car.

They stopped there, waited for him. "Mr. McNeil," Shea said smoothly, "I'd like your assurance that you won't say anything to Mark Robillard. It might be better if you can avoid even seeing him, without being obvious."

Anger, hot and welcome, shot like a knife blade between Scott's ribs. "You think I'm going to rush up there and tell him you know he murdered Shelly Lange? And, oh, yeah, you're coming for him tomorrow?"

"You wouldn't be the first person to decide there has to be another explanation. That if you just ask, your buddy will straighten it all out."

Eyes watchful if brighter than they should have been, Meg stood silent beside her partner. In daylight he saw how tired she looked, shadows and puffiness beneath her eyes, skin tight over elegant cheekbones.

He refused to feel guilty.

"I won't say anything," Scott said curtly. "I was fond of Shelly when she was a kid. I'm not about to foul up your investigation."

"That's what I wanted to hear," Shea said in the tone of an adult congratulating a kid for using his head for once.

Scott let the irritation slide away. He didn't give a damn about Shea. He'd save his anger for Meg Patton, who offered him a vague nod and opened the passenger side door on the patrol unit.

At the last minute, she glanced back. "Thank you for doing this, Mr. McNeil." Without waiting for an answer, for *You're welcome,* she climbed in and slammed the door, looking straight ahead as she waited for her partner to join her.

Shea gave him an odd, direct look over the top of the vehicle. He shook his head and got in, too.

From that moment, Scott might as well have been invisible. The patrol unit backed out of the parking slot. Through the windshield, he could see them talking, neither of them even glancing his way. He was still standing there when they drove away.

He wouldn't feel guilty. Anger was a waste of energy. Which left…?

Searing emptiness he'd prayed never to feel again. It was like losing part of himself. Not his "good right arm." No, he hadn't lost anything that obvious, he could go through the motions, he looked the same in the mirror. Inside was different.

Inside he hurt, and knew something irreplaceable was gone.

What was left of his heart.

THE HOUSE WAS EMPTY and quiet. Meg found the note scrawled on the white board on the refrigerator.

"Mom, I'm shooting hoops with some of the guys at the H.S. Open gym until six."

She sank dispiritedly into a chair at the kitchen table. Will was finally making friends. Before she knew it, he'd never be home. And then he'd be gone to college, and she would be really alone.

All of her felt leaden. Even her mind moved slowly. No, she thought at last, being alone wasn't what she minded. It was the contrast between what-would-be and the glorious what-could-be she had briefly imagined. Just last night.

Could it be that recently? she wondered, the amazement dulled by the lassitude that had hit her the minute she walked in the door.

A nap. She needed to sleep.

But, despite last night's lack, she wasn't really sleepy.

Something else, then. A pile of chocolate chip cookies and a glass of milk. Or…ice cream. Chocolate mint. A bowl so big she'd gain five pounds just looking at it.

But she wasn't really hungry, either. And getting out a bowl, dishing up, all seemed to require too much energy.

She wanted Scott. Will. The mother of her distant childhood memories, not the one dying attached to monitors in the hospital. She wanted home. Family. Not to be alone.

Staring blindly, Meg thought, *Renee.*

Pictures tumbled through her memory: a little towhead toddling after her; herself walking a nervous kindergartener to class the first day of school; the two of them, almost teenagers, giggling over a dirty joke; and Renee, big-eyed and solemn, flopped on Meg's bed listening and nodding sympathetically as Meg ranted and raved about their father.

On the very thought of her sister, Meg was out of the chair and heading for the phone. It was only four. Would Renee be working? Home?

She tried there first. Renee answered on the second ring.

"Renee, this is Meg."

Her sister heard the ache in her voice. "Something's wrong. Meg, are you all right? Will? Will's not hurt, is he?"

"No. No, it's nothing like that." Closing her eyes, Meg leaned her forehead against the cool wood of the kitchen cupboard. "Can I...can I come over? Are you busy?"

"Don't be silly. Of course you can. Unless you want me to come there?"

"No. I don't mind." The exhaustion retreated; she would make it. She had a purpose. Someone who cared.

Maybe.

Renee met her at the door. She took one good look at Meg and held out her arms.

Meg found out she'd been wrong. She could still cry.

AN HOUR LATER she articulated one of her worst fears.

"I thought...maybe you hated me."

"Never!" Renee launched herself from her end of the couch to hug Meg with fierce strength. "We're sisters! I just...I was so scared without you! And I missed you so much!"

Meg gave a watery sniff. "But you were mad, too, weren't you?"

"Of course I was!" Renee pulled back to gaze earnestly into Meg's eyes. "But I never, ever, quit loving you. That day you walked into the station was one of the best of my entire life. I'd dreamed of it so many times, just looking up and there you were. And then it happened, and you were home. I feel like..." She gestured helplessly. "I don't know. As if some circle is closed. My life is complete. Like at my wedding. It didn't feel right, not having you there."

Meg was the one to hug her sister this time. New tears wet Renee's shoulder. "I wish I'd been there. If I'd just come sooner..."

"But you didn't know Dad was dead."

"No, but…" Meg sank back, grabbed a tissue and blew her nose.

Hearing something new in her voice, Renee followed suit, then waited.

Meg sighed. "I think maybe Scott's right. Could I have been petty enough to want to keep Will from Jack just because I was angry at him? Because I felt betrayed? I'm thirty-one years old! I knew Jack wasn't a kid anymore. Why didn't I quietly contact him years ago? Why didn't I stand up to Dad years ago? Once I was a working, responsible adult, no court would have taken Will away from me. Maybe I still could have rescued you and Abby. I just…" She bit her lip. "I keep thinking back. *Why?* And…and I don't know. It was like…I wouldn't let myself even consider the possibility. I couldn't trust Jack, I'd tell myself. I couldn't take a chance. Dad would find a way to hurt me, I just knew he would. It was too late for you guys, I convinced myself. And so…I didn't do anything."

Meg had never let herself face the pain she'd caused so many people by her choices. Will must come first, she had always believed. But how could contact with his father, with his aunts, have hurt her five or eight or twelve-year-old son?

No. By that time, she wasn't afraid for Will. She was just afraid.

"I think," her sister said softly, as if reading her mind, "we've both let Dad shape our lives in ways we never realized. You and I, we fought so hard. We would have both denied we feared him. I never, never, let him see my fear. He'd hit me, and I'd stare back at him until he hit me again. Oh, what pride I had in defying him, in seeing his frustration! But in the end, it took me six months after he died to change even one tiny thing in the house, because…I don't know. Because he'd come back and torment me some more? Because secretly, I was terrified of him. I'd just never admit it to him or myself." She reached out and took Meg's hand. "And maybe you felt the same."

"Yes. Yes, I did." Meg blinked back moisture. "That's the real truth. I got away, and I was afraid to come back. Even for your sake. Oh, Renee, I'm so sorry!"

They hugged again, wept some more. Daniel strolled in and tried to tiptoe back out, but Renee said, "It's okay, Daniel. We're just…venting. Meg, where's Will?"

"Oh…" She glanced at the clock. "Home, I hope. I'd better call. No, he'll be getting hungry. Maybe I'll take him out for pizza."

"How about if we all go out for pizza?" Renee looked at her husband. "Mario's. Even if we do have to wait at this time of year."

They smiled at each other, and Meg had a feeling she was missing something.

"Why not?" he said. "Shall I pick up Will? Meet you ladies there?"

Meg phoned her son, who said, "Yeah, cool."

On the way, Meg updated her sister on the murder investigation and the plans for tomorrow.

"You don't think he kept the gun, do you?"

"Probably not," Meg conceded. "Chances are it's buried under ten feet of snow somewhere out in the woods. But you never know. He wouldn't be the first perp to be arrogant enough to figure no one would ever suspect him."

"But now," Renee pointed out, "he knows you do."

"Maybe. An affair and murder are two different things. He knows we're talking to other people, too."

Meg turned into the parking lot next to the restored brick building that housed Mario's. Daniel wasn't there, yet. Neither woman reached for her seat belt clasp.

"Are you watching him?" Renee asked.

"You kidding?" Meg stared at her in astonishment. "Do you guys in the city P.D. have that kind of budget?"

"We wish." Her sister gave an odd sort of shiver. "I just have a bad feeling about this guy. Like you said, he has a lot at stake. Be careful when you make that collar, okay?"

"I'll be careful," Meg promised.

"And give McNeil time." Renee touched her hand lightly. "He'll come to his senses. If he doesn't, he's not worth losing sleep over."

"Right," Meg said wryly. "I'll remember that."

But probably not tonight, which she would spend asking herself the same questions again. Why had she kept Will from his father? Was Scott right in thinking her petty, even cruel?

Her father must be chortling in his grave, Meg thought with sudden bitterness. How he would enjoy knowing that, after all, she had been afraid of him! That, because she let her fear rule her, now the man she loved was rejecting her.

Oh, yes. Death hadn't stopped Ed Patton. He had reached from the frozen earth to punish his wayward daughter.

WILL LIFTED HIS SKIS from the rack atop his father's blue Toyota 4x4. It was Sunday morning and Mom had to work again, but Will's dad had agreed to take him skiing. A bank of snow towered fifteen feet or more above this stretch of parking lot. Blue sky arched overhead, and the glitter of morning sun reflecting off snow dazzled Will's eyes.

"This is going to be great!" he said, blinking from the brilliance and turning to watch his father lock up. "Mom keeps promising to bring me, but she's always working." He eyed some older boys who were passing, and said enviously, "I want to learn to snowboard. I'll bet it's even better."

"Living here, there's no reason you shouldn't," his dad said. "Your mother working today?"

"She's *always* working." He lifted the skis to his shoulder and added grudgingly, "I mean, she's got that murder investigation. I guess she can't help it."

"She getting anywhere?"

"I think so." They started the length of the parking lot. His skis dug into his shoulders and his boots weren't that comfortable—they weren't made for walking anyway, and rentals never fit quite right. Maybe now his feet were done growing and Mom would buy him his own equipment. "She and Aunt Renee were talking about it last night. Mom said something about getting a search warrant today."

"Ah." His father wore all black except for a white hat; even the band on his goggles, pushed up on his head, was black. *Darth Vader,* Will thought. Or like George Clooney in *From Dusk to Dawn.* Really cool. His best friend Colin's dad had had a pot belly and always wore these super ugly plaid shirts.

Impulsively, Will blurted, "Do you ever wish you and Mom had gotten married? I mean…stayed together. You know." His father's arched brow had him stuttering. "I mean…"

"I know what you mean."

They turned from the parking lot and climbed the snowy, boot-packed slope to the lodge and ticket booths. He didn't say any more for a minute, and Will thought he wasn't going to.

Finally he said, "Your mom didn't give me a choice back then. For a long time, I was sorry. But when I think back… We were so young. Who knows what would have happened?" He stopped by the ticket booth and thrust the base of his skis into a snowbank. "Water under the bridge," he concluded.

"But neither of you is married," Will persisted.

His father gave him a look that wasn't unkind but didn't lift Will's hopes any, either. "Whatever we had together is gone. The years do that. Even to married people, if they aren't careful."

Not until they had their lift tickets, had shuffled through the line and were on the chair, swinging out over the snowy slope, did Will say, "Do you ever want to get married?"

This time his father laughed. "Why the obsession with marriage?"

"Mom's dating this guy," Will said glumly. He swung his skis, one tip up, one down, careful not to rock the chair.

Jack squinted and seemed to be studying the summit. "Seriously?"

"I don't know." A lie: his mother really liked the guy. That's what had scared him. Into telling McNeil something Will knew he wouldn't like? He swallowed. "Maybe. He's an okay guy. I guess. It's just…"

"You thought maybe your mother and I would get back together."

The chair clanked past a lift pole.

"Yeah."

"Well, we're not." His dad straightened. "We're almost there."

Like Will couldn't see the lift house coming up. He rolled his eyes. Ski tips up; the chair lurched, and he and his father stood and skied down a short incline to the top of the run.

Both pulled their goggles over their faces and gripped their poles.

But his father didn't take off right away. He ignored the skiers pouring off the lift behind them, parting to go around them, giving them looks as they passed.

"Will," his father said. "I'd like to live with you. But your mother and I…it's just not going to happen. This guy she's dating…I hope she finds happiness. I hope you let her."

He had to say that. After Will had already fouled everything up, made Mom cry.

Will couldn't think of anything to say.

A second later he was watching his father's back as he drove into the first mogul.

CHAPTER FIFTEEN

WILL TOOK A HUGE windmilling fall on the sixth run. Clambering up, he had to spit snow out of his mouth and shake it from under his collar. His goggles had to be unburied. He put on one ski, did a hopping turn and sideslipped to the spot where the other one was sticking out of the snow.

"You okay?" his father called from down the hill.

"Yeah!" He waved. "I'm the Herminator!"

The best part of the Olympics had been watching Austrian Hermann Maier's fall in the downhill. Everyone thought he was going to be dead or something. Instead he went on to win two gold medals in the Super G and the giant slalom. Talk about comebacks.

At the bottom Will took off his hat to shake the snow from it. "Did you see me?" he asked. "I mean, I was flying!"

"Spectacular fall," someone said quietly from behind him.

Will swung around so fast he crashed down. Again. But this time—jeez!—in the lift line! Some guys farther back laughed. And it hurt.

With as much dignity as he could, considering, Will got back to his feet. "Mr. McNeil," he said stiffly.

Neither man laughed. Scott McNeil's gray eyes were

steady, nonjudgmental. "Will," he said with a nod. "Murray. We've met."

They all shuffled forward. The line was short; Will's and his dad's turn was next. The chair was coming. In a rush, Will said, "Mr. McNeil, are you by yourself? Can I ride up with you? Is that okay, Dad?"

Jack Murray took a second, sharp look at Scott, and inclined his head. He skated into place and sat as the chair moved under him.

When Will and Scott McNeil followed, the guy operating the lift greeted him. Will bet he was extra sharp helping people when his boss was around.

They settled into the chair and let it swoop them forward and out over space.

After a moment, when Will didn't say anything, McNeil pointed up the hill. "We're planning to put a new lift down the other side of that ridge. It'll open some pretty steep terrain." He talked about it, the numbers here over Christmas break, the competition between skiers and boarders, the racing— "Are you interested? We have a junior program."

Will could tell McNeil was filling the silence to be nice, which gave him this crawly feeling of shame. The guy probably *was* okay; Will knew he hadn't given him a chance.

Finally he interrupted, saying hurriedly before he could chicken out, "What I said the other night—about Mom not ever telling my father about me…"

Those clear gray eyes trained on his face. "I could tell you're angry about that."

"No." Will watched skiers swooping down the wide smooth slope beneath them. "See, I'm really not. I mean, my dad's great. I'm glad I know him now. But

Mom…the thing is, we were cool together. You know? She's the best."

"Your father might not agree," the man beside him said dryly.

Starting to feel desperate, Will said, "But he's not that mad at Mom. It's…it's weird. Like he understands why she never told him about me. I think…" Mom might kill him for this—she said you never tell family secrets to outsiders—but Will thought this once it was justified. "Mom says he—my dad—let her down really bad back then. *Her* father hurt her. She says Dad has changed, but that she couldn't take a chance then that he would, or else she would have lost me. And she says not for anything would she have let her father raise her kid. And so you see…" He took a nervous glance toward the approaching lift house. "She did it to protect me. And…and I think you should know. That doing what was right for me is all she cared about. And if that's wrong…"

"My son died." McNeil sounded hoarse. "He wasn't even six months old."

Will gave him a startled look. At the last second he saw the net below them and he lifted the tips of his skis.

"I expected to see him grow up." They both rose to their feet, let the chair nudge them forward. "If I found out my ex-wife had lied, that Nate hadn't died after all… That all those years were gone, for whatever reason…"

Will stopped beside the man he was pretty sure his mother wanted to marry. He could only think of one thing to say.

"But if you found out she'd lied to you to protect your little boy? Because that was the only way she thought she could?" Will swallowed, lifted his chin.

"Wouldn't you want her to put him first? Even if…if it meant you couldn't see him?"

Scott McNeil stared at Will. His voice sounded odd. "Why are you saying this?"

"Because it's true. And—" he looked down, poking at one ski with his pole "—because Mom never cries. But she did after you left. For a long time. And I know it's my fault."

"No. Not your fault. Mine."

"I'm the one who opened my big mouth…"

"But I wouldn't listen to her."

"Well…" Will looked over to where his father waited, watching them. "You still could. When you're sorry, Mom never stays mad. At least, not at me, but I bet…"

"She might not hold a grudge against me, either." McNeil gave this twisted smile that almost hurt to look at. "Thanks, son. We'll hope you're right."

With that he took one skating step, skied past Will's dad with a quick word and kept going, shooting right over the brink and straight down The Wall, just whisk, whisk, whisk, these little snappy turns that were so pretty to watch, they took Will's breath away. And he'd thought his dad was good!

"What…what did he say?" Will asked his dad as they both watched.

Jack Murray smiled. "He told me I have one great kid."

"WHY…I DON'T KNOW WHERE he is," the secretary said worriedly. "Mr. Robillard's wife called just a minute ago, and he talked to her and then he went running out of here. I asked him if his children were all right, but he didn't answer!" She looked from Ben to Meg. "Did something bad happen?"

Damn it! Meg thought furiously. Atherton and Dailey had jumped the gun and served the warrant on Robillard's wife early. They'd *agreed,* all of them, to exactly coordinate the two searches so neither Robillard could warn the other; they'd checked their watches. What in hell had gone wrong?

"I'm sorry," Meg said formally. "To the best of my knowledge, his children are fine. But we do have a search warrant for Mark Robillard's home and office, and I suspect his wife warned him we were coming."

They overcame her shock, presented the warrant and hastily checked: no gloves. Ben swore viciously.

"Let's find him," Meg said. "We must have just missed him on the way in. Where does he park?" she snapped to the secretary as they raced past.

"The employee lot…" Her voice trailed them.

He drove a one-year-old Toyota 4x4, green; their warrant included it.

"If he ditches those gloves, we don't have a case," Ben growled as they bounded down the stairs.

Stating the obvious had never been her favorite hobby. "Unless Atherton or Dailey have big mouths, he doesn't know we want gloves or why."

"They're usually good. Goddamn idiots."

People turned to stare as they sprinted past the clothes and rental shops. Down the hall. Ben slammed open the back door. They slipped and slithered along the path between banks of snow until the parking lot opened before them. Sun glinted off windshields; roof racks obscured their field of vision.

Ben swore again. "It's a big lot."

The only named slot was the general manager's: Scott's. Robillard's 4x4 could be anywhere.

"A ton of people work here." She thought quickly. "You get the car and try to block the highway, if we're not already too late. Radio for a patrol unit to head up the mountain loop highway looking for him. I'll hunt here."

He didn't argue, just took off at a run. Miracle of miracles, was he learning to trust her? Meg wondered wryly. Or did he just not trust her behind the wheel?

She edged between parked cars. Bumped her hip on one. The parking lot was slippery, as if the sun had varnished the packed snow. She should have worn boots; hadn't expected to be doing anything more than walking into the lodge, maybe waiting for Robillard to come down from the ski hill.

Movement flashed to her left. She swung around, pulled her revolver.

A young brunette got out of a car and slammed the door. Meg must have made a sound, because she turned, saw the gun and gasped.

"Go on, go on." Meg held her finger to her lips and gestured toward the lodge. The young woman took off at a trot.

Meg dodged through the next double row of cars, her frustration growing. Where was Robillard? Would he have parked elsewhere? Or wasn't he running, after all? He must know it would be futile. Her mind worked feverishly as she scanned the lot.

What was Robillard doing? What was he thinking?

Metallic green caught her eye; no, it was a van. Next to a tan Bronco; half the population of Butte County drove utility vehicles.

Only part of her mind was on the search. The other part was still thinking motive, behavior.

What if Robillard had kept the murder weapon—had had it all along? Maybe after the call from his wife he'd taken off to toss it in a snowbank, or figured he could throw it out the window of his vehicle halfway to town, if he could slip past them now.

He wouldn't know they were after the gloves.

Meg banged her shin against the bumper of a pickup and mumbled a curse. If she weren't careful, she'd shoot herself in the foot. Or take out somebody's windshield.

She looked one way up the next row, then the other.

And saw him hurrying toward her, maybe fifty yards away. Wearing a parka, hands black-gloved. He spotted her at the same moment and plunged between cars. Paralleling him, Meg pursued.

"Stop!" she called.

The green Toyota was parked in the next row. As she slid and almost fell, she saw Robillard fumbling with something. Keys. Must be keys. He disappeared behind his vehicle. Unlocking it.

She headed right down the middle of the row.

He'd parked nose out. She was thirty yards away when the Toyota rocketed out of the slot directly toward her. Why hadn't he gone the other way? He'd seen her; she knew he had. He could have reached the exit either way, and he didn't know Shea waited for him there.

The sun reflected off the windshield. She couldn't see him, only the blinding glare.

He was accelerating, the snow tires gripping the icy surface with ease. She was smack in the path of the 4x4, the footing slick as a wet bar of soap.

Too late, Meg realized: the bastard was going to run her down.

HE'D GOTTEN ONLY ONE RUN, and his pager was already beeping. Trapped in the lift line between two packs of teenagers, Scott felt tension eat at his stomach the second he saw the number: Robillard's office.

He grabbed his phone and dialed even as he automatically moved forward in line.

"Oh, Mr. McNeil!" cried the secretary. "I don't know what to do! It's terrible, and I don't understand, and..."

Usually unflappable, capable of handling a multitude of minor crises in her boss's absence, she babbled on. Something about a search warrant, a call from Mark's wife, him taking off—he'd looked so upset, and he hadn't said where he was going—and now the cops had gone after him.

"Oh, please. What should I *do?*"

Cops. Her story hit Scott, a slam in the gut. Not "cops." *Meg.*

No simple serving of a warrant. Somehow Robillard had known what was coming and taken off. Meg was after him. After the man who might have murdered Shelly.

Scott swore, inciting another burst of worries from the secretary. He ignored them, thinking hard.

Meg wouldn't be alone, would she? No, Melissa had said "cops." Plural.

He still didn't like it. If Robillard would drag Shelly across the snow, shove her down into that snow well and shoot her in cold blood despite her pleas, why wouldn't he kill a cop if he thought he could get away? *God.*

"Nothing, Melissa," Scott snapped. "Don't do anything. Don't call anybody. Sit tight."

Shoving the phone in his pocket, he backed up, bumped one of the kids. "Excuse me."

He lifted the bright orange rope that prevented skiers from cutting the line and skated under it. He scanned the area in front of the lodge.

Nobody was running. The ticket booths were busy. People were coming out of the lodge, going in, putting on skis. A mom pulled two little ones in a blue plastic saucer, all of them laughing. A teenage girl threw a snowball at a boy. A couple, leaning on their poles, talked intensely, even hotly.

All normal. He'd had momentary visions of a hostage situation, a shoot-out among the families skiing at Juanita Butte. Thank God they evaporated.

He used the drop-off from the lift line to send him shooting past the nearest ticket booth. From here the ground rose to the back of the lodge. He'd never climbed so fast on skis; sweat blurred his vision.

Scott reached the back of the timbered lodge and poled forward to the edge of the snowbank. From this vantage point he could see the parking lots.

Somebody ran between cars, yelled something. Olive-green uniform, pale blond hair. Meg. She had her gun held two-fisted.

Oh, crap. There was Robillard, farther down the same row. He dove in behind his Toyota. Meg was running toward him, yelling.

Scott had never felt so impotent in his life. Even when his son died. That had happened behind his back, the soft breaths stopping sometime during the dark hours, when Nate was alone, asleep, unknowing—or so Scott prayed. But this—God Almighty, this was spread out before him, too far away for him to help, but all crystal clear, brutally real.

That SOB drove straight for Meg.

With a bellow, Scott shoved off the top of the bank and arced through the air. Still on his skis, he hit the icy parking lot with a force that slammed through his body like a pile driver, but he stayed on his feet. The momentum kept him shooting across the ice toward the drama ahead.

For a second Meg's stance widened; Scott thought she was going to shoot the oncoming vehicle.

And then she must have realized, as he did, that the Toyota was going too fast, too straight. It would hit her even if she killed Robillard.

She scrambled, slithering, crashing to her knees. She wouldn't be able to get out of the way. The 4x4 was too close, really moving now.

Scott wouldn't make it, couldn't do any good if he did. His throat was raw from the bellow rending the air. "No! Meg! Goddamn it, no!"

Somehow she got to her feet and flung herself sideways. Just as the Toyota reached her.

He heard a dull thud. She fell to one side, flopping on the ice.

Rage filled Scott. He had his skis off before he knew what he was doing. Grabbed one of them, hoisted it in both hands above his head as if it were a javelin. Waited. If he could kill with this ski, he would.

Wait. The Toyota came on. Robillard would run him down, too. One more second.

Now!

Weight behind it, Scott slammed the butt of the ski into the windshield, aiming at the driver behind the wheel. The force flung him to one side as a crazy web of cracks bloomed. The glass had stayed intact. He'd failed. The vehicle's momentum slammed the ski against his head. The side mirror got his ribs. Already vomiting, fire lacing his torso, Scott was on his knees on the icy lot when the smash of metal shook the ground. He rolled onto his side and saw the Toyota sliding, entangled with another car, shoving it. Robillard had lost control. Maybe slammed on the brakes in the icy lot. Now more metal screamed as they hit a van. The domino effect.

His stomach heaved; pain lanced his ribs—or his belly, he didn't know. Only dragged himself to his knees. Meg. Meg was hurt. He pushed up. Wobbled to his feet.

And saw her. Walking toward him.

Her face—something was wrong with it. Blood and swelling. And she limped. But she was walking. Steadily. Alive. In better shape than he was.

Scott crumpled to his knees again, grabbed a bumper for support.

"You're hurt!" She reached him, crouched, and he saw the terror in her eyes. For him.

"Okay," he managed, although the effort of speech made him want to throw up again. "Robillard."

"I've called for backup and an ambulance." Her hand touched him, softly. A woman's hand. Loving.

Her other hand held a long-barreled black gun.

"Go," he said.

She walked away. "Robillard," she called. "Don't move. I want to see your hands."

A man lay halfway through the now shattered windshield. Blood trickled down the green hood onto the snow.

Meg reached him, checked his pulse. And lifted a gun from the bloody hand.

"I'M NOT ABOUT TO STAY in the hospital if I don't have to," Scott growled from inside the turtleneck he was yanking over his head, half an inch at a time. Who would think broken ribs could hurt so much?

"You won't be able to hold Emily," Meg pointed out, from her unseen spot beside his bed.

"Watch me."

"You're bullheaded."

"Damn right."

His head emerged from the turtleneck and he discovered he had visitors. Her son and Jack Murray. He had a hazy memory of them in the parking lot along with EMTs and cops and… Hell, half the skiers up at Juanita Butte had clustered around, it had seemed like. He hoped he was exaggerating; he hadn't been at his best about then.

"You're okay?" Will said, eyes bright and interested.

" 'Okay' being relative," his mother said dryly.

"Mr. McNeil looks better than you do," her son told her.

She gave a crooked smile, all she could manage with one side of her face skinned, purple and swollen. "Thanks, buddy. I am stingingly aware—a pun, get it?—that I don't look my sharpest." She pretended to think. "Hey, was that a pun, too?"

"Jeez, Mom." Will rolled his eyes. "You're the one who is always telling me to take *some* things seriously."

"Oh, I took this seriously." Meg's eyes met Scott's, and he saw a shadow of her fear in them.

"It's almost too bad Robillard lived," Jack commented. He'd been paged on the hill, too, by a dispatcher who knew where he was. *Officer down.* Every cop within twenty-five miles had come running. He and Ben Shea had been the closest.

"Oh, no," Meg said softly. "I want him to stand trial. To have lots of time to think about Shelly Lange.

Remember her face, hear her sobs, see her blood. Fifty years would be good."

Scott couldn't look away from the courageous woman who had yet to remind him of what an idiot he'd been. But he had to know. "The gun matches?"

"They're still messing with it," Murray said, "but I hear it looks good. The bastard would be sent away for trying to kill a cop anyway."

"He might wriggle out from under that, though," Meg said. "Claim the sun was in his eyes and he didn't see me."

"It was morning. He was heading west."

She cocked her head, winced. "Still. How can we prove what he saw or was thinking?"

"Thanks to good, solid police work, you'll get him for Shelly Lange's murder." The Elk Springs police chief clapped her lightly on the back. "You want me to take this kid away?"

Meg looked up at her son, and suddenly her eyes were misty. "Nah. I'll keep him. But thanks, Jack."

They looked at each other a moment; smiled, nodded. Scott knew what she was thinking: if she had died today, Will would have had a father. A good one.

"Then I'll see you all later." Jack said something quiet to Will and left.

Meg sat on the edge of the hospital bed beside Scott and went right back to her original point. "Will Marjorie keep Emily tonight?"

Talk about bullheaded. "I'll manage."

"Will? Can you wait outside for a minute?"

"Yeah. Sure. But you know, we could, like, stay with Mr. McNeil. And get up with the baby and stuff." He flushed. "I mean, if he wants us."

Meg's smile was radiant. And, apparently, painful,

because a whimper escaped her. "Took the words out of my mouth. But do me a favor, kiddo. Whatever you do, don't make me laugh."

He opened his mouth as though the challenge was irresistible, then took a good look at his mother and closed it again. "I'll, um, be out in the waiting room."

Meg waited until the door closed behind him. Head bowed, she said, "I was going to make the same offer. Unless there's someone you'd rather have. No strings attached. I'm not asking you to change how you feel. But…" Her gaze turned up to him, her eyes so huge and blue he felt as dizzy as if he were staring up into the heavens. "Let me help. You're hurt because of me."

"I thought you were dead." His voice was hoarse. He forgot the pain in his ribs. He reached for her, felt a rush of gratitude that she came into his arms without protest. Against her hair, Scott said, "The way you hit. Bounced." A shudder walked up his spine. "I wanted to kill the bastard. I've never wanted to kill before."

"The fender grazed me. That's all." She seemed unaware that she was patting him, tracing the line of the bandages wrapping his rib cage, checking for other damage. "When I saw you…"

"Will talked to me today."

Meg tilted her head back. "Just now? That was nice of him, wasn't it?"

"No. Earlier. We rode up the chair together. He told me you'd been justified in keeping his existence secret. And he said…" What the kid had said sliced into his gut, worse than the scraping edges of broken ribs. Scott swallowed. "He asked me a question. What if Nate could have lived, but only if Penny hid him from me? Wouldn't I have wanted her to do whatever she had to do to protect him?"

Meg went completely still in his arms.

"Yes." Scott's voice was as raw as Meg's cheek. "Yes. Of course, I would have. I would have done anything to protect Nate. Just like you did what you had to for your son."

She tried to argue, to tell him that she thought maybe she'd been a coward, unwilling to admit that she was so afraid of her father she was irrational. Scott wouldn't listen.

"You did what you thought you had to," he repeated. "You've raised a great kid. I was…lashing out from my own misery. I couldn't see beyond my own loss."

"Damn it," the tough cop in his arms mumbled, "I'm crying again. That's all I seem to do these days."

"In between having wild sex and arresting murderers."

She lifted her head and looked at him straight on, new tension humming through her, causing the faint tremor under his hands. "Do you mind? That I'm a cop?"

"No." He tried a smile of his own, though it didn't match either his voice or the anxiety suddenly swelling under those tight bandages. "Meg…I know it's too soon. We hadn't met a month ago. We've had—what?— three, four dates."

"Yes," she said.

"Three? Or four?"

"I wasn't answering that question."

The anxiety was transmuting to hope, as painful in its way. "I'm going to try to adopt Emily. I don't know how you feel about that. Maybe it's stupid, but I believe Shelly meant for me to have her. And for Emily to have me."

"I think—" Meg's smile was as soft as a mountain

dawn "—that it would be wonderful if you adopt Emily."

"I'll share her if you share your son." That was as close as he dared come to what he was thinking.

"Deal." Meg feathered a kiss across his cheek, then groaned. "That hurt. I can't even kiss the man I love!"

"You love me." He turned his head so that their mouths touched. He nibbled gently on the good side of her lips, on her earlobe. "Did you really say it?"

"I said it." She gave a huge sigh. "You could try."

He swore, and his voice went rough again. "God, I love you. It's too soon, but will you marry me anyway?"

Bruised and swollen, her face shone. "Yeah. Don't tell Will—we'll have to get him used to the idea first—but, yeah. Of course I'll marry you."

His mouth swooped for hers, stopped short, and Scott groaned. He couldn't kiss her; he sure as hell couldn't make love to her. Not today, or tomorrow.

But soon enough, he thought with satisfaction and a huge welling of life and joy he'd never expected to feel again. They had time, and then some.

"Well, then, Deputy Margaret Patton," he murmured, "shall we collect our children and go home?"

"Oh, yes," she breathed, the tears she hated in her eyes again. "Home, it is."

Everything you love about romance...
and more!

*Please turn the page for Signature
Select™ Bonus Features.*

Patton's Daughters

BONUS
FEATURES
INSIDE

Author Interview:
A conversation with
Janice Kay Johnson

Tell us a bit about how you began your writing career.

Reading, reading, reading! Yes, like most authors, I've been a bookworm since I learned to read. I'd bring fifteen books home from the library and be back a few days later for another pile. Inevitably, I started making up stories in my head. As far back as I can remember, I had serial ones going. I actually looked forward to going to bed at night so I could get back to my story! I didn't seriously start to write until I'd graduated from college with a degree in history and had a boring job while I waited for my then-husband to graduate. I wrote perhaps 100 pages of an historical romance and learned a great deal. About the same time, my mother also started writing—she took a class and wrote a couple of romantic suspense novels that never sold. My mom and I decided to collaborate on a romance novel, and actually sold it! We wrote four together, all published by Signet, before branching out on our own. I've been going strong ever since.

Have you been to the places where your books are set, or do you rely on research?
I set the majority of my books in the Pacific Northwest because I'm familiar with the locales. I like to know what the *feel* of a place is. The setting for the Patton's Daughters series is particularly meaningful to me, as I grew up in central Oregon. Elk Springs is very much modeled after Bend, where I lived for three years. Our house was near Pilot Butte, the cinder cone in the center of town, for example. My father was a college professor during the school year; during the summer, he was a naturalist who set up the museum atop Lava Butte, a classic red cinder cone amidst lava fields. I remember spending days up there while he worked, feeding the chipmunks that lived in the crater. I fear that I may have defiled my beloved cinder cones by sprawling a body on one in *Dead Wrong!*

What was your inspiration for the protagonists in Patton's Daughters?
At their heart, virtually all of my books are about family. I'm always fascinated by how siblings, who have—to all appearances—grown up in the same environment, are impacted in such dramatically

different ways by that family environment. In *Patton's Daughters*, I had three sisters who reacted quite differently to the loss of their mother and their father's brutality: Meg with defiance and finally the decision to take her life in her own hands, Renee, by letting their father shape her life and haunt her after his death, and Abby, by learning to manipulate him and all men. Of all my characters, the Patton sisters and the men in their lives took on real life to me—obviously, since I'm still writing about them!

When you're not writing, what do you love to do?
I'm actively involved as a board member and volunteer at a no-kill cat shelter. The past several years, I've chaired the annual auction (despite my once-upon-a-time vow to never do fund-raising!). I love to garden and have dozens of old roses surrounded by perennials. I quilt when time allows, I read, read, read (even at stoplights), and perhaps most of all I love to spend time with my daughters, now nineteen and twenty-two.

Do you believe in inspiration or plain old hard work?
Honestly—a combination. Nobody would ever get a book written by waiting for the mood to strike. Every writer I know has days where she drags herself to the computer and writes even though she really, really wants to do something—

anything!—else. On the other hand, I find that for me writing is very much a subconscious activity (and isn't that what inspiration is?). I'll quit for the day when I haven't figured out what to do next, but by the following day some part of my brain has apparently worked it out. Handy, since my conscious self sure hasn't! Ideas for stories sometimes just pop. If the whole process was work, in the traditional, consciously-aware-of-making-myself-do-things sense, I probably wouldn't be a writer. The "work" turns out the pages; the inspiration (i.e. magic) makes it fun!

What are your top five favorite books?
Because I'm a *huge* reader, this is a tough one. I'll leave out the nonfiction I read and go with the books with romantic elements that I think edged me toward becoming the writer I am, and which are frequent rereads. Hmm. I could choose a dozen by Elizabeth Peters, aka Barbara Michaels, but I'll say *The Crocodile in the Sandbank, Beauty* and *The Blue Sword* by Robin McKinley. Many by Georgette Heyer, but I'll say *Regency Buck*. And, to deviate from the romantic theme, *Doomsday Book* by Connie Willis. I guess the obvious question is, why am I not writing historical or fantasy novels? We'd better save that one for another interview!

Is there one book that you've read that changed your life somehow?
I think the beginning of my rich fantasy life was *The Black Stallion,* by Walter Farley. Oh, I loved his books when I was a kid!

What's the one thing you don't have enough of, but wish you did have more of?
Energy! I was going to say money, or time...but ultimately both come down to the fact that I don't have enough energy to get as much done as I'd like. I want to be one of those superwomen who only need four hours of sleep a night and are active from their 6:00 a.m. rising until their middle-of-the-night bedtime.

What makes for a happily-ever-after, whether it be in life or marriage?
Clearly, the easy answers don't work. We'd all like to have wealth, fame and success, for example, but the wealthy and famous are often terribly unhappy. I think patience, tolerance of other people's quirks and the ability to see the humor, even in the midst of humiliation and disaster, make for the greatest happiness!

What matters most in life?
Family, friends, empathizing with others and acting on that empathy.

Recipe: Pumpkin Bread

This recipe came to me originally from a good friend and fellow writer (thanks, Pat!), but I've altered it quite a lot in my quest for better health and more energy. The wonderful thing is, it tastes better now that it's low-fat and more nutritious than it did in its original incarnation! How rare is that?

Pumpkin Bread

2/3 cup of applesauce

1 1/3 cup of sugar

1 1/3 cup of Splenda

8 egg whites (or equivalent)

1 can (1 lb) of pumpkin

2/3 cup of water

3 1/3 cup of flour (I use half whole wheat)

2 tsp soda

1 1/2 tsp salt

1/2 tsp baking powder

1 tsp cinnamon

1 tsp cloves
2/3 cup diced nuts
2/3 cup of raisins

Heat oven to 350°F. Grease two bread pans. In large bowl, mix applesauce, sugar and Splenda. Stir in eggs, pumpkin and water. Blend in flour, soda, salt, baking powder, cinnamon and cloves. Add nuts and raisins.

Pour into pans. Bake about 70 minutes or until knife inserted in center comes out clean.

*Feel free to keep tinkering! Some bran might be good, or oat flour, or soy flour if you're trying to add protein. Let me know if you come up with a winning addition!

Here's a sneak peek...

DEAD WRONG
by
Janice Kay Johnson

Six years ago, prosecutor Will Patton's girlfriend stormed out on him. That night she was brutally raped and murdered. Wrapped up in his own guilt and anger, Will developed a powerful thirst for justice...and was determined that no criminal would ever walk free again. Now, he's returned to his hometown, but his return is greeted by a gruesome discovery—another body and an all-too-familiar calling card. In order to track down this serial killer, Will teams up with rookie detective Trina Giallombardo—only to realize that if he falls for her, she'll be next....

CHAPTER ONE

GETTING THERE five minutes quicker wouldn't make any difference. They weren't racing to the rescue. They were going to view a corpse. Nonetheless, Meg Patton drove fast, with fierce concentration. If Detective Giallombardo said anything, Meg didn't hear.

This wouldn't turn out to be anything like the other murder, she kept assuring herself. The detail the kid who called 911 had blurted out would be an aside, something dropped at the scene, not a deliberate choice of murder weapon and staging. She'd feel like an idiot for tearing out here when she was supposed to supervise detectives, not respond to calls. She'd seen the way heads had swiveled when she'd stood abruptly and said, "I'll take this one."

She'd garnered more surprise when she'd glanced around, choosing young Giallombardo almost randomly. Eeny meeny miney mo. "Are you tied up? Then come with me." Everyone in the squad room had stared after them.

Butte Road ran yardstick straight for miles between rusting barbed wire fences holding back brown heaps of tumbleweed before terminating at a small volcanic cinder cone. The pavement turned to gravel not much beyond the Elk Springs city limits. Most of the year, their SUV would have raised a red cloud of cinder dust to trail them like a tail. Today, the hard-packed surface was frozen solid.

She drove this road every few weeks. Her sister Renee, the Elk Springs Chief of Police, lived out here on the Triple B Ranch with her husband, Daniel, and her two young children. Meg barely spared a glance for the gate when she tore by it. Renee would want to hear about the murder, even if it was outside her jurisdiction. Cops didn't like brutal murders happening in their own backyards. Even if, in this case, that backyard was a whole heck of a lot of empty country.

One of a half dozen in the immediate vicinity of Elk Springs, this lava cone, no more than a couple hundred feet high, wasn't even dignified with a name, as far as Meg knew. The county had once contemplated using its cinders for road construction, until Matt Barnard of the Triple B

BONUS FEATURE

made a stink about having trucks roaring up and down his road all day long. After that, it was left in peace, except for Friday-night beer parties and fornicating teenagers.

A lone pickup truck sat in the turnaround at the end of the road. Two heads in it, real close together. Kids, cuddling against the horror they had suddenly understood walked their world.

Meg was careful to pull in right behind them, so as not to further damage any possible tire prints.

Uh-huh, her inner voice jeered. *On frozen cinders.*

She killed the engine and got out, slamming the door and then pausing for just a minute to take in the surroundings. The bitter cold stung her skin.

Funny how a dead body could give a familiar landscape a surreal look. The view out here was spectacular, with high country desert stretching to the horizon in one direction, brown and stark in winter. The jagged peaks of the Sisters sliced the sky to the west, while Juanita Butte seemed to float to the north like a perfect scoop of vanilla ice cream. A few thin patches of snow clung to the cinder cone and the red-brown soil between tumbleweeds. The sky was a cold, crystal-blue, the stillness absolute.

Until Detective Giallombardo also slammed her door and crunched around the rear of the Explorer to join Meg.

In silence, the two women walked forward, both staring at the woman's naked body sprawled low on the slope of the cinder cone. Head uphill, resting on the pillow of a patch of snow.

In life, she had been long-legged and shapely. In death, she was bluish-white against the rust-red cinders, with the dark stain of bruises discoloring her flesh. Even before they closed the distance, Meg could see that her left breast had been mangled. Torn by an animal after death, maybe, although Meg thought that unlikely.

But the detail that riveted her was the jock-strap. The elastic of the waistband sliced into the victim's neck. The cup had been twisted to cover her face.

A message, or a gesture of contempt for the victim. Maybe for all women. Meg never had known. The man who had killed in exactly this way, who had left the body posed just as this one was posed, had insisted he was innocent. Was still protesting his innocence from the state penitentiary, where he was serving a life sentence.

Feeling sick, she said, "I'll talk to the kids. You call for a crime scene crew. We need pictures."

Detective Giallombardo nodded and went back to the Explorer.

Meg knocked on the window glass of the pickup and then opened the driver side door.

"Chris Singer?"

The girl, a waif with a blotchy face and red, swollen eyes, nodded.

"And you are?" Meg asked the boy.

"Colin Glaser." He was trying to sound manly. The squeak at the end undermined his effort. He gazed through the windshield toward the ghastly sight. "That woman… She's like, *dead*."

"Yes, I'm afraid she is." Meg heard the grimness in her own voice.

16

He shuddered.

Meg looked at both of them. "Can you tell me when you arrived? Did you get out of the pickup? Touch anything?"

In unison, their heads shook violently. "We never got out," the boy said. "I wanted to get the hell—the heck—out of here, but when I started to back up, Chris said we should call 911. And wait until the cops got here. So we locked the doors and that's what we did."

"We were only here like a minute before we phoned," the girl said.

They'd been cutting school, Meg learned, because they had been having a relationship crisis. Despite the boy's comforting arm around the girl, Meg guessed the relationship was dead now. Chris had called her dad, who was on his way out here. He wasn't going to be a happy man.

She thanked them for being responsible, then left them to wait for the girl's father.

"Let's take a closer look," Meg said to Detective Giallombardo, who obediently followed her. Both slipped on the slope of red cinders as they scrambled the eight or ten feet up, then edged toward the body.

Unless bloodstains provided a trail—and they were going to be a bitch to spot on volcanic cinders this color—it was going to be impossible to tell where the UNSUB parked, whether he dragged or carried the body. How much Luminol did it take to spot blood in a landscape this vast? Footprints and ruts didn't last in loose cinders, which tended to rattle downslope to fill any hole even when there was still a foot in it. Meg knew, because she'd climbed up to the crater several times as a teenager.

She crouched beside the victim, Giallombardo standing right above her.

Legs splayed in a grotesquely inviting gesture of sexual come-on. The savage bite marks on the breast were made by human teeth, if Meg was any judge. Maybe they'd get lucky and at least get a decent bite impression to match up with a suspect later. Arms spread to each side. The victim had been allowed no dignity in death.

And then there was the jockstrap. To appearances, it had been used to strangle the woman. It looked brand-new. Bought for the purpose.

This wasn't chance. The staging was identical to the murder six years ago that had cost Meg her son in every meaningful way, though he still dutifully arrived at her door for family holidays.

She didn't realize she'd spoken aloud until Detective Giallombardo said, "Identical to what?"

Meg froze, her instinct to keep family history private until such time as there was no option. But when it came down to it, she'd been a cop too long to hide evidence.

"The crew's coming," she said.

"And Dad," the young woman cop observed.

A red SUV was gaining fast on the official convoy. It fishtailed once but didn't even slow. As a parent, Meg understood.

She and Giallombardo scrambled and slid their way back down to the foot of the lava cone. Crime-scene techs bundled up as they climbed out of vehicles. Meg estimated the day hadn't reached ten degrees Fahrenheit when the sun was at its height, and the temp had probably already dropped to six or eight degrees with subzero to come tonight. Her cheeks and nose were numb.

She directed the crew to get them started, some spreading out to search for evidence, the photographer beginning to snap pictures, the coroner waiting to get to the body. The girl's dad erupted from his SUV almost before it skidded to a stop, and she flung herself right over her boyfriend into Daddy's arms.

Meg introduced herself, explained the situation and asked if he'd drive both kids back to town. "We've got his pickup boxed in." To the boy, she said, "Colin, can you get someone to bring you out here tomorrow after school to get your pickup?"

He nodded.

To his credit, the father squeezed the boy's shoulder and said, "Come on, son. Your mom home from work yet?" He led the two away and was soon backing out.

Meg leaned against the fender of her black Explorer. The young cop who'd been promoted to detective all of a month ago waited with a patience Meg admired.

Trina Giallombardo had risen fast in the ranks. She was only twenty-seven. A local girl who had gone to college at Oregon State, then come

BONUS FEATURE

home. As a cop, she was smart, steady, mature beyond her years and dedicated. When Meg interviewed her for the promotion, she claimed to have always wanted to be a detective.

She wore thick, shiny, dark hair drawn tightly into a bun. Big brown eyes dominated an olive-complected face that gave an impression of stubbornness and intelligence rather than beauty.

Meg would have given anything to have Ben Shea, her longtime partner and brother-in-law, here instead. But Ben had broken his idiot leg—thank God, not his neck—trying to keep up with Abby on the ski hill. His leg was still in traction.

But why did I have to bring a novice? Meg asked herself. Instinct? She didn't have a clue.

Gaze on the crew, spread out like giant ants below their hill, she said, "Six years ago we had a murder that looked just like this one."

"Six years…" Giallombardo frowned. "I was away at college. Wait. Not Will's girlfriend?"

"You know my son?"

"Only by sight." Did red tinge her cheeks? Hard to tell, with both their faces damn near frostbitten. "I was two years behind him in school. But I saw him play basketball. And since he was president of the student body…"

Meg nodded. "His girlfriend was raped and murdered when she came home with him for spring break from college. She was strangled with a jockstrap, and the cup was pulled over her face. She was posed just like that."

"Oh." The young cop exhaled the single, soft word.

They stood in silence while she processed the implications. "Isn't that your brother-in-law's ranch we passed up the road?"

The fact that this body had been dumped so close to her sister's home was already bothering Meg. Their family had been targeted once before. Surely not again. Surely this had nothing to do with the Pattons. It was happenstance that the previous victim had been Will's girlfriend. She'd gone to a bar on her own and left with the killer. She'd probably never even mentioned her boyfriend or the fight they'd just had.

Giallombardo interrupted her thoughts. "Did you catch the killer?"

Meg nodded. "He's supposed to be serving life."

They both glanced involuntarily toward the body.

"Paroled?"

"We'll find out."

The photographer signaled the coroner, and the two women joined him. Sanchez, an elected official, had run unopposed for as long as Meg had

BONUS FEATURE

been with the Butte County Sheriff's Department. Unlike some elected coroners or medical examiners, he was good.

"Don't see any surprises," he said after a minute. "Looks like strangulation. See how deep the elastic has cut into her throat?"

They saw.

"Time of death?"

He hemmed and hawed. This cold made it harder to tell. It was like putting a body in deep freeze. "You find any I.D.?"

"So far, we haven't even found her panties."

He nodded. "I'm thinking last night," he finally concluded. "Maybe twelve hours ago. You might look for a young woman who waited bar, say, and didn't make it home."

"Okay." Meg was trying to take notes. She hoped they were readable. Either she wore gloves, or her fingers went numb. She alternated.

"Let's take a look at the face," the coroner suggested. "Then roll her."

Meg struggled to pull a latex glove onto her right hand, then reached out and tugged the fabric of the jockstrap to one side.

The victim's mouth was frozen open as if in a scream, the grotesquely swollen tongue protruding.

"Was he hiding her face?" Giallombardo whispered. "If anything would shock you…" Before Meg could comment, the young detective was already shaking her head. "No. He posed her. He didn't kill her out here. She'd be scraped by cinders when she struggled. And if he, uh, penetrated her, he'd have had to expose his penis."

The coroner actually hunched, as if the very idea of baring himself to the subfreezing air was so hideous he couldn't prevent a physical reaction.

"Plus he'd have had to kneel on the cinders… No."

Meg agreed. "She was already dead when he carried her here. A man horrified by his crime flees. He doesn't lay out the victim so carefully."

"He has to be a local. To know to come out here."

"That thought has occurred to me." Meg nodded at the victim. "*You're* local. Do you recognize her?"

Giallombardo swallowed. Meg watched as she focused on the face, made herself look past the distended tongue. To study glazed eyes that might have been hazel, the tiny mole on one high cheekbone…

"Oh, God," she whispered.

"You do know her."

Her breath rattled in her chest and she nodded dumbly.

"Who is she?"

Giallombardo swallowed again. Against nausea, Meg guessed. "Amy Owen. She might not be anymore. I mean, she might have gotten married. But in high school that was her name."

Disquiet struck again. "That sounds familiar."

"I think—" the detective was taking quick, shallow breaths "—I think Will dated her."

Air hissed from between Meg's teeth.

"He brought girls out here. Sometimes."

With quick alarm, she thought, Not Trina Giallombardo. Boy, would that complicate things. "How do you know?" she asked, aware she sounded harsh.

The gaze slid from hers. "Not because…" She closed her eyes, obviously struggling to regain her composure. When she spoke again, her voice was devoid of emotion. "I heard girls talk. That's all."

Meg's eyes narrowed. Was there some history here of which she was unaware? Damn it, had the young Trina Giallombardo had a crush on Will? If so, should she be jettisoned from the case?

But they didn't know that this had anything to do with Will.

Please God.

"I came out here when I was a teenager," she heard herself say. She was distantly aware that the other two were gaping. "With Will's father."

After what she realized was an appalled silence, Giallombardo said, "Um…I suppose almost everyone in Elk Springs has."

The coroner looked up at Meg with shrewd eyes. "You sure Mendoza is still locked up?"

"We should have been informed if he came up for parole." Meg stared down at the body. "Let's roll her."

Between rigor mortis and freezing, the job wasn't easy. Despite the cold, Giallombardo looked green by the time they were done.

The backside revealed lividity and more bruising, nothing more.

Meg raised her voice. "Let's bag her. People, has anyone found anything?"

General shakes of the head. No tracks, no discarded clothing, no convenient cigarette butts that didn't look as if they'd been left last summer. Truthfully, Meg hadn't expected anything different. The unknown subject—or UNSUB, to cops—had likely driven out here with the dead woman in his trunk. Maybe at night, maybe this morning. He'd carried her a few feet up the slope of the lava cone, splayed her limbs, adjusted the jockstrap like a man adding a flourish to his signature and left.

How in hell had he known every detail? Had he *seen* the body? Could there have been two murderers? Had he stumbled on the body before the cops found it? Or, she thought with a jolt, *was* this killer a cop?

And, whoever he was, why had he waited six years to imitate the previous rape and murder?

"Lieutenant?"

She knew on one level that Sanchez was talking to her, but still she stared down at the body and asked herself the one question she'd been avoiding.

What if Ricky Mendoza's protestations of innocence were real? What if he didn't do it?

And what if the real killer *had* been shocked by what he'd done? What if he'd been able to suppress his sexual perversion for six years—until something triggered his rage?

Something, say, like the fact that Will Patton had just moved back to Elk Springs?

Common sense revolted. No! Damn it, they had Mendoza cold. She'd been sorry, because she liked the kid, but he had to have been the killer. She was letting a mother's fear intrude, and if she couldn't think with the cool logic of a cop instead, she'd be the one who had to step back from this investigation.

"Sorry," she said, forcing herself to look up. "What's your question?"

"HEARD ANYTHING last night? Or early this morning?" As withered as the winter sagebrush, the old woman stared suspiciously through the six-inch gap between door and frame. Either she was worried about keeping the heat in, or this intruder out.

"Yes, ma'am," Trina said politely.

"We're to bed by nine o'clock."

Trina wouldn't have minded being invited inside. She was freezing out here on the doorstep with the sun sinking fast. This was the fourth house she'd stopped at, and at only one had she been asked in and offered coffee. The few swallows she'd managed were a distant, tantalizing memory.

She strove for a conversational tone. "You must not get much traffic out on Butte Road at night."

The old woman looked at her as if she were simple. "Saturday nights, it's like living next to Highway 20. All those young hands that work the ranches, they come hootin' and hollerin' by, two, three in the morning. Lean on their horns, stereos blasting to shake the windows. They even race sometimes." Her mouth thinned. "They turn onto our property, we get out the shotgun."

Trina considered mentioning that the law did not entitle a property owner to shoot someone for turning into his driveway.

Instead, she surreptitiously wriggled her fingers

inside her gloves to see if they still functioned and said, "Last night wasn't Saturday."

"Some of them get drunk other nights, too."

Heaven send her patience.

"I'm sure they do." She shook her head as if scandalized. The old biddy. "Was last night one of those nights? You hear anybody heading home late?"

"Might have."

"Can you recall what time that was?"

Mrs. Bailey's lips folded near out of sight, as if it pained her to give a straight answer. Finally she sniffed. "Two thirty-five. On a Thursday night. Then the fool turned around and went back to town. Bars shouldn't be open that late."

Despite her surge of excitement, Trina pointed out, "Someone might have been giving a friend a ride home."

Silence, followed by a grudging, "Might could have been."

"Are you certain you heard the same vehicle coming and going?"

"'Course I am! Wouldn't have said it if I hadn't meant it."

Maybe it was perversity that had her suggesting, "One pickup truck sounds an awful lot like another."

The woman didn't like explaining herself.

After primping her lips and thinking about it, she said, "This one sounded like my Rufus out there. Don't bark often, but when he does, you best jump."

"A deep, powerful engine."

"Isn't that what I said?"

Her own lips were going numb. "Did you notice when the truck came back by?"

"Didn't look at the clock." She chewed it over. "Twenty minutes. Half hour."

The timing was just right.

"Mrs. Bailey, do you think you've heard this particular engine before?"

"Can't say."

"Would you recognize it again?"

"Might."

Trina gave her most winning smile, which considering she couldn't feel most of her face might look more like a death mask. "You've been a great help, Mrs. Bailey. We may need to speak to you again. In the meantime, I appreciate your cooperation."

With no "You're welcome" or even a "Mind you don't slip on the steps," the old lady slammed the door shut in Trina's face. A deadbolt lock thudded home.

If she wasn't so darn cold, Trina would have laughed. She hurried to the Explorer she was driving, started it and cranked up the heat. Intermittent shivers racked her. But at least she'd learned something that might be useful, she thought with a small glow of triumph. Useful enough, maybe, that Lieutenant Patton would let her keep working the case.

She couldn't believe her luck to have been singled out today, and by Lieutenant Patton, of all people. Trina had become a cop because she wanted to be just like Meg Patton and her two sisters, the one Elk Springs' police chief, the other an arson investigator. From the time she was eleven or twelve she'd read about their exploits in the newspaper, and since Will went to the high school people had talked, too. Lieutenant Patton had been the county Youth Officer back when Trina was in high school, so she'd talked at assemblies or in Trina's classes a couple of times a year. Trina thought she was amazing—beautiful and brave and smart. Everything Trina wanted to be.

In her interview for the promotion to detective, Trina had almost blurted out something about how much she'd always admired the lieutenant. Thank goodness she'd been able to stop herself. Even if it was true, it would have sounded like the worst brown-nosing.

Now here she was, hardly a month later,

partnered with her. Despite her shivers, Trina still marveled. Junior partner, of course. The lieutenant had gone back to the station to find out whether the killer from six years ago had somehow gotten out of prison and also to try to discover whether other jurisdictions had had murders with this same M.O. Lucky Trina had been assigned one patrol officer to help her canvas the houses along Butte Road.

But it had to be done, and she was pretty excited to have actually learned something. Maybe. Unless the deep-throated pickup or SUV *had* just been dropping some drunk ranch hand back at the Triple B or the Running Y. Except she'd stopped at the Triple B herself and no ranch hands had admitted to being out late last night. She'd find out from Officer Buttram whether the same was true at the Running Y. Those were the only two working ranches past the Baileys' place.

An hour and a half later, she hadn't learned a thing. Buttram and she agreed to meet back at the station.

There, he shook his head. His ruddy face glowed. "Bitch of a night."

"I would have traded my right arm for a thermos of coffee."

"With a dash of whiskey." He took off his sheepskin-lined gloves. "Nobody heard nothing."

"I found somebody who did. A Mrs. Bailey."

Her sense of triumph dimmed at the sight of his face.

"Oooh. There's a nasty one."

"She calls in complaints?"

"Once a month or so." He shook his head. "Hates the neighbors, hates teenagers, doesn't much like cows. You believe her, somebody is always being noisy or trespassing."

Noisy? "I don't remember a house near hers."

"She has damn fine hearing."

Trina quizzed him about who he'd talked to at the Running Y, then went to Lieutenant Patton's office.

Through the glass inset, she saw the lieutenant lift her head at the sound of the knock. She waved Trina in.

"You look cold."

"Yes, ma'am."

Her superior scowled. "Quit ma'aming me."

"Sir…"

"That isn't any better. You make me feel old."

"Lieutenant."

"A slight improvement." She sighed. "I suppose that was an exercise in futility?"

"Actually, I did get one report of unusual traffic."

Brows rose. "Really?"

Trina repeated what Mrs. Bailey said. "I understand she's something of a crank…."

"She?"

"Mrs. Bailey?"

"Not Luella Bailey! She's a thorn in the side of anyone who has dealings with her. Daniel—my brother-in-law—counts his blessings daily that he's not her next neighbor. Pete Hardesty of the Running Y gets hell every time a steer finds a fence break."

Crushed and trying to hide it, Trina asked, "Does that mean she's not reliable?"

"Hmm." Meg Patton rubbed her chin as she thought. "Well, she's not delusional. When she says a steer is eating her dahlias, by God there it is. Kids do drag race out on Butte Road. So…no. She might actually be a good witness. Most folks out there wouldn't pay any mind to a passing vehicle. Luella, though, lives to find grievances." Her gaze sharpened. "Tell me again what she said."

Trina did.

"Twenty minutes to half an hour. That would be about right."

Trina nodded at the phone. "Did you learn anything?"

"Ricky Mendoza is right where he should be. That lets him out. No sign of Amy's Kia. I sent someone by to check her apartment complex and the lots outside the brewhouses and restaurants that seem like the most obvious choices. Otherwise, I've put out calls. Any kind of match through VICAP will take time." The federal data base was a godsend to local law enforcement. Unfortunately, it had limitations; many small jurisdictions didn't input crimes.

Trina nodded.

"I've already talked to Amy Owen's parents. They still live here, only a few blocks from where I grew up in the old town."

"She hadn't married, then?"

"Married and divorced. The ex is next on my list."

"He's around?"

The lieutenant consulted her notes. "Doug Jennings. He's a ski bum, according to the parents. Amy wanted to think about buying a house, starting a family. He wasn't interested."

"So the divorce wasn't ugly?" From what she'd read, Trina was willing to bet this killer and Amy had been strangers, anyway, but you had to consider all possibilities.

"Not according to them. They say he'll be broken up to hear about her murder. I went by his place and he wasn't home." Meg Patton rose. "What say we go talk to him now, then take a look at her apartment?"

"Am I going to stay on the case, then?" Trina asked, rising, too.

The lieutenant looked surprised. "I tagged you, didn't I?"

This didn't seem the moment to ask why. "Thank you, ma...um, Lieutenant."

Exhilaration wiped out her weariness. Her mind buzzed. She'd want to read the file on the six-year-old murder. Look for details that were the same—and ones that were different. Talk to whomever had found that body. The cops who worked the murder. If this one was as similar as Lieutenant Patton claimed, this killer had to be close in some way to the previous crime. Copycats had a motive. What was this one's?

Wow, she thought, feeling giddy. *I'm a detective. A real detective.*

Not even missing the cup of coffee she hadn't yet poured, she followed Lieutenant Patton out.

...NOT THE END...

BONUS FEATURE

Look for DEAD WRONG in bookstores February 2006 from Signature Select.

**A breathtaking novel of
reunion and romance…**

THE F⊙RTUNES OF TEXAS: Reunion

Once a Rebel

by Sheri WhiteFeather

Returning home to Red Rock after many
years, psychologist Susan Fortune is reunited
with Ethan Eldridge, a man she hasn't gotten
over in seventeen years. When tragedy and grief
overtake the family, Susan leans on Ethan to
overcome her feelings—and soon realizes that
her life can't be complete without him.

Coming in February

Silhouette®

Where love comes alive™

If you enjoyed what you just read,
then we've got an offer you can't resist!

Take 2 bestselling
love stories FREE!

Plus get a FREE surprise gift!

Signature Select™

COMING NEXT MONTH

Signature Select Spotlight
THE PLEASURE TRIP by Joanne Rock
Working as a seamstress on a cruise ship called the *Venus*,
Rita Frazer hasn't been feeling very goddesslike lately. But when
the ship hosts a fashion show, Rita figures she has a chance at
being a designer until she finds *herself* on the runway, instead of
her designs. But Rita's found her muse....

Signature Select Collection
AND THE ENVELOPE, PLEASE...
by Barbara Bretton, Emilie Rose, Isabel Sharpe
Three couples find romance on the red carpet at the glamorous
Reel New York Awards—where the A-list rules and passion and
egos collide!

Signature Select Saga
DEAD WRONG by Janice Kay Johnson
Six years ago, prosecutor Will Patton's girlfriend stormed out on
him. That night, she was brutally raped and murdered. Wrapped
up in his own guilt and anger, Will developed a powerful thirst
for justice...and was determined that no criminal would ever walk
free again. Now he's returned to his hometown, but his return is
greeted by a gruesome discovery. In order to track down this serial
killer, Will teams up with detective Trina Giallombardo, only to
realize that if he falls for her, she'll be next....

Signature Select Miniseries
FIREFLY GLEN by Kathleen O'Brien
Featuring the first two novels in her acclaimed miniseries
Four Seasons in Firefly Glen. Two couples, each trying to avoid
romance, find exactly that in this small peaceful town in the
Adirondacks.

The Fortunes of Texas: Reunion Book #9
ONCE A REBEL by Sheri WhiteFeather
Returning home to Red Rock after many years, psychologist
Susan Fortune is reunited with Ethan Eldridge, a man she hasn't
gotten over in seventeen years. When tragedy and grief overtake
the family, Susan leans on Ethan to overcome her feelings—and
soon realizes that her life can't be complete without him.